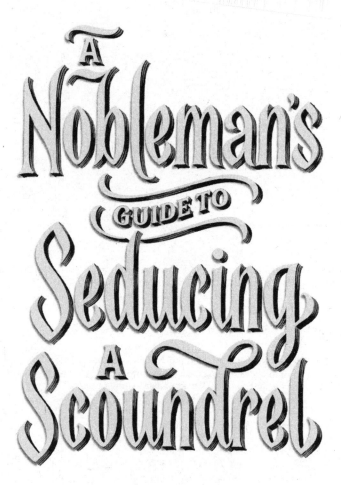

A Nobleman's Guide to Seducing a Scoundrel

KJ CHARLES

sourcebooks
casablanca

Copyright © 2023 by KJ Charles
Cover and internal design © 2023 by Sourcebooks
Cover art © Jyotirmayee Patra
Internal design by Laura Boren/Sourcebooks

Sourcebooks and the colophon are registered trademarks of Sourcebooks.

Published by Sourcebooks Casablanca, an imprint of Sourcebooks
P.O. Box 4410, Naperville, Illinois 60567–4410
(630) 961-3900
sourcebooks.com

Cataloging-in-Publication Data is on file with the Library of Congress.

Printed and bound in the United States of America.
LSC 10 9 8 7 6 5 4 3 2 1

This one's for Courtney Miller-Callihan, best of agents.

One

THE ISLE OF OXNEY, ROMNEY MARSH
APRIL 1823

RUFUS D'AUMESTY, NINETEENTH EARL OF OXNEY, TWENTY-second Baron Stone, and inheritor of the ancient and unbroken d'Aumesty lineage, glared at his uncle Conrad and said, "Balls."

"Your vulgarity is regrettable." Conrad wore a little smirk on his smug face. Rufus regretted the twenty-year age difference that prevented him knocking it off.

"We've been through this," he said in lieu of violence. "The Committee for Privileges took seven months to assess my right. You dredged up every calumny and speculation you could think of against my mother and invented God alone knows what nonsense about me in your effort to claim the title, and you still lost. They said so, it's done with, and you cannot start it all again!"

Conrad's smirk stayed in place. "Of course I have accepted the decision of the Committee. I can scarcely be blamed for taking pains to ensure the title continues down the true line in lawful fashion—"

"You speculated my mother bore a girl and switched me at birth with an orphan boy, as though she were a Bourbon queen, not a draper's daughter," Rufus said with all the patience he could muster, which was scant. "Then you said I was an impostor who'd stolen a dying man's identity on the battlefield."

"I merely raised the question."

"You called my mother a liar and me a fraud, and I've had enough of it. The title has been awarded. The matter is closed."

"Then it must be reopened. Some very serious information has only recently come to light, as a matter of chance. It requires investigation."

Rufus's back teeth were grinding together. "It does not, because the title has been awarded. I'm the legitimate son of Raymond d'Aumesty which makes me the sodding earl, and there is no more to be said!"

"Certainly you are Raymond's son. The question is your legitimacy."

Rufus clenched his fist to prevent himself saying something his uncle would regret. He was going to stop trying to hold on to his temper very shortly. "The Committee examined the proof thoroughly. My mother was married to my father. That is incontestable."

"Oh, the marriage is unquestionable," said the man who'd spent months questioning it. "I do not argue that Raymond went through a ceremony with your mother. The question is whether he was legally able to do so."

"Legally able to—what, marry?"

"Indeed."

"He was twenty-seven years old and of sound mind, insofar as any d'Aumestys are of sound mind, which—"

"He was already married."

"What?"

Conrad plastered on a sympathy-shaped smile. "Or such is the allegation. Raymond was my brother, but he was a rash, irresponsible, foolish man, easily led, with uncontrollable enthusiasms—"

"What do you mean, already married?" Rufus demanded. "Get to the point!"

"Before Raymond became...entangled with your mother, he had a dalliance with a local girl. A housemaid who abandoned her duties to sport with a son of the house."

"You mean he pestered one of the staff. And? If my father had married all the girls he bothered—"

"He married this one!" His uncle spat the words out, then went on in his usual condescending tone, "Or so it is suggested."

"By whom? And why wasn't it 'suggested' while you were scrabbling round for a way to make yourself earl?"

"I could not say." Conrad looked sour. "But I have now received this information, and it must be investigated. Whatever the Committee for Privileges has ruled, this would change everything. If your father was already married at the time he wed your mother, that second marriage is invalid and you are not legitimate."

"If," Rufus said. "Where's the proof? Who is this woman, and if she was married to my father, why hasn't anyone heard of it till now?"

"Her name is Louisa Brightling. She is or was a local woman, from Fairfield. She no longer lives in the area and her whereabouts are not known."

"Then who's making this claim?"

Conrad gave him an exceedingly unpleasant smile. "Her son."

❧

They sent the claimant orders to present himself at Stone Manor the next day. Rufus would have preferred to ride down and confront the fellow at once, but he lived in Dymchurch, halfway across Romney Marsh. It would probably be bad tactics anyway: he didn't want to treat this latest freak of Conrad's as having any more substance than all his other accusations.

He needed to get out of Stone Manor. It was raining, as it always did in this blasted place and this blasted country, but he ordered his horse anyway, and rode out for Buds Farm. He'd been meaning to go, given the numbers of complaints that had come from that source, and hopefully an unheralded visit on such a dismal day would make him look like a good landlord who took his duty seriously.

Little chance of that, he reflected as he rode along the wooded, dripping lane to Wittersham, what with the pile of unread or half-read letters accumulating on his desk, and the nightmarish labyrinth of accounts to which he had no clue, and the state of his lands, which showed itself to be worse and worse the closer he looked.

This was, or should be, a prosperous area, since the Weald supported an amazing number of sheep per acre. The d'Aumestys ought to be a prosperous family with prosperous tenants. He might easily have inherited the earldom as a well-run concern, with a smooth transition of authority from his grandfather to himself. No such luck.

Rufus had spent seven miserable months in the legal mire as the Committee for Privileges examined his claim to the title. It had been scarifying, but he'd won. He was the Earl of Oxney, immovably in place unless he committed treason, which he didn't intend, or was proven illegitimate, which he was determined not to worry about. This was a last desperate throw of Conrad's, and Rufus was tired of putting up with nonsense because his uncle couldn't let go of his disappointment.

In fairness, Conrad had good reason to be disappointed, and angry too.

The previous Lord Oxney, Waleran by name, had had three sons, of whom Conrad was the youngest. The eldest, Baldwin, Lord Stone, had never married; Raymond, the second son, had eloped with a draper's daughter, Mary Hammond. The old earl had promptly disowned him, and disavowed any responsibility to Rufus, his grandson. He didn't respond to pleas for help when Raymond abandoned his young wife and child, or send for the body when Raymond died, and when Rufus was reported killed in action, and his grieving mother wrote to let the Earl know, he had replied that he was glad to hear it. Mary never forgave that cruelty, and Rufus didn't blame her. But it meant that she didn't trouble to write to Stone Manor when Rufus turned up thin, ill, scarred, but alive after five months as a prisoner of war. She hadn't wanted the Earl's poison tainting her joy.

And then the eldest son, Baldwin, died. Mary saw the notice in a newspaper, and took vengeful pleasure in advising the Earl that his despised commoner grandson was alive and now his heir. The Earl replied with a single line of crabbed acknowledgment. He did not suggest meeting, which was a pity because Rufus would have enjoyed refusing: he had nothing civil to say to the man.

Rufus had gone on with his life as a soldier, since it seemed ghoulish to think of himself as an earl in waiting. Still, he'd known the position would be his one day, and when the old man shuffled off at last, he'd expected to assume it without too much trouble.

He'd expected wrongly. Because, over the three and a half years since Baldwin's death, the old earl Waleran had not broken the news to his family that Rufus was alive.

For all that time, his third son Conrad had been under the impression that Baldwin, Raymond, and Rufus's deaths made him heir. For all that time, Conrad had awaited his decrepit, bedbound father's death in the belief that the coronet was a breath away from his own brows, and the old earl hadn't troubled to disabuse him.

That absurd, cruel silence had given Conrad years of hope and anticipation and expectation, and then snatched everything from his grasp. Rufus could not imagine what had been in the old fool's mind unless he'd had a particular dislike of Conrad, which was understandable.

Rufus shared that dislike, but despite that, or perhaps because of it, he intended to be scrupulously fair. So he'd meet this individual who claimed Rufus's father had married his mother first, and he'd hear him out and examine the evidence fairly. And if it proved to be a pack of lies, he'd kick the swine all the way down the Isle, and into the Marsh he came from.

On that invigorating thought, he arrived at Buds Farm.

Rufus wasn't a countryman. He'd been brought up in the household of his stepfather, a successful draper; he'd followed the drum from the age of sixteen. He didn't know anything about farms, or farming. But he knew what makeshift repairs looked like, when you had to keep shoring-up and patching-up because there was no time or money to do a proper job, and he saw it here.

The tenant farmer, Hughes, didn't seem overjoyed by a visit from his new landlord. He spoke respectfully, but there was a lot of resentment under the polite words.

"Been asking for repairs a long time now, my lord. I wrote to Mr. Smallbone time and again. Didn't happen when the old master was alive, and as for after he died, with you and Lord Oxney—Mr. Conrad, I should say—fighting over the title for seven months..." He let that hang meaningfully.

"Surely the work of the estate was carried on in that period," Rufus said.

"No. It weren't. And I've an agreement says what costs I bear, and what the Earl, and that ain't been done. I've got *rights*—"

"Now, Hughes," his wife said, warning in her voice, and something more than that. Alarm, perhaps.

Rufus had a temper. He was well aware his face showed his feelings, and he was undeniably angry at this moment, so he made an extra effort to look and sound calm. "Have you given Mr. Smallbone the full list of repairs due?"

"Three time."

"I'll talk to him," Rufus promised, trying not to make it sound like *I'll wring his neck.*

Hughes snorted. His wife dug a finger into his side with an urgent expression, and he shot her a glower. "Stop that, woman. I've talked to Mr. Smallbone, and written too, and he's made plenty of promises of this and that. Well, it ain't happened yet and I don't see it happening now, and I'm weary of asking for the same thing over and over. I got my rights!"

The battle cry of an Englishman digging in to be an awkward son of a bitch. Rufus knew it well. "Yes, you have rights, Mr. Hughes, and the estate has duties to you. I'm going to get this under control. Can you tell me, this situation, with repairs due—"

"All over," Hughes said, with a sort of gloomy glee. "There's nothing been done to speak of anywhere on the estates, not since Lord Stone died, and that's the truth. Everyone'll tell you the same. The loss took the heart out of old master, your lordship, and nobody could blame him for that, but it's been more'n four year now—No, I will not mind my tongue!" he snapped at his wife. "His lordship asked, and we've had nothing done in all this time, and if he wants to turn me off my land for saying so—"

"I shall do no such thing," Rufus said. "I asked you a question because I wanted you to answer it. I'm grateful for your frankness."

Hughes gave him a short nod. Mrs. Hughes didn't look convinced.

⁂

Rufus was still turning over that unsatisfactory encounter in his mind the next morning as he sat in the study, swamped by paper

He was supposed to have the assistance of his cousin Odo, Conrad's younger son, who had acted as his grandfather's clerk. Unfortunately, Odo was a vague sort of man, nervous to the point of imbecility, who only seemed happy talking about ancient history and the family heritage, subjects in which Rufus had no interest at all. He reacted as though he might be struck whenever Rufus expressed the slightest sign of annoyance, and since Rufus did that a lot, matters were not going well. Rufus didn't want to upset the fellow, since Odo was the only one of his family to show any sort of civility, and he was clearly trying. But he was also useless, and Rufus had been obliged to send him away earlier, in case he swore at him.

There was a lot to swear about. Odo's hand was appalling, a chaotic close-written chicken-scratch that slanted erratically up the page, with endless crossings-out and insertions, so a wooden rule under the lines was no help. It danced in front of Rufus's eyes, the words tangling themselves into incomprehensible knots, and the most ferocious concentration wasn't giving him anything more than a headache. There were entire books of this that he needed to make sense of, but he could barely get through a page in an hour, leaving him in a state of shame, rage, and frustration.

And there were sheaves of unanswered letters from the seven-month interregnum, when it seemed nobody had taken any responsibility at all, and new ones coming in every day, and Rufus was beginning to panic. The steward Smallbone seemed entirely useless, affairs were all too visibly deteriorating, and everyone he spoke to was hostile. The family hated him, and the staff were stiff and unwelcoming, siding firmly against the interloper who had stolen Mr. Conrad's birthright. They eyed Rufus with distrust, and took his orders to Mrs. Conrad for confirmation.

It was enraging, miserable, and exceedingly lonely. Rufus would not have compared his situation as earl of Oxney with his time as a prisoner of war, or at least not out loud, but in the last weeks he had sat through too many meals where the company was even colder than the food, and spent too much time mired in the study, struggling with books he didn't understand and an inheritance he didn't know how to manage, and he was beginning to feel something rather like despair.

He didn't intend to give in to that. Still, he sat in the study alone, achieving nothing, cursing Conrad and the books and this damned pretender fellow, until he was informed that the visitor had arrived.

Odo was in the hall, looking even more like a surprised owl than usual. He gave Rufus one of his twitchy smiles. "Oh—ah—Oxney."

"Busy," Rufus said, to head off whatever gibbering he was likely to be subjected to.

"Is it the, uh, the—"

"Fellow who claims he's the earl. Some ridiculous name."

"Perkin Warbeck."

"What? No, nothing like that."

"No—I mean the claimant—Perkin Warbeck was a pretender to the throne," Odo explained earnestly, falling into step by him. "He declared himself to be one of the Princes in the Tower, you know, and attempted to take the throne from Henry the Seventh."

"Good for him. Did it work?"

"Well—er—no? He was captured, and Henry hanged him."

"Even better," Rufus said, and kept walking.

Conrad was waiting for him in Stone Manor's drawing room, along with the pretender, who Rufus was now inevitably going to call Perkin at some point. Conrad was in a flow of oratory; the other man was listening in silence.

He stood when Rufus arrived. "Lord Oxney. Good day. I'm Luke Doomsday."

It was a ridiculous name. Perkin Warbeck would be better, and come to that would suit him better. Someone named Doomsday should be villainous-looking: shabby and sinister and scarred.

This fellow was not shabby. He was respectably dressed, even rather smartly, with a well-fitted coat that showed off a pair of decent shoulders for his height. He had a bright head of guinea-gold hair that gleamed in the little sunlight allowed by Stone Manor's miserable windows, and a clean, clear look to him, with nothing sinister or piratical about it.

But by God, he was scarred.

It was a hell of a scar, a raised welt easily four inches long that slashed down his temple, made a jagged curve around his left eye, and ended over his cheekbone. It was clearly old, which invited questions because he looked to be in his mid-twenties, and it must have made a bloody mess of his face at the time. It was the kind of scar someone called Doomsday ought to have. People of a sensitive nature would recoil from a scar like that.

Rufus wasn't sensitive, and had seen a lot worse, and the face it bracketed was otherwise rather pleasing. Dark brown eyes that made a nice contrast to the shining hair, finger-thick near-black brows over them—as though a couple of caterpillars had found a resting place, Rufus thought unkindly—and a generous mouth.

Doomsday, Rufus reminded himself. *Pretender.*

"Sit down," he said. "So. You think you should have my earldom."

Those thick brows went up like hands on a clock. "No, Lord Oxney."

"No? Am I misinformed?"

"Really, Oxney," Conrad began.

"Let's hear it from the horse's mouth," Rufus said. "You've had plenty of opportunity to coach him already."

"Excuse me!" Conrad said furiously.

"I beg your pardon, Lord Oxney," Doomsday said. "I have not been coached, and I have no claim on your title."

"Then what are you doing here?"

"You ordered me to come." His voice had just a slight edge. "I'd be very happy to state my position and answer your questions, but I have travelled a long way at your summons, my lord, and I don't feel I should be insulted for it."

That was plain speaking. Confident, too, excessively so in the circumstances. Rufus eyed him. "Stop me if I'm wrong, Doomsday, but I understand you bear a name of some notoriety on Romney Marsh. I hear your family are a pack of smugglers."

"Were," Doomsday said calmly. He was well spoken, without the thick accent of this part of Kent. "There is some history to the family, but they operate as respectable traders these days."

"Moral reformation?" Rufus suggested sarcastically.

"Lower taxes," Doomsday retorted. "It makes all the difference. I'm not a smuggler, Lord Oxney, I'm a secretary. I have letters of reference from Mr. Acheson Wood, Viscount Corvin, and Sir Gareth Inglis."

Rufus had met Sir Gareth, a tall, thin, pale-haired fellow with a peculiar hobby. Beetles, that was it: he'd written a book about the beetles of Romney Marsh or some such thing. Rufus had an untouched copy somewhere. It was a respectable reference, and could be checked easily enough. "Well," he said, trying to sound a bit less hostile. "But you're here with a story, aren't you?"

"I'm here because I was asked to bring my information." Doomsday sounded a little tight. "As follows: My mother was Louisa Brightling, from Fairfield. She worked at Stone Manor as a girl. I understand that Mr. Raymond d'Aumesty expressed his intention to marry her, that she was dismissed by Lord Oxney on that account, and that Mr. Raymond was sent to relatives in Oxfordshire to get him away from her influence. She was fifteen," he added without inflection. "That was in 1789, years before my birth, so please correct me if I'm wrong."

Rufus frowned. "He married my mother in 1789."

Conrad shook his head with pantomime regret. "From the frying pan into the fire."

"My mother was also fifteen," Rufus said. "And my father, at their marriage, was twenty-seven, so if you're saying he was stupid enough to be manipulated by girls half his age—"

"I should not use that term about my brother, but if the cap fits." Conrad smirked. Rufus bit back his annoyance at laying himself open to that hit.

Doomsday's jaw tensed a fraction. "Louisa did not marry, despite many offers and many suitors. She did, however, have a child some years later. She named the father as Elijah Doomsday, deposited it—me—with the Doomsdays, and left the Marsh."

"That's a sorry tale," Rufus said.

"And a revealing one," Conrad put in. "Why would a woman not marry the father of her child? Surely the only reason would be that she was legally unable to marry. Or, should I say, to marry *again*."

Doomsday gave a very slow blink. Rufus rolled his eyes. "I'm yet to hear the meat of this."

"Louisa left the Marsh, and has never been heard from again. I don't know where she is or what became of her. But I did speak to her father, Mr. John Brightling, a few years ago. He was ailing; he died not long after. And when we talked, he spoke—rather wildly—about a secret kept for thirty years. A secret marriage." Doomsday paused, apparently bracing himself. "He told me, 'She married the lord's son. She married Mr. Raymond.'"

"And there we have it," Conrad said triumphantly.

"If by 'it', you mean this fellow's unsupported word," Rufus pointed out. He did not like the sound of this. "Who did you tell about this at the time you heard it?"

"Nobody," Doomsday said. "Mr. Brightling spoke to me in confidence."

"You didn't mention this to anyone else? Lord Oxney, say—you didn't think he should know?"

"Lord Oxney was an old man then, bedridden. Mr. Raymond was long dead; so was his son. Or so I understood. Everyone said his son was dead."

"I was wounded in battle, spent five months as prisoner of war. The gazettes had me dead. I wasn't," Rufus said testily. It hadn't been an entertaining period of his life and he was tired of talking about it. "So you didn't think you needed to tell anyone."

"No, Lord Oxney. I thought it would cause distress to no purpose. I should certainly not spread such a story as gossip. It was not my affair."

"Not your affair who your mother was married to?"

Doomsday slow-blinked again. "Lord Oxney, it makes no difference if my mother was married to Mr. Raymond, Mr. Conrad, or Mr. William Pitt the Younger. My father was Elijah Doomsday. Louisa made that very clear, he acknowledged me, and it is impossible to doubt for anyone who knew him. I have his eyebrows."

"They're hard to miss," Rufus said, though he was already getting used to those thick black brows, and their pleasing contrast to his bright hair. "And what about when the Earl died, and I was known to be alive?"

"I didn't hear about it. I was offmarsh—away, working. I haven't spent much time here in recent years."

"Oh, come off it. You weren't aware of seven months of legal wrangling over the earldom?"

"I'm from Dymchurch, Lord Oxney. The doings of the Isle aren't our concern."

Rufus had heard that the Marsh was parochial but this was absurd. "You can't be serious. It's, what, twenty miles away?"

"Fourteen," Doomsday said without embarrassment. "I'd have

heard if I'd been here, of course, but my family don't write letters. As it is, I came back last month for a visit. That's when I learned of the dispute about the succession, and I realised Mr. Brightling's story had become relevant."

Rufus frowned. "So what did you do?"

"My cousin Emily works here, as a housemaid. I asked her what was going on, to understand the situation before mixing myself up in it. I didn't want to betray a confidence if I didn't have to. She spoke to Mr. Pauncefoot, who went to Mr. Conrad."

"Why the devil did he not bring it directly to me?" Rufus demanded. It was rhetorical: he knew damned well that the butler took Conrad's side. "And why this pussyfooting? You must have realised it was important. Crucial, damn it!"

"If true, my lord. But all I have is a story told me by a man who's been dead five years. I don't know if it's true; I can't prove it if it is. And I didn't greatly want to invite anger or resentment for raising the issue."

That put Rufus's hackles up. "Are you suggesting I'd punish you for speaking the truth?"

"I don't know," Doomsday said. "Will you?"

Rufus opened his mouth, and stopped himself. Nobody here knew him; it wasn't an insult. "I will not. I suppose your concern is not unreasonable, in principle."

"I'm more concerned by the practice. I really don't want to be involved in this. It's nothing to do with me."

"On the contrary," Conrad said. "You had a moral obligation to disclose what you knew, and you should have done so at once. However, I do not consider it blameworthy that you did not go directly to—my nephew." He glanced at Rufus. "After all, that might have been misinterpreted. Some persons might have questioned whether your silence might be for sale."

Rufus had to take a second on that. Conrad was all but accusing him of wanting to bribe this fellow, and he would have exploded with outrage if Doomsday hadn't got in first. "I am a confidential secretary, sir. My silence is for sale on a purely professional level. There is a name for amateur sellers of silence, and I have done nothing to deserve its application to me."

Rufus gave him a nod. "That was a blasted insulting implication, Conrad. And talking of implications, can we move to facts? Because if all you have is a claim of what a dead man told you—"

"And the fact that the Brightling woman never married when it would have been to her advantage," Conrad said. "And the letter from my father talking about Raymond's secret marriage—"

"He said *secretive*, not secret, and it referred to my parents' marriage!"

"We don't know that," Conrad retorted. "It is dated September 1789. It could have been written before Raymond's ceremony with your mother. Not to mention that my father also referred to you as a bastard when he wrote to your mother at your birth."

"That was an insult. One of many my mother received at his hands."

Conrad ignored him. "I consider this a great deal of cumulative evidence. Doomsday's allegations must be investigated."

"Investigate them, then," Rufus snapped. "Find this Louisa Brightling, and get proof of her story from the horse's mouth. Otherwise you have nothing but hearsay."

"An excellent idea, nephew. Doomsday, you will seek out your mother at once."

"I beg your pardon, sir," Doomsday said, and added, at Conrad's blank look, "No."

Conrad turned to eyeball him. "You will oblige me by obeying my orders without argument."

"I don't work for you, sir." This seemed to stagger Conrad. Doomsday went on before he found his voice. "With the utmost respect, my concern is to find another post and I cannot take the time to hunt for a woman I have never met. Or, at least—"

"Wasn't formally introduced to?" Rufus suggested.

Doomsday's eyes flew to his, sparking with sudden amusement. Rufus would have called him a good-looking man anyway, but that expression, with his eyes gleaming and his full lips pressed together against an unwary laugh—

"Nonsense," Conrad said. "This is your duty and I require you to do it immediately. If your mother was married to Raymond then, most regrettably, that renders this gentleman, my nephew, illegitimate. Ill-eg-itimate," he repeated, relishing the syllables. "And as such, not entitled to the position and honours he currently bears, in which case I should be obliged to take up those dignities as my father always intended. The fate of a noble house depends on this matter."

"It would if this was more than a tissue of rumour," Rufus said. He was damned if he was letting Conrad set the terms of this discussion: he'd learned his lesson there. "Until you have proof, this is just another story, and you've tried plenty of those already. And stop throwing orders around. If this fellow's to do it, he should be paid."

"It is hardly a great matter to ask a man to see his mother."

"It is if she's been gone for however long it is!"

"Twenty-six years, with no communication to her family, still less mine," Doomsday said. "I'm afraid I have no idea—"

"Sorry, wait, stop," Rufus said. "*How* long was that?"

"Twenty-six years, Lord Oxney."

Rufus felt unholy glee dawn in his soul. "So you are how old?"

"Twenty-six?" Doomsday said, with just a hint of 'is there something wrong with you?' in his tone.

"You don't look it. When were you born?"

"February ninety-seven. I was left with the Doomsdays on the eighteenth of that month, when I was a day or two old."

Rufus rapidly checked his mathematics. "Well, now. Well. February ninety-seven. Well, there's a thing."

"What?" Conrad demanded.

Rufus grinned at him. "Born February ninety-seven, so he was got in, what, May or June ninety-six. My father died in October ninety-six. Which means, Doomsday, he could be *your* father."

Doomsday gave another of his slow blinks, which Rufus was starting to suspect were secretarial code for *This man's an idiot.* "But he wasn't. My father was Elijah Doomsday. That is beyond question."

"Not if Raymond married your mother, it's not," Rufus said. "At least, not in law. Right, Conrad?"

Conrad didn't get it for a second, then his eyes bulged. "Now, just a moment!"

"I don't follow," Doomsday said. "If they were ever married, they'd been separated seven years."

"That might do for normal folk," Rufus said. "But the law's the law. If Raymond and this Louisa were legally wed, well, a child born in legal wedlock is legitimate." Rufus smiled savagely at his uncle, whose face was a mask of horror. "You taught me that, Conrad, with your foolery in front of the Committee. The child's legitimate unless the father goes out of his way to disavow it as soon as he learns of its existence, and even then he'd have to prove he couldn't have done the fathering. The courts don't just take a fellow's word for it. Raymond d'Aumesty was alive and well when you were conceived, Doomsday. If you're the oldest son of his lawful wife? *You're* the earl."

Two

CONRAD TOOK IT EVERY BIT AS BADLY AS RUFUS HAD HOPED.
He couldn't believe the man hadn't thought of the flaw in his scheme, but then again, Conrad was native to these parts and had doubtless heard stories about the Doomsdays all his life. Rufus had asked Knaresford, his grandfather's valet and now his, for an account of this notorious criminal clan, and begged him to stop after a quarter hour with no end in sight. Clearly, it hadn't occurred to Conrad that an avowed Doomsday could be a legal d'Aumesty, and now he was faced not only with his own exclusion, but with the ending of a line unbroken in eight centuries in favour of a family of scoundrels.

It went down poorly. He had a great deal to say about how no Doomsday scum would disgrace the halls of Stone Manor, and added that one merely had to look at Luke Doomsday to see he was a wretched villain, at which point Rufus suggested that he go away.

Conrad stormed out and slammed the door, leaving Rufus alone with the object of his ire, who was massaging the bridge of his nose. He looked annoyed rather than shaken, but all the same Rufus said, "Drink?"

"Ah—yes. Yes, please. Lord Oxney, are you serious about this?"

"Entirely. If Louisa was lawfully married to Raymond, any child born to her in his lifetime is his by default."

"But I'm obviously a Doomsday!"

"In fact, yes. In law, you're a d'Aumesty if this tale is true, and a Doomsday if it isn't. Rather a coincidence, don't you think?"

Doomsday gave him a wary look. "What is?"

"Doomsday, d'Aumesty. You'd barely need to change your name."

"It's the same name," Doomsday said. "Or, at least, Mr. Pagan d'Aumesty says so. He said, specifically, that 'Doomsday' is a corruption of 'd'Aumesty', bestowed on our bastard offshoot of your noble family by unlettered rustics. He said that to my cousins' faces."

From what Rufus had seen of his great-uncle, this was all too likely. Pagan d'Aumesty, the old earl Waleran's brother, rambled around the place both physically and verbally, subjecting the unwary to impromptu lectures with entire disregard for their feelings on the subject. "How did that go down?"

"It will not be forgotten or forgiven in my lifetime."

"Fair enough." He handed the man a glass of sherry.

Doomsday took a healthy swig. "Thank you, my lord. May I ask something?"

"Go on."

"Well, Mr. Conrad clearly feels there is something in Mr. Brightling's story. And now you're suggesting, if there is, that I, a smuggler's bastard, will put you out of your place as earl." He cocked his head. "Why are you so cheerful about that?"

"Honestly? Spite."

"Oh."

Rufus shrugged. "If I am to be turfed out, I'd rather it was in your favour than Conrad's. It would be highly entertaining if you took the earldom. The combined blue blood of the d'Aumestys would clot on the spot."

"What a delightful prospect for me," Doomsday said, rather sharply.

"Were you expecting them to be pleased?"

"I wasn't expecting any of this!"

"No. You came with a story, and now the stakes are considerably higher than you'd thought, and you might be wishing you were well out of it. So between us, Doomsday, you, me, and a closed door. What's the truth here?"

Any hint of humour fled Doomsday's face. His eyes were very brown, and his brows very heavy over them. "I'm not a liar, Lord Oxney. I've told you everything I was told; I don't know if it's true or false. Mr. Brightling was adamant, but he was also an old, sick man who had wanted better for his daughter. For all I know, he wished it to be true until he came to believe it."

"By Mr. Brightling, you mean Louisa's father, your grandfather? Why not call him that?"

Another slow blink. "Elijah Doomsday had his way by force. He made Louisa an unwed and unwilling mother, and drove her away from her home by it. Mr. Brightling had no interest in the result of that crime. When he finally sent for me, it was because he was dying and desperate for something of her." He gave a tight smile. "He said I look like her. The hair. It seemed to make him happy."

"Christ," Rufus said. "I'm very sorry, Doomsday."

"My mother was the sufferer. I can't say I'm happy at the idea of tracking her down, Lord Oxney. I have always believed, or hoped, she made a new start, with people who treated her well. I wouldn't like to be a reminder of a past she wanted to forget."

"No. I see that."

"But you need to know: I see *that*. Could I make a suggestion? Two, in fact?"

"Go on."

"First, I have some extremely competent cousins with a taste for adventure—"

"Smugglers?"

"Marshfolk. I could trust them to look for Louisa. To do it subtly, to recognise her and find a way to speak to her without risking the new happiness she may have."

Rufus found that hopeful to the point of implausible. Anyone could predict the kind of life Louisa had fallen into, alone, away from her home, with that past. But Doomsday had clearly developed a fantasy of his mother safe, well, and not ruined by his existence, and Rufus wasn't going to besiege a harmless castle in the air. "I'd need someone to verify her identity independently."

"There's still family here. People who would remember her."

"Very well. And the other suggestion?"

"If Mr. Raymond did marry a Marsh girl, the news would have spread like wildfire without someone powerful and ruthless keeping the matter quiet. That means the last earl. Which in turn means there may be something in the records here. I'm good at paperwork, and I'd recognise names. And I'm between jobs. I could look for proof."

"You think I should give you the opportunity to do that?"

"Who else? If you get your own man in to look, and he finds nothing—"

"Conrad will say I destroyed the evidence," Rufus completed with weary certainty.

"Whereas if *I* don't find it, that surely suggests it doesn't exist to be found, since you say I'd benefit from finding it to a ridiculous extent."

Rufus cocked his head. "That's not a bad point. You have time to do this, but not look for your mother?"

"She didn't want me as a baby. It would be remarkable if she wanted to know me as a man." Doomsday spoke as if that were a simple statement of fact, and perhaps it was. "Also, you indicated you'd pay me, and that would be welcome."

"Mph. And if you find proof?"

"Good question. What if I find proof that I'm the rightful, or at least legal, earl? What then, Lord Oxney?"

They looked at each other. Doomsday's eyes were intent, and there was just the touch of a smile on that generous mouth. Rufus wondered if he knew it. He wondered, too, if he was being asked for a bribe, and hoped that he was not. He'd taken rather a shine to this excessively confident young man.

"If you are the lawful son of Raymond's lawful wife, then you are the earl, and I will relinquish the title without complaint. I am not a thief, and I don't take what is not mine. If this whole thing is rumour and nonsense, I shall not hold a grudge that you played an honest part in it." He leaned in, deepening his voice. "And if this is a fraud and you are lying to me, I will make you sorry you were ever born."

Doomsday's eyes widened. It might have been alarm, but Rufus didn't think so. It looked almost like anticipation. "Noted, my lord. But I'm not lying. I don't think Mr. Brightling's story is true, but I've reported it as accurately as I can."

"Why not true?"

"Because earl's sons don't marry housemaids. In my experience, powerful people take what they want from the less powerful, and they don't put a great deal of thought into the consequences for their victims."

"While that's true of my father in general, he unquestionably married a draper's daughter. He had a taste for young girls of the lower classes."

"But marriage? That seems highly eccentric behaviour from a nobleman."

"I take it you aren't familiar with the d'Aumestys."

That won a quick, sharp grin. "Notwithstanding, they're famed for their high opinion of their heritage. I struggle to see Mr. Raymond defying that on the Marsh, even if he was ready to do so in foreign parts."

"Oxfordshire?"

"Foreign, yes."

Rufus did like him, he decided. "We shall see. Tell me, has Conrad spoken to you about this? I'm not implying anything about your probity by that question." *Only Conrad's*, he didn't say.

Doomsday considered him rather than answering at once. "May I speak frankly?"

"Carry on."

He made a face, twisting his mouth to one side. The grimace pulled at the scar, distorting his expression into a caricature. "You're outmarsh, not from here. I don't know if you were familiar with your grandfather's ways?"

"Never met him."

"He was a bad man to cross. He had a great deal of power, and he liked to control people. If he owned one's freehold, for example—"

He stopped there as if struck. Rufus said, "What?"

"Only that he may have owned Mr. Brightling's freehold," Doomsday said slowly. "Certainly he had a lot of property in Fairfield. I could check that. Anyway, my point was that he had ways of commanding obedience—financial and otherwise—and used them freely to put pressure on people and their families. With that in mind, I feel a little vulnerable."

Rufus thought back to Buds Farm, and the alarm on Mrs. Hughes's face as her husband made his complaints. "I see. Right. Well, he may have gone on in that way but I do not, and I hope you're not concerned that I will strong-arm you into anything."

"I meant Mr. Conrad."

"Ah." Rufus frowned. "Can your family, the famous smugglers, not look after themselves?"

"Oh, I didn't mean them," Doomsday said. "I'd like to see anyone try. No, I was entirely thinking of myself. I need to find another secretarial post, and I could do without being dogged by bad references. Whispers of dishonesty, claims that I have ideas above my station. You know how these things travel."

"I'm not sure Conrad has the sort of power you're suggesting."

Doomsday looked as him as though he were a rather slow child. "He was going to be earl for close to four years."

"Yes, but—" Something else from the other day nudged at Rufus's mind. "Wait. Were people calling him Lord Oxney while the title was being disputed?"

"I'm told he insisted."

"Did he. Right." This was explaining a great deal, with more clarity than he'd had from the sum total of his conversations in Stone Manor for the best part of two months. He wondered if he could reasonably pick Doomsday's brains while he was here.

"Right," he said again. "But he *isn't* Lord Oxney. I am."

"Yes, my lord. But Mr. Conrad is the man with connections here, and that matters on the Marsh. And he's made his wishes clear to me."

"Has he, by God?"

Doomsday rocked a hand. "By inference and implication as to the outcome he wants, which he clearly wants very much. I am not willing to be forced into a lie, or dragged into court, and I don't like what I've got involved in here. So I think...I think I'm asking for your protection."

Doomsday seemed a fraction less confident as he said that, something in the set of his shoulders, and Rufus could no more have refused than he could have taken flight. Doomsday might well have reason to fear Conrad, and even if the bloody man couldn't really do anything, fear was debilitating. Rufus did not propose to stand by when his help was sought, or needed.

And, a small and unworthy part of himself added, he'd do well to have Doomsday on his side. He might come of a bad family but he radiated competence, and Rufus did not want him taking Conrad's side in this business, which meant he had to clasp the man to his own.

"You have it," he said gruffly. "If you deal honestly by me, you will not be the sufferer for it at my or anyone's hands. I will keep you from harm: you have my word."

Doomsday's lips parted and curved in a little, almost shy smile. "Uh—thank you. Thank you, my lord."

The door banged open. Conrad walked in, accompanied by his wife.

Matilda d'Aumesty was a cool, imperious woman. She had an excellent figure, an air of such aristocratic authority that Rufus occasionally felt the urge to salute, Norman lineage to rival her husband's, and no regard whatsoever for underlings. She looked at Doomsday, who had stood and bowed with prompt and respectful humility, made a moue of distaste, and said, "Ugh. Certainly not."

"What was that?" Rufus asked.

She turned her icy gaze on him. "You continue to regard our heritage with contempt. Let me be clear: if your mother's marriage is shown to be invalid, Conrad will inherit. That is all, *Oxney*." She always enunciated his title as if handling it with tongs, to convey her doubts that he owned or deserved it.

Rufus glanced at Doomsday, who wore an expression so blank Rufus had only ever seen its like on dead people. "It's not up to you. The law will decide."

Her nostrils flared. "You may find it amusing to speak of such a"—she waved her hand at Doomsday, averting her eyes—"in dear Father's place. I do not."

"Then you're missing a good joke." Rufus didn't feel minded to placate her. Doomsday hadn't flinched in the slightest at Matilda's contempt, so maybe he was used to it, maybe he didn't care. Rufus damned well cared. He'd known many good, brave men who'd sacrificed limbs, faces, abilities to the war; he'd seen the revulsion and contempt that greeted them back home, and how shame hollowed them out. Doomsday's scar was a deal too old to be a war wound, but it must have been excruciatingly painful, and it was a shocking disfigurement on an otherwise very attractive face. The sneers would hurt. Rufus didn't know whether Matilda and Conrad didn't care if they inflicted hurt or didn't understand that the lower orders felt it, but neither was tolerable.

Matilda was glaring at him. "I do not know what you mean."

"Let me be clear, then," Rufus told husband and wife. "You brought this matter to me, and I'm taking it extremely seriously. I shall set on a search to find this lady who may have been Raymond's wife, and in addition we will search the records of this house for any evidence Lord Oxney knew of a secret marriage. Doomsday—*Mr.* Doomsday—is going to be part of that. Moreover, as a claimant to the title, until this matter is resolved, he will stay here."

"*What?*" Conrad yelped.

"You heard. You'll be glad of the prior acquaintance if he's the new earl, won't you? You're always complaining about being surprised by my existence." He swung to Doomsday, who looked as slack-jawed as Conrad. "Treat the place as your own, old fellow. Luke, was it? Luke, these are your cousins Conrad and Matilda."

"Lord Oxney—"

"This is absurd!" Matilda said furiously.

"Is it?" Rufus asked. "Is it really? Because Conrad was quite convinced of this secret first marriage, right up until the point he realised he wouldn't be the beneficiary. Have you changed your mind, Conrad? Do you now think this story is a lot of rubbish that needn't be taken seriously?"

Conrad shot a look at his wife. She said, "Of course it must be considered. That does not mean inviting this individual into Stone Manor. A cousin to the housemaid! I trust you are jesting."

"I am not," Rufus said. "If you believe the story, he's the rightful earl. If you don't, I'm the rightful earl. Pick a side."

Doomsday rubbed a hand over his face in a thoughtful manner that hid his mouth. It did not hide the malicious amusement that brimmed in his eyes, and Rufus looked at him and thought, *This man likes trouble.*

"Your behaviour and frivolity only indicate your gross unfitness for the coronet," Matilda informed him. "Come, Conrad."

She swept out. Conrad followed. Doomsday waited for them to leave, walked over, shut the door, and then leaned against it very much as if attempting a barricade. "Do you always do things like this? My lord."

"The particular situation hasn't arisen before," Rufus said. "But I'm sure you've heard the best defence is a good offence."

"You must be an excellent defender, then. Do you seriously intend me to stay here? Have I a choice?"

"Of course. But you wanted my protection. And if it's fourteen miles to Dymchurch you'll need to stay anyway while you're searching the records: you can't do that journey twice a day. How long should it take you to look?"

"It depends on the state of things. Maybe a week?"

"Well, then. Stay here. I'll keep an eye on Conrad and make sure he leaves you alone; you look for evidence in the books. I'll pay you a fair rate for your time, and by the end of a week either you'll be the

earl, or Conrad and Matilda will be so appalled at your presence in
these hallowed halls that they'll be grateful to give this one up."

"That isn't a terribly inviting prospect."

Rufus considered him. "Been a secretary long?"

"Eight years."

"And you don't want a chance to make the noble family miserable,
for once?"

"If you're asking me to turn up dressed like a smuggler, my lord—"
His lips twitched upwards, suddenly and irrepressibly. "I could do
that. Talk like a decent Marshman, too, not fancy-like with your
anointed cramp-words." That was in a startlingly broad Kent accent.

Rufus gave a crack of laughter. "Do it. I beg you."

"Tempting though it is..." Doomsday grinned at him. He had a
very, very appealing grin. "I doubt it's needful. I'm a Doomsday and
my cousin is your housemaid. That should be quite enough."

"I hope so." Rufus wouldn't actually ask the fellow to take on
Conrad and Matilda, but it was a pleasant fancy to share. "Don't
let them walk over you. You'll be here as my guest, paid or not, and
you'll be treated as such. Be here tomorrow at ten. I'll have a room
made ready."

Three

LUKE WAS AT THE ISLE BY NINE THE NEXT MORNING: NO POINT in risking lateness. He jumped off the cart at the crossing, told Young John Groom (who was nearly sixty, but his father was still going strong) to take his things up to the Manor, and walked up the canal a little way.

He knew where he was going: the point where the Royal Military Canal ran alongside High Knock Channel, under the shadow of the Isle of Oxney. Its wooded slopes rose over him, and he could make out a corner of Stone Manor's looming grey bulk on the skyline, amid the trees.

He was looking up because he didn't want to look around. He didn't need to look; he could find this place in the dark. He made himself pay attention to his surroundings anyway. It was good practice.

He walked to the point where a thorn tree grew by the Channel. A man had died here thirteen years ago, his neck wrung like an unwanted dog's in the dark. He'd been little mourned then and was mostly forgotten now, and if any part of his life had done any good to anyone, Luke wasn't aware of it. All the same, he stood watching the ripples on the water and thinking about the ripples from that long-ago death until he heard the faint bell of the half-hour roll down from St. Mary-the-Virgin in Stone, and echoed by St. Mary's in Appledore.

Time to go.

He walked up to Stone Manor. It was a pleasant spring day on the Marsh, which was to say it wasn't currently raining, and the Isle of Oxney that had seemed so steep in his boyhood was laughable now that three years in the Peak District had given his legs some climbing muscle.

Lord Oxney had muscle. Luke had read up on his military career—1806 to the triumphant end—and clearly he hadn't let grass grow under his feet since. He was bulky, even barrel-chested, carrying a solid amount of weight with ease.

He didn't look much like the other d'Aumestys. They ran to thin height; Lord Oxney was about five feet ten, and thus notably taller than Luke, but no towering presence. His build made up for that, though: broad-shouldered and very solid, with arms that looked like they were used to, or for, hard work, and powerful thighs made for riding. Luke certainly wouldn't mind riding them, a thought he put firmly aside. The Earl wore his hair cropped unfashionably close and his hazel eyes had a greenish tinge against browned skin that suggested he spent a lot of time outdoors. In his loosely cut and carelessly worn practical clothing, he looked more like a farm labourer than an earl. Luke, who liked a strong man, was all in favour of that.

He didn't sound like a farm labourer, or at least not like most people's idea of one. He was clearly used to giving orders, and very much not to tact or circumlocution. Luke liked that too. In fact, he liked a lot about Oxney.

He'd initially assumed he'd be on Mr. Conrad's side. But Conrad was a prick, and his wife every bit as bad as Cousin Emily said. Luke would have taken orders and insults if necessary—that was life when you worked for rich people—but Oxney seemed the far more entertaining option.

Entertaining, physically impressive, and yet something of a calamity by all accounts. Luke had questions about that. He would have called Oxney a decisive, competent sort of man based on what he'd seen, but that wasn't the keg-meg. Luke had made sure he heard all he could using his family connections, which covered the Marsh like a spiderweb and were just as sensitive to the slightest vibration. Emily knew everything about the Stone Manor household; one of the main Doomsday henchmen, Matt Molash, was married to a sister of one of the grooms; and the Doomsdays between them knew plenty of people who lived on d'Aumesty lands and paid d'Aumesty rents. Luke had wrung everything he could from all those sources, and what he'd heard was a hostile family, an unsettled household unsure where its interests lay, a catastrophically managed estate, and a resented and incapable new master. He'd heard Oxney called *uneducated, do-nothing, fool.*

Yes, Luke had questions. More, he had ideas, and if he couldn't make something of all this, his name wasn't Luke Doomsday. Which, of course, it might not be. Perhaps it was Luke d'Aumesty. He was grinning at the thought as he came to the door.

He'd gone to the main entrance. Secretaries could do that, but the butler, a very grand fellow, looked at him with bleak contempt. "You're to go to the study. And I'll thank you to use the back door, as befits your sort."

Well, that was a flag planted. Conciliate or clash? Luke weighed it up and chose a middle path. "I have orders from his lordship, Mr. Pauncefoot. Thank you very much."

Pauncefoot narrowed his eyes, but stepped back, and crooked his finger at a footman. "Take *Mister* Doomsday to Lord Oxney's study."

Luke followed the man down a series of corridors, noting land-marks that included two full suits of armour, and knocked at the Earl's study door just as the clocks chimed ten.

"In!" came a bellow.

Luke pushed the door open. Oxney was seated at the desk, wearing a ferocious scowl. The study was horrifying: teetering piles of papers on the desk, and shelves, and floor, double or triple stacked, odd sheets everywhere that had clearly slid out of place. Oxney looked red in the face and profoundly exasperated. With him was a tall, flustered-looking, spindly man with very round eyes and a pointy nose.

"About time," the Earl said. "Odo, this is Luke Doomsday. The pretender. He'll be working on the archives. Show him where they're kept, will you?"

"Archives? But—should not I—"

"No. You're meant to be my secretary, God help us both, and we have hell's own job as it is to make head or tail of this, so no, you're not going to disappear into the damned archives for weeks on end and leave me drowning in paper. Go on, move."

Odo moved, or rather jerked in a panicky sort of way, throwing a desperate look at Luke. "But really, can you—do you, familiar—historical record—back to the Normans—parchment? Palimpsest?"

Luke waited a moment, but that appeared to be the whole question. "I've plenty of experience with documents, Mr. Odo. And I'll only be looking at the years seventy-eight to, say, ninety-five. Of the last century," he added, in case that was in doubt.

"Oh. Oh, good. Although, uh, you should understand, you should, uh—"

"Show me," Luke said soothingly. "I'll understand if you show me. You can tell me where to look and make sure I get it right."

Odo sagged a touch. "Good. Yes. I will. Unless, Oxney, if you need me—"

"No, carry on," Oxney said. "Actually, no. I'll come with you."

"To the archives? You said you'd as lief set fire to them!"

"Temper," Oxney said with a slightly guilty look. "I've not had time, that's all. You might as well show the whole thing to the both of us at once. Give us that tour of the place you've been pressing me to take while you're at it. Settle him in."

⁓

The tour did not settle Luke in.

Stone Manor was large, ancient, and baffling. You might not call it a castle, but it wasn't far off. The main part of the building was the medieval Manorial Hall, a stone-walled, four-square tower dating from the fourteenth century, extended in the sixteenth, and with a new wing added in the seventeenth to connect it to the oldest part of the place, a plain stone relic of Norman times called the Chamber Block. The various extensions meant that the Manor formed an approximate and asymmetrical U shape, linked by a disorienting maze of corridors in unpredictable alignment. Odo kept up a running commentary as they went around, very much in the vein of, "Note the groined and vaulted roof, with its heavy chamfered ribs." Luke let that slide off his ears without touching his brain. He did listen to Oxney's interpolations, which were more along the lines of, "The front of the house is that way."

He restricted himself to murmurs of admiration he didn't feel as they trudged round, but he couldn't avoid stopping dead as they passed a window at the rear of the Manor. "What is *that*?"

Odo glanced out. "Oh, yes. The Cathedral."

It was indeed, to all appearances, a cathedral in the Gothic style, with flying buttresses, gargoyles, tall windows, and a lofty spire for its size, which was that of a large cottage, and it was sitting across

Stone Manor's courtyard as though dropped there. Luke turned to check Lord Oxney could see it too. "Is that the chapel?"

"Goodness, no, the chapel is in the North Wing," Odo assured him. "The Cathedral isn't consecrated, of course. We just call it that as a jest. It's a folly."

"Don't they put those in gardens usually? Big ornamental gardens, far away from the house?"

Odo sighed. "I know."

Luke stared out at the absurd structure. He was beginning to have serious concerns about Stone Manor.

He did pay attention to the disposition of the family. The Earl lodged in the Manorial Hall itself; the Conrads in the Stuart-era New Wing, where, Lord Oxney pointed out with some bitterness, it wasn't quite so cold and the chimneys didn't smoke. Mr. Pagan, the old earl's brother, slept in the ancient Norman Chamber Block for its historical associations, regardless of the intense inconvenience this caused the staff, who had no other reason to go there. The North Wing was, it seemed, unused.

It did have a portrait gallery, though, to which Odo took them as a sort of grand finale. This included indecipherably dark fifteenth-century images painted on boards, and crumbling parchments, reverently kept, that Odo said went back to the thirteenth. "These show that William le Bâtard, the Conqueror himself, bestowed the barony of Stone on Aymer d'Aumesty in 1068. Henry the First created the earldom, making Pagan d'Aumesty the first Lord Oxney in 1129. Of course Henry founded the Angevin dynasty"—his tone suggested that this was a regrettable faux pas—"but as the Conqueror's son, he was of the true Norman blood, which we have the honour of carrying in our veins. Aymer was a paternal cousin of the great William, as you know."

"I didn't," Oxney said. "So as the twenty-second baron, I'm William the Conqueror's first cousin twenty-two times removed?"

"Well, the exact number—"

"And that's impressive?"

"Of course! The unbroken lineage—"

"Everyone's got an unbroken lineage," Lord Oxney said. "We've all got a father and a grandfather and a twenty-two-times great-grandfather. Can you name your twenty-two-times great-grandfather, Doomsday?"

"Aymer d'Aumesty," Luke said without thinking.

"I beg your pardon?"

Luke cursed himself mentally. He ought to have learned about keeping smart remarks inside his head a long time ago. At least Oxney looked startled rather than annoyed. "Well, if the Doomsdays are an offshoot of the d'Aumestys at some point after the Normans arrived, then logically—"

"Good point," Oxney said. "Excellent point. So the d'Aumestys have however much of the Conqueror's first cousin's blood after it's been diluted by twenty-two generations. And the Doomsdays have just as much of the Conqueror's first cousin's blood as us. And other than that, the difference between the d'Aumestys and the Doomsdays is, what, one lot wrote the names down?"

Odo looked startled and upset. "The Barony of Stone is one of the most ancient in the land. Our ancestry is a living heirloom, a connection to the history of the land and the people." He gestured around him at eight hundred years of dark, damp, chilly history. "It matters!"

"Does it?"

Odo straightened. He had a scholar's stoop, or possibly a younger son's cringe, but when he stood properly he was several inches over Oxney's height. It transformed his appearance from a surprised owl to a tall surprised owl. "This is your inheritance, Oxney. Your birthright. You must take your place seriously."

"I intend to," Oxney said. "I have the land and the people of which you spoke depending on me to do just that. And I cannot see how this ancient mummery aids me in the slightest."

He looked decidedly belligerent. Odo's eyes were bulging. Luke slid gently between them. "Mr. Odo, do you know when the Doomsday line branched off the d'Aumesty family? I'd be fascinated to learn."

"Oh." Odo's ruffled feathers subsided. "Well, I couldn't say, but one might discover—parish records, perhaps—"

He turned away to contemplate the shelves. Oxney threw Luke a glance that mingled thanks and a touch of guilt. *All part of the service,* Luke thought. "Perhaps Mr. Odo could show me the archives next, Lord Oxney? I'm sure you have things to do."

"Yes. Right. Thank you, Odo. I'll have you shown your room in an hour or so, Doomsday."

He went off. Odo looked after him with an expression Luke couldn't interpret. "Oh dear. I don't know why I can't make him appreciate this. It would be so much better if he was more like us."

Luke had no intention of getting embroiled in that conversation. "The archives," he suggested.

It was much as he had expected: a lot of shelves, a lot of books, and leatherbound ledgers, and paper tied in scrappy heaps. Odo gave him a brief tour, indicated where the years he wanted were to be found, and then stood and looked around longingly. Clearly, this was his territory.

"This is all most comprehensive," Luke said. "When does it go up to?"

"The year nine."

"Nine? Why no later?"

"Well, those are all in the study. For reference, you know."

No wonder the study looked like a library had rutted with a law office and littered, if they kept the last fourteen years' worth of accounts to hand. "Do you need those for reference very often? Since it's now the year twenty-three," he added, in case Odo wasn't sure.

"Ah, well, possibly not. But what with everything that happened, and the costs—Grandfather mentioned them a great deal to Baldwin, and no wonder—and I've never really found the time to move it all back, you see. Now, what else do you need?"

"I think I have everything, Mr. Odo."

"And you have worked with older books and records?" Odo asked, not for the first time.

Luke reached for his most soothing voice. "If I have any problems I'll come to you."

"I wish you would." Odo was hovering. "And I do wish Oxney— well, of course he could not, he does need me to help—though really, I don't know how much good—"

This was going to give him a headache. "You're acting as his lordship's secretary, is that right?"

"Yes!" Odo looked grateful at having a noun to latch on to. "Secretary. Or clerk. Or something, only, you see, I'm not trained to it. My grandfather dismissed his secretary after—and he ordered, so of course I—and one tries to learn, but it's not my métier, you see. I want to do it!" he added hastily. "I want to be useful to the family. I just wish I thought I *was*."

"You've been doing the books for the last...?"

"Four and a half years. Since Baldwin died, Lord Stone, you know."

Luke gave a sympathetic nod. "It must be hard work."

"Oh, awful. You're a secretary, aren't you? Do you like it? Are you, well, good at it?"

"Yes, to both," Luke said with a modest smile. "I like order and organisation."

Odo's eyes rounded as though he'd said *I like sharp spikes and mantraps*. "Really? Could you—I don't suppose—"

"If I can be of any service to you, Mr. Odo, I'd be delighted to help."

He found his hand clasped in both of Odo's. "Thank you! You're very good. Very kind. Thank you. I must—but perhaps we can speak soon?"

"Absolutely." Luke ushered him out, shut the door, and put his back against it for a moment. Then he hauled out everything from 1789, the year of Raymond's notional marriage to his mother, spread it all on the table in a way that showed willing, and leafed through an account book as he considered his position.

Archives that only went to 1809. What the devil use was that?

He had an obvious way into the study. Odo was clearly useless by reason of nerves if nothing else, so Oxney was badly in need of a secretary, and Luke had established that he was badly in need of a job. It would mean working here longer than he'd thought, but he'd have been hard put to stretch his 'investigations' in the archives over a week, and that was not much time at all.

Try to do everything in a week and get out, or take his time, with all the associated risks of spending much longer here? There were advantages on both sides, primarily that it would be no bad thing if he could secure the place as Oxney's secretary. Of course, if luck was on his side, he would never need to work again, but there was always the chance he'd fail, and in that case a reference from an earl would go some way to wiping out the last humiliation. Not to mention he would benefit from free range over the house, preferably with Oxney's imprimatur to do whatever he saw fit.

And he liked Oxney. That was a poor reason, but he did. The Earl had a brusque, burly appeal, and a touch of humour under the temper, and when Luke had asked for his protection, he'd responded instantly. That was something Luke found very appealing indeed, especially since he didn't need it.

Oxney wasn't managing. Perhaps Luke could do him some good.

That would, if one thought about it, be a very fair trade, even if it wasn't one Oxney was aware he was making.

Decision made, Luke leafed on through pages he barely glanced at while he schemed.

Oxney arrived an hour or so later. "Hard at work already? Found anything?"

"To my great surprise, my lord, no."

"Cheeky swine," Oxney said without heat. "Come on, I'll show you your room."

"You?"

"Why not?"

"You're the earl."

"Don't remind me," Oxney said. "I doubt I could safely leave you to the staff. Oh, but you've got a cousin here. Which one?"

"Emily. She's an upper housemaid."

"Is she a Doomsday?"

"Yes, but she's called Tallant here. They wouldn't let her go by Doomsday."

"Of course not. Tallant—brown hair, bit older than you, bit shorter? How does she find the place?"

"I couldn't speak for her, Lord Oxney."

"I dare say not. Come on, then."

Luke followed him out into the hallway. Since his lordship had thrown off his shamefully baggy coat at some point and was in waistcoat and shirtsleeves, this gave Luke a back view he could only admire. He did so for a couple of seconds, then lengthened his stride to catch up.

"I don't know all the house yet," Lord Oxney remarked as he led the way. "Still get lost. Ridiculous place. That's some ancestors there, or someone's idea of them." He waved at a large oil painting of men in chain-mail armour and unflattering egg-like helmets posing in a warlike, historical sort of way. "Idiocy. We're back in the Manorial Hall now. Drawing room is through *that* door, and from there you get to the Countess's Drawing–Room—not that there's been a countess since before the French Revolution but why change a name just because it hasn't applied in four decades? Are you oriented? That way is the dining hall, then the New Wing is beyond it, turn right. That's where the Conrads live, so I'd avoid it if I were you. I certainly do. Up."

He led the way up the broad flight of stairs. Luke lagged slightly, because the Earl's back view was really *very* impressive.

"More Normans." Oxney flicked a finger at the oil paintings they passed: two large battle scenes, with knights in egg-shaped helmets against men wearing hairy sacks. "Everything on the walls is history paintings of Normans, portraits of the family with half of them dressed as Normans, or etchings of the Isle of Oxney and even some of *those* have Normans. And along here is the Earl's Salon. That's mine."

He ushered Luke into an extremely depressing room. It had small leaded windows that needed cleaning, dull and very dark wood panelling, a rug on the floor that had had the pattern walked out of it, as his Aunt Mary might say, a couple of etchings of Stone Manor with some suspiciously egg-headed figures in the foreground, and an extremely faded armchair which was sprouting horsehair and had been sat on to the point that the seat had an arse-shaped dint. A clock ticked like doom.

"Apparently my grandfather sat here every day for eighty years," Lord Oxney said, adding sourly, "You can hardly tell."

"New furniture?" Luke suggested.

"When I've summoned up the energy."

"Would you care for me to organise it?"

Lord Oxney cocked an eyebrow. "Really?"

"Well, I'm a secretary," Luke said. "This is the kind of thing I do. And if you don't have anyone else to do it—"

"Won't you be busy in the archives?"

"I like to be busy. And I'd like to be of help."

"Very kind, but I'd advise you to make sure of your ground before you go into battle," Oxney said. "Changing anything from how 'dear Father' liked it is a mortal insult round here, and while it might be amusing to pit you against Matilda in full tragedy-queen voice, it would be a little unfair on you."

Luke tilted his head. "Have you heard of Ma Doomsday, at all, Lord Oxney?"

"My valet mentioned something. A local legend, yes? Some appalling ogress who led smugglers into pitched battles, and whose name is used to frighten the children."

"My Aunt Sybil," Luke said. "She chased the Aldington gang off Dymchurch turf outnumbered two to one, and broke their leader's arm with a fence post. I grew up in her house. Do you have an idea of what you'd like for the room?"

Oxney took a step back and surveyed him. "I am having trouble placing you, Doomsday. Are you a smuggler or a secretary?"

"I had an unusual upbringing," Luke admitted. "And I tend to be quite, uh—"

"Cocksure?" Oxney suggested.

"Confident, perhaps."

"Overbearing?"

"Helpful. Competent. Invaluable."

"And unquestionably modest," Oxney concluded, with a grin. "What would you do with the room, given your head?"

Luke had no idea. He looked around. "What colours do you like?"

"God, I don't know. Red."

The room was north-facing, with its windows set in deep bays, and the wood panelling meant it was dark even at close to noon. "I'd recommend golds and greens."

"I'm sure I just said red. My mouth moved, and I distinctly heard sounds emerge."

"Yes, but you were guessing."

Oxney choked. He generally had a rather grim expression—Luke wasn't sure if that was natural to his face, habitual after the war, or just the effect of Stone Manor—but when he laughed, the effect was transforming. It made him look like a man you'd laugh with, shoulders shaking, eyes meeting, joining in pleasure.

"Insolent, but accurate," Oxney said. "What's wrong with red?"

"Too dark. Paler colours will reflect the light better." Green would bring his eyes out, too. "I'd suggest we—you have the furniture reupholstered"—he gave the chair a careful prod—"replaced, and perhaps add a mirror or two. That's an excellent way to increase the light. Although, if you had the panelling removed—"

"It's a few hundred years old, apparently. It's linenfold oak, Odo says, or possibly oakfold linen. Special, anyway."

If Luke were the earl of Oxney, he'd rip all this ancient rubbish out without thinking twice. He inclined his head. "Shall I send for some samples? And look for paintings more suited to your tastes. Less Norman."

"What, in this house? You'll be lucky."Oxney said. "All right, yes, why not. Carry on. And come on." He led the way through a second door, into a room with a four-poster bed.

Luke couldn't help an exclamation. It was a spectacular piece of furniture, about seven feet long and the same width, obviously extremely old and made of very dark wood. Headboard, columns, and canopy were ornately carved with flowers, foliage, and fruit, through which fantastical creatures rioted, like some monstrous physical version of a Hieronymus Bosch painting. The little light in the room caught the edges and depths, so that the strange shapes gleamed. Luke stepped sideways, and the shift made dragons twist and writhe, a monk wink.

"Good heavens. That is quite a bed."

"It is, isn't it."

"Imposing."

"Ancestral," Oxney suggested.

"A challenge to live up to?"

That came out of his mouth faster than his brain could stop it. He glanced over, but Oxney was grinning. "You're not wrong. It's made for begetting warriors, or possibly being murdered in, nothing so mundane as sleep. I ought to be exercising my droit du seigneur in it at this very moment."

Luke's mouth opened. Oxney added, hastily, "Not this moment, obviously. That was a joke. I'm not a Norman." He coughed. "Poor taste."

It was a joke that had given Luke some very vivid ideas. The room was hung with ancient tapestries, the windows even less generous than in the Earl's Salon, and he could just imagine how it would look at night, lit by lamplight, with deep shadows leaping on the walls and darkening the bed, and maybe the heavy-set master of Stone Manor giving him a severe look...

He put the notion to one side for private enjoyment at a more convenient juncture, resisted the impulse to check how sturdy the posts were, and glanced around the otherwise very plain room. "Redecoration in here too?"

"Why bother? It would be like putting ear-bobs on a wild boar. You're through here." Oxney led the way through a side door and a small anteroom used for dressing, which in turn led to a much plainer bedroom with whitewashed walls. Luke's bags had been put on a chest of drawers, but not unpacked.

"Is this not your valet's room?"

"I'm using my grandfather's valet, greatly to his dismay, and he's always slept down the hall. It's a servant's room, though, which is very clearly the message you're expected to take. As you will gather,

Matilda's writ runs in the household. I can put you somewhere else if you want, but I thought I'd check first how much of a battleground you'd care to be. I'm starting to draw conclusions on that, myself," Oxney added.

That was thoughtful. Luke considered the question. It would be preferable not to be so close to Oxney, but at least there was a room in between, and he didn't want to find himself billetted with the Conrads, still less under curious gazes in the servants' quarters where people moved around at all hours. "This is very well, thank you. So the staff are loyal to the family they know?"

"That's one way of putting it," Oxney said. "Of course, if the family welcomed me with open arms, the staff would take their lead from that. But here we are."

"Are you looking to make changes? A new butler or valet?"

"I won't dismiss people unless I have to."

Oxney led the way out of the other door as he spoke. He headed down the corridor with a series of disobliging remarks as to the house's windproofing, convenience, and state of repair, and strode round a corner right into a tall, yawning man who wore good clothes with studied neglect and had a somewhat dissipated look.

"Fulk," Lord Oxney said, without warmth. "Good morning. If it's still morning."

"We don't all rush around at crack of dawn pretending we're busy." This was Fulk d'Aumesty, Conrad's elder son and Odo's elder brother. He was regarding the Earl with a level of open dislike that justified Lord Oxney's sourness about his family. "I prefer to keep gentlemen's hours, rather than drapers' ones. What's this fellow?"

"Luke Doomsday. The pretender."

"That mountebank?" He actually looked at Luke then, and his eyes widened at the scar, as people's eyes always did. "Christ, what a spectacle."

"Mind your damned offensive tongue," Oxney said. "And get used to him. He'll be working in the archives for a while."

"Someone else to help you read?" Fulk said. "Well, you clearly need a few."

Lord Oxney's reply was short, to the point, and astonishingly obscene. Fulk recoiled in shock, but gathered himself rapidly with a sneer of, "I expected no better," and strode off.

"Prick," Oxney said after him, not quietly, then swung to Luke. "Well?" His voice was challenging, even aggressive.

Luke wondered if he'd considered being less confrontational. His cousin Joss was famed for his ability to get his own way, which he usually did with the application of intense charm, good humour, and a very close eye on what people wanted. In Oxney's position, Joss would probably have won his new family's hearts already. Luke might have tried to do the same himself, as the smoothest route. He rather liked that Oxney wasn't trying.

"Not kissing cousins, then," he said.

"That's one way of putting it." Oxney waved an irritable hand. "It's one damn thing after another round here. The family believed I was dead, and don't hide their resentment that I'm not. The only one who talks to me is Odo, and he doesn't make any sense. If you'd prefer to switch sides, I shouldn't blame you: you'd probably find it more comfortable."

"It's challenging, certainly. Luckily, I hate being bored."

"Do you now." The Earl's smile lit his face, which had been looking decidedly grim. "We have that in common, then. How do you deal with boredom? I've always found getting into trouble works wonders."

"Same. The trick is to have that be your job." He let that hang a moment. "Thank you for the tour, my lord. I should get back to the archives."

Four

His chance came the very next day.

Luke was in the archives when he heard a familiar carrying voice raised from several rooms away. He gave it five minutes, and then knocked cautiously on the study door.

"What the bloody hell is it?" the nineteenth earl of Oxney bellowed.

Luke slid in. "I hoped to consult Mr. Odo, my lord. If it's convenient."

The study looked significantly worse than before. Someone had either dropped or thrown a bundle of papers, apparently from a height because they were all over the floor, and an inkstand had spilled. Oxney was red-faced and visibly frustrated, Odo on the verge of tears. Luke glanced between them and said, "My lord, may I assist?"

"At what?"

"I'm a secretary," Luke said, not for the first time. "Mr. Odo mentioned you have a great deal to do—"

"And I cannot do it," Odo said. "I d-did my best and I'm sorry it's not good enough—"

"It isn't," Oxney said through his teeth. "And the fault for that lies with the decrepit old fool who gave you a responsibility you weren't suited for and no training to help you do it, and I wish to Christ he hadn't done the same to me. Just—go away, Odo. Get some fresh air. I should not have raised my voice at you and I'm sorry, but please, go for a walk outside while we both calm down."

Odo retreated, visibly shaken. Oxney leaned forward and put his elbows on the desk and his head in his hands.

Luke shut the door. "Again, can I help?"

"Do you think you can help with this?"

"Yes."

Oxney groped for an account book and thrust it at him without looking up. "Try again."

Luke took it and flicked through the pages. He'd been expecting bad; he was hard put to keep his countenance. "I...see. It's all like this?"

"Four and a half years of it," Oxney said. "For four and a half years, all the paperwork's been left to Odo, who mostly lives in the eleventh century and can't string a sentence together, and as far as I can see nobody at all has been superintending the estate, or the steward, and nothing has been done to stop the rot, literally. My grandfather must have had rats in the attic. And Conrad just let it happen, the useless bone-idle sneering son of a bitch!"

From what Luke had heard, Conrad hadn't been permitted to act, but he wasn't here to make Oxney think better of his uncle. "The estate should be grateful you inherited, then."

"I wouldn't say that." Oxney threw himself back in the chair and met Luke's eyes. "You want the truth, Doomsday? Actually, you're getting it, want or not. I don't know what I'm doing. I can't make head or tail of the books, I've no idea what it means to manage an estate, and nobody here wants to help me even if anyone is competent to, which I'm beginning to doubt. I'm in the middle of a slow disaster and there's nothing I can do about it. We'd all better pray that you're the true heir, because I'm not fit for the role."

"I take leave to differ, my lord." Luke took Odo's abandoned chair and pulled it over, without waiting for a nod to sit. "Lord Oxney, you cannot possibly tackle this alone. That's not your failing or fault: you're unfamiliar with this work and faced with years of incompetence, mismanagement, and neglect. Therefore, you need help. You need an excellent secretary as a matter of urgency, to deal with the details while you start taking control of the overall situation." He waited a second for that to sink in, and went on, deliberately, "Whereas I need a post with someone who will shield me from any retaliation over this affair, and if that someone was titled, it would be very useful for my future career. It seems to me, my lord, we could help one another."

Oxney gave him a long look. "I see. And are you an excellent secretary?"

"Yes. I am." He glanced around at the distressing piles of paper on the floor. "Not supernatural; this will take a while. But good."

"What can you do?"

"Anything you require. Correspondence, organisation, accounts. I can hire staff, manage household affairs, arrange events, and make things happen as you wish them to. If there's anything I haven't done before, I will find out how. I'm extremely good at putting things in order and keeping them there."

Oxney gestured at the study. "How would you start?"

"I'd like to spend a few hours acquainting myself with the situation and clearing the decks, then have a discussion as to your priorities."

"The estates. I'm getting daily complaints of neglect and undone repairs, and no sense at all from that damned incompetent excuse

for a steward. Talking of priorities, what about that proof you're supposed to be looking for?"

"You could ask Mr. Odo to do that," Luke said. "He'd probably
prefer the role, and it would mean you weren't dismissing him. That
might help family harmony."

Oxney's head lifted and he gave Luke a very long, straight look.
Luke had to resist an urge to shift in his chair. "You take a lot on
yourself. I don't recall asking for advice on my family relations."

"No, my lord."

Oxney's eyes narrowed. "On the other hand, that's a damn good
idea. Just...keep within bounds. What experience have you?"

"I worked for Mr. Acheson Wood for three years, as an under-
secretary, and then for Viscount Corvin for another three, mostly at
Wrayton Harcourt, his home in Derbyshire. My last role was with
Sir John Grayson. It's given me a good range of experience."

"References from all of them?"

"From Mr. Acheson Wood and Lord Corvin."

"And the last one?"

"No," Luke said. "Or rather, not a reference I would care to share.
I left following a difference of opinion."

"About who was the master in the house?"

"Not that, no. The difference was, ah, personal."

"Meaning?"

Luke considered him. "I will have to request this be absolutely
confidential, my lord." Oxney waved a hand. "Thank you. The difference was that Sir John felt my duties included bedding his wife
while he watched, and I did not."

Oxney looked blankly at him. "You're not serious."

"It was a regular marital arrangement of theirs, apparently: she
was involved in the hiring process. When I declined, he sacked me,
and assured me he would give the worst possible reference, which

he did. I've been out of work for five months, and if I tell that story to explain myself, it makes any prospective employer consider me as someone who might spill his secrets too."

Oxney was going red again. "That is an outrage. Absolutely disgraceful. The man is a villain. Good God. Very well, I see you can't explain that widely. But you told me?"

"Yes," Luke said. "I had an idea you might listen. And, to be frank, I don't have many options left. I will work for you to the best of my ability, Lord Oxney, if you give me the chance."

He could see that taking effect. Lord Oxney was so obviously a man who gave people chances: there was a very kind heart under the thick muscle and temper. It made him staggeringly easy to manipulate. Luke made a silent vow that nobody else would be doing *that* while he was here.

"Your family," Oxney said. "Is this going to be a problem?"

"People who know of my family's reputation might think you're a fool to take me on. People who actually know us will think it's a clever move on your part. Unfortunately, an earl's circle is much more likely to include the first group than the second."

"The local nobs will disapprove?"

"Not all of them. I should say that I've greatly benefited from Sir Gareth Inglis's friendship. I've been staying with him."

Oxney blinked. "You? With Sir Gareth? Why?"

Gareth's house had been home to Luke for thirteen years; it was so natural, he found the question jarring. "He's a good friend of the family. He sent me to school, and he's godfather to my cousin Sophy's daughter."

"This is a damned odd place, your Marsh. Still, if a baronet can mix with smugglers, I dare say I can. And—you spoke of my grandfather abusing his power. Your family aren't beholden to mine?"

"The d'Aumesty holdings in the area are mostly up on the Weald, with those on the Marsh on the Guildford Level. My family are on the coast and have our own freehold. We've no financial or personal connections to Oxney."

"Unless it turns out you're the earl."

Luke winced. "Could we work on the assumption that I'm not? I really would prefer to make as little of that tale as possible. The jokes will be endless, and I'd rather not have future employers think I'm grasping at privilege above my station."

"That would be a damned unfair interpretation to put on things."

"But it will be put on. I'd rather be here as a secretary than a pretender."

"Is that you knowing your place?"

"A secretary's place is quite flexible," Luke said. "Let me know what you want from me, and I'll do my best to provide it."

He should probably not have said that, because Oxney's eyes widened. Just a little flicker, just there, that sudden crackle of awareness at a second meaning. Still, he sounded level enough as he said, "Well, let's try it. Shall we give it a month and see where we stand? As for salary...what did your last employer give you?"

"Two hundred a year."

"Are you worth that?"

"No, Lord Oxney," Luke said with absolute assurance. "I'm worth twice that."

Oxney gave him a long look. It was hard and assessing, penetrating even, and once again made him want to shift in his seat. Oxney had been a major in Wellington's army, which implied a force of personality and determination that hadn't gone away just because he was out of his depth in a study full of paper. Possibly this business—this master—might not be quite as easily managed as all that.

Still, he liked a challenge.

At last, Oxney nodded. "Two hundred and fifty per annum, then.

The fifty's for putting up with the family, or making them put up with you."

Luke bowed in his seat. "My lord, it will be a pleasure."

❧

"Feet *right* under the table, then," Cousin Emily said. "Secretary, la."

Luke was eating alone in a spare drawing room, of which the house had many, as he had the previous night. Oxney had ordered it as he was currently neither a servant nor a suitable guest for the Family's table. He'd move to the servants' hall once Oxney had broken the news that they had officially joined forces. "Conrad's going to fly up into the boughs," he'd said with a grin.

It suited Luke very well. He'd let Emily know and she'd arranged to bring his meal, a lavish quantity of food to which she'd helped herself lavishly. They were enlivening dinner with a very useful conversation.

"Where do the staff stand?" Luke asked.

"Mr. Pauncefoot, the butler, he's the one to watch," Em said. "Mrs. Conrad's man through and through, and can't stand his new lordship. Nor can Bunting, Mrs. Conrad's lady's maid, evil old stick. They bully everyone between them. They're saying his lordship won't stay. He's no use, can't do the work, he'll go off and spend all the money in London and everything will go back to how it was."

"Why are they saying that?"

"Want it to be true, I expect. All those years waiting for the title while the old master rotted in bed. Honestly, I thought he'd never die. And after, when it went to law, we had to call Mr. Conrad 'my lord' anyway, and woe betide if Mr. Pauncefoot heard you say anything but what he'd win."

Luke poured her a second glass of wine. She gave him a look. "Free with your master's things already?"

"Excuse *me*," Luke said. "I'm merely being treated as I deserve."

She increased the intensity of the look, which gave her a fleeting but unlovely resemblance to Aunt Sybil. "What are you up to, bettermy? The things people are saying, about Mr. Raymond and this secret marriage—"

"I can't help what people are saying."

"Like heck you can't. Does Joss know what you're about?"

"I'm on the Isle, not the Marsh," Luke pointed out. "It's not Joss's business."

"*You* tell him that," she said firmly. "If he asks me, I'll answer."

That was standard self-preservation for any Doomsday, so Luke didn't argue. "Anyway, the wine's for me. His lordship said so."

"Nice for some."

Housemaids didn't get wine. Luke had never been sure why Emily, the most literate Doomsday other than himself, had settled for a domestic role and stayed in it for six years now.

"Enjoy it. And while you're drinking, what happened in or after the year nine? Here, I mean. Mr. Odo mentioned something expensive, but when I asked what, he just said words at me."

"Oh, bless him," Emily said. "He's not nearly so bad once he gets away from the rest of them, but he's scared as a cat of his family. Can't blame him. The way the old master used to go on at him, and Mr. Fulk always calling him an idiot, and his ma and pa the worst of the lot. Not surprising he can't hardly get a word out. It's a crying shame."

"Poor fellow," Luke said. "The year nine?"

As expected, she had the story. It was long before she'd come to Stone Manor, but she was an intelligencer.

The old Earl Waleran had first become ill in 1808, fifteen years back. He was soon confined to bed and thought likely to die, so Baldwin, Lord Stone, his eldest son and heir, had assumed control of family affairs.

Unfortunately, Lord Stone had not been a respecter of the d'Aumesty heritage. His first act had been to build the ridiculous undersized Gothic cathedral over the Elizabethan herb garden, and he'd been working on plans to level Stone Manor and construct something more suited to his own taste. He spent a fortune on works over a couple of years as his father languished; once the earl had recovered, he'd been furious.

"Never forgave him. Used to shout at him all the time," Emily said. "Mr. Pauncefoot says they fought, but I can't see Lord Stone fighting, myself. He'd just smile in this bland sort of way and do as he pleased. He'd drawn up a whole set of plans for a new building, with an architect. The earl burned them, and cut his allowance off, never gave him another a penny so he couldn't hire another man. It was like that for ten years and more, the old earl cursing him up hill and down dale, and Lord Stone cared not a whit. He just had to wait for his father to die, and then he'd tear the house down. And the old master knew it."

Luke whistled. "How old was Lord Stone then?"

"Well in his fifties."

"And he lived here? Why do they all live here?"

"His lordship didn't want them anywhere else. Lord Stone, Mr. Conrad, all of them. He sent Miss Berengaria to have a London Season, but said her husband would have to come live here."

Miss Berengaria was Conrad and Matilda's daughter, elder sister to Fulk and Odo. Luke had vaguely expected her to be either the spoiled darling of the house or a general dogsbody; as yet he had seen no evidence of her existence.

"Unusual," he said. "Why would a husband want to come here?"

"And get pushed around by the Earl, or Mrs. Conrad? Well you might ask." Emily sniffed. "You'd come if you loved her, course, but it didn't arise. She didn't 'take', like they say, and Mrs. Conrad won't let her forget it. Same sort of thing with Mr. Fulk. He was supposed to make a good marriage and bring his bride here as future countess. Lord Stone wasn't married or going to be, so Mr. Fulk would have got the title in due course, but Mr. Conrad's not much over fifty, and the old man lived to be almost ninety, and I wouldn't sign up to be Mrs. Fulk, still less Mrs. Conrad's daughter-in-law, on a promise of being a countess in thirty years."

"So the earl wanted his family around him?"

"Even though he hated half of them. Well, all of them but Mr. Fulk and Miss Berengaria, really."

"Still, he couldn't *make* them stay."

"Purse strings," Emily said succinctly. "And the glory of the Family and that. And mostly, Lord Stone and then Mr. Conrad were just biding their time to inherit. Must be a thing, sitting about waiting for your father to die."

Emily's father had drowned when she was a baby. Luke's, regrettably, had not. They exchanged shrugs.

The current situation was because the old earl had sickened again five years ago, becoming more and more cantankerous and domineering. "Arbitry," Emily said, a Marsh word for a cruel old clutchfist. "He dismissed staff, cut spending on the estates. Ordered Mr. Odo to act as clerk though anyone can see he's all the use of a glass hammer, and there was Mr. Fulk and his father fighting like cats in a sack, because Mr. Fulk's expensive and the old master paid his debts, but he wouldn't fund Mr. Conrad. Imagine being jealous of your own son."

"It happens," Luke said.

She shot him an apologetic glance. "Well, he was though, because Mr. Fulk had his father's favour and the money. Miss Berengaria too. The old master paid for her paints and didn't care if she married. He said she could do as she pleased. *That* wouldn't have lasted when Mrs. Conrad took charge of the funds. And all of them on at poor Mr. Odo, and him worrying himself to a wreck, and the old master spitting bile at Lord Stone. Like back home when your old man and Joss were always at each other's throats, but three times as many of 'em at it, and nobody caring to keep the peace. And then Lord Stone died. That was a shock. He wasn't young, but even so, nobody expected it."

"What did he die of?"

"Were you on the Marsh for that bad storm in the year eighteen? It was then. He told Mrs. Conrad he was going to commune with Nature, went out in the rain, and died."

"Rain doesn't kill you," Luke was forced to observe. "If it did, the Marsh would be empty."

Emily gave him another look. "Not like that, bettermy. It was his heart. What it was, he stayed out overnight in the storm. Miss Berengaria says that's what communing with Nature is if you're a proper romantic sort, like poets."

"Sir Gareth communes with Nature all the time, and he's got enough sense to come in out of the rain."

"Maybe he's not romantic. Anyway, they found Lord Stone lying on the ground in the morning, not thirty yards from the Chamber Block." She dropped her voice to a low, thrilling tone. "He'd beaten his hands bloody to be let back into the house."

"He was locked out, in a storm?"

"Course not," she said, reverting to her normal voice. "He'd ordered a side door left open for him, which it was, and if it had been locked, there was the Cathedral to shelter in, or he could just have rung the bell, for goodness' sake. But there he was dead, with his hands all battered. I suppose he panicked. Silly old fool."

"You didn't like him?"

"No," she said. "Not that he ever did anything to me. But you ever seen those beetles pinned on cards, all nicely arranged? Does Sir Gareth have those?"

"No. He likes looking at live creatures, not owning dead ones."

"Good. Those things are mucky. But that was how Lord Stone was. Not cruel, but distant. He looked at you like beetles."

Luke couldn't help a shudder. Emily nodded. "I doubt anyone mourned him, and the old earl downright hated him, but he was knocked sideways all the same. We all thought that was why he never gave Mr. Conrad the title. Mrs. Conrad wanted to be Lady Stone and she was in middling order about it, but he wouldn't. I suppose that was because he knew that Mr. Raymond's son was alive."

"About that," Luke said. "Why on earth did the old earl not tell Mr. Conrad he wouldn't inherit?"

"I don't know. Funny way to go on, with the Conrads strutting round proud as peacocks. Maybe that's the why. They were sat there waiting for him to die, so could be he thought it served them right not to be told. And he *didn't* die, anyway, or not for ages. He couldn't leave his bed, he was skin and bone, but he dragged on, worse and worse, for years."

"Lord," Luke said. "I'm so glad Great-Uncle passed suddenly."

Emily gave his hand a squeeze. They'd both adored their great-uncle Asa Doomsday, who had taken charge of their educations. "That's right. Your heart stops and you go, best way. Not the earl. He lingered on till we all thought he'd live forever." She shook her head. "This is a dismal house."

"And what about his lordship, the new man? What's he like?"

It was a silly question that he didn't need to ask. He just felt the urge to know what she thought. Perhaps she'd have insights.

Emily cocked her head. "You'd know better than me, Mr. Secretary. Temper, we've all heard that. I heard he threatened to kick Mr. Conrad round his house for insulting his mother. Always polite to the staff, though, and the grooms love him, just ask Perce in the stables. Fills his breeches well, not that I'm supposed to notice *that*. Ooh, I've had too much wine." She put her glass down. "And not stupid, I don't reckon, for all the Family say he is."

"Do they?"

"All the time. They say he's had no education, never learned to read proper-like."

"That doesn't make a person stupid."

"It does not," Emily agreed. "Reading too much, that's what gets you, so be warned. I'm off, bettermy. And whatever you're up to, take care of yourself, because I won't be blamed when it goes wrong."

Five

TAKING DOOMSDAY ON MIGHT HAVE BEEN THE BEST IDEA RUFUS
had ever had, except for the calamitous parts.

His new secretary was as good as he'd proclaimed himself to be.
He'd sent Rufus away with a humble request—Rufus knew an order
when he heard one—that he stay away from the study until permitted
to return, and brought Odo back in to help him sort out the paperwork disaster by identifying what went where. It took two days, at the
end of which the study looked like it belonged to a rational person,
and Odo was speaking in complete sentences.

(Rufus had asked how the devil he managed that. "I didn't shout
at him," Doomsday said, "and I let him tell me all about the family
history while we worked, in full detail. I think we reached the reign
of Queen Anne." Rufus had not pressed further: he could see when
a man's eyes held pain.)

Superficial order restored, he'd set to work on the issue of spending on the Oxney holdings over the last years. This was Rufus's first
concern. It seemed that his grandfather had become miserly, prone
to rages, locked in hatred of his sons. He'd despised Baldwin, Lord

Stone, with his plans to demolish Stone Manor, but he'd seemingly also despised Conrad, who couldn't be more concerned with the family heritage. He hadn't given Conrad any power to manage affairs, and Conrad hadn't tried to force his hand with legal action.

Which went to confirm the man was a useless prick, because what Rufus was looking at now was an extensive patchwork of holdings, farms, and buildings where not even the bare minimum of repairs had been done in long enough to turn small nuisances into large problems. He had a lot of angry tenants, though their anger was held down under a lid, like steam in a boiling pot, meaning they were just as likely to explode. He couldn't blame them: it was a damned disgrace. Doomsday had made a complete list of repairs requested and what action if any had been taken, while Rufus had spent a couple of days in the saddle speaking directly to his tenants, hearing their complaints, and assuring them that things were going to change as quickly as he could make them.

He and Doomsday were to spend the day on this. It was urgent. Doomsday was already downstairs. And yet Rufus was still in the Earl's Salon, looking out of the window, wasting time.

It wasn't as if there was much of a view. Granted he had the best vantage point over Romney Marsh that one could ask, but the problem with that was it showed him Romney Marsh. No rolling downs, no peaks, not so much as a hill, and he could only see the sea as a vague grey line even when the air was clear of rain, which was not often. It was just an endless stretch of dead-flat reclaimed land unpleasantly reminiscent of the Low Countries, where he had spent several months trying not to be killed. The whole thing was enough to dishearten a man, and he was looking out at it purely to delay several conversations he needed to have.

Several he needed to have; one he absolutely must not even hint at, because Doomsday was a man in a risky position. Odo was wallowing in the archives like a pig in shit, happily reading every page of endless spidery incomprehensible letters in search of anything that might be a reference to a secret marriage, but he'd been at it more than a week now. Rufus very much doubted he'd find anything, and Conrad was furious about it. His last hope was leading nowhere, he had brought a 'scoundrel Doomsday' into the rarefied precincts of Stone Manor, and the scoundrel in question had promptly usurped Odo's role and become Rufus's ally. Conrad was spitting nails, and he'd doubtless take it out on Doomsday if he could.

Well, he couldn't, that was all. Doomsday had asked for Rufus's protection and he'd get it, and that meant Rufus was not even going to think about the wicked smile, a touch lopsided because of the scar's pull, the way his eyes laughed even when his face was sober, those thick brows that begged for the stroke of a finger, the bright, glowing hair.

Doomsday was an excellent secretary. He couldn't help how he looked, or smiled, or the way his shameless insubordination tickled Rufus's...call it, his fancy. And he was waiting downstairs, so Rufus needed to be the responsible nobleman he was and not slaver like some cursed predatorial rake over a man in his employ.

With that severe self-rebuke in mind, he went down to the study. Doomsday was at the desk, caught in a shaft of morning light from the window. His hair glowed like an angel's halo in an illuminated manuscript, the savage scar just a misplaced scratch of ink, and Rufus felt the breath stutter in his lungs.

Then he looked up and smiled. "Good morning, my lord."

Lord, Rufus reminded himself. Lord and master—Christ, no, lord and *employer*, and thus keeping his hands to himself. "Morning. Got that list?"

Doomsday picked up the papers in front of him and held them, halfway between demonstration and offer. They were neatly but closely written, and Rufus's heart sank.

"It's long," Doomsday said. "And involved. Would you prefer to read it first? Or if you wanted to refer to the plan of the estates at the same time, I could go through it, and take notes on your comments?"

He knew. He had to know, because that was close as dammit to *Shall I read it out to you?*, so why the hell wasn't he saying anything? Rufus had a strong urge to snatch the papers from his hand just to show him he didn't need any bloody help, and enough self-discipline to recall that, in fact, he did.

"Good idea," he said, knowing it was a paper-thin excuse. "Helps me learn it all. All right, I have the plan: go on."

"Prawls Farm," Doomsday said. "On the Isle, east of here—"

"Keeps pigs. Outbuildings in shocking repair."

"He's requested work four times, starting March twenty, to which he is unquestionably entitled under the terms of the leasehold. It wasn't done because Lord Oxney instructed Mr. Smallbone not to carry them out under any circumstances. He said, I quote, 'Prawl is as much a pig as his beasts.'"

"Why?"

"He's a Dissenter."

"My grandfather refused to carry out his legal obligations to a tenant because he didn't like the man's beliefs? Christ. Get them done. Next."

"Pick Hill Farm, near Small Hithe. Bad damage from the storm of the year eighteen, when Lord Stone died. Lord Oxney refused to pay on the grounds that he was the greater sufferer."

"You aren't serious."

"There's seven significant claims for damage from the storm of eighteen, and he wouldn't pay any of them. Mr. Smallbone's been putting them off ever since."

Rufus tossed his plan of the estate on the table. "Why the devil did Conrad not take action? He sat there watching his father abuse the tenants, deny his obligations, run down his bloody inheritance, and did nothing even once the old bastard was dead? This is going to cost a fortune to put right, and God knows how much resentment's built up. And he just bowed the knee and let the senile bedridden avaricious old fool do as he pleased!"

He was too loud, he realised. "I beg your pardon. I'm not shouting at you."

"Just near me." Doomsday looked unintimidated. "Is that a rhetorical question, or would you care for an answer?"

"Have you got one?"

"After Lord Stone's death, I understand Lord Oxney became irrational, insisting that no power would pass from his hands. People thought he resented Mr. Conrad for taking Lord Stone's place. There were furious arguments over his refusal to grant the courtesy title, with Lord Oxney screaming that Mr. Conrad would have nothing while he lived. Of course, we now know that Lord Oxney could not grant the title because it was yours if anyone's, but at the time, it was seen as hatred of his heir."

"He couldn't give away the title, but he could have let Conrad manage the lands for him," Rufus said. "I have wondered if he ran down the estates so badly because he knew it was all coming to me."

"It's entirely possible," Doomsday said, in very much the matter-of-fact way he'd suggested that his mother wouldn't want to see his face. "But Lord Oxney could also have lavished money on Mr. Conrad while he lived, and he didn't do that either. I'm told he said that, if Mr. Conrad tried to assume any of his dignities or privileges in advance, Lord Oxney would throw him out of the house."

Rufus had a number of questions about that. The most pressing was, "Told by who?"

A smile glimmered in Doomsday's eyes. "Do you want to know,

my lord? If I can assure people they may speak to me in confidence, that might be more useful to you."

An information-monger. Of course he was. Rufus had known a few men like that in the Army. They always heard everything first; they could generally obtain supplies to which nobody else had access, or put you in touch with whoever you needed, for a price. Rufus, who vaguely suspected such men functioned by witchcraft, disapproved strongly.

On the other hand, he had to admit this was useful. "Hmph. Nobody ever gossips to me."

"Well, they wouldn't," Doomsday said. "You're a great deal too straightforward. Gossip requires a bit of give and take. Flexibility. Everyone talks to my cousin Joss on the Marsh because he knows what things to keep quiet and when to tell people."

"*Flexibility.*" Rufus rolled his eyes. Doomsday flickered his brows, conveying wordlessly that that was not one of Rufus's talents. It was insolence and insubordination, and Rufus fought back a grin. "Are you sure of your sources?"

"Yes. The arguments were loud, and your family tend not to notice people of less importance."

In other words, they had flaming rows with the servants in the room and expected them to pretend they didn't hear. Rufus had been raised in a household where the maids regularly put their halfpenceworth into any argument, but of course nobility were different.

"Still," he said. "The level of neglect—surely Conrad should have acted. Found someone to talk to the old man, someone he respected."

"I'm not sure who that would have been. My understanding is that Mr. Conrad was in a state of constant expectation—apprehension, I should say—of his father's death. Perhaps he felt legal action would be unnecessary, and ruin his last days?"

"As if Conrad ever gave a damn about ruining anybody's day."

"I try to be charitable," Doomsday said, a lopsided grin marking the obvious lie.

"See if you can be charitable about Smallbone, then," Rufus said. "Because given the deliberate neglect over which he's presided as steward, and the number of people who've told me of promises of 'repairs next year without fail', not to mention that he's spent the last two months being absolutely bloody useless to me, I'm inclined to dismiss him for gross dereliction of duty. I wanted to give the swine a chance, but he's had that and more." His grandfather's lugubrious steward had not endeared himself to Rufus in general, but it was the string of broken promises he disliked most.

"I don't know about charitable," Doomsday said. "Mr. Smallbone brought all the requests to Lord Oxney. Mr. Odo has confirmed that he pleaded for help and raised the problems that the neglect caused, but Lord Oxney told him to economise, and to stop exaggerating. He said that he lavished money on his ungrateful tenants and wanted to hear no more complaints, or Mr. Smallbone would be replaced himself. Perhaps he should have resigned on principle, but he has a large family, and lives in a cottage owned by the Oxney estate." He raised his hands. "I suspect he isn't a negligent man, just a badly downtrodden one. He can't do his job with self-respect, he can't afford to leave, he fears supporting you because it will earn Mr. and Mrs. Conrad's hostility, especially if you go to London and leave the estate in Mr. Conrad's hands. And, I suspect, he can't make himself believe that you will do better, because he's more afraid of being disappointed again than he is willing to hope."

That was too much at once. "Hold on. Go to London? Why would I do that? And why would I leave Conrad of all people running the place?"

"That's what Mr. Pauncefoot is saying you'll do. The idea is that you will enjoy your newfound status in the fleshpots of the big city, and Mr. Conrad will rule here. Which, if true, would make it a very poor idea for the staff to side with you against the Conrads. It's why you're having so much trouble making people listen to you."

Rufus stared at him, wordless. Doomsday looked a question. "No?"

"Yes. Or—are you sure of this?"

"It's what's said in the servants' hall. Not in front of me, but…"

His cousin. "Right. I see. That was the very devil of a briefing, Doomsday. I know you said you liked to be invaluable, but I didn't realise you meant it."

Doomsday actually flushed, his cheeks reddening with pleasure. It was delightful. "Not at all, my lord," he said, with an airiness that the blush undermined. "All part of the service."

"Consider yourself licensed to be as flexible as you need with information, as long as you pass it to me like that. Can we get Smallbone back up to scratch? Or rather, can I retain a man who nobody trusts any more?"

"If you wished, I think you could. Everyone knows about the old earl, and Mr. Smallbone did the job well for twenty years before this. Perhaps we might make a list of the most urgent works from this and put him on it, with the money ready, and you can see if he applies himself to your satisfaction. A last chance."

"I would prefer that."

Doomsday hesitated. "If I might suggest…"

"We both know you're going to, whether I like it or not. Spit it out."

Doomsday grinned at him. "I will of course keep my opinions to myself if required, my lord."

"I'd like to see the day," Rufus said darkly. "Go on."

"Mr. Smallbone had a great deal of respect for your grandfather, and was badly affected by the change in his character. If you approach this, not as repairing your grandfather's gross neglect, but as restoring his life's work, I think you'd have Mr. Smallbone's enthusiastic support."

That was exactly the kind of thing at which Rufus was dreadful. It made perfect sense when he was told, but he never seemed to think of it before someone told him. "Understood. You may make suggestions whenever you like, if you continue being this useful. I'm beginning to feel your salary is a bargain."

"I hope you find it so." He said that almost urgently, as though it might not be true. "And speaking of suggestions..."

"Already? Good God."

"It's about the matter of you going to London. Is that your plan?"

"Of course not. Can't stand it, stinking filthy pit. What the blazes would I do there?"

"I think you're intended to court ladies at Almack's."

"No," Rufus said firmly. "Damned if I'm going, even if they'd let me in."

"Why would they not let you in? You're an earl."

"Wouldn't do me any good. I've heard about that place. Fancy manners and no trousers."

Doomsday spluttered. Rufus pointed a warning finger at him, grinning. "I meant, you have to wear black silk knee-breeches and dress up as though it's the last century. Drink ratafia and mind your language. Bugger that. And how am I supposed to take charge of the estate from London?"

"Well, you couldn't, that's the point. This is, let's call it wishful thinking on Mr. and Mrs. Conrad's part, as passed down through the staff by Mr. Pauncefoot. And it doesn't have to be Almack's; the point is very much the courting of ladies. You are the earl, and, well, heirs."

"I couldn't give two shits for that," Rufus said, once again forgetting he was an earl, although in fairness, the most foul-mouthed of his fellow officers had been a marquess's son. "And I'm not courting anyone. Wouldn't know how to start."

"You could court!" Doomsday said with a touch of indignation. "Perhaps not in the most conventional manner, but you'd have no trouble."

"I would. I never learned to dance—would you believe that's all but demanded of officers? Bloody ridiculous cavalry twiddle-poop." As a proud member of the 54th Foot, Rufus had views on cavalry officers. "And I've no idea about fine words or wooing, and I'm cursed if I know what one's meant to *do*. If you want me to continue the d'Aumesty line, Christ knows what for, you'll need to give me a list of instructions, or find me an etiquette guide or some damn thing."

"A nobleman's guide to courting a countess? Step one, take the lady's hand and praise the delicacy of her skin with a salute." Doomsday adopted a decidedly effete upper-class voice for that, simultaneously turning his hand and arm in a wonderfully elegant manner, offering Rufus his palm just like a lady.

Rufus took it, bowed over it, and kissed it.

He hadn't intended to do that. It was just a joke, spur-of-the-moment, continuing the banter, except that he'd *kissed* Doomsday's *hand*, not just the hand but the sensitive palm, had pressed his lips against warm skin, and even as he stood bowed over it wondering at his own incredible stupidity, he still held that hand in his. "Uh—"

"That's very good." Doomsday's fingers rested lightly in Rufus's, so that all Rufus would need to do was close his own fingers on them and pull. His long eyelashes were lowered modestly, as part of the joke. His voice sounded a bit constricted. "Perhaps a little forceful, but flattering enthusiasm is very hard to resist."

"I'm glad it meets your approval," Rufus managed. *Play along*, he told himself. *Banter.* "What's step two?"

"That would be a compliment on the radiance of her complexion, or perhaps the lustre of her eyes."

"Madam, your eyes are as brown as, uh. I don't know. Bread?"

Doomsday's downswept eyes swept right back up. *"Bread?"*

"I couldn't think of anything else brown. Hot chocolate? A good beef stew?"

"Stop talking now," Doomsday said, extracting his hand. "And by that I meant: Maybe I should send for an etiquette guide, my lord."

"I'm glad you meant that, or it would have sounded damned insubordinate," Rufus told him. *Banter. Joke.* "Nonsense aside, no. I'm not going to London or courting anybody, so what was your point?"

Doomsday looked at him for all the world as if he'd forgotten the point. "Uh—right. Yes. The point is, you need to say so. Make the staff understand that you're here to stay, you are the earl, and they are your people. They have to understand that the authority lies with you, and not with Mr. or Mrs. Conrad."

"You'd think that would go without saying."

"But it doesn't. Mr. Conrad was to be master here for a long time; he spent seven months being called the earl; and he is still questioning your right. Mrs. Conrad runs the household, with Mr. Pauncefoot very much her loyal lieutenant. The maids and footmen and grooms are being told that you'll be gone soon and the Conrads will be here, that if they serve you well, it's disloyalty. It's an impossible situation for them: they can't do their work properly because of your family argument. You need to make your position clear."

"My position as earl?"

"I'd say, your position as the man who will dismiss anyone who isn't up to scratch."

"No," Rufus said flatly. "I'm not dismissing people because they're caught between me and Conrad." So many of his men were jobless now, soldiers abandoned by the country they'd spent years serving, returning to find themselves placeless and unwanted.

"It would help them," Doomsday said. "The threat would constitute the excuse people need to ignore Mr. Pauncefoot. If they can say 'I have to do my job properly, I need the pay'—"

"I'm not going to bully anyone into siding with me, and that is the end of the matter."

"I understand that, my lord. But—"

"Not 'but'. If I can't win loyalty without forcing it, that's my failure, and it's time and past I amended matters. Tell Pauncefoot I want to inspect the staff tomorrow. I'm sure you'll have a way to put it."

Doomsday watched him with an expression Rufus couldn't read. "Yes, my lord."

Six

THEY SPENT ANOTHER COUPLE OF HOURS GOING THROUGH THE list of urgent repairs before luncheon. Rufus left Doomsday alone after that, because he had other things to be doing than hanging around his secretary. Instead he rode out to speak to Smallbone, since it had temporarily stopped raining. He needed every opportunity he could get to familiarise himself with his lands, and he also had to do some hard thinking.

He had been overwhelmed by the situation, that was the problem. He'd known he'd be unwanted as heir but he hadn't imagined the scale of hostility he'd meet from the family. The seven months in front of the Committee for Privileges had left him helpless and humiliated, a grown man in his thirties borrowing money from his stepfather to pay for a lawyer. He'd been a soldier since he was sixteen years old, and had no experience of being a gentleman of leisure, or of much else outside the Army. And his ennoblement had created a distance between him and his real family that Rufus hated but couldn't blame anyone for. His mother had no happy memories of the d'Aumestys; she, his stepfather, and their children were content in their own life, which had nothing to do with earls and manor houses.

Rufus had been pulled violently out of his own sphere, and flung into a new and very different one where he wasn't comfortable or wanted, and he hadn't known how to handle it. He felt like an inexperienced terrier thrown into a ratting pit, so swamped by the sheer number of problems that he flailed and snapped frantically to no effect.

Doomsday went in like a seasoned ratter: catch problem, break its back, catch the next. He was young to be so methodical, but Rufus had sat and watched him work a few times, telling himself it was to assess the fellow's capabilities. He could see the way he slid into deep concentration. His breathing changed, becoming shallower; he propped his elbows on the desk and ran his thumb unconsciously over the scar, up and down its curve, in a way Rufus had yet to see him do at any other time. He went through tasks and put things in motion as though he lived to get them done. If he'd been Rufus's aide-de-camp in the war, they'd have been unstoppable.

The difference was, in the war, Rufus had known what he was doing and been bloody good at it. So he wouldn't have left important things undone or unaddressed, and a competent aide-de-camp wouldn't have given him this vague sense he was being run rings round by a cleverer man.

And here he was thinking about Doomsday again. Bloody fool.

Why, why, why had he done that? It had been horseplay, he reminded himself, just foolery, not done for the feel of Doomsday's hand in his, the skin warm against his lips. He had at least resisted the temptation to describe Doomsday's eyes as they deserved, although in fairness their deep brown was more than anything the shade of a cup of long-brewed tea, which probably wouldn't sound any better than 'bread'. The colour didn't matter: it was their expression, the laughter and intelligence and occasional wariness, the life and light and just sometimes a flicker of something that Rufus could very easily persuade himself was desire.

"For Christ's sake, control yourself," he said aloud, and set heels to his horse.

When he returned to the house, it was to a message requesting his presence in the Manorial Hall's drawing-room. He had no idea why the Conrads couldn't confine themselves to the New Wing and leave him be, but he walked in to find Conrad, Matilda, all three of their children, and Doomsday, whose face was tight and very blank except for a red flush over his cheekbones.

Rufus opened hostilities. "What is this, an ambush?"

Matilda gave him a frozen look. "Good afternoon, Oxney. Would you care for tea?"

"No. What are you doing with my secretary?"

"We wish to know the progress of the investigation into your father's first marriage," Conrad said. "This fellow has been most unhelpful, indeed obstructive. I have a multitude of questions, important ones about this exceedingly serious matter, yet he has barely responded—"

"You've barely let him," Berengaria said.

She was a tall woman with an air of distant unconcern about her, hands and dress usually smeared with paint. She barely spoke at meals and was almost never to be seen round the house; Rufus had chalked her up as one step above the family ghost. Given the unexpected intervention, he might need to revise that.

Matilda was glaring at her daughter. "Hold your tongue."

"Tell that to Father and you might get somewhere. You've both shouted over him every time he opened his mouth. If I were Oxney, I'd want to know why you were bullying his staff. As I'm not, I'll merely ask why I have to sit and watch it."

Fulk and Odo were wincing but not obviously shocked. Rufus inferred that Berengaria stood up to her parents in a way they did not.

"Berengaria!" Matilda snapped. "You would do well to remember that dear Father is no longer here to indulge you. And if you wish—"

"I've better things to do than witness your family squabbles," Rufus said over her. "As to the investigation—" In truth, he'd all but forgotten about it. Doomsday was so convinced it wasn't true, and had fitted so perfectly into the role of Rufus's secretary, it had been easy to disregard how they'd got here. "First of all, kindly don't talk about my father's 'first marriage' as though it's an established fact, because it's not. Doomsday will report, and then Odo. Doomsday?"

"I have put several people I trust and respect on the task of looking for Louisa Brightling, my lord," Doomsday said. "I have heard nothing back."

"'Several people looking for her'," Fulk mimicked unpleasantly, putting on a Kentish accent Doomsday didn't have. "Ridiculous. She's your mother. How can one lose one's mother?"

"Careful, Fulk," Rufus said. "You sound like you're asking for tips."

Matilda's mouth opened in silent rage. Berengaria said, "Ha!" Doomsday's hand came up very much as if he'd been about to put it over his eyes, and who could blame him.

"I beg your pardon," Rufus went on swiftly, "but I will not have my secretary barracked. Go on, Doomsday."

"In answer to Mr. Fulk," Doomsday said, "Louisa left the Marsh when I was a couple of days old. Neither her parents nor my family were able to find where she went at the time, and that trail has been cold for twenty-six years. She could be anywhere in the country or out of it, under any name, or she could be dead. I would be most grateful for Mr. Fulk's advice on how best to proceed in this situation."

Fulk reddened. Conrad said, "That is insolent, sirrah. Oxney, you will oblige me by making this fellow mind his tongue."

"Two minutes ago, you believed he was the future earl," Rufus observed.

"I accept no such thing. The first marriage disqualifies you; *his* claim is flagrantly false. He admits himself he is a foundling and a bastard. I have written to an attorney for an opinion. This man is a scoundrel and a pretender and he will not be earl of Oxney."

Doomsday's mouth was tight. "I never suggested I should be."

"Be silent!" Conrad snapped.

"My secretary, Conrad," Rufus said. "Not yours to rebuke or insult: *mine*. Odo, what about the archives? Found any evidence of this supposed marriage?"

Odo's eyes darted nervously to his father. He launched into a stumbling explanation that didn't so much as reach a main verb before Conrad shouted, "For God's sake, boy, get on!"

"Let him speak," Rufus said. "Without interruption. Or I might think you're trying to bully him into doing your bidding."

Odo stared at the carpet. "I, I have found no references to any marriage in the books between January 1788 and the date of Raymond's marriage to Oxney's mother. The Brightling marriage, if it occurred, could surely not have been done under banns without word spreading here, so I wrote to the Archbishop of Canterbury to discover if Raymond requested a special licence. It, uh, it appears he did."

"Ha!" Conrad shouted.

"He did?" Rufus demanded. "Why didn't you say?"

Odo flapped a hand in an agonised way. "No—but— There is a record, an allegation as it is known, but it is not of a marriage. A licence *permits* a marriage; it does not prove one was carried out. And we knew already that Raymond intended to marry Miss Brightling: that was why Grandfather sent him away. And, and, also, unfortunately, you see, a special licence permits marriage anywhere at all, a private house, without the requirement for residency. If we don't know *which* minister carried it out—where—no parish record—a deliberately clandestine manner—very little chance—" His syntax was disintegrating under his father's stare. "I, I, I nevertheless consulted the parish records at Stone-in-Oxney, and also Fairfield, where Miss Brightling—and I sought advice from the curate there, too, most helpful, he and his daughter, remarkably well informed and quite charming—"

"For God's sake, stop wittering," Fulk said.

"Will you be quiet!" Rufus told him. "Odo, that is an outstanding piece of work. Thorough, comprehensive, and impressive. Doomsday, can you suggest any additional courses of investigation?"

"No, my lord. Mr. Odo has done everything I would have and more. I could not do better."

Odo had gone bright scarlet, but in a good way. "Um, thank you. Thank you very much. I did my best."

"Exceedingly well. So, your conclusion?"

The proud smile faded. Odo's eyes darted to his father. "Uh. Um. None."

"None?" Conrad repeated. "*None?*"

"None, Father. Unless some record is found—over thirty years ago—I have no evidence that any such marriage took place."

"What use is that, you stammering fool?" Conrad bellowed.

"It's ascertaining the truth," Rufus said as Odo shrank away. "I thought that was the purpose of the exercise. If you've got any better ideas on how to track down this probably non-existent marriage, feel free to offer them. And by 'ideas', I mean practical suggestions, not ranting about the answer you want."

"This fellow has attested there was a marriage!" Conrad snapped, stabbing a finger at Doomsday.

"No, Mr. Conrad. I repeated a story told to me by a dying man," Doomsday said. "I have no idea of its truth."

"But you have found nothing to say it is *not* true?" Conrad demanded of Odo. "No evidence against it?"

"Well, I suppose—"

"Precisely. You have not disproved the marriage, and in the absence of disproof—"

"May I ask what 'disproof' could be offered, Mr. Conrad?" Doomsday enquired. "What evidence, exactly, could show that a marriage didn't take place? I am not married, but I don't know how I could prove that. And I believe, in law, the burden of proof is on the shoulders of he who makes the allegation."

"Quite," Rufus said into Conrad's pop-eyed silence. "Which is to say, put up or push off. I'll be about my business. Come on, Doomsday."

"Excuse me," Matilda said. "It is evident you do not intend to admit this claim, no matter its likelihood—Be quiet, Berengaria! You must, however, realise it is quite inappropriate to put the claimant under obligation to you."

"I beg your pardon?"

"This man now takes your pay. Naturally he will do and say as you tell him. Clearly this renders his protestations in your support worthless, and when we take this to court, the judge will know what weight to give his word."

"You are insulting the integrity of a man who is unable to return the compliment," Rufus said. "I can and will do it for him. How dare you? How *dare* you assume I would bribe or bully to get my way, and how dare you assume he would take a bribe? It is a cursed insult to an honest man, and I am tired of insult at this family's hands."

"Protesting too much, coz?" Fulk sneered. "Come, now. You've brought in some scoundrelly Doomsday to Stone Manor and you expect us to believe you're keeping him around for, what, his good looks? Of course you're paying him off."

The force of rage all but lifted Rufus off his feet. "You are a bone-idle, insolent, rag-mannered swine who knows nothing of hard work, and if you want to continue in this house you will keep your damned vicious mouth shut!"

"And now you threaten my son," Matilda said. "Rather than accept the clear impropriety of having this man in the household, not just as a claimant but as a member of such a notorious family—"

"My staff are not your business!" Rufus bellowed. "Will you understand that! You have no say in who I employ!"

"A village boy of infamous family that you put in authority over my son, your cousin—"

"Mother," Odo pleaded. "It is Oxney's choice who he has as secretary, and Doomsday is awfully good. I am very happy to assist him."

"A d'Aumesty as a smuggler's assistant! It is a degradation!"

"Absolute rubbish," Rufus said. "Odo has done good work, which is more than I can say of anyone else in this family, and Doomsday is an excellent secretary, which is the beginning and end of why I employ him, and that is the end of this discussion."

"You employ him as a means to conceal the truth!" Conrad said.

"Oh, be fair, Father," Fulk put in viciously. "Oxney does need someone to read to him."

"We are all aware of the shortcomings of your education," Matilda added. "It is disgraceful that the earl of Oxney should have been so poorly taught as to stumble over his letters like an unschooled hobbledehoy."

"There was nothing wrong with my education," Rufus managed through a throatful of mingled shame and rage.

"Then clearly there are sad limits to your ability," Matilda returned, words clipped, precise, and calculated. "Whether it is your breeding or your upbringing at fault for your incapacity."

"Go to the devil, you damned scold!"

Fulk leapt up as Matilda gasped. "Don't talk to my mother like that!"

"Tell her to mind her tongue, then," Rufus snarled. "You, the lot of you, are in my house on my sufferance, and I'm coming to the end of that. If you don't like it, leave."

Matilda was on her feet as well. "You may be the earl in name, but you have no right—"

"You are a usurper!" Conrad shouted. "The title was meant for *me*! You don't belong here!"

"Who the devil would want to? Every fucking one of you is worse than the next, you arrogant, whining, inbred pack of scrounging cu—*What?*"

Doomsday had a hand on his arm, fingers digging in hard. "Excuse me, Lord Oxney." He sounded absurdly calm, despite the grip. "I believe you have business elsewhere."

His brown eyes were speaking. Rufus bit back an expletive and inhaled deeply through his nose. "We'll return to this conversation later."

"You will not walk away!" Conrad bellowed, but Rufus was already stalking out, fists and shoulders tight with tension, Doomsday at his heels. He kept up as Rufus strode out of the main door and set off, cutting through the woods at a clipping pace.

He'd lost his temper. He'd sworn, repeatedly, at his whole family, including his aunt, an older woman, and no matter how far he'd been provoked, that was simply wrong.

Shit.

He breathed deeply. The ground was muddy and the air wet, but it wasn't actually raining for once. Sticks crunched underfoot.

He took the path to a gap in the tree cover, on the edge of the Isle. From here he could see across the whole Marsh to where the escarpments rose to the north and west, a damp green-brown plain

cut with waterways and speckled with sheep, and the shifting grey
of the distant sea.

"It's so damned flat," he said aloud.

"The Isle was the biggest hill I ever saw until I was seventeen,"
Doomsday said from beside him.

"You're joking."

"I didn't leave the Marsh until I was nearly fourteen, and then
I went to school in Hastings. The first time I saw anything really
geographical was when Lord Corvin brought me to his house in
Derbyshire. I saw the land rise as we travelled of course, but when
the carriage stopped in the Peaks, when I truly understood what a
mountainous region looked like and that I had to live in it, I wanted
to curl in a ball on the floor and cry."

"Really?"

"I felt like being sick. It was awful. They just went up and up. Or
one went up them, and then the land went *down*." He shuddered
demonstratively.

Rufus laughed despite his roiling anger, mostly now directed at
himself. "You're a Low Countries man at heart?"

"I did come to love the Peaks. Well, it's beautiful. And large,
which also made a change, along with its more pointy qualities. But
going from here to there..."

Rufus could see that. The Marsh, in his view, was trammelled
beyond toleration, a hundred square miles of mud. Doomsday must
have felt like a bird let out of a cage. Rufus felt like a bear inside one.

"I lost my temper," he said.

"I saw."

"Thank you for stopping me. And I'm extremely sorry for the
insults you were exposed to."

"That is hardly your fault."

"You're here in my service, and what they said was unforgivable."

Insulting his parentage, his family, his honesty, his *face*. Which was in itself extraordinary. Fulk had asked if Rufus employed Doomsday for his good looks and he'd meant it as sarcasm. If he'd asked seriously, he'd have been a damned sight nearer the mark. How could anyone see nothing but the scar? "You don't have to put up with that, and I shouldn't blame you if you wanted to leave."

"Do you want me to?"

"Good Christ, no."

Doomsday's mouth twitched. "That sounded heartfelt."

"You would leave me alone in this house. Must I offer you half my fortune to stay?"

"No need." The twitch turned into a smile, and not Doomsday's usual cocky grin, but something else, something oddly vulnerable, a little uncertain. "I was grateful that you intervened on my behalf. It was... Well, thank you."

Rufus should probably turn that off with some light remark, that he'd do the same for anyone in his employ. Perhaps it might even be true. He couldn't say it.

He cleared his throat. "What they said. About me."

"That you struggle to read."

So matter of fact. "Well?"

Doomsday cocked his head. "I thought the work today went smoothly. I can summarise letters or papers easily enough, and read out the ones you want in full. And if there is anything I can change in the way the books are kept—wider lines in the ledgers, or writing in capitals—"

"That makes it worse."

"Noted. I've seen you with a newspaper: is there something about type that helps?"

It was an intelligent, incisive line of questioning that offered practical assistance, and Rufus should not find it grating on his nerves.

"If you're so damnably acute about how I read, or fail to, why the devil haven't you said something before? You're hardly backward in putting yourself forward."

"I've got a four-inch scar where my face was cut open with a knife, and you haven't brought that up either."

That left Rufus entirely wrong-footed. "What? That's your affair. It doesn't affect your ability to do your job."

"On the contrary. I once went in for interview and my prospective employer said, 'Good God, how dreadful,' and waved me straight out again."

"Christ. What's wrong with people?"

"'If you have no compassion, have you not even manners?'" Doomsday murmured. It sounded like a quotation. "Some people don't care to look past a disfigurement, or a difficulty, and that is their loss. You struggle, so you need support. I'm sure you had someone who read dispatches and so on in the army. I'll do what you need, if you tell me what helps."

"I don't want bloody help. I want to be able to read with the fluency of an average schoolboy," Rufus snapped. "Or, failing that, not to be the object of contempt because I can't."

"I can't mend the first. For the second, you could throw the Conrads out."

"Are you seriously recommending evicting my family from their ancestral home?"

"Well, I would."

Somehow, Rufus didn't doubt him. "You would, wouldn't you? Maybe you *should* be the earl. I can't."

"Why not?"

He said it like a serious question. Rufus found a tree and leaned against the trunk. "Because they've lived here all their lives. Well, Fulk's spent time in London, but the rest—Conrad's never left.

Matilda came here at her marriage and then *she* never left. I doubt Odo's been as far as Dymchurch. It's ridiculous that a third son never got off his arse to do something for himself or his family, but here we are, and God knows how they'd manage if I turfed them out. They'd be helpless. And for what? So I can live in a twenty-bedroom house by myself?"

"But you don't like living with them," Doomsday said. "And it's your house."

"I've lived with people I disliked since I was sixteen. That's what barracks are. And this business has not been fair to Conrad. He was led to believe he'd inherit; he spent years in that expectation. And it would be one thing if it had been a misunderstanding, but the old man knew the truth and concealed it, and that is the devil of a thing to do to your son. Conrad lost the earldom, but he also—" Rufus groped for his meaning. "To discover the old bastard knew all along, had let him hope—"

"Yes. I see."

"Conrad's a prick, but he's been truly wronged. I took his future; I don't want to take his home if I don't have to. I may yet have to, if that pair can't resign themselves to the situation, but then God knows what I'll do with Odo and Berengaria. They haven't merited being thrown out, but to kick out their ageing parents and not them—Ugh. It would be a blasted mess however I proceed. I can put up with a bit of talk while things settle down, and at least give everyone a chance to do better."

Doomsday simply stood, looking at him. Rufus said, irritably, "What?"

"Just, I think you are a very good-hearted man, my lord."

"Tell that to Matilda," he muttered. "God rot it, I swore at her. Bloody fool. Now I'm going to have to apologise to the damned woman." He rubbed the heels of his hands against his eye sockets.

"Is there something I can give Odo, that you can delegate to him, when he finishes searching for the—" He waved a hand.

"Non-existent needle in a very boring haystack? Why?"

"Well, you saw him. Poor fellow just wants to be useful—second son of a third son, can't blame him—and you've taken his occupation from him, not that he was any good. But it seems he can be competent when it's his area and nobody's shouting at him."

"Yes, he can, but I would really prefer him to stay out of the books. He's done quite enough damage."

"He could clear the study," Rufus suggested. "There's any amount of rubbish going back fifteen years that we don't need there. I'll tell him to take those to the archive, get it all tidied up."

"No, don't," Doomsday said quickly. "I'd rather not have him in there: he's still got the family history from Queen Anne's time to tell me. Um... Oh. You could ask him to write a history of the family."

"I don't want a history of the bloody family."

"But you have an excellent excuse not to read it."

Rufus turned on him, caught his eye, and threw his head back with a crack of laughter. "You damned swine. How often is it that you've been dismissed in disgrace?"

"Just the once, to date."

"Keep counting," Rufus said with menace.

He felt better for this. Better for being outside; better for speaking frankly about his incapability at last, instead of avoiding the subject in the vain hope it hadn't been noticed. Maybe even better for Doomsday's practical response. His mother had always been practical about it, and his fellow officers had cared a great deal less about the pen than the sword, but he'd had enough sneers, enough frustration, first tearful then angry, at his own struggle to do something that so many people found simple. It was a sore point that had never healed, and which both Fulk and Matilda had prodded viciously.

They'd meant to hurt. They'd intended to provoke him, and he'd been provoked, and not for the first time, either. He'd been a deal more level-headed than this in the Army, but in the Army he'd had a place, and a purpose, and a majority of people who preferred him alive to dead if he didn't count the French.

"It just occurred to me that I enjoyed being a soldier at war a great deal more than I am enjoying being an earl at peace," he said.

"I should think you were a very good soldier. Perhaps you need to put your talents into being an earl."

"I've been trying." Except he hadn't been frank with his secretary about his struggles with reading, and he was on the back foot with his family although he held the purse strings and the power, and he'd let the discipline of the manor staff slide away. "But not hard enough. Are you telling me to pull myself together?"

"I think this house might be a very intimidating place."

"Are you intimidated?"

"No, but I'm a Doomsday."

Rufus turned to look at him. He shrugged. "The Marsh is my home ground. The Isle is not, its lords are not my affair, and with the greatest respect, I don't give a curse for Mr. Conrad. Whereas the family must have loomed quite large for you, in the past, and that can cast shadows."

Rufus contemplated him. He looked serious, the thick brows drawn together, a slight frown tugging at the scar. Rufus wondered if lovers touched the scar, if they ran their fingers over it when they cupped his face. He wanted to know how the devil a boy—he must have been a boy—had got his face sliced open, and how many flinches he masked behind the cocksure facade.

"Shadows. What do you mean?"

"Your father was cast out, disowned. To grow up knowing that's a thing that could happen is unnerving."

"You think I care about the d'Aumestys disowning my father?"

"Families can be frightening things when they band together against one."

"I wouldn't know," Rufus said. "My father walked away from me and my mother. He cast us out, or away. I was four years old. My mother was only twenty—too young to wed by any reasonable standard, let alone be left with a son, and her parents hadn't forgiven her for the marriage. They gave their consent because my father had already spent the night with her, then told her she'd made her bed and to lie in it. And knowing that, knowing she had nobody in the world but him, *because* of him, he abandoned us."

Doomsday was watching, brown eyes intent. "I didn't know that."

"I don't remember much. My mother crying, and trying to hide it. She wrote to the earl for help because she was desperate, even though she was terrified the d'Aumestys would take me from her, and he didn't even trouble to reply. He had disowned Raymond, he didn't want me, and he was utterly indifferent as to whether we lived or died."

The surge of anger and resentment was startling in how fresh it felt. Doomsday said, softly, "I'm sorry."

"I despise my father's sort. All he thought of was his own wants. God knows what he put your mother through; he left mine when she was increasing a second time. She was probably too grown for his tastes by then. She lost that child." He rubbed his face. "She brought me up to be honest, and made sure I understood that a decent man shoulders his responsibilities and fulfils his obligations. She was always afraid I might grow to be like my father."

"Mine feared the same of me, or so I expect," Doomsday remarked. "Hence she didn't take the risk. That sounds like a very difficult time."

"Oh, we survived. My stepfather took us in out of kindness—that, and he was a business rival of my grandfather—and married my mother three weeks after they heard Raymond was dead. I'm a damned sight better off having grown up in his household than with any cursed d'Aumesty."

"Agreed," Doomsday said. "But even if you weren't fully aware of what was happening at the time, it will have been there—the fear of power, and hostility. Knowing you have been abandoned and could be again. Feeling you should be a part of something but you aren't."

"That sounds like experience."

"When people are frightening, you want to please them." Doomsday sounded a little distant. "Certainly, it's harder to oppose them."

"I opposed the French, and they frightened the shit out of me," Rufus pointed out. "Especially on horseback."

"But you knew how to fight those battles. You knew how to be Major d'Aumesty. Whereas Mrs. Conrad telling you that you don't understand your position and aren't fit for it is probably very unnerving if—well, if you fear she might be right."

Rufus exhaled. "At least you said it out loud."

"I think you understand your position very well, for what that's worth," Doomsday said. "It's simply that your understanding of how you should be and what you should do doesn't match Mr. and Mrs. Conrad's. And of course they're far more familiar with nobility and earldom and living in a castle, which might easily set even a confident man to wondering if you were wrong and they were right. It's very hard to be out of your accustomed place."

"Experience again?"

Doomsday gave a tiny shrug. "I was the first in my family to have more than dame school and my great-uncle's tutoring. My father hated the idea of my education; he thought it was an insult. Treachery. My great-uncle pushed for it, but in the end it was Sir

Gareth who found a school and paid for me to go. A lot of things were easier outside the family."

Rufus wondered what that meant to a man for whom family loomed so large. "I'm very grateful he, and you, did it, because you are damned useful to have around. I hope you know that."

"I like to be useful," Doomsday said. "Life is precarious when one isn't, as you observed with Mr. Odo." He gave a little frown. "I wonder if Mr. Fulk needs to make himself useful too."

"Him? Does he do anything but drink and gamble?"

"Well, no. I understand his grandfather funded him to do so for years, as the eventual heir, and now his father can't and won't, and he has nothing to do. That was my point."

Rufus didn't give a damn for Fulk. "Where's Dymchurch?" he asked instead.

"Over there." He pointed. "Eastward of here, on the coast."

"Do you want to go back? You have yet to have a day off."

"Perhaps next week."

"If you want to take a few days there, or to borrow a horse or whatnot, let me know."

"That's very kind."

He didn't sound enthusiastic. Rufus didn't press: he wasn't in any position to give other people advice on their family relationships, and it was Doomsday's business. He just wished he could do something, *anything*, that would tell his secretary that he had indeed made himself indispensable, that Rufus was relying on him to an alarming extent, and not just for paperwork. That it meant everything to have a true ally, a loyal lieutenant, an irrepressible, confident, cocky little bastard of a rat-catcher by his side. That he did not want him to leave.

He wasn't going to say any of that. If he started blurting things out, God alone knew where he'd stop.

Seven

THEY WALKED BACK TO THE MANOR TOGETHER IN SILENCE.
Lord Oxney was clearly bracing himself to go and apologise for
his language. Mrs. Conrad was not obliged to apologise in return,
because among the gentility, you could say whatever vile things you
liked as long as you expressed them with civility.

Luke didn't want him to apologise. Oxney had flown up into the
boughs when pressed about his reading, and thank God that was
finally out in the open, but he'd been getting steadily more outraged
on Luke's behalf, which was warming. Not that Luke needed defending, or protecting, or any of the shelter Oxney offered as though it was
natural, but still, he appreciated it. His whole life had turned on the
moment Sir Gareth—not a friend or even a relative, but a man with no
obligation at all—had stood up for him as a child. To have Oxney do
it for him now was quite unnecessary, but Luke liked it all the same.

Accordingly, his lord would not be humbling himself to an *arrogant, whining, inbred pack of scrounging*—he rather wished he'd let
Oxney finish the phrase. Which meant Luke needed to give him
something else to do instead.

"My lord?"

"Mmm."

"A thought," Luke said. "That incident came after I advised Mr. Pauncefoot of your intention to inspect the staff."

"So?"

"Mrs. Conrad runs the household and I don't think she likes the idea of that passing from her control. Hence restating the doubt of your legitimacy. It's to distract you from infringing on her authority."

Oxney frowned. "I suppose you're right. Curse it. Do I have to apologise for that too?"

"The very opposite, my lord. I think we should make it clear you're here to stay. Plant a flag. Claim your territory."

"Which territory?"

"The Earl's Salon. Did you look at the fabrics?"

Oxney gave a rueful grin. It was a very likeable expression. When he scowled he could have been a medieval baron, the kind that won wars and shouted at people and threw bones around at meals. He could have played the overbearing master of the house to perfection, if only he didn't smile.

Luke didn't want him to smile any less. He might even be wasting his time solving Oxney's problems because he wanted him to smile more. Professional pride, he told himself.

"I did look at them," the Earl said. "Unfortunately, and this is a devil of a thing for a man of my background to admit, I've no feeling for cloth or patterns at all. My stepfather despaired of ever making me a draper."

"How fortunate you had the earldom to fall back on."

Oxney gave a bark of laughter. "Yes, it was that or walking the streets. Sometimes I regret my decision."

"I'm sure you would have made an excellent lightskirt, my lord."

That was unquestionably going too far, except that Oxney simply swiped a hand at him, grinning. He gave himself a mental kick anyway. *Stop flirting. You tried that and look what happened.* Oxney's hand on his, the brush of lips over his skin—Christ, he'd made a fool of himself, and it could have been a lot worse. Thank heaven his master had simply played along with the joke.

Or, not-joke. Luke knew appreciative looks when he got them. He could also see Oxney was trying damned hard not to give them. If he'd said something flattering about Luke's brown eyes then, if he'd teased Luke's palm with his finger, or his lips, or his tongue—

He had not. He could have, and he'd chosen not to, and Luke had been pestered rather too often himself. He would do well to mind his manners before he became a nuisance.

To business, he told himself. "So did you like any of the fabrics? Do you want to see them again?"

"I dare say they'd all look very well. You pick one; you seem to know what you're about."

Luke sighed. "What do you want the room to feel like?"

"Feel?"

"The mood that it has, or that you want it to have when you walk in. You don't sit in that room at all; you only pass through it to go to bed. What should it feel like to make you want to stay there, with a book or a drink or a friend?"

"Cheerful, I suppose?" Oxney said dubiously. "Alive, unlike the rest of this mausoleum. What sort of questions are those?"

"When I was with Lord Corvin, he decided to renovate his Derbyshire house. He put the work in the hands of a good friend of his who is a noted artist. The rooms were beautiful when he'd finished, and suited Lord Corvin perfectly. I don't have his talents, of course, but I observed his technique, and he always started with the feelings he wanted to evoke, that Lord Corvin wanted to have. He said you use colour and light to make the mood of a room."

"Good God," Oxney said. "Is there anything you don't know?"

I don't know why I'm doing this, Luke thought. *God knows I've more important things on my plate. I don't know why you have to sit so close when we work, and watch me the way you do, if you're not going to reach for me. I don't know—*

He did know. He knew exactly what he wanted; he'd wanted it for long enough. When he had it, he could move on to other desires.

"I do my best, my lord. Could I look at the room again?"

"Yes," Oxney said. "Claiming my territory, you say? Yes, let's do that."

The Earl's Salon was every bit as dingy as Luke recalled. "Damned if I can see what you'd do to make this cheerful," Oxney said, looking around. "Well, burn it. A fire would be cheerful while it lasted."

Luke wasn't sure either. He'd done well in life by making limitless assurances without worrying about how he'd fulfil them: so far he'd always kept up with himself. He doubtless would again, but he had to admit that the task of turning this gloomy room into a delightful one was, perhaps, not quite as straightforward as he might have thought. "What does your idea of a cheerful room have?"

"Chairs?" Oxney offered vaguely. "Who's this fellow your chap used?"

"An artist named John Raven."

"Could we get him?"

"I believe he's travelling with Lord Corvin. I'm sure I can find someone to advise you—"

"What about Berengaria? She's an artist, I'm told. Always covered in paint, anyway. And she seemed a bit friendlier—less hostile—than the rest, earlier."

This was true. Then again, Luke had yet to hear any sense from a d'Aumesty, present company occasionally excepted. "Which are her paintings?"

"No idea. Unless she's the one painting all the Normans. Christ, I hope not, we've got enough of those."

Miss Berengaria lived with the rest of the Conrads in the New Wing. Luke had been quietly roaming the house in spare hours, but he hadn't yet found an excuse to spend time where he knew he'd be exceedingly unwelcome. He might as well take the opportunity. "Perhaps a visit to her studio, to see?"

They walked through the New Wing mostly in silence. "Feel like we're reconnoitring enemy territory," Oxney muttered, which was so close to Luke's own feelings that he gave a startled laugh. "Conrad's family have this part—two drawing rooms, don't know why they're always underfoot. I believe Berengaria has her studio around here; they all moan about the smell of paint. Maybe it's through this way? Damn: we've come too far."

Luke looked about him. Bewilderingly, they'd gone from papered walls to stone. "Is this part older?"

"We're in the Norman chamber pot. Chamber Block. The oldest bit, anyway. Have you not been here yet? No reason you should, nobody uses it except Pagan, who lives on the top floor. God knows why, must be even colder than my rooms. They built the New Wing to connect it to the Manorial Hall—that's our bit—in James the First's time because that's what passes for *new* around here. I'm sure Odo will explain it in detail if you ask. Do it when I'm present and you're sacked."

You might take that at face value if you didn't know him, Luke thought. He had a voice that had been trained and plentifully used for orders and shouting, and he seemed to assume his hearers would understand what was a joke, or a momentary flash of temper, and what a serious remark. The staff probably found that unnerving.

"I will live in fear, my lord," Luke said politely, as they retreated to the New Wing, and Oxney opened doors at random. "Mr. Raven, the artist I mentioned, insisted on the best light for his studio. That would be high up and south facing."

"Good idea. Let's try this way."

They did some stair-climbing and knocking, until Luke noticed the sharp smell of paint, and they followed that.

"It's coming from here." Oxney knocked at a door. A female voice, irritable, shouted, "Go away."

"It's Rufus!" Oxney shouted back. "Oxney, I mean."

"So?"

"My house," Oxney muttered, and opened the door.

The room was large, with reasonably generous windows compared to the Manorial Hall, though nothing like the light that artists demanded in Luke's experience. It still seemed bright, because the walls were covered in large, unframed paintings of quite extraordinary hues, a riot of vibrant colour.

"Good God," Oxney said.

Berengaria stood at an easel, brush in hand. Her plain brown dress was smeared with bright paint. She scowled. "What are you doing here, Oxney?"

"Disturbing you. You've encountered my secretary, Doomsday."

"I have, yes. I'd apologise for that nonsense earlier but I dare say you're accustomed to it. Which are you?"

That was to Luke's address. "Which what, Miss Berengaria?"

"Doomsday."

Oxney raised his brows. "There's more than one kind?"

"I was down in Dymchurch a few years ago, sketching. I met Ma Doomsday—there's a character—and a few others. There was a brother and sister, dark: he was remarkably charming, and she swore dreadfully."

"My cousins Joss and Sophia," Luke said, needing no further clues. "Ma Doomsday is my aunt."

"I drew all three of them. Interesting faces. And there was a very fine old man, too, and Tallant, of course. The maid," she told Rufus.

Gareth had acquired an excellent pencil drawing of Joss, which he had framed and kept in his bedroom. Luke had never asked where it came from. He rapidly adjusted his ideas.

"I didn't see you," she went on. "I'd remember." Her finger traced a shape over her own cheek in what looked like unconscious mimicry of the scar. "You don't take much after the rest of them, but there's a look, something about the eyes. Why's a Doomsday being a secretary?"

"It's my profession, Miss Berengaria."

"If you say so. What was it you wanted, Oxney?"

Oxney didn't answer because he wasn't paying attention. He was, rather, standing in the middle of the room, looking around with an expression of astonished joy.

Berengaria scowled. "Oxney?"

"I, uh, wanted to ask..." The Earl sounded distracted. "Did you paint these?"

Berengaria's head went back. She didn't lack composure and her manner was decidedly forbidding, not unlike Oxney's. All the same, Luke thought the gesture was defensive. "What if I did?"

"They're marvellous! Marvellous. The colours, my God. Glorious. This is the first room in the house that feels alive. It's—" Oxney turned on the spot, gesturing in a dramatic way as if to make up for his lack of words. "Look at these, Doomsday!"

Luke wasn't sure what he was meant to be looking at. The painter John Raven had once spent half an hour trying to explain art to him, then told him he was a philistine and thrown him out of the room. "They're speaking to you?" he tried. It was a phrase he'd heard used, though never understood.

"Yes! Yes, they are. You said colours. *These* are colours."

"What's that?" Berengaria enquired, attention caught.

"Oh, my rooms. The Earl's Salon. Ghastly. I want a room I might want to sit in, so Doomsday wanted me to think about colours. Turns out we've neither of us any idea. Whereas *this*—" He waved wildly. "Why aren't your paintings all over the house?"

"Mother finds them vulgar," Berengaria said, with precision.

"What? God, she's a raging—"

Luke coughed very loudly, but Oxney was already correcting himself to, "She's wrong. I'd put these everywhere. I *want* these everywhere. Is that right, for the paintings? Can you do that in a pile like this? Would you allow it?"

Luke melted backwards, out of the way, and drifted gently around the room as the cousins conducted an increasingly animated discussion— which was, he realised, the first time he'd seen Oxney actually enjoying a conversation with someone other than himself. All the rest of the time he'd been either holding on to his patience or losing it.

That wasn't fair. He was energetic and huge-hearted and a force of nature, and he ought not be trapped in the miserable grinding atmosphere of Stone Manor. No wonder such an extremely vibrant man liked these extremely vibrant paintings. No wonder he was flailing in this cobwebbed and stifling place. He looked entirely different waving his hands and talking at the same time as Berengaria, whose stiff, reserved features were lighting up. They could hardly not: Oxney's enthusiasm was a near-physical force, and Berengaria would have to be made of stone to not be delighted. Luke wondered what it might be like to be the undivided focus of all that energy.

He was going to do something about Stone Manor while he was here, he vowed. Loosen Conrad and Matilda's death-grip, at least, and help Oxney bring the sunshine in.

He wandered around as the cousins chattered, looking at the paintings and trying to see what Oxney saw. They were very bright. Some were fantastical landscapes: a few of the usual Gothic sort with crags and mountains and apocalyptic volcanoes, but more that seemed to be images of an English Paradise, with lush woods and meadows, and brilliant dawns. Some were of gardens, thick with flowers he didn't know, possibly imaginary. A couple of those had insects; one in particular crawled with bright butterflies and beetles. He wondered what Gareth would make of it.

The one he stopped in front of was different.

It showed the Marsh, an endless plain of grey-green-brown, studded with gnarled black thorn trees and cut by dull grey dykes. It looked like February, a dead water-land in a dead month, except that over it stretched a rainbow so strong and bright that its stripes were reflected in the water below. Flashes of colour leapt from dyke to dyke, setting the Marsh aglow.

It was just a painting. Just the Marsh, lit with imaginary beauty. All the same, he looked at it for a long time with a feeling he wasn't sure how to interpret, and moved on because he had the oddest feeling, just for a second, that he wanted to cry.

The next few paintings were of a conventional ruined-architecture sort, which he could ignore forever. That came as something of a relief, until one quite extraordinary composition caught his eye. He stopped and stared.

"Found something?" Oxney said over his shoulder. "God almighty, what the hell is that?"

"Ah, the tauroctony," Berengaria said. "That's just a preparatory work for something Great-Uncle Pagan asked me to do."

The image was somewhere between sketch and painting. It looked vaguely classical to Luke's eye, and showed a young man in a short red tunic and a peculiar floppy hat. He had one knee on a white bull's back, and was pulling its head back by the nostrils, knife at the ready above its shoulder. The bull was simultaneously and rather unfairly being attacked by a dog, a snake, and a scorpion. The last of those had affixed itself lobster-style to the bull's prominent scrotum. Oxney made a choking noise, suggesting he had also noticed that detail.

"What did you call it, Miss Berengaria?" Luke asked.

"Tauroctony. Bull-slaying. Do you know about Mithraism?"

Luke shook his head. Oxney said, warily, "I've heard Pagan mention it."

"I imagine you have. It's a Roman cult. Pagan believes this area was a centre of Mithras-worship. There's an altar with carvings of the sacred bull in the vicarage garden in Stone."

"Really?" Luke had never heard anything about this down on the Marsh, but it sounded the sort of thing Isle folk would do. "Is it used often?"

She gave him a look. "An ancient altar. It's been there forever, hence the names of Stone Manor and Stone, the village: the place of the altar stone. It once stood in the churchyard, but it was being used as a horse block so some past vicar had it moved. Pagan has always thought there was a mithraeum here."

"A—?"

"Mithraic temple. Underground, very dark, very secret. Lots of smoke and incense, with the practitioners wearing strange masks and everyone chanting. Nama Mithras! Nama Mithras!" she intoned with relish. Luke flicked a glance at Oxney and had to bite his lip.

"You should ask Pagan about it," Berengaria went on, voice returning to normal. "No, you really should. Mithras was a soldier's god, you see, just the thing for you, Oxney. And a trader's god too, hence the temples across the far-flung corners of empire, wherever merchants and soldiers went. Lord of the Contract, he was called, and God of the Exchange. You like that?"

She addressed that to Luke, startling him. "In what way, Miss Berengaria?"

"God of the Exchange. You looked like you liked the sound of that."

"Well, my family has a long history of trading—"

"We all know *that*," Oxney muttered.

"So I'm interested to hear there was a god for it," Luke finished, pointedly ignoring him.

"Yes, of course. Ha: soldier and trader. Oh." She contemplated them both. "Hmm."

"I'm a secretary," Luke said, slightly unnerved by the scrutiny.

"Contracts! Of course. Oh yes. Oh, I think—"

She paused there, mouth slightly open. Oxney said, "Berengaria?"

She shook her head. "Don't mind me. I had an idea. Will you sit for me if I want you? Both of you."

"Absolutely," Oxney said at once. Luke, who had sat for a painting before and did not want to repeat the experience, reminded himself that one couldn't kick one's noble employer on the ankle. "So what has all that to do with this toro...thing you said?"

"Tauroctony. It's the essential image of the cult, as the crucifixion is to Christianity. The scorpion always goes there, by the way."

Oxney snorted amusement. "Not your idea? I'm relieved. I don't think this one for the Salon, on the whole."

"Heavens, no, you couldn't decorate a wall with it. Great-Uncle would call that blasphemous."

"I'd have a few words myself. What was the one you were looking at, Doomsday?"

"Me?"

"You were standing like a stock. Must have been five minutes."

Luke hadn't realised he'd been noticed. "I..."

"It was this one." Berengaria indicated the Marsh painting.

"Hmph." Oxney examined it. "You like that?"

"Er. Yes. Yes, it's, uh." Luke couldn't think of something to say that was more intelligent than 'good'; for some reason, none of the usual platitudes about art were coming to his tongue. "I liked looking at it?"

"Do you know, that's the first time in our acquaintance you've been speechless," Oxney said. "Can I have this too, Berengaria? I think I need it."

"If it's going to be looked at like that."

"Too?" Luke asked.

"You really were caught up, weren't you? Berengaria is lending me these." He indicated three of the fantastical landscapes. "And she's going to come and tell us about colours."

"And you are both going to sit for me," Berengaria said firmly. "Fair exchange."

Luke chalked that one up to his running tally against the d'Aumesty family. "Certainly, Miss Berengaria."

Oxney clapped his hands. "Right. Let's get these to the Salon."

The three of them carried the pictures through the lengthy corridors rather than ring for assistance. That was the Earl's impatience, and Berengaria's indifference to protocol, but Luke enthusiastically supported the idea: it was exactly what he would have recommended. He hoped they'd meet people.

They duly did, the first being Fulk in the New Wing's hallway. "What the devil are you doing?" he demanded.

"Redecorating my rooms," Oxney said.

Fulk gave an incredulous snort. "With those ghastly daubs? You're as mad as she is."

"And you're a damned ill-mannered swine. Get out of the way."

Fulk began to retort but Berengaria hissed at her brother, a sharp warning of the sort you gave a dog, and he took a step back, letting them pass.

"He'll tell Mother," she remarked as they made their way into the main hall. "He always does. You know she'll be furious if you change Grandfather's rooms."

"Will anything I do not make her furious?"

"Unlikely." There was a smile in her voice. "Though who you ought to watch out for—"

"Lord Oxney?" That was Pauncefoot, in the hall, looking appalled. "My lord, we have footmen for this purpose. Miss Berengaria! Please, allow me—"

Luke got in his way, aided by the large painting he carried, which he used to screen himself and the butler from the cousins. "You were ordered to have the old furniture removed some days ago, Mr. Pauncefoot," he said quietly. "You didn't do it then, and it's too late now. We'll do it ourselves."

"Do what?" the butler demanded.

Luke smiled up at him. "His lordship will be getting rid of a lot of old things that aren't useful to him. That starts today. Excuse me."

He sauntered up the stairs, insofar as he could saunter while carrying a damn great painting. He could feel the butler's stare between his shoulder blades.

The next two hours were exhausting but entertaining. Berengaria became thoroughly immersed in creating a new vision for the Earl's Salon. She and Oxney moved the paintings around, shouting about colours, while Luke ran up and down stairs removing unreadable books, gilt-framed etchings of architecture and Normans, and spindly incidental tables. He turned away every attempt at assistance from the accumulating footmen, repeating, "The Earl wanted this done days ago," and watching the increasingly unnerved stir that created.

He dumped the previous earl's furniture in the entrance hall in a pile. That was not tactful, or meant to be.

Mrs. Conrad arrived as he and Oxney were lugging the horrible old horsehair armchair down the last few stairs. "What is the meaning of this?" she demanded. "That is Father's armchair!"

"Drop," Oxney ordered. Luke let go, possibly a little

enthusiastically. As Oxney had done the same, the chair thumped unceremoniously to the floor, teetered, and fell on its side. Oxney wiped his brow. "That's right. I'm clearing out the rooms. Pauncefoot, get this rubbish dealt with, why's it still cluttering the place up?"

Mrs. Conrad looked outraged. "You propose to throw out your grandfather's most favoured things? His—his relics?"

"That's right."

"Pauncefoot! Have this chair taken back to its place!"

Oxney turned to the butler and said, quite pleasantly, "Don't."

"At once!" Mrs. Conrad shouted.

Pauncefoot, caught between a rock and a hard place, said, "Your lordship..."

"Yes, Pauncefoot?" Oxney said, still in that pleasant voice, which Luke noted as a warning sign.

"That chair was the earl's for many years, your lordship. It is of great sentimental value to the family."

"If anyone wants it, they can take it for their own quarters. Otherwise, throw it away. I don't care what happens to it as long as I don't see it again. Stop standing around, Doomsday, there's plenty more to do."

"You may not be aware, with your humble background," Mrs. Conrad said, voice vibrating with rage. "But it is not customary for the earl of Oxney to do his own manual labour."

"Thank you for that advice," Oxney said. "But it will become customary if I do it, because, in the absence of evidence to the contrary, I *am* the earl. Pauncefoot, order the carriage while I bring down the other chair. Berengaria and I are going to Rye. Doomsday, get the settle taken out."

He took the stairs two at a time. Luke followed, grinning. This particular skirmish, he felt, was theirs.

Eight

By his fourth week of employment in Stone Manor, Luke had learned a certain amount, reached a number of conclusions, and done very little to achieve the purpose for which he'd come.

That was not a problem, he told himself. He was running a long race, not sprinting. He'd had plenty to do to establish himself, to learn his master and the house and the situation. There was no point rushing to his goal: he'd be more likely to misstep.

Those were excuses. The fact was, he was enjoying himself. He relished the work, he'd plunged with gleeful malice into the fraught politics of Stone Manor, he liked his employer. He liked his employer too much, but the man was so infuriatingly likeable. Under other circumstances, he would have been congratulating himself on finding the ideal post: a great deal to do; an entertaining employer who saw him as an ally, not a serf; excellent status; and it didn't hurt that Oxney was so very good to look at, with his powerful build and ridiculously endearing smile. It might have come to hurt if he was staying, because 'look but don't touch' was not a maxim Luke cared for, but he wasn't staying. So he'd improve Oxney's position while he was here. He deserved it, and so did Conrad and Matilda, although differently.

It was the small things that caught Luke. The little jokes, the tiny considerations. Some that were less small, such as the Earl's Salon, where Oxney had ordered two new armchairs, and designated one as Luke's. Or the riding. Oxney insisted Luke should have plenty of exercise and fresh air, and demanded he ride most days. That was easily done since the stables were firmly the Earl's territory, causing Fulk immense resentment. Luke had had a chat with the head groom, Joss's henchman's brother-in-law, to ensure the stables took the correct side in the family war, but no pressure had been needed: Oxney's obvious care and enthusiasm for horses had won them over by itself. So Oxney had first dragged Luke along on a couple of his many visits to farms and tenants, and then stopped bothering with the pretext and just took him out for rides: slow, rambling excursions where they chatted idly. Like friends; like people together, learning each other, taking pleasure in one another's company—

Oh God, he was making such a bad mistake.

He knew it all too well, but Luke was very good at not thinking about things he didn't want to face: he'd been well trained. The realisation only hit home at occasional moments, such as when he found that he'd been daydreaming of Oxney at his desk, and realised his prick was thick and heavy with it.

This was stupid beyond belief. He'd lost his last position because his employer had wanted his body as well as his talents; he ought to know where that led. Admittedly, he'd been very happily seduced by his employer in the position before that, to no ill effect, but Lord Corvin was an excellent man to be seduced by, mostly because he was quite frank about what he offered. *Entertainment if you care for it, no hard feelings if you don't,* he had said in so many words, and Luke had indeed been entertained.

That wasn't this. That was nothing like this, because while Luke had liked Corvin, he hadn't cared for him in the slightest. That was *why* he'd fucked him: because for all his vaunted brains, Luke was painfully aware that he did not love intelligently.

So he tried his best not to love at all. He chose as partners men who could fuck with friendliness and part without dramatics, because he had control of his life these days, and didn't intend to lose it again.

But there was still a kernel of him that was a desperate, lost, hungry thing, and no matter how hard he tried to starve it out, it was always there, poking its head out at a sniff of affection, howling for more, making him hopeful and vulnerable and stupid.

Fortunately, Oxney—a good man, a responsible master—was clearly determined not to act on the attraction between them. Unfortunately, he wasn't doing the sensible thing of ignoring Luke and confining himself to orders, or behaving like a prick so as to earn a healthy dislike. Instead he was kind, he was amusing, he cared for Luke's well-being and his feelings, and thought of his wants, and appreciated his work, and stood up for him, and was in every respect the sort of man one could fall hopelessly in love with if one didn't know how staggeringly stupid that would be.

And yet here Luke was, shilly-shallying, instead of doing what he'd come to do and getting out. Worst of all, he had nobody to blame but himself. (And Oxney, if one could blame a man for being too protective, smiling too much, and possessing an excessively nice pair of forearms.) Luke knew exactly what he was doing, and he couldn't seem to stop himself, justifying every intimate moment, every smile, every casual touch with *Just one more*, and *This won't hurt*, like a drinker eyeing the last inch in the bottle.

Foolish. He had a goal here. He wanted to win and to show people he'd won, to rub their faces in it. To make them all understand—no, *admit* that Luke Doomsday was more than an unwanted ill-begot, a smuggler's bastard who didn't know his place, an overambitious scrabbler after position. He was more than his surname, or his service, or his scar, and he was damned well going to prove it, and when he did, it would make up for a lifetime of sneers and dismissal. That *mattered*. It was all that mattered.

Or, it had been. Only somehow Oxney mattered too, with his bursting energy, and his pugnacious looks that belied a laughing, generous soul, and his endless interruptions that meant Luke couldn't get a damn thing done, a fact he resented far less than he should. He needed to go through the records of thirteen years ago for his own purposes, but he wanted to rip apart the slovenly books of more recent times and make them make sense for the Earl.

Doing the latter would salve his conscience too. Not that he was doing anything *wrong* here, not really, no material harm to Lord Oxney at all, and yet he felt more unpleasantly aware of his false colours with every day that passed. Guilty, even.

It couldn't be helped. He was here for a reason. He *deserved* this. And he was earning his wage, even if he wasn't dedicating all of his time to the job. When he left Stone Manor in triumph, he vowed, he'd also leave the household in the right frame of mind, the books in good order, and the d'Aumestys a cowed, subservient rabble.

The first of those was going to plan. Mrs. Conrad had downed tools, demanding a full apology for Oxney's many offences and submission as to her right to direct the running of the Manor and its staff. He had apologised for his language but stood his ground otherwise, and she had accordingly refused to instruct Cook or the housekeeper any further since her labour went unappreciated. That had been a tactical error since, while the butler adored her, the others did not. Under Emily's guidance, Luke had made sure both women knew that this was their opportunity to claim their domains, while encouraging Oxney to offer them profuse apologies, well-merited praise, and thanks for their assistance in a difficult situation. They had both risen to the occasion with a show of competent authority that suggested they preferred not to work under Mrs. Conrad's close supervision. Emily assured him that the phrase 'His lordship's orders' was starting to trump 'Mr. Pauncefoot says'. Factions had formed. Several of the upper servants weren't speaking to one another. Luke lived for it.

The second aim was also going well. Odo's bookkeeping hadn't been dishonest, just extremely Odoesque, and while Luke still cursed his name, he'd begun to get the hang of how the man thought. He'd communicated that to the Earl, who suggested he take a long lie-down with a cold compress, but it was allowing him to get on top of things, while Mr. Smallbone, invigorated at last by Oxney's energy, had enthusiastically embarked on the first steps of a very large programme of repairs.

And talking of getting on top of things...

He felt a little nervous as he waited for Oxney to come in. He'd been out inspecting the work on one of the farms all morning. Luke had made himself do a solid couple of hours on the books from 1810, to annoyingly little effect since half his mind had been on what he was going to propose. He very much hoped the works were going well.

Oxney turned up after lunch, sauntering into the study. "Ah, Doomsday. What have you been up to?"

"This and that, my lord. How are the works?"

"Not bad."

He recounted a few details they needed to cover. Luke took notes, nodded along, and finally said, "My lord, may I show you something?"

He indicated a paper on his desk. He was going to hand it over, but instead Oxney came around to stand by him, leaning over his shoulder, painfully close.

Breathe.

"Family expenditure?" Oxney asked. "Berengaria—that's not how much her paints cost? Christ alive. Are these annual figures?"

"Yes, my lord. I wanted to see what the old Earl gave the family in the way of allowances and support. It's a remarkably small amount. Bills paid, generously, but very little actual money for anyone except Mr. Fulk, and that was cut three years ago."

"The old man had them on a damned tight leash."

"Lord Oxney used the finances to keep his family around him. Miss Berengaria had her painting equipment paid for, lavishly, and her clothes also"—not that she looked it, but Emily assured him Miss Berengaria was uninterested in finery rather than deprived of it— "but no pin money at all. Same for Mr. Pagan and Mr. Odo. Lord Oxney let them have whatever they wanted in terms of books and so on, but the bills had to be presented for his approval. They had nothing to spend on their own account. Nor did Lord Stone."

"What?"

Luke produced another sheet, twisting over his shoulder to watch Oxney's eyes move. "He used to receive an allowance, which was cut off after the business with the Cathedral. From then until his death, he had to supply his father with his bills and had no independence. And your grandfather did the same to Mr. Conrad. He had received an allowance, though not a generous one, but once he became the heir—or, rather, once Lord Stone died—it was taken away entirely."

"What the devil—Why? What does he have now?"

"Aside from a small income brought by Mrs. Conrad on their marriage—I believe a hundred pounds a year—nothing. They are all entirely dependent on the estate."

"Good God, the old man was a swine. Any particular reason you've brought this to me?"

"Two," Luke said. "Firstly, I thought you should be aware that the family have been both encouraged and obliged to live here by your predecessor's financial arrangements. You might want to change that."

"Are you plotting to evict the Conrads?"

"That would hardly be my place, my lord. But if you *did* want to evict them, you'd need to know this."

"You really are well named, aren't you? An apocalypse in action. What was the other reason?"

He sounded in a good mood. Luke took the plunge. "I wondered how you found the handwriting."

"Eh? It's fine. It's...very clear." He frowned. "It's different. Isn't it? Have you changed something?"

"I've been looking at the things you find easier to read," Luke said. "The newspaper, and some of the correspondence. I saw some patterns, or thought I did, and I wondered if a rounder, better spaced style with more distinct letters might make a difference—"

Oxney put a heavy, silencing hand on his shoulder and picked up the papers in his other hand. Luke didn't quite feel able to twist round and look up at his face. He just waited, with Oxney's fingers warm on his shoulder, feeling every tiny twitch.

"It's better," Oxney said, after forever had passed. "It is—I didn't even notice when you showed me, but it is easier, somehow."

"I thought we could work on it. Try variations. Distinguishing the shape of the letters more, see if the lines should be further apart. Refine it until it works as best it can, and then I can adopt that myself and have a model you can give other secretaries."

"Yes. I see. The lines—a little further, maybe." Oxney's voice was rough and his grip had tightened almost painfully. "I get lost when they're close. God damn it, Doomsday, are you proposing to change your *hand* for me?"

Luke knew he should find a secretarial way to reply, some mass of polite words. What he said was, "Yes."

There was another long pause, and Oxney was so near, his body's warmth burning across the space between them. His fingers were digging into Luke's shoulder, and Luke could reach up and put his own hand over them. Just a few inches of space to cross.

He could. He shouldn't. He should. He couldn't.

"We can work on it," he said again, and couldn't help, "Together."

Oxney exhaled, long and hard, breath ruffling Luke's hair and the nape of his neck, then he let go, and retreated to the other side of the desk in two paces. There was a sheen in his eyes that made Luke's heart hurt, but he spoke with determined cheer. "This is beyond the call of duty, Doomsday. I believe I offered you half my fortune to stay the other day. I think I should make it the whole thing."

"No need."

Luke said it as lightly as he could. It didn't sound nearly light enough, and nor did the Earl when he said, "I would."

Luke couldn't reply. He should, he knew it, something to slacken the awareness that had snapped to life with that incautious exchange, but he simply couldn't come up with a riposte when two words had pulled the air from his chest.

Oxney looked equally at a loss, the unconvincing smile fading from his face, as if he'd startled himself with a truth. They stared at each other, trapped in words and silence, for a few endless seconds, then Oxney said, "Thank you," in a stifled voice, turned on his heel, and left in a few long strides, not looking back.

Nine

RUFUS DIDN'T KNOW WHY HE WOKE. HE SIMPLY FOUND HIMSELF awake, and wide awake at that. He lay in the darkness, wondering why, and had the vague memory of a noise.

It was dead silent now, and felt like the middle of the night. He ought to turn over and go back to sleep but the thought that he had heard something had burrowed into his brain, and he found that his ears were straining.

This was absurd. The odds of a burglar breaking into the Manor, still less coming within earshot of the Earl's Salon, were negligible. He'd probably been woken by a dream. All the same, he lay listening, and, after a moment, groped for the tinderbox and lit a candle.

The light made the shadows of the room and the oppressive monstrosity of a bed all the more noticeable. He sat up a little longer, trying to convince himself that he could go to sleep without care, then swung himself to sit on the edge of the mattress, wincing as his bare feet hit the cold floorboards.

Damned if he cared if the house was being burgled. Good luck to the bastards finding anything worth taking: he hoped they liked paintings of Normans. All the same, he wouldn't be able to go back to sleep in this state of alertness, not without checking whatever had woken him.

It was probably nothing. No: it was probably Doomsday, getting up to relieve himself or some such. Which would mean he was awake, two rooms away. Rufus sat for a moment, thinking about Luke Doomsday awake and two rooms away.

He was so bright, in every way. The hair, the intelligence, the vibrant force of personality. A bright spark in a dark house, worth his weight in gold, and Rufus would be a damned fool to jeopardise that simply because he couldn't stop noticing the man.

Rufus wasn't generally speaking a slave to his desires. He'd been a late developer in the petticoat line; he'd felt no urge to trouble the camp-followers, and nobody had troubled him, since he hadn't been a pretty youth, but rather an awkward, bulky lout. He had discovered tupping in due course, but he also discovered he only cared for it when he liked his partner, when you could share a laugh and you both enjoyed yourselves. He couldn't see the point of putting his prick in someone for whom he had no affection, as a merely physical act. In short, where his fellows all seemed to have spent years in thrall to the beast with two backs, Rufus had never found it particularly compelling.

That was probably a blessing, given his desires had always seemed to run towards men. He'd assumed he'd eventually meet a woman who would spark his interest, or at least those interests, enough for marriage, but that was yet to happen. At the age of thirty-three, Rufus thought he might be set in his ways, and wasn't troubled by the fact. It was his body and he'd use it as he pleased, whether that was with men or with nobody at all.

He'd been entirely content with that last. And then, Doomsday.

Rufus knew his face so well now: how he frowned in concentration, the wicked way he smiled, the look of pleasure when he was up to something clever, the cocksure self-possession that shone the brightest in his most insubordinate moments. Rufus knew all those expressions, and wanted more. He wanted to touch, to stroke his hair and find out if it was as satin-smooth as he imagined; he wanted his name, not his title, on Doomsday's lips. Curse it: he wanted his lips on those lips.

Rufus didn't lust where he didn't like. But he liked Luke Doomsday so very much, and now lust was flooding him in a way he'd never experienced in his life.

He wanted his secretary. He wasn't sure how you went about worshipping a man in bed but he wanted to find out and do it. He wanted to know what pleased him and do it all, piece by piece, until one or both of them was a babbling wreck. He'd been unable to resist quite a lot of speculation over what Doomsday might like to do in bed, preferably in this bed, ludicrous carved nonsense that it was. He couldn't stop imagining the bright hair and that marred, perfect face framed by the twisting devils of a warped medieval mind. He might be going mad.

How was he supposed to get any work done like this? Desire was playing hob with his will, his self-control, his schedule, and the pure hell of it was, he could not possibly indulge it. He had thought sometimes that there was something in Doomsday's eyes, that he might feel the breathlessness Rufus felt around him, that his secretary watched just as Rufus did—but all that was a guess, or maybe wishful thinking, not to be relied on, and the consequences of unwanted advances were far too serious to take the risk. He didn't think Doomsday would flee in fear: he surely knew Rufus better than that. But it would be impossible for him to turn down his employer and then keep working with him on terms of trust and intimacy, and it would be grossly unfair of Rufus to force him out of his position in such a way, especially given what he'd already suffered.

He wasn't going to think about what might happen if Doomsday welcomed his advances, because he wasn't going to make any. It would be wrong, and stupid, and there were more important things than fucking, although he was having difficulty remembering what they were.

He shook himself out of this frustrating morass of thought, in which he'd been floundering for what felt like months. Doomsday was safely asleep and Rufus had nothing to say to that. He was going to look around, to put his mind at rest and because he'd managed to wake himself all too thoroughly, and then he would go back to sleep, probably with the joint assistance of his imagination and his trusty right hand.

He pulled on breeches under his nightshirt. Apart from anything else, if Doomsday was awake and he appeared bare-legged and bare-arsed—well, he would not do that. He took up the candle, went out into the hall, and saw Doomsday's door was open.

That was odd. Needed checking. Nothing to do with a sudden urge to see how he looked asleep: that would be intrusive and frankly peculiar, and there was quite enough peculiarity in this damned house. Rufus edged to the door as quietly as he could, purely in the interests of security.

The room was dark. There was no sound of breathing. Rufus felt a sudden, unreasoning pulse of alarm that led him to lift the candle high, regardless of the sleeper he might disturb, and saw—nothing. A neatly kept room, several neat stacks of books, a pair of slippers neatly by the door, and the one point of untidiness, an empty, rumpled bed.

Doomsday was abroad, at—he glanced at the clock—ten past two. Rufus came into the room, feeling like a trespasser, and touched the sheets.

The linen was cold. Doomsday had been out of bed for some time.

That was damned odd, and he was very awake now. He padded on cold feet down the icy stone stairs, moving as silently as he could through the silent manor house, not sure what he was looking for but determined to find it. The stone seemed to soak up his candlelight, as if the small defiance of flame made the night shadows deeper. He paced along the corridor, and down the grand stair to the ground floor, and saw a light.

It was faint but there as he looked over the banisters, flickering on the walls below. Either the servants had left a lamp burning, or someone was up and about, and whoever it was had better have a good explanation.

He made his way down with careful stealth, rounded the end of the stairs to look along the hall, and saw his secretary.

Doomsday was standing with a lantern, fully dressed. As Rufus approached, he said, "Good evening."

"Evening? It's two in the morning!"

"Yes. Could you not sleep?"

"Me? What are *you* doing out of bed?"

"I sometimes don't sleep. I got up."

He'd looked tired in the last week. Rufus had noticed the shadows under his eyes. "What, so you came down to find a book or some such?"

"Getting up for a little is better than lying in bed, I find."

"And you put your boots on to do it?"

Doomsday glanced down, as though he wasn't aware of his own footwear. "The floor's cold."

"I know it's cold, I'm standing on it. And you own a pair of slippers so why are you wearing boots? Muddy boots, God damn it! You've been outside!" He wasn't sure what precisely he feared, but this was Romney Marsh, a world away from anywhere, and he had a sudden, unwelcome remembrance of all the warnings about Doomsday's criminal family. He stalked closer, putting his candlestick down on a side table, not liking that he wanted his hands free. "What the devil are you up to?"

"I realise we didn't spell out my working hours," Doomsday said, "but they end. Or at least, I consider them to. I don't think I owe you my time at two o'clock in the morning."

"I'm not asking you to work. I want you to explain why you're roaming the house, or the grounds, at this hour!"

"I am conducting my life," Doomsday said, with something of a hiss. "I don't see I need to account for that."

Rufus had dressed down too many misbehaving junior officers not to spot evasion when he saw it. "Oh, yes you do. I won't have my staff creeping round doing God knows what at God knows when. Explain yourself. Now."

"If you insist. I had an assignation."

"A—"

"Assignation. An appointment to get fucked, if you want it spelled out. Which, sadly, did not come to pass, so it seems I got up for no reason. I trust that suffices?"

"No, it bloody doesn't," Rufus said, on a wave of feelings he didn't stop to examine. "Your private life is your business, but my household is my responsibility. I won't have local girls popping out my staff's bastards—"

Doomsday's head went back as though he'd been slapped. "It is my business, and I am not basket-making, and if I were, that would also be my business and I would deal with the consequences. Which will not in any case happen, so—"

"You know damned well you can't promise that, and don't try to distract me," Rufus said. "This is a bloody lie. Why the devil would you be meeting girls at two in the morning?" Sneaking off for a roll in the hay was a time-honoured country activity, but nobody was wandering around the Isle of Oxney at this hour for that. There was no shortage of opportunity for a fumble in this barely-populated place: a girl could surely evade the most watchful parents, meet a lover in the evening, and still get a good night's sleep. Anyway, he knew it was a lie. There was something about Doomsday's bearing: he could simply tell.

He glared at his secretary. "I asked you a question. Well?"

Doomsday met his glare with an equally aggressive look, and then something in his face changed. He shut his eyes for a second, his expressive eyebrows twitched, and he gave a tiny shrug, as if he'd made a decision. "Who said I was meeting girls?"

"What?"

"I told you I was going out to get fucked. Did I say it was by a woman?" He sounded impossibly casual. "I intended to meet a gentleman, or at least a man, for that."

"You can't do that," Rufus said. It was utterly unacceptable that he should be sneaking around outside, with all the risks male assignations carried, in order to meet someone else. To meet *someone*. "Absolutely not, I will not have it. Are you trying to get yourself pilloried?"

"Don't be ridiculous."

"Ridiculous?!" He just managed to turn the shout to a hiss. "The law—"

"I know the law; I've broken it plenty of times. I know Romney Marsh better than you. And I will conduct my life as I please."

"Not under my roof!"

"I was outside," Doomsday pointed out.

"You know damned well what I mean."

"I do, and no." Doomsday folded his arms. "I don't accept your authority in this. I told you the truth; if you don't like it, dismiss me. But the only say you get in who or how or when I fuck, my lord, is—"

He still sounded calm, but his chin went up a fraction. "If it's you fucking me."

Rufus made an entirely involuntary choking noise. His lungs and brain seemed to have shut down abruptly and simultaneously, although his prick was still functioning, and making itself felt.

Doomsday held his gaze. "Well?"

"Well—uh—what?"

Doomsday went to the side table and put his lantern down with a click. "You heard. Sack me, fuck me, or leave me be. Pick one."

Rufus moved, fuelled by anger, frustration, arousal. He took two furious paces forward, grabbed Doomsday by the shoulders, and let go almost at once, before he could do anything stupid, such as pushing him away or, worse, pulling him in. He slammed his hands against the stone instead, which trapped Doomsday between his arms, against the wall. His blood surged with the awareness of how close they were; his voice came out a growl. "What the devil are you playing at? How much trouble do you want to be in?"

Doomsday raised an eyebrow, the cocky little bastard. Their faces were inches apart. "Am I in trouble?"

"Yes, and you know it!" Of course he did, because he wasn't a fool, and he wouldn't have said that without thinking, not unless he *wanted*—

Doomsday was watching him. Rufus's mind was snarled up with alarm and hope and throbbing need. "You work for me, rot you! Do you not realise the position you're putting yourself in?"

"I was hoping you'd do that."

Rufus stared at his secretary. Doomsday stared back, chin high, eyes a little wide. "Specifically, I hoped you might get over your moral scruples and give me the tupping we both want." His lips curved suddenly and irrepressibly, a painfully familiar, lovely sight. "I've been waiting for you to exercise your droit du seigneur for weeks."

Rufus couldn't think of a thing to say. There *were* things, he knew, important ones; there was common sense to be exerted, and an entire array of second thoughts and warning signs to be taken into account. Unfortunately, he couldn't see any of them because his vision had shrunk to Doomsday's guinea-gold hair, the dark eyes on his, the reddened lips, just slightly parted, waiting.

He lifted one tentative hand to his secretary's face, and found it caught at the wrist in a hard, almost convulsive grip.

He tried to jerk away, horrified. Doomsday didn't let go. "Sorry, sorry. Just, not the scar, that's all. Don't touch it, don't talk about it. I'm open to more or less anything else."

Rufus might have thought of that for himself. At least now he knew Doomsday had no hesitation in raising objections. It ought to have been a reassurance. "Would you please, in simple words, tell me what you want?"

Doomsday relaxed his tight grip, but didn't altogether let go. Instead he slid his hand up to intertwine his fingers with Rufus's, sending shivers down his skin. "I want you, my lord. I want you to kiss me. And quite a lot more, but that—"

Rufus pushed their linked hands back against the wall, high, so Doomsday's arm was stretched up. Leaned in, trapping his body with Rufus's own larger one. Kissed him.

It felt so good. That pretty, cocky, clever mouth yielding under his own. Soft lips and the faint rasp of stubble, the touch of tongue. Doomsday's mouth greedily open, demanding to be plundered. Rufus kissed him carefully, then just a little harder and felt him moan response, and then he could be sure at last, and the relief was bone-melting. He slid his free hand between Doomsday's legs, found a substantial bulge already straining against his breeches, and cupped it in palm and fingers. Doomsday made a delightful noise in his mouth, and brought a thigh up over Rufus's hip, and Christ, this was everything he'd wanted and needed for weeks. He leaned in. Doomsday grabbed his skull, since Rufus didn't have much hair to grab, and pushed his hips up to grind against Rufus's hand, and it was suddenly frantic.

They kissed and rutted against each other with wild abandon. Doomsday's mouth was demanding, his hands moving frenziedly over Rufus as if he was trying to get them everywhere at once, and the tiny, urgent sounds he was making resonated through Rufus's nerves. Rufus was swamped in sensation and stiff as a post, prick almost painfully hard, and, he realised, in grave danger of spending in his breeches in this draughty hallway.

Absolutely not. He needed Doomsday where he should have been all along, making use of that absurd bed.

He dragged his mouth from Doomsday's lips to his ear, nuzzling the warm skin under gold waves. He'd intended to make a suggestion, but the hair distracted him, and Doomsday got in first with, "Jesus. Can we take this upstairs?"

"My room. Now." He reluctantly let go to grab the candlestick, feeling the lack of Doomsday under his hands. Doomsday followed, extinguishing his lantern so that they moved in near-darkness and near-silence. He was as quiet in his boots as Rufus on his painfully cold bare feet.

Rufus led the way into the Earl's Salon. Doomsday, behind him, went instead into his own bedroom, and Rufus had a terrifying second of *oh shit, he doesn't want*—before he heard the faint sound of a key turning. By the time Rufus was in his bedroom, Doomsday was coming through the anteroom door, which he closed and locked behind him.

"Cautious," Rufus said.

"Good practice."

Rufus walked him against the wall, this time pressing the length of his body against his secretary, holding both his hands palm to palm, curling their fingers together. "Doomsday. Luke," he tried. The name suited him, the smooth sound, closed off with a determined click. "Luke," he said again, enjoying the way the name felt in his mouth. "What do you want?"

"Is a damn good fucking out of the question?" His breath was warm on Rufus's face.

"Tell me you've thought of oil."

"In my pocket."

"Absolutely enragingly competent," Rufus said. "I may have mentioned that." He hauled Luke bodily off the wall with a hand under his—yes, as firm as it looked—arse. Luke yelped. Rufus half carried him the couple of steps across the room, and dropped him on his back on the bed.

He stared up, eyes very dark, that irresistible mouth curving. "Seigneur."

Rufus climbed onto the bed, over him, trapping Luke's arms with his knees, saw his eyes widen. Luke licked his lips with a slow, entirely deliberate tongue, wetting them so they gleamed in the dim light.

"To be clear," Rufus said. "I'm not a man for hints. If there's something—something particular—you want of me, spit it out."

"Spitting it out is the last thing I'm going to do. I want you in my mouth. Like this, now."

Rufus fumbled with buttons, pushing cloth out of the way with clumsy urgency till he had his stand clear. He leaned forward as Luke curled up to meet him, and then his mouth was on Rufus's prick and the pleasure spiked so hard he gasped aloud. He had to put his hands on the bed, gripping the coverlet in an effort at self-control. Luke's tongue and lips were greedy on him, straining. "More," he mumbled around his mouthful, and Rufus leaned forward, felt his secretary take him deeper. Mouth sliding, lips tight, tongue caressing, and Jesus, Rufus could die happy here.

On the other hand, Luke had made his feelings clear earlier. Rufus indulged himself a moment more, then pulled back, looking down at his own spit-wet stand and Luke's reddened, smiling lips.

"More?" Luke asked.

"I want to touch you. All of you."

"At your pleasure," Luke murmured, and Rufus had to give himself a sharp squeeze.

"Christ. You—Get your damn clothes off."

He clambered off the bed to make that possible. Luke sat up to remove his boots. Rufus went to pull off his nightshirt, and stopped. "Shit."

"What is it?"

"I have scars," Rufus said reluctantly. "Quite a few. Is that bad?"

Luke's head came up sharply, and the look on his face could have broken a man's heart, so shocked and raw and yearning. "I," he said, and then started again. "Thank you. Thank you for thinking of that, but there's no need to worry."

"Are you sure?"

"Entirely. At least, not on my account. What about you?"

"God, I don't care. I came by them honestly." Luke's eyes widened, and Rufus could have kicked himself. "I mean, at war. I was a soldier, we all got knocked about. I don't care about the things. Touch them or don't, as you prefer."

"Noted."

Rufus would have liked to apologise for any inadvertent insult, but he didn't want to infringe on the prohibition he'd been given. He concentrated on stripping off his breeches to recover himself, pulled his nightshirt over his head, and stood naked in the dim light.

Luke sat on the bed, bare-chested himself, staring. "You're

magnificent." He rose to his bare feet, with a hand out, face almost awed. "That's exactly what I thought you'd look like." His fingers skimmed Rufus's chest, dragging through the tangle of hair, sliding over a hard nipple. Rufus reached for his head, getting his hands into the gold hair—thick, smooth, wonderfully grippable—feeling Luke's hands roam over his sides, his belly, his thighs. Both touching their fill, because they had been waiting far too long.

Luke's fingers paused on Rufus's right thigh, where gnarled scar tissue told its story of the musket ball and, far worse, the camp doctors. By comparison the various sabre-slashes were quite tidy. "You don't mind this?"

"I minded a great deal at the time, but there's no shame in scars." Christ, could he not say anything right tonight? "I mean, nothing to it, for me. I see it as a useful reminder, that's all."

"Reminder of what?"

Rufus shrugged. "To stand a foot to the left next time."

Luke burst out laughing. Rufus dragged him closer, clamping his hands on that absolutely irresistible arse, and kissed him, feeling the smile against his mouth. "You bloody beauty. Get these off." He was working at Luke's buttons as he spoke. Luke took a hand, wriggling breeches and drawers off and kicking them away, and Rufus pushed him back onto the bed again.

He was stunning naked. The gold of his hair was carried down in the thick chest hair, the line that arrowed down to his groin, even the tangled curls around his jutting prick. Rufus knelt to wrap his fingers around that, feeling Luke strain into his hand, watching his face. Learning the feel of a cock that seemed made for his big palm. "God, I want to stroke you off. Watch you spend."

"On the other hand, we mentioned your droit du seigneur," Luke said. "A Norman French phrase which I believe translates to 'fuck me like you own me'."

Rufus almost swallowed his tongue. Luke's lips curled, wicked, provocative, hungry. "At his lordship's pleasure, of course."

"His lordship pleases," Rufus assured him. "Oil?"

Luke squirmed to his feet and retrieved a bottle, and a cloth. He returned to lie across the bed, arm behind his head, one leg crooked. He looked like a painting, a fallen angel.

Rufus tipped oil into his palm, slicked a finger, and called Luke's extremely free translation to mind. "Spread your legs."

Luke moved his thighs apart. Rufus knelt between them, and took possession, sliding his slippery hand over Luke's core. His stand, his cods, his buttocks, his inner thighs, all the forbidden parts, slicking them as though he marked them his own. He could see the muscles tense and flex in his lover—his secretary's stomach.

A little more oil, and he traced a finger over Luke's entrance, winning a gasp. "Droit du seigneur. Does that make this mine by right?"

"Right of conquest," Luke suggested breathlessly. Rufus pushed his fingertip in, playing with the ring of muscle, feeling it flutter. Probed deeper to find the pleasure-point, and watched his secretary stiffen as finger brushed nub. "God!"

Rufus leaned forward to put his free hand, and his weight, on Luke's smooth shoulder, and pushed his oiled finger in as deep as it went, plastering the rest of his slick hand over balls and arse. Luke moaned. Rufus leaned harder, with both hands, working his finger around. Luke thrashed against his grip. "Yes. Fuck. Will you exert your damned rights before I die of waiting?"

"You are blasted insubordinate," Rufus told him. "I don't know how to handle this level of shameless insolence."

Luke's lips curled. Sprawled naked over the ancient bed, he didn't look remotely like the subject of his master's lust. More like the Sun King, waiting impatiently for his pleasure. "Mercilessly."

Rufus got his hand free and nearly spilled the oil as he tipped more into his palm, liberally slicking his prick. Luke rolled to hands and knees; Rufus moved behind him. The blackened, twisted posts and the heavy canopy of the bed were closing in around them both, or possibly his vision was failing. He took hold of Luke's tense, perfect arse and pushed in.

"Ah. God."

"You asked for it." He was stronger than his secretary, physically at least, and he used that, his size, exerting his muscles. "Legs wider. Oh Christ, Luke, I wanted you—"

"Have me."

Pushing past the internal resistance, feeling the ring of muscle tight around his prick. Luke whimpered with every movement, a desperate little sound deliciously at odds with his usual demeanour.

"Not so cocky now, are you?" Rufus gritted out, and felt him quiver. "Is this what you want?"

"This. You. God, I want you. Jesus, like this. More." He shifted his hands one by one to grip the bedstead, fingers pale against the dark ancient wood.

Rufus took hold of his shoulders, feeling the strength in them, pushing deeper. "Luke. Say my name."

"Rufus." It came out on a breath, almost a whisper. "Rufus."

His damn fool name had never sounded better, and particularly because it came out decidedly Kentish, with a rolled R and rounded vowels. Luke Doomsday losing his self-possession? More of that, Rufus decided. He tightened his grip on those sturdy shoulders and thrust hard.

Luke gave a whispered cry, pushing back toward him, golden head bowed. Rufus did it again, and Luke sobbed his name, and he had said *mercilessly*. So Rufus fucked him harder and deeper, thrusting as forcefully as he dared until Luke was shuddering, thrashing, begging incoherently, and Rufus put one hand between his secretary's shoulders, put his whole weight on that hand, and pushed him down onto the ancient bed.

Fuck me like you own me.

"You," he said. "Mine."

He got his other, still oil-slick hand to Luke's prick, rigid and leaking, felt the body under him jerk at the touch. He needed, desperately, to feel Luke spend like this, while Rufus held him and fucked him, while his palm was spread across hot skin and his cocksure secretary was out of control under his hands. Luke was hard and hot, and so close to spending that Rufus could feel it.

"You asked for it," he said again, for the pleasure of feeling Luke's spasm of response, and set himself to win that climax, holding back his own pleasure, but nothing else. He fucked Luke hard with cock and hand at once, fucked him through his muffled cries with his own teeth savagely gritted, rode him as he thrashed under Rufus in helpless release, and only then let himself go, emptying himself into his secretary's body in his own glorious completion.

He fell forward, so drained it took him a moment to remember about breathing, then shifted his weight slightly in case Luke was suffocating.

"Christ," Luke said into the bedclothes. He was splayed on the bed, flattened under Rufus. *"Jesus."*

Rufus was still trying to refill his lungs. He grunted. Luke made a sort of gurgling noise in reply, and Rufus buried his face in the crook of neck and shoulder.

"Jesus," Luke said again, after a moment. "If that's how you do your rights, I can't wait for wrongs."

"You're a menace. Ah—you're all right?"

"Me, very much so. Your bedclothes may have suffered."

"I'm sure the bed's seen worse over the last few centuries."

"I doubt it's seen much better. I don't want you to get off, but I do actually want you to get off."

Rufus pulled out carefully, and reached for the cloth to mop up a bit. That done, he tugged Luke to him, and the coverlet over them both. With the sweat drying, it was decidedly cold.

Luke yawned, reminding Rufus irresistibly of a kitten. "Don't let me fall asleep here."

"Knaresford doesn't come in." His valet, who had served his grandfather for years, didn't want a new master. Since Rufus didn't actually want a valet, they had reached a very satisfactory equilibrium by avoiding one another.

"Even so."

Rufus traced his ear and jawline with a finger—the right side of his face only, staying well away from the scar. "You're devastating. I have dreamed of this for days. Weeks."

"Well, I've dreamed of it for years, so I win."

"What?"

Luke grinned sleepily. "There's a book, a cross between a Gothic novel and *Fanny Hill*, but for men's men. The hero goes through many tribulations, including spending about half the story in a castle at the mercy of a wicked earl. And also the earl's henchman, and occasionally his groom. Sometimes all three at once."

"Good God."

"The story parts are enjoyable, and the filthy parts are exceptionally filthy. I'll lend it to you if you like. It's not that I wanted to re-enact my favourite scenes for myself—"

"Are you telling me that you only want me for my title?"

"And your Gothic mansion." He curled into Rufus's chest, nuzzling. "And maybe some other things, too. But it's mostly the title."

He was delightfully warm, a little sweat-damp, slightly sticky, and this was the best Rufus had ever felt in the earl of Oxney's bed. "Lend me your book," he said. "I clearly need it. This is the most effective way I've found to shut you up, and I will be using it in the future."

"It would be my pleasure. Quite literally." Luke yawned again. "I'm going now, or I will fall asleep here. But—" He tugged Rufus's hand up and kissed the knuckle. "That was glorious, seigneur. Truly glorious."

He slid out of bed. Rufus watched him gather his things and go, then made his way under his own sheets, which were badly rumpled and felt empty. He was asleep within minutes, exhausted, sated, and deeply content.

It didn't occur to him that he should have asked any more questions.

Ten

RUFUS HAD AT LEAST A MINUTE OF PURE, UNBRIDLED SATISFAC-
tion when he woke the next morning before the second thoughts arrived.

He stared up at the dark canopy of the monstrous bed, wondering
what happened now. Luke had made his wishes and his pleasures
clear last night, but things one did at two in the morning often seemed
less sensible in the light of day. What would happen if he decided—
very reasonably—that he couldn't be a secretary and a bedmate?

Rufus needed Doomsday the secretary, not just for his superla-
tive ability, but for his companionship, his care. That painstakingly
worked, gloriously legible page had forced Rufus out of the room
before he'd said something he couldn't take back. Which, of course,
was redundant now. He needed the secretary, but he wanted the
man, because he was irresistible and he laughed, and last night had
been a joy. He didn't want to choose. He might not be able to choose,
because it wasn't up to him.

If Luke regretted what they'd done, if he had changed his mind, if
Rufus had been wrong about him and this had been a mistake, what
the devil would they do?

He swung himself violently out of bed, and saw a book on the table that hadn't been there the night before. He picked it up. It had plain though excellent quality leather binding, with a crow stamped in gilt on the spine. He opened it at the title page, which read, *Jonathan: A Novel, by A Gentleman*.

The book looked well-thumbed and had a slip of paper as a bookmark. Rufus opened it to that page. The type was a nice clear one, and the print good size and well-spaced, not cramped. He wasn't surprised: of course Luke would not have left him something he'd find an excessive struggle. He considered everything. Rufus sat on the bed and read.

Some fifteen minutes later, he put the book down with two very firm convictions. Firstly, this was not a book you'd give a man if you'd changed your mind about fucking him. Secondly, Luke had not been joking about the villainous earl in the book. The scene he'd read was absolutely filthy, and spectacularly effective: Rufus's convictions were not the firmest thing about him right now.

He took a moment to calm down, and got dressed with a decided sense of anticipation.

Fortunately nobody was in the breakfast room to spoil his mood. He appropriated a coffee-pot, two cups, and the milk jug, and strolled off to the study, where Luke was, inevitably, deep in the books.

"Good morning." Rufus kicked the door shut and put his tray down on the desk, on top of an account book. Luke looked up at him with unalloyed malevolence. "Didn't get enough sleep?"

Luke's lips tightened in an effort not to smile. "Not much."

"Any other problems to report?"

"I know you want me to say the chair is strangely uncomfortable, and I won't be giving you the satisfaction."

"Pour the coffee," Rufus told him, grinning, and went to lock the door. When he turned, it was to meet a very quizzical eyebrow.

"We need a private conversation," Rufus said. He took the cup he was handed, and cleared a space to perch on the desk by stacking a double handful of books and papers on top of another pile.

"As long as you realise you're paying me to sort that out again," Luke said with resignation.

"That's all right. Luke?"

Brown eyes snapped up to his. "My lord?"

Wicked little bastard. "I found—" Rufus extracted the book from his coat pocket. "Looks fascinating."

"I think you'll enjoy it."

"I have no doubt." He reached out, putting just the tip of a finger to his secretary's chin. Luke tilted his head a fraction, a tiny gesture that squeezed Rufus's lungs, and his groin. "I want you to do me a service."

"I'd be very glad to do that, my lord."

"Don't," Rufus said. "Or— Look, I want to know what you thought about last night."

Luke's eyebrow flickered. "Fishing for compliments?"

"I'm serious. *This* is serious. Last night was—well, I hope as good for you as for me, but we're now in rather an awkward situation. I have my thumb on the scales, like it or not. I'm your employer, you're in my house, I have the title. All the power is on my side—"

"It really is not."

Luke said that with a smile, but not one that looked quite right, and it gave Rufus a prickling sensation, as though there was the hint of a threat. "What do you mean?"

Luke shook his head, tossing golden locks out of his eyes. "I suppose I understand what you're saying. You don't want to abuse your position, and you very easily could. You could have made it clear to me at any time that my employment depended on granting you my body—"

"It does not!"

"I know that," Luke said patiently. "I seduced *you*. I wouldn't have done it if I didn't want to. And this is my home ground. If I sent to my cousin Joss for help against the wicked earl who had imprisoned me in his dungeon—"

"Be serious."

"I am serious. I'm a Doomsday. I know you don't know what that means on the Marsh, but just fourteen miles away there is an inn full of people who spent years running rings round the Revenue, the law, and some very ruthless rivals, and they will come if I call. I am not powerless."

"But you need this job, you told me so yourself. I'm paying your wages—I am, aren't I? Have you arranged that?—and that's not an equal position. So I'm asking you, what now? Where does this leave us?"

Luke tipped his head. "Wherever we choose, surely."

"Where's that?"

"It is up to me to say?"

"Yes," Rufus said. "Again: you're in the more vulnerable position here, even if you have more useful cousins than I do, which God knows isn't hard. So I need you to tell me what you want. Not what you think I might want, but what *you* do."

Luke looked at him, an examining look with a little frown between his eyes. "Is that your concern?"

"Of course it is. And not because I'm afraid of any blasted smuggler," he felt obliged to add. "I don't want you to fear for your position any more than for yourself. I had told myself I would not touch you for exactly that reason."

Luke gave a tiny shrug. "I also intended to be sensible."

"Good intentions," Rufus muttered. "Not worth the paper they're written on."

"And I realise that last night, ah, overstepped the boundaries. You may not wish to do that again."

Rufus didn't know if one could overstep boundaries again when they had already been thoroughly and mutually trampled into the ground. Perhaps he ought to re-erect them. If he only knew where they should be.

He knew where he wanted them to be, in this moment, with Luke inches away and the memory of his touch, his taste.

"I do wish to do it again," he said. "I'd sodding love to do it again, repeatedly. Just not at the cost of your job, or your well-being, or our friendship. I hope you count us friends."

"Yes," Luke said, voice rather constricted. "Yes, I...have come to do that."

"As your friend, I don't want to hurt you. As your employer, I don't want to lose you. As the man whose bed you adorned last night, I'd very much like you back there, but not at the expense of the rest. So tell me what you want, and I will do my best to do right by you, which includes taking your 'no' with all the grace I can muster."

Luke's dark eyes looked huge. "I believe that you would hear my 'no'. Could I persuade you to hear my 'yes'?"

"I would take that with pleasure." Rufus's chest felt rather tight. "A *lot* of pleasure."

"Promise?"

The fallen-angel curve of Luke's lips at that was everything Rufus wanted. "To the best of my ability," he managed, and saw Luke's smile widen and darken. "As soon as you like. Only, you'll tell me if you change your mind?"

"I will let you know if you do or suggest anything I don't want. I won't gloss my objections, spare your feelings, or worry for my employment. Does that satisfy you?"

"Make sure you say it clearly. I'm not good at subtlety."

Luke's eyes gleamed. "I have observed that, my lord."

"Rufus."

"Uh—"

"Not Oxney or 'my lord'. Use my name."

"No, that's a terrible idea," Luke said. "I'm not sure you should be using mine; I absolutely ought not get in the habit of using yours."

"I cannot bed a man who calls me by my title. It's absurd."

"Don't ruin my fun. I told you how I feel about Gothic earls in castles."

"I'm not a Gothic earl, and this isn't a castle. It's a Norman manor house."

"If I wanted accurate historical detail I'd fuck Mr. Odo, and don't ever make me have that thought again."

"And to think I was worried you wouldn't say what you meant," Rufus muttered. "Leave my relatives out of it. I want to hear you say my name."

Luke's lips parted. He looked at Rufus a second, then his eyelids, fringed with lashes as dark as his brows, swept down. "Make me."

"What did you say?"

"You want me to use your name? Make me."

"God damn it," Rufus said. "I am going to find out if this bloody place has a dungeon. Come here."

Luke rose. Rufus, aware of the window, retreated a few steps. Luke came round the desk, and Rufus grabbed him by the lapels, hauled him over, and pushed him against the wall, safely out of sight.

"My lord," Luke said softly, tauntingly.

Rufus looked down at him, with all the glower he could muster. "That's right. And I am sure my authority extends to telling you what to do with that mouth of yours."

"Arguable. Although, on the other—mph."

That was because Rufus had kissed him, rather hard. His hands came up, snaking around Rufus's neck and into his hair, pulling him in, and they were kissing wildly once more, mouths colliding with sharp, hungry pleasure, clumsy with need. Luke wrapped his leg round Rufus's thigh, and Rufus got a hand under his taut arse, felt Luke hold on around his shoulders, and hoisted so that he came off the floor. Then they were face to face, hip to hip, Rufus pressing him into the wall in an effort to defy gravity and because he liked him there, Luke clinging on like ivy on oak. They kissed with bites, with moans, fingers hard on skin, Luke's thighs clamped over Rufus's waist, open and willing and gloriously enthusiastic.

Rufus pulled his mouth away. "Say my name."

"I told you."

"Helpless youths at the mercy of Gothic earls"—he had to stop to kiss him there—"do what they're told. Droit du seigneur, damn it."

"There's no such thing as a right you can't enforce."

"I refuse to debate legal theory now." Rufus leaned in, nuzzling his way through golden hair to kiss Luke's ear. It was a particularly fine ear, elegantly curved, with a generous lobe. Not that he'd previously looked at ears with any great attention, but he was quite sure this was a superior specimen, and he very much liked the way Luke arched his neck to give him access to it. He used that well, licking the lobe, the sharper curves. Luke shuddered and clung tighter. Rufus gave the lobe an exploratory nip, and won a tiny gasp that went right to his prick.

Oh, he liked that. He worked on the ear a little longer, with Luke straining helplessly against him, his stand stiff and rigid against Rufus's belly, gasping and whimpering. "Fuck. Oh God, what are you doing, that's perfect. Ngh."

"Shameless little—" Rufus kissed his neck hard, aware his grip had slipped badly, along with his self-control. "Putting you down."

Luke slid his feet to the floor. "You mentioned my mouth?"

Tempting, but no. Rufus got a hand between his legs, pressing firmly on a very satisfactory handful, starting to massage. Luke's head went back and he sagged against the wall, eyes shut, mouth open. Rufus worked his palm, pressing and stroking, kissing that lovely neck again, bright wisps of curls tickling his face, until Luke gasped, "Oh, please."

"Please what?"

"Almost anything."

"Absolutely anything," Rufus said. "Anything you want." Luke's hips were straining against his, and he probably wouldn't want to spend in his clothing. Rufus increased the pressure and speed of his strokes accordingly. "I will suck you or fuck you, bring you off or kneel for you or any damn thing you want. Just ask me." He gave it a second. "By name."

"You anointed fucker," Luke gasped, gloriously if incomprehensibly Kentish. "Oh God. Your hand, and kiss me. *Rufus!*"

Rufus went for the buttons with frantic haste, fingers fumbling with urgency. Freed Luke's prick, felt it strain into his hand, rubbed the wetness at its tip over the smooth skin for a blissful moment. His other hand was braced against the wall. Luke's hand found it, and their fingers entwined, and then Rufus was kissing him, frigging him, holding him. So magnificently close, Luke so magnificently pliant, crying softly into Rufus's mouth and shuddering as he spent.

He sagged. Rufus pushed closer, holding him up, or just holding him.

"God," Luke said after a moment. "You."

"You."

"Rufus." He whispered it. "In private only. *Not* as a matter of course."

"You see? You can find a perfectly reasonable compromise, given the right inducement."

Luke opened his eyes, which looked hazy. "That wasn't an inducement. It was extortion."

"Fair means or foul." Rufus kissed him again, rather more gently. "You are unjustly lovely. Your eyebrows are an offence in themselves. It's distracting."

"Me, distracting? I was at work when you came in."

"True. You should get back to that now."

Luke looked up, startled. "What about you?"

Rufus ran a finger down the scarless side of his face. "Well, I thought I might sit quietly in here and read a book for a while. Since I had one lent to me this morning. And if I should feel the need to tell you what to do with your mouth, in due course, I might mention it. If that suits you?"

"That would be *extremely* distracting," Luke said. "I'd be sitting there trying to work, wondering what part you were reading and expecting you to make demands at any moment. It would be quite impossible to concentrate."

"Oh. Well, we don't have to—" Rufus began.

Luke grabbed his face. "Yes, we do. Read the book."

After that magnificent start to the day, Rufus found himself in a generous mood. He also recalled something Luke had said, and accordingly, that afternoon, he sent for Odo.

His cousin arrived, looking nervous. "What can I do for you, Oxney?"

"Good question," Rufus said. "How are the researches going?"

"Oh, very—down to Fairfield, which—necessary to address certain points—"

Rufus waited patiently while he stumbled through the maze of his sentence, which led to the conclusion that nothing had changed. "Good, excellent. When you feel happy to let that go, I have another task for you."

"Oh. Well, of course. If I can, ah, very happy if, within my powers—"

"Could you write a book?"

"...what?"

"Book. You. Write one."

"What book?"

"A history of the family."

Odo's eyes bulged. "A history?"

"We don't have one, do we?"

"Well, in 1679, Arnulf, Lord Oxney commissioned—"

"So we need a new one. A full history of the d'Aumesty line from our Norman beginnings to the present day." That should surely keep him busy for a good few years. "Could you do it?"

"Well—I—me?" Odo clasped his hands, his face transfigured. "Really?"

"I can't think of a better man for the job." Rufus clapped him on the shoulder. "Give it some thought, let me know."

Odo's mouth worked. He quivered a second, then grabbed Rufus's hand and shook it violently, which was a relief, because Rufus had feared he might go in for an embrace. "Thank you, Oxney. Thank you. I *knew* you'd find your place here. I won't let you down."

"Excellent," Rufus said. "Send Fulk to see me, will you?" He was in a mood to get things done.

Fulk arrived a little later, looking supercilious in a way that didn't quite hide tension. "You summoned me, Oxney."

"I did," Rufus said. "Sit down. What do your debts come to?"

"Not beating about the bush, coz?"

"If you want tact, talk to someone tactful, though Christ knows who that would be in this house. If you want money, I'm the one who has it."

Fulk stiffened. "I can't say I like your tone."

"I don't like you running up bills you can't pay, but we all have our cross to bear," Rufus said. "If you don't care for this conversation, you're welcome to find the money yourself. Otherwise, how much?"

Fulk's lips thinned. "Oh, around two thousand, five hundred."

"Jesus. You felt that, since your father was to become earl, the estate would bear the costs?"

"It was a reasonable assumption," Fulk said, looking rather white about the nose.

"No. There's years of neglect that needs repairing. You can't just wring money out of land, or tenants, as if they exist only to feed you: you have to put it in too, and nobody seems to have understood that in some years. It's disgraceful, and it is changing now. *However.*" He let that hang in the air a moment. "You had an honest expectation of inheriting and have not been treated well over that, so I am going to see what I can do for you. Bring me a full list of your tradesmen's bills."

"Don't trouble with those. They can wait."

"No, they can't."

"A gentleman's debts of honour—"

"I'm not a gentleman," Rufus said over him. "I am the son and grandson of drapers, I don't give a damn for debts of so-called honour, and not one penny of mine goes towards your gambling friends until every bill is presented and paid. That is, money you owe people for goods and services you have received, because when you don't pay your tailor's bill, Fulk, you might as well stick your hand in his pocket and steal his watch while you are at it, and I will have no thieves in my household. Get them together, all of them, and while you do that, you can consider how you intend to proceed. Because if your sole aim, once hauled out of the River Tick, is to plunge straight back in and waste your blunt all over again, don't imagine I will save you a second time. If you want to drive to the devil, pay for your own horses."

Fulk was scarlet, which was unsurprising: Rufus had experience in administering well-merited rebukes. "By *proceed*, I take it you mean find some drudgery."

"Work is a thing that people do for money, yes. If you prefer to be idle, that's your choice." Rufus leaned back in his chair. "But I'd be sorry for it."

"Would you really."

"I could use your help. You seem an intelligent enough man, you grew up here, you will have insights I don't. I'm trying to acquaint myself with the entire estate at once, and I'm running both Smallbone and Doomsday ragged in the process. I could use a lieutenant."

Fulk looked, for once, entirely nonplussed. "Me? But—No, really, Oxney. You must be aware my grandfather never permitted me to take an interest in the lands, even while he allowed me to believe they would one day be mine. He was very happy for me to waste my blunt in London, as you so delicately put it: he liked to have a rake in the family and saw no reason I should do anything else. I have no idea how to go about the management of tenants and buildings and such."

Rufus snorted. "You think I do?"

"As has been established…"

"Of course I don't. Don't have the first idea. So I'm learning, because damned if I'll sit around this mouldering barracks all day feeling useless."

Fulk's eyes met his properly then. "One can see you have not been brought up in the ways of gentlemanly idleness."

It could easily have been a sneer. It *was* a sneer, in fact: Rufus just didn't think it was entirely aimed at himself.

"No, well, I'm not a gentleman," he said. "Just an earl, one up to his neck in work. And I'd rather not be running this place entirely against the grain of my family."

"Tell that to Mother."

"No, you tell her."

"I beg your pardon?"

"If you care to dabble in being of use, you can start there. I want a deal less quarrelling and a deal more cooperation. I've heard enough about my shortcomings, my staff, and especially my parentage. I will pay your tradesmans' bills whatever happens; persuade your mother and father to meet me with the appearance of civility, and we can talk about the gambling debts. And if you choose to work with me further, I'll be grateful in a very material sense."

"Some might call that a rather mercantile approach," Fulk remarked with a curling lip.

"Don't think of it as a transaction," Rufus assured him. "It's a bribe."

Fulk stared at him, then gave a sudden, sharp crack of laughter. "You're a piece of work, coz. You'll pay up if I smooth your way with the old folk? Well, I dare say I might speak to them on your behalf."

"It would be in their interests more than mine. Right now, I'm strongly tempted to say that anyone who can't make themselves either pleasant or useful will soon be required to make themselves scarce. Pass that on however you see fit."

Fulk nodded and rose. "Very well. Although, do you know, it's rather a shame you didn't address that last to Mother directly? She might have been pleased. It was Grandfather to the very life."

He sauntered out on that. Rufus had to admit, it wasn't a bad last word.

Luke applauded wildly when Rufus recounted his work that evening, sprawled over the bed. "Marvellous. Lovely pincer movement to split the older and younger Conrads into opposing factions."

"That wasn't my intention." He frowned. "Was it yours? You were the one who suggested both those things."

Luke leaned up to kiss him. "I thought those might be effective tactics, yes. Whereas you were being both practical and kind, and merely happened to be so in a very effective way. I think you will be a very good earl."

"I hope to. Whether I achieve that remains to be seen, but I'm trying. At least I'm better than Conrad would be."

"That goes without saying, but you're also a great deal better than I'd ever be. You care so much, Rufus. I don't think I quite realised how much you care, and—and you deserve better. That's all."

"Better than what?"

Luke hesitated, then gave a sudden, jaw-cracking yawn. "D'Aumestys. Normans. Sorry, I'm exhausted. I should probably go to bed now: I doubt I'm making sense."

"Do that," Rufus said. "Get some rest. Sleep as late as you can." He pulled Luke over to kiss his hair. "We've a lot to do tomorrow. I'm damned glad you're there to do it with me."

Luke pushed his head against Rufus's chest like a cat. "So am I."

Eleven

LUKE HADN'T MEANT TO DO IT. HE REALLY HAD INTENDED TO ignore the crackling attraction, repress his desire. To keep the situation simple, or at least not make it more complicated than it had to be. But he'd been pushed into a corner, he'd had no other way out— That wasn't true and he knew it. He'd wanted Rufus so much, and when the temptation had been there in front of him, along with the perfect excuse to give in to it, he hadn't resisted. If you could describe grabbing what he wanted with both hands as "not resisting".

He'd thrown caution to the wind, and he was paying the price. Because if he'd thought the pull between them was strong before, he'd known nothing. He'd been a heap of dry tinder and Rufus was the match.

The problem was, he *liked* the bloody man. Rufus made him laugh, and laughed at him. He valued Luke's thoughts, and gave him his head while never disavowing responsibility. He wanted to make things run properly, which spoke to Luke's own love of organisation and control. And he was a magnificent lover, not because he was particularly skilled or experienced, but because he listened. He asked what Luke

wanted, and then did it with force and enthusiasm. He was consider-
ate in ways that made Luke feel stupidly soft and vulnerable and cared
for; he was brawny and bulky and mouth-wateringly good to look at,
and it was all so unfair that Luke could have cried.

At least, he could in the nights, when he returned alone to his
room on grounds of discretion, and lay staring at the darkness with
Rufus's touch still tingling on his skin, the taste of him in his mouth.
Then he thought about the borrowed time he was living on in too
many ways and how he would have to leave—how he would have
had to leave *anyway* because for all the fun they were having, Rufus
was an earl, and that would start to mean something one day. That
he was going to hurt Rufus. That he didn't want to.

He thought about those things at night, even while he prowled
Stone Manor's dark corridors pursuing his own midnight goals, ears
twitching madly, because if Rufus caught him out of bed again he'd be
in trouble he might not be able to fuck his way out of. He rose too early,
pushing through the tiredness to do what he needed before Rufus
started the day. And then his lover, his employer, his seigneur would
crash into the room like a gale, and Luke would once again forget all
the reasons he shouldn't be doing this in the pure glory of doing it.

That first time in the study, Rufus had sat in the chair reading
Jonathan, the erotic novel—it had a good-sized, clear typeface, and
the content offered a powerful inducement to take the trouble—for
far longer than Luke had found reasonable. Turning pages, occasionally licking his finger to do it, all but forcing Luke to calculate
where in the story he'd got to. Luke had impressive powers of concentration, but that morning he'd had all the focus of a four-year-old
who'd eaten too many sweetmeats. He'd almost cried with relief
when Rufus had finally crooked a finger. *Come here. Suck me. Bring
yourself off while you do it.*

That had been copied from a scene in the book, and Luke could only applaud. Applaud, obey, tumble headlong down the primrose path because it was so very, very pleasant to be on.

It had been a week now, in which they'd fucked at least twice a day. Luke didn't have the time for that, and did it anyway. He *wanted* to do his job. He had work to do and the books were crying out for deliverance. But there were only so many hours in the day and night, and Rufus was claiming so many of them.

Obviously, he could say no. *No, I will not put down my pen and come to your arms; no, I don't want you sitting there reading* Jonathan *in the corner of my eye; no, I will not join you for a brandy in your rooms after dinner, and end up on or over the settle at midnight when I ought to be searching your house. No.*

Chance be a fine thing.

He was currently in those very rooms. Miss Berengaria's paintings, newly framed in carved and gilded wood, glowed on the walls like windows to a brighter world. The furniture had arrived, upholstered in peacock blues and greens with a thread of gold. Luke felt mildly smug that he had said gold and green himself, though he hadn't envisaged anything like this. Gold-framed mirrors and an abundance of candles made it all glow.

Rufus had hung the rainbow painting of the Marsh opposite the chair he'd designated as Luke's, so he could sit and look at it as he pleased. A painting on his own walls for Luke's pleasure, and nothing about that was fair. He was on the settle instead where he didn't have to see it and be reminded, curled up inside the Earl of Oxney's sprawling limbs having his hair stroked as though he were a cat, and that wasn't fair *either*. How was he supposed to do what he was here for, the important thing, when Rufus kept making other things matter?

"Is something wrong?" Rufus asked.

"Wrong? No."

"You look..." Rufus's finger traced the delicate skin under his right eye. He had a very light touch for a forceful man, and Luke hadn't missed how carefully he avoided the left side of his face. "Tired."

"You're exhausting me."

"I do that. Are you not sleeping well?"

He was lying awake till he heard Rufus snore, then prowling the house and grounds at two or three in the morning. Of course he wasn't sleeping well: he was barely sleeping at all. "I sometimes suffer from insomnia. It's nothing."

"Nonsense. You need sleep. You need more fresh air and exercise. We'll ride tomorrow and don't argue. There's nothing that can't wait, and you'll do a better job for the rest. You haven't taken a day off this whole time. I feel like a monster."

Luke sighed heavily. "I don't—"

"It's an order. Do you want to ride down to Dymchurch and see your family on Sunday? It's been a month and you haven't visited them, and I should rather not be the reason for your absence."

"You aren't, at all."

"Then why not go? Lord knows I'd like to see my family; I don't want you kept from yours."

"It's not you doing that."

"Then what is stopping you? You talked about being estranged from one's family, cast out. Is that...?"

Christ Jesus. Either Rufus was more perceptive than he'd realised, or one simply couldn't be this intimate without being noticed, which was yet another reason he should never have done this. Luke knew that. It didn't stop him burrowing a little closer into the comfort of Rufus's warm, solid body as he searched for an answer. "No. I'm not that. But—well, I told you about my birth. I was left with the Doomsdays at a bad time for the family, when two of my uncles had recently drowned and my father was the only young man left. Everyone was struggling to cope, and an unexpected, unwanted baby was one more problem, and that was how it went on. I was on the outside, underfoot, nobody's in particular. I didn't fit."

Rufus's hand was brushing the hair on the left side of his face, perilously close to the scar. His fingers were hesitant and it wasn't hard to guess why. If he asked, it would be an excuse to end this conversation, but he didn't. He just waited, stroking, listening, until Luke felt compelled to go on.

"Then—well, various things happened. Mostly, Sir Gareth stepped in. Everything changed then. I went to live with him, went to school, discovered wider horizons. Left the Marsh. You might say I turned my back on my home by getting educated; my father felt that very strongly. It created a distance."

It was true in essence if not detail. It wasn't the whole truth, not even in essence, but he wasn't going to talk about the guilt he could and would not assuage, his father's anger which he'd soaked up until it filled him, his own poisonous resentment.

"I'm not cast out at all," he went on. "They would be there for me in a heartbeat, but I don't belong in the same way the others do. That's all. Really, if I'm avoiding visiting, it's because I don't care to ride fourteen miles in order to be called a bettermy young rascal."

"A what?"

"Bettermy. It's a short way to say 'you think you're better than me'. I heard it a lot growing up although, in fairness, they were right. That and Goldilocks, which was what everyone called me until Sir Gareth made them stop."

"Also in fairness—"

"No. I hated it."

Rufus chuckled, his chest shaking under Luke. "It's not far off, though. Walking into someone else's house and decreeing exactly how the porridge and the stools and the beds should be—"

"Well, yes, that would be reasonable," Luke admitted. "But I got it for my hair. Everyone else is dark, but apart from the eyebrows, I look very like my mother. So I'm told."

"I love your hair." Rufus gave it a very gentle tug. "I can also imagine that you were a fairly intolerable boy. I say this as an absolutely intolerable one myself."

"What was wrong with you?"

"Loud. Always fighting. Broke everything."

"Sounds right."

Rufus caught his hand, lacing the fingers together. "I don't think I or anyone should be excessively blamed for the dreadfulness of youth. I also hope your family can see your achievements as something to be proud of, and if they can't, it's their loss." He hesitated, in a manner that suggested he was trying to think of a tactful way to say something. Luke braced himself. "Do I need to know anything about your relations with Sir Gareth?"

"He's the best man I know. He changed my life out of nothing but kindness and took me into his home and paid for my education, and if you're looking askance at that, get your mind out of the gutter."

"I see. Well, if he's been such a good friend to you, with no ulterior motive—"

"He is and has," Luke said, bristling.

"Then you clearly owe him at least a visit. And I certainly do: I am grossly behind on doing the pretty to my neighbours. Suppose you ride down on Saturday and stay. I'll pay him a call on Sunday and we can ride back together."

"You," Luke began.

"If you were about to say that I take a lot on myself, I hope you paused to recall how often I have said that to you."

"That doesn't make it less irritating."

"Now you see why I keep threatening to sack you."

Luke glowered at him. "I can't go on Saturday. Miss Berengaria made me promise to sit for her in the afternoon." He glanced up into Rufus's face and gave in. "But Sunday would be very pleasant. All *right*, I'll send him a note. Do you know what this painting is, and why she wants me?"

"Something to do with that pagan god of Pagan's. A history painting, she said. I told her, I'm not dressing up in a tunic for anyone's money and nor will you be."

Luke hadn't realised that might be a possibility. "Thank you," he said wholeheartedly.

"And if you'd rather go than sit for her—"

Luke wanted, suddenly and desperately, to go back to Gareth's for a few days. To be coddled and fed too much, to pour his heart out. To tell Gareth all of it, the secrets he'd harboured for so long, the plans he'd made and the lies he'd told...

He couldn't do that. This was his to do alone; this was how he would get his deserts for every wrong that had been done him, and he couldn't let anyone stand in the way. Not that Gareth would want to do that, but he wouldn't understand, not properly, because he wanted Luke to let go of the past, whereas Luke wanted to put a stake through its angry, miserable heart.

He couldn't risk it. He'd come too far and done too much to give up now, and he didn't like that his will was being sapped this way. It had all been a lot clearer when he'd first made his plans.

"Let's keep Miss Berengaria on our side," he said in lieu of all that. "Never thwart an artist in the grip of inspiration. I've seen it done and the results aren't pretty."

Rufus snorted, but pulled his hand up, kissing the fingers. "If you insist."

Miss Berengaria did indeed try to make him wear a tunic, but Luke dug his heels in as politely as possible, and she compromised on him stripping off coat and waistcoat. The eye with which she examined him was entirely professional, but it was still not a comfortable business to sit in front of a lady of the house in his linen.

"Chin up. Higher. Look serious." Her pencil scratched rapidly on the paper. "Look up a little. Better."

"What is this for?" Luke had to ask. "Lord Oxney said a painting of the god you mentioned?"

"Mithras, the soldier's god. Oxney's the soldier. You're the god."

"The—"

"Turn your face a little. No, other way. Good heavens, you've superb eyebrows. I dare say Oxney won't mind me casting you as his deity. It's the hair. Mithras was a sun god, which makes very little sense to me given they worshipped him underground, but there we are. You didn't get your hair from the Doomsdays."

"I take after my mother."

"Mph." She frowned at him. "Who may or may not have married Raymond. What's the truth in that claim?"

"Mr. Odo has found nothing to support it, and I can't say I expect him to."

"Say what you like about Odo, he's thorough, at least when it comes to mouldering documents. If he hasn't found anything, I doubt there's anything to be found. Which, I may say, is driving Father to distraction, since he can't accuse Oxney of suborning his own son. Or at least, he hasn't yet. It's probably a matter of time."

That was startlingly frank. Luke could see why she and Rufus had hit it off so well once they started talking. "I doubt he'd be suborned, and I am sure Lord Oxney wouldn't suborn him if he could. He's an extremely honest man. But I don't think it would be necessary anyway; there's nothing in it."

"Good," Berengaria said. "Not for you, I suppose, or Father if he's right that he'd take the coronet instead of you, but otherwise, good. Oxney's exactly the breath of fresh air we needed here after Grandfather's unconscionable time a-dying. Mrs. Greening says he's a godsend."

The housekeeper was a powerful voice in the Earl's party now. Emily had passed her remark on to Luke the other day. He wondered who'd told Berengaria. "Am I right in thinking that you have lived in Stone Manor all your life, Miss Berengaria?"

"Mph. Why?"

"I'm attempting to make a list of works that were done on the house some years ago, but the records are in something of a disordered state. There's a lot of expenditure and no detail given, and it's unclear what was actually built then."

"You're talking about Uncle Baldwin's exploits? The Cathedral and the rest?"

"Yes," Luke said. "If you could tell me about that?"

"Raise your right arm a little, as if you're holding the sun—just holding *something*, use your imagination—and turn your head. Chin up. Baldwin's foolery? Well, this was when Grandfather was very ill—not his last illness but the one before. He was bedridden for close to two years, I think. His vision was affected and his moods dreadful, and to be quite honest, nobody expected him to recover." She paused to dab at her work. "Baldwin certainly didn't, because he went ahead and did as he pleased, and bribed the others not to mention any of it to Grandfather. Well, *that* was a fine mess. Baldwin did it, Pagan was in on it, my father didn't stop him, and Grandfather never forgave any of them."

"And this was in the year nine or thereabouts?"

"Around then, or a little later. I was in London for my Season. Ridiculous waste of time."

Luke's skin was tingling. "What did Lord Stone do, exactly?"

"He had the Cathedral built, right over the ornamental herb garden. You must have noticed."

"And the other works you mentioned?"

"The ice house for Father. That was quite useful, even Grandfather had to admit, though he'd refused to build one himself. And Pagan's folly. That wasn't expensive but it was—well, Pagan. I didn't think Grandfather needed to be quite so rude about it, but he was very angry."

"What, exactly..."

"A mithraeum. A temple to Mithras."

Luke wasn't even surprised. "Where is it?"

"He put it in the undercroft. Really, there wasn't very much work needed, mostly the carving, and it's not as though anyone sees it. Not like the Cathedral. That was really what did it, along with Baldwin's plans for the future, and of course the fact that he had it erected as Grandfather lay dying—or not dying, as it turned out—and they all conspired to keep it from him. It would be best not to trouble Grandfather with any decisions, was what they said. Cowards. Mother wouldn't have let it happen, but she was in London with me. When Grandfather recovered to find a monstrous Gothic folly in the middle of the grounds, he was apoplectic. It's astonishing the business didn't finish him off by itself. Good heavens, the rows."

"I'm sorry to hear it."

She shrugged. "You've doubtless gathered, there's not a great deal of love lost in this family. If you're interested in anything to do with the history, talk to Odo. And if you'd like to see the mithraeum, ask Pagan: he holds the key. You'll get a lecture with it, mind."

"Thank you," Luke said sincerely. "Thank you very much."

Once released from Berengaria's scrutiny, he went to find Odo, who was in the archives, as usual. He gave Luke a hopeful look. "Ah, Doomsday. Does Oxney want me?"

"I haven't come from him, Mr. Odo. I wondered if you might spare me a little time to talk about the alterations to the house some fifteen years ago, or a little later."

"Oh, the Cathedral? Poor Grandfather. Baldwin behaved appallingly. The Cathedral was quite bad enough, but what he intended was unspeakable. Do you know, he wanted to demolish—demolish!—Stone Manor? To raze it to the ground. And to replace it with—" He paused dramatically. "*Gothic Revival.*"

Luke attempted to arrange his features into a suitable look of horror. "Gothic Revival? Not really?"

"Yes! He actually went to see Fonthill Abbey, that monstrous creation in Wiltshire. Do you know of it?"

"I have visited it, as it happens," Luke said. "A little while before Mr. Beckford sold it. A previous employer made his acquaintance." Lord Corvin's relentless air of sexual availability had got them in; Mr. Beckford's skin-crawling manner had driven them rapidly out. "It was a quite extraordinary building but to be honest, Mr. Odo, not a very reliable one, for all that was spent on it. The kitchens had already collapsed once and the tower did not feel entirely safe to stand under. I certainly don't think it will last a thousand years. Not like the Manor."

"Exactly," Odo said. "Exactly! Was it impressive?"

"It was astonishing in its way, but it didn't seem real. Spires and arches and endless empty halls, nothing solid about it. My employer said it was a dream in stone. It wasn't like this house, a living monument to a great heritage."

He wondered if he'd laid that last part on too thick, but Odo's frantic nodding suggested no such thing was possible. "Exactly! And that was what Baldwin wanted to do here. He said he loathed the Manor, that the walls were too thick and the rooms oppressive and dark. He had a terror of the dark, you know. He left candles burning all night, didn't like enclosed spaces, couldn't even think about being underground, so perhaps one can understand to a degree—but to *hate* it, to want to destroy it—can you imagine?"

Luke shook his head, adopting a dismayed look. "I'm astonished, Mr. Odo. To disregard your family's history, and lineage—"

"Outrageous. Appalling. He was a fantasist of the most absurd kind. Imagine dreaming, yes, dreaming of such nonsense while our true, our noble history is all around us."

The true history was, in Luke's view, ugly, inconvenient, and cold. He didn't have any more time for the grotesque waste of ill-gotten money that was Fonthill Abbey, pretty though it had been, but if Rufus razed Stone Manor to put up something sensibly-sized where the chimneys didn't smoke, Luke would cheer him on. "And that was the reason for the Cathedral? Lord Stone making a start on his plans?"

"Exactly. He said, quite openly, that when he was earl the whole Manor would come down. Grandfather was livid, with him and everyone who had allowed it to happen. Baldwin wasn't sorry in the slightest. He kept working on his plans for a Gothic Revival mansion. Grandfather cut him off so he couldn't pay the architect, so he just made his own designs which really were—" He shuddered. "If he'd succeeded Grandfather, heaven knows how much damage he would have done. Thank God he—no, I don't mean that, but I must be grateful he never had the chance. I don't know if Grandfather felt the same way," he added thoughtfully. "He seemed to hate Baldwin, but he hated Father as much for taking his place. Which, working for him, having to pass on messages and refuse his bills—it was all very difficult."

"Your grandfather made *you* tell your father he wouldn't have his bills paid?"

Odo winced. "Yes, it—well—punishment, you see. For him, or possibly both of us."

Luke was not a sympathetic man, as a rule. Odo had a kicked-puppy air that ought to evoke compassion, but Luke didn't like dogs. He did, however, know all about being trapped with people who set out deliberately to hurt you, and he added another mental line to his tally against the elder d'Aumestys, this one thick and red. "That was not kind, Mr. Odo. Not kind and not right."

Odo's eyes flew to his. "Well, perhaps—but he was the earl. Really it was just—well."

"It was not right," Luke said again, because sometimes one needed to hear that out loud. "Why did he want to punish your father?"

"I asked him that, you know. It was just a few days before he died, so probably it was foolish of me, it wouldn't have made any difference, but Father had been so angry and I wanted so much for it to stop—anyway, I asked him. Henry the Second, he said." He sighed. "I suppose he was right."

"I don't follow," Luke said, with some restraint.

"*You* know. Henry the Second," Odo explained earnestly, as though Luke had simply not heard him the first time. "That was the position he was in with my father."

"Could you assume I'm not up to the mark with the Angevin monarchs?"

"Henry was a Plantagenet," Odo said, with a touch of rebuke. "He was the father of Henry the Young King—not to be confused with Henry the Third—"

"I'll try not to."

"—and Richard, later the Lionheart, and John. The Young King and Richard both rebelled against Henry in his lifetime, and on his deathbed he learned that John too had joined forces with Richard, just as Father had joined Baldwin. A father dreadfully betrayed by sons trying to snatch power from his grasp."

"I see."

Odo's shoulders sagged. "I dare say it's why Grandfather was so hard to please. He was awfully disappointed. And angry. And very unwell for a long time. And of course he must have known that Raymond's son was alive, which would have made everything worse. I wish—no, I don't." He shook himself, apparently remembering that none of this was Luke's affair, and added rather stiffly, "I beg your pardon, I have been rambling."

"I'm very grateful, Mr. Odo," Luke said. "So they worked on the ice house, the Cathedral, and Mr. Pagan's mithraeum. Is that right?"

"Yes. Yes, I believe that was all. Quite enough, really."

"Thank you, that was very informative. Is it possible to see inside the Cathedral?"

"There's nothing to see. The interior was never finished and it's just used to store lumber and a lot of old chests and so on. Family clutter."

Luke could have kicked himself. He'd asked at the wrong time; he shouldn't have asked at all. Rufus would have demanded the key for him and handed it over without question. But now Odo knew Luke was interested, and if he pushed further, the man would wonder why. Damn it. He was too tired, and he was just a little too excited that he might have found his answer.

He'd already searched the ice house. He could go and consult Mr. Pagan on the mithraeum, but the old man was reclusive, eating most of his meals alone in the Chamber Block, and, when he did emerge, prone to endless monologues about his peculiar interests which caused everyone in the house except Odo to avoid him, by hiding in cupboards if necessary. Seeking him out would strike people as odd enough that Luke would need to come up with a good reason for his interest.

No: he'd start with the Cathedral, which meant getting the key, which would doubtless be in Mr. Pauncefoot's possession. This was what family was for, he thought, and went to have a quiet word with Emily.

Twelve

THE NEXT MORNING, LUKE WOKE UP IN THE WRONG BED.

He couldn't even tell where he was at first, except that the bed felt oddly different and there seemed to be more of it, and the warm presence of a breathing body close to his...

He'd fallen asleep in the great d'Aumesty bed last night. With Rufus. Naked.

And missed his usual night-time exploration even though he had the Cathedral's key in his pocket, but that was the least of his worries. If the valet had come in—

"Morning." Rufus's deep voice rumbled through him.

"You let me sleep here!"

"You fell asleep. I didn't have the heart to wake you."

"Brains," Luke growled. "It's *brains* you lack, not heart."

Rufus gave a snort of amusement. "Ye of little faith. I locked the door."

That was something. Luke let himself relax slightly. "Still. That was reckless."

"How? I don't have tea brought to me; I don't wear anything that requires professional help to put on." This, regrettably, was true, as he'd look magnificent in the sort of tight-fitting coat that had to be wrestled on to its wearer. "My family avoid me as far as possible. Nobody is coming in. And—" He rolled over, slung a heavy arm over Luke's side, and brushed a kiss to his eyebrow. "You looked exhausted. Do you always sleep so poorly, or is it this damned barrack giving you nightmares? You didn't look this tired when you arrived. Sir Gareth will think I'm working you to death."

"It comes and goes." He didn't want Rufus to care about his fictional insomnia. "I certainly slept like the dead last night. What time is it?"

"Half past seven by the clock. We should set off around nine, I think."

Today was to be a holiday. Rufus had made his will clear, and there was no point spoiling it with thinking of other things. He would ride with Rufus, see Gareth. He'd take the day off, and enjoy it as he would if he wasn't lying to anybody at all, as if he were what Rufus thought him to be, and nothing else.

And since his holiday was beginning in this ancient bed...

"So we have an hour." He rolled over onto his side, under Rufus's arm, and ran his hand down the strong flank, noticing—it was hard to miss—that Rufus had an admirable case of morning wood. "And the door is locked. Both doors?"

"Both...? Ah."

Luke made a strangled noise, rolled out of bed, and locked the door that led to his own room, then tested the other door was in fact locked as promised, because Rufus was an idiot. He turned back to see that the Earl had kicked off the coverlet and was sprawled naked over the sheets.

An idiot, but a glorious one. Luke took the time for a good look at his thick, muscled body, pale in the dim light, framed by the weird carving of the bed that caged him. "God."

"What?"

"You look like... I don't know. Like the Baron Stone and Earl of Oxney."

"What did I do to deserve that?"

"I don't mean badly." Luke moved forward, got onto the end of the bed rather than round the side, kneeling erect in every sense so he looked down at Rufus's long-limbed sprawl from an unaccustomed height. "You look like the master of the halls and lord of all he surveys, in the ancient bed of his ancestors, and I want to do something absolutely filthy to you."

"Well, if you put it like that. What do you have in mind?"

"I don't know. Stroke your cock while I think about it."

Rufus's hand moved. "You're in an authoritative mood this morning."

"Does that suit you?"

"It always does. I'm just pointing out your mask has slipped."

"I *don't—*," Luke began, but when Rufus grinned at him, he had to admit that, well, maybe he did.

Rufus's fingers were wrapped loosely round his stand, moving gently, thumb flicking over the top. Luke made his way forward, so he sat on Rufus's powerful thighs. Those green-tinted eyes, muted by shadow, were on his, and Rufus's hand was still moving, pleasuring himself gently, almost absently, as he watched. He wasn't entirely sure what he wanted to do, only that he wanted whatever it was to reduce Rufus to a whimpering boneless heap.

He ran his hands up the inside of his lord's thighs. "Put your hands out."

Rufus let his prick go and stretched his long arms up and out, in a way that made the muscles cord interestingly. He knew very well Luke was a weakling for his arms. Luke clambered over his stand and positioned himself so he was on all fours over his supine master, knees either side of his thick chest, hands over Rufus's so their palms kissed, their fingers interlaced.

"I want you to pleasure me," Luke whispered. "I want you to suck me like this, with your prick hard. I want to fuck your mouth and spend in your throat, and then—we'll see what next."

"I'll tell you what next." Rufus's eyes were on his. "You take your pleasure now, exactly as you like best, as long as you like, and then I will turn you over and take mine, as long and slow and hard as I like. Think about that, you blasted apocalypse, and be aware that when it's my turn, I'm going to make you know my rights."

Deliciously taunting words, laughing eyes. His hands were so tight on Luke's, their fingers entwined. Luke shifted forward, dreamlike, bumping his stiff length against Rufus's lips. Rufus swiped with his tongue, and it sent a shock spiking through Luke's nerves.

He leaned in. Rufus's lips tightened round him, and sucked gently, and Luke's fingers spasmed. He rocked forwards, moving slowly, an inch or so moving in and out. Rufus's mouth around him, wet and warm, lips like an embrace. His lord, lying under him, Luke fucking his mouth in gentle strokes of slow pleasure, taking his time because he could. The Earl's mouth, the Earl's bed, the Earl's domain, and he, Luke Doomsday, ruling it all for these few private moments.

Rufus shifted under him, fingers curling. Frustration, Luke thought: he was a highly active lover and this passive role must be maddening. He pulled out accordingly, till just the tip of his prick rested against Rufus's lips. "Was there something?"

Rufus's tongue lashed at him, futile. "I'm going to fuck you till you scream. Just a warning."

"I'll look forward to that," Luke said, and leaned in again.

He'd have liked to keep it going forever. The enforced passivity was driving Rufus wild: his hips were moving under Luke, fingers clutching, and he was making urgent noises in his throat, even as he pleasured Luke with lips and teeth and tongue, making him giddy with power and arousal and anticipation, and he didn't want to wait any longer. He leaned in once more, a little harder, meeting Rufus's straining mouth, and thrust a bit deeper, and again, and let himself be swept up in the ascent to pleasure as it built in the rhythm, the suction, the warm wet depths of ecstasy as he rubbed against the roof of Rufus's mouth and came, biting his lip against a shout, spending in near-painful spurts of relief in his lord's throat.

He made himself pull out, and sagged backwards to sit on Rufus's chest, head resting on his shoulder, their hands still tangled. Rufus coughed thickly and swallowed. They lay in silence for a moment, warm and together, perfectly close.

"It strikes me," Luke managed, when he could speak. "It strikes me I could tie you to this bed and take three times as long over things."

"You could," Rufus agreed. "The consequences might be three times as severe, though."

"Consequences? I haven't seen any—"

Rufus didn't even release his hands. He simply moved with unexpected speed and strength, heaving Luke up, over, and down, so he thumped onto his back on the bed, hands still trapped. Rufus knelt over him, smiling into his eyes. "You will, my End of Days. You will."

⚜

It was ten o'clock before they set off for Dymchurch, and Luke found the riding wasn't entirely comfortable.

Not that he intended to complain. Rufus had been as good as his word, fucking him so long and slow that he spent a second time. Flattened on the bed under his lover's weight, with Rufus's hand round his prick, his other arm round his waist, holding him up, he'd felt entirely mastered, entirely cherished. He'd also ended up begging incoherently, not for the first time.

He was definitely going to tie Rufus to the bed at some point, if only because the bloody man knew exactly what Luke liked, and you couldn't reduce someone else to a pile of jelly while they were doing it to you.

It was a two-hour ride to Dymchurch. They didn't meet anyone on the way to speak of, which was a relief; they talked a little, mostly while walking the horses. Nothing important, nothing meaningful, just casual words that the breeze whipped away as soon as spoken. Luke pointed out the very few landmarks, and explained the system of dykes that drained the Marsh; Rufus shared some memories of his time in the Low Countries. It felt like friendship, or something more than that.

"So is there much smuggling here still?" Rufus asked as they passed St. Mary's, approaching Dymchurch. "I had heard Kent was a hotbed of crime, but you said your family was mending its ways."

"There's far less than there was. The Coast Blockade put a stop to a lot of activity in the past few years, and now that the Coastguard Service is fully manned, it's making life much harder for the smugglers. And the taxes are lower than they were, too, so there's less need. A lot of people are moving away from the trade."

"Good. Damned sneaking scoundrels."

Luke bit back his immediate response. Rufus glanced round. "Offended? Don't expect sympathy. I was fighting Napoleon while these greedy bastards were making a profit from the war."

"The biggest profits were made in London, and in Parliament," Luke said. "Smuggling has been a way of life here for a long time. Not to sound like Mr. Odo, but owling—wool-smuggling—on Romney Marsh goes back to the reign of Edward the First."

"How do you know that?"

"Because that's when they first levied taxes. Impose taxes, create smugglers."

"Are you defending trading with the enemy in time of war?"

Luke sighed. "I'm not defending anything. But you're seeing it as a simple issue, black and white, and it's not. Your grandfather had all his brandy and wine and tobacco from free traders."

"How do you know that?"

"We supplied a lot of it. Sir Anthony Topgood is the same," Luke added. "He was a well-known friend to the Gentlemen, so it might be best to avoid the topic of smuggling with him—or really, with most people here."

"You mean I shouldn't mention that they're hand in glove with criminals?"

"Yes. You'll make enemies to no purpose. And don't say you don't want friends who tolerate smuggling. You're in the wrong part of England."

Rufus growled. "Not the first time I've thought as much. It's a bloody disgrace. Is there a single honest man on the Marsh? What about Sir Gareth?"

"Entirely honest, and godfather to a Doomsday. You need to understand before you make judgements."

"Ever the cry of the villain. I understand the difference between right and wrong perfectly well. *However*," he went on over Luke's objection, "I am capable of keeping my opinions to myself, believe it or not. I'll ride up for luncheon with Sir Anthony, do my best not to offend his delicate sensibilities on the subject of collusion with criminals, come back here around three o'clock, and we'll ride back together after I've done the pretty. Does that give you enough time?"

"Plenty. Thank you. This is Tench House." He indicated Gareth's red-brick home, which had seemed so magnificent in his boyhood, before he lived with viscounts and earls. "The road takes you to Dymchurch and Sir Anthony lives two miles the other side. Ride along the Wall: there's a path along the top and the tide's in, so it should be lovely today." The sun was bright; the sea would be glittering, and the Wall gave a good vantage point over the flat land. He would like Rufus to see the Marsh at its best. "You can't go wrong, except by riding into the sea. And anyone you ask will be able to tell you where Sir Anthony and Sir Gareth live. Most of them will know who you are," he added.

"Best behaviour. Right." Rufus smiled at him, warm and affectionate. It felt like a kiss. "Have fun."

Luke waited for Rufus to disappear down the lane before knocking at the door, and was greeted by Catherine, Gareth's companion and housekeeper, with a warm embrace. "Luke, my dear. How lovely to see you. Gareth!"

Gareth had already emerged from his study, hands out in welcome, and Luke grasped them with a flood of desperate relief that he hadn't expected in the slightest, and that almost brought tears to his eyes. "Gareth. I have missed you."

"You're only at Stone Manor," Gareth pointed out. "It's hardly Derbyshire, you could visit at any time. Come and sit down."

Luke had lived here for several years. Even so, walking into the drawing room after an absence always brought back the first time he'd come here as a boy: shaking, frightened, sticky with his own blood, his face aflame with pain and his heart as badly torn. Gareth had brought him home and told him he was safe. Catherine had given him tea and fruit cake, found him a clean shirt, gently dabbed the dried blood away. They had given him refuge in the worst moment of his life, and Luke would never be able to repay that but he was bloody well going to try.

Gareth was looking at him with a tiny frown, and Luke realised his hand had gone to the scar. He took it away. "How are you? How's Joss?"

"I'm very well. Joss has made himself scarce to avoid your noble employer, as per the not terribly subtle hint in your note. That was a little hurtful, Luke."

"I would like to see him," Luke said, with a stab of guilt. "I just felt—well, two worlds, Gareth. *You* know."

"And never the twain shall meet? I know what you mean but I should observe that, when I let go of that particular shibboleth, my life became infinitely better."

"You're a baronet," Luke pointed out. "You can decide for yourself whether you want to mix with smugglers. I can't decide that for Lord Oxney, and he has Preventive views. He was a soldier."

Gareth held up a hand in acknowledgement. Lord Oxney could not be asked to sit at a table with a Kentish-talking smuggler, even if that smuggler was the almost-respectable Joss: they both knew that.

"I think they'd get on like a house on fire," Luke added. "Metaphorically or possibly literally: Lord Oxney is quite explosive. But while I'm his secretary, it's all a little too awkward."

"I dare say you know best. Though if any man in England knows what it is to have awkward relatives, I should think Oxney does. I've met some of them."

"Aren't they ghastly? A set of crows cawing about their Norman blood."

"I can well imagine. Tell me about the Manor. How is your new post? What's Oxney like?"

"Good. Excellent. Perfect."

Gareth blinked. "That's very enthusiastic."

"The *position* is perfect. There's a great deal to do, which I enjoy, and it's interesting work. Did you know the old earl?"

"I paid a few calls on him over the years. Dreadful old man, astonishingly arrogant and dictatorial. As far as he was concerned, the recent creation of my baronetcy put me on a level with his groom, and didn't he let me know it. As did Conrad d'Aumesty: what a shocking fellow. Mrs. Conrad could give your Aunt Sybil a run for her money, Pagan d'Aumesty is the biggest bore unhung, and as for Lord Stone, good heavens." Gareth looked quite ruffled. "If ever there was a man not to be trapped in a small space with."

"Really?"

"Not like that. More...how can I put this...he smiled very pleasantly, and talked about his interests with great enthusiasm—it did not occur to him to ask about mine—and I had the distinct feeling that if he'd thought my head would look nice in a jar on his mantelpiece, he would have cut it off without further ado. That may sound absurd."

"No, I can well believe it," Luke said. "It's a family trait. To varying degrees, of course, but that selfishness, or self-absorption—yes. Except the Earl, my earl. He's not like that."

"It's very fortunate that he inherited. I can't imagine what havoc Lord Stone might have caused in the role. He was obsessed with turning Stone Manor into Nightmare Abbey."

"The current building is ghastly, to be fair."

"But you wouldn't put up Strawberry Hill-on-the-Marsh in its place, would you? His family were probably quite relieved he died."

"I haven't heard anyone mourning him," Luke agreed. "Do you know what happened to him? Emily had a story but it sounds implausible."

"He was found outside the Manor, the morning after that dreadful storm in the year eighteen. Apparently he went out in the night to embrace the sublime majesty of nature, and got so worked up that his heart failed. Typical," Gareth said without sympathy. "The Marsh whisper was that his family let him die like a dog in the storm, which mostly tells you what the Marsh thinks of the d'Aumestys. Lot of Gothic nonsense. I suppose that means he died as he lived."

Luke grinned at him. "You're all heart."

"Takes one to know one. So how is Lord Oxney tackling the situation? I've heard he's struggling."

"He is not. Or, not because of his own fault," Luke said. "He's doing his best to sort out an ungodly mess and get the estate in order, and the family resent him bitterly for it. At least Mr. Conrad does, and his wife. Goodness me, she wanted to be the countess. The younger ones seem to be coming to terms with things. Perhaps they've worked out that running the estate properly might be better than doing it badly, if only because there would be more money."

"Ah, families," Gareth said drily. "I rather liked Miss d'Aumesty, myself. She came to the Marsh to paint a few years ago. Lodged in Dymchurch for two weeks and did any amount of sketching people and wandering around the Marsh. She and Emily hit it off wonderfully: I believe she arranged Emily's post at the Manor. And Catherine took to her very much. She came for tea once or twice."

"She did your drawing of Joss, yes? I have no idea where she gets her talent. There's a painting she did of the Marsh which is, uh. I'd like you to see it one day." He described the rainbow painting, trying to convey the magic of it. "It doesn't make the Marsh beautiful, exactly, but it also doesn't make you think that the rainbow is beautiful and the Marsh isn't. It shows...oh, that there's glory in the world, and some of it is here too. Do you know what I mean?"

Gareth was watching his face. "I would love to see it. I don't think I've seen you moved by art before."

"I have it on good authority that I'm a philistine, but that painting...it made me see why people care about art. It made me feel like the sort of person who cares."

"Good. I would like you to feel that way more often."

Luke looked up at that, startled. "I care about lots of things. I care about—" His goal, of course, reaching it for himself and to show everyone he'd reached it. Rufus: he cared far too much about Rufus. "You, and Catherine, and Cecy."

Gareth's smile didn't look as happy as it might have. "I know you do. You seem to have studied this painting very closely."

"It's in Rufus's rooms. He hung it there because he saw I liked it."

Luke dwelled on that little piece of generosity rather too often for his own good, but it was so very Rufus and he couldn't help boasting of it, if only to Gareth. "Of course those are his private rooms, but we spend a certain amount of—what?"

Gareth was staring at him, pale brows at a very steep angle. Luke ran back over the last few seconds of conversation in his mind, and shut his eyes. Shit. He'd *told* Rufus this would happen.

And he needed to say something plausible now, but he hated lying to Gareth, and as he hesitated, his mentor's expression changed from startled to decidedly sardonic. "'Rufus' being Lord Oxney? I *see*."

"I, uh—"

"Perfect, I think you said?"

"I meant the job!"

"No you did not. And you're going red. Good God, Luke, what are you playing at?"

"I don't know! It just happened. You needn't tell me it's a bad idea."

Gareth frowned. "You are all right?"

"Of course I am. He's very—" Caring. Kind, strong, funny, bloody good in bed, and entirely, utterly, the wrong man at the worst time. "I like him a great deal. It's all well. There's no problem at all."

"Except that you're bedding your employer, the most powerful man on Romney Marsh."

"And I'm a Doomsday. I *know*."

"You aren't 'a' Doomsday. You are Luke Doomsday, with a sheaf of well-deserved references and the best brain on the Marsh. Any employer should be proud to have you, although not in that sense of the verb."

"*Gareth.*"

"Sorry. My point stands, though. There is nothing wrong with you and there is no shame in your surname, and if Oxney makes you feel there is—"

"He doesn't make me feel that at all. He's a draper's son and proud of it, and he has a very high opinion of me. Stupidly high. He thinks I'm *marvellous*." The word was choking.

There was a frown between Gareth's eyes. "Why is that bad?"

The urge to pour it all out was overwhelming. He'd always told Gareth, if not everything, more than he told anyone else: painful truths and little hurts and secret shames. He couldn't tell Gareth, of all men, this. "Because I'm not marvellous. How could I be? Look at where I come from. Look at *me*."

"Luke..."

"I don't want to talk about it."

"I know you don't: you never do. But you've come back, and you seem to be staying, and I had an idea that you might want to face the past now, not avoid it."

"I face the past every time I look in a mirror. The past defaces me."

"That's not true," Gareth said sharply. "Don't say that."

"What else would you call it?" The anger rose in him, sickening and familiar. It came so easily when he was with the people he loved most, as if he couldn't let it out anywhere else. He hated that. "Am I supposed to pretend it didn't happen, that none of it happened, that I'm not walking evidence it happened? Should I just get over it?"

"I didn't say that," Gareth pointed out, in the tone he always used in argument. It was just a little too calm and controlled, as though he was watching his words. Luke found it maddening. "Nobody's asking you to pretend it didn't happen. Everyone wishes it had not. But it did, and here we are, and the only part of all this you can control is yourself."

"Stoic philosophy?"

"Or common sense. I'm not telling you to get over it. But I wish, all these years later, with everything you've achieved and all you might do—I wish you could come to terms with it. I wish you could let go."

"How?" Luke demanded. "Forgive and forget?"

"I've never known you to do either of those things in your life," Gareth said. "I don't know, Luke. I don't know how you might come to terms with things because it seems to me that you have set yourself not to, and I cannot see that it's making you happy."

"I'm...," Luke began. "No, I *am* happy, some of the time. A lot of the time. I—" He was happy with Rufus. Happy scheming his way through the tangled mess of Stone Manor and upsetting the Conrads; happy as Rufus's invaluable, valued right hand; happy beyond words when it was nothing but the two of them. As for the rest of the time, and the things he didn't tell Rufus, or Gareth... But one couldn't expect to be happy all the time; that was absurd. "And I have not set myself against anything."

"But you don't come home," Gareth said. "The Doomsdays miss you."

"They didn't seem to when I left," Luke flashed back.

"You wanted to go. Joss said nobody was to stop you."

"Did they try?"

Gareth sighed. "Luke—"

"Anyway, you're wrong," Luke went on over whatever he might say. "There *are* things I can control, and I'm going to. I'm going to show you, show everyone. I'm not going to be the victim of this the rest of my life, Gareth, do you understand? I'm going to make it right, for myself, and when that's done, we'll see who's getting over things!"

Gareth's eyes had widened. "That sounds rather ominous."

Luke made himself breathe out the choking anger. "Don't worry about it. It's my affair."

"*Luke—*"

Catherine knocked lightly on the door. "Come, you two. Luncheon is ready."

Thirteen

RUFUS WAS NOT IN A PARTICULARLY SOCIABLE MOOD AS HE RODE back from his visit to Sir Anthony Topgood. The elderly Squire was as bluff, gouty, and tedious as before; his daughter was flirtatious in an overt, almost hungry way. It couldn't be much of a life in this isolated place for a woman who craved marriage, especially if her pool of suitors was limited by her desire to maintain her status. He wondered if he ought to offer Berengaria another chance to go to London and meet men, and decided she'd laugh in his face. Maybe she'd want to meet artists, though, people who'd understand her in a way nobody in the family did.

It was important to be understood. That wasn't something Rufus had ever considered before—he was himself, and other people were themselves, and one just got on with it. Whereas Luke thought about whys and wherefores, and what people wanted, not in the way one might find in a novel of sentiment, but like a man taking a clock apart to see how it worked.

Maybe other people would have looked at his cousins and seen people desperate to be valued. Rufus hadn't, but Luke had, and the results were magical.

Luke made things clear. That was what he did. When he'd compared Rufus's incapability to his scar, a thing that simply existed and
that everyone had to get used to, and which Rufus would happily
punch anyone for using as an insult—that had helped immeasurably.
It's not going away, so live with it. That was Rufus's natural tendency
with most problems, but the reading had stuck in his craw. Somehow
the acceptance felt easier with Luke on his side, making it work.

Although, he couldn't but notice that Luke wasn't as matter-of-
fact as all that about the scar. Hadn't said how he got it. Didn't want
it touched, or mentioned.

Well, it was his right to shy away from any subject he chose. As it
was his right sometimes to sit with his eyes on Berengaria's Marsh
picture for long stretches of the evening, sometimes to shift position
so he couldn't see it at all. Rufus had noticed that and hadn't com-
mented, and felt vaguely proud of himself for both.

One might think a man who made things so clear might be easy
to understand. Luke wasn't, quite. Or, mostly he was. Mostly he was
the cocksure, clever, outrageously competent man who was Rufus's
friend and ally and lover, and that was marvellous. There were just
those other moments, when something twitched behind his eyes,
when the confidence slipped and he looked almost furtive. Almost
afraid.

Rufus wasn't sure of any of that: he wasn't used to considering
finer feelings. He just knew that sometimes he didn't understand,
and it was those moments when he most wanted to pull Luke to him
and tell him—

Tell him what?

Rufus was thirty-three, and not prone to whims or enthusiasms.
He'd cared for previous partners, naturally, but he'd never been what
the poets called 'in love'. Not for lack of wanting to: it just hadn't
happened. Probably he wasn't that sort of man. *You'll never fall in*

love in your life, one of his partners had told him. *That or you'll do it once and once only, and God help you if it's a mistake because you'll be stuck with it.*

He was thinking about that in a rather unsettled way as he halted his horse by Tench House.

Sir Gareth greeted him at the door with friendly words, if an oddly examining look. Luke was in the drawing room, along with a Mrs. Catherine Inglis who seemed to be a relative, Sir Gareth's half-sister Mrs. Cecilia Bovey, and her extremely boisterous sons aged three, five, and seven, all of whom regarded Luke as a tree to be climbed. She was increasing again, Rufus couldn't help noticing. He admired her optimism.

After ten minutes of polite conversation repeatedly interrupted by growing volume on the part of the boys, Luke scooped two of them up and said, "I think we'll go outside."

Rufus grabbed the third boy as he sprinted past a table. "I'll bring this one."

"Lord Oxney!" Mrs. Bovey protested. "You need not."

"Please let me. I haven't played with children since I left home, and I miss them."

Which led very shortly to a riotous game of chase in Sir Gareth's garden, with Rufus being a bear, a role in which he'd excelled with his own nephews, Luke as wolf, and Sir Gareth playing a trapdoor spider, lying in wait and leaping out to attack from hiding. Mrs. Bovey and Mrs. Inglis drank tea and called unhelpful advice. There was a great deal of shrieking and laughing, not least from the adults involved.

Rufus had pictured Luke in many ways over the last month. 'Pouncing on small children for tickle attacks' hadn't been one of them, but he now realised it should have, because, laughing in the garden, Luke shone like the sun.

They stayed significantly longer than intended: Rufus was enjoying himself too much to leave. Catherine Inglis insisted on a break for a cup of tea and some excellent cake at half past four. The conversation flowed far more easily with the ice broken; then the boys wanted another game; and it was half past five when Luke reluctantly said that they had to go, given the long ride back. The seven- and five-year-olds immediately attached themselves to his legs and begged that he stay. Rufus was amused and a little moved to find the three-year-old wrapped around his own calf, incoherently but insistently repeating his brothers' demands.

"That is a delightful family," he said as they set off. "You're very close?"

"Yes. Cecy is four years older than me, and neither of us has any siblings—well, she has Sir Gareth of course, but they had only met a few months before at that point, and he's ten years older than her. She tried to mother me when I moved in, but after that, we became excellent friends. And I love her boys."

"I could tell. You make a very fine wolf."

"You're a wonderful bear. Are you missing your family?"

"Painfully," Rufus said. "I didn't appreciate it before I enlisted, you know. I was a tiresome young hothead barely interested in the younger children. Coming back to a family was everything. I can't complain about inheriting an earldom, but I miss them."

"You should visit."

"Not after a month, with such a tiresome journey. That's absurd. But I will invite them as soon as I have wrestled the family into submission—I might see if my younger brothers would make a long stay—and be damned to any d'Aumesty opinions. What on earth is a trapdoor spider?"

"Some eight-legged abomination that lurks in holes in the ground. Not here, thankfully. I believe they live in hot, dry places."

"That's one reason to love the Marsh."

"Gareth always plays trapdoor spider because he doesn't like running around. Joss is usually an eagle. He swoops down and carries the boys away."

"Joss—your cousin Joss?"

Luke looked a little startled, as if he'd been thinking of something else, or not thinking. "Oh. Yes, my cousin. Sir Gareth is godfather to his sister's daughter, who is the same age as young William Bovey, who is inseparable from my cousin Tom's boy. There's usually a horde of Boveys and Doomsdays at Tench House. Gareth loves children."

Rufus would have liked to know how a baronet came to be godfather to a smuggler's brat, but suspected the question might sound offensive, however carefully he phrased it. "But he has none of his own?"

"No." Luke glanced at him. "He's not the marrying kind, but you had guessed that."

"Mmm. He seems happy."

"He's the most contented man I know."

"And you were happy there. I haven't seen you look like that before."

Luke looked a little shocked by that. "I *am* happy," he protested. "I like to work. And I like the parts that aren't work," he added, with a waggle of a thick brow.

Rufus didn't doubt that was true, but even so, he knew he was right. Luke had forgotten something, perhaps just himself, in playing with the boys. He'd been caught up in the game, laughing, and something that Rufus was used to seeing had been missing from his face. Not calculation precisely—that had an unpleasant ring to it—but a habitual wariness or concentration or some such.

"Use your Sundays," he said firmly. "You promised to come back and play soon: I heard you. I won't be responsible for you breaking a promise to those boys."

Luke rolled his eyes. "Yes, Lord Oxney. If you insist."

"I do."

They rode back to Stone Manor at a leisurely pace. This, as Rufus had expected, meant that the family's dinner had already been served. He assured his apologetic staff that they had been quite right not to wait on his arrival, and requested a plate of something for himself and Doomsday in the Earl's Salon. That meant they sat together in the luxury of his refurbished rooms, with a bottle of good wine, a lavish spread of cold meats and cheese, a blazing fire against the chill of the ancient stone walls, and each other.

"This is the best day I've had since I came here."

Luke looked up at him with a slightly surprised smile. "Really?"

"Without doubt." A damned good fuck in the morning, idle time on horseback, the making of new friends, the uncomplicated pleasure of children, and this quiet evening together. "A day with you, and you letting me into your family. Thank you."

Luke didn't reply. He sat silently, something going on behind his eyes that Rufus couldn't read. Then he rose, putting his wine glass down. He walked over, and went to his knees in front of Rufus, hands sliding up his thighs.

Rufus put a finger to his chin, tilting it up, examining his face. Those thick brows over glorious brown eyes, the jagged scar. He wished he could talk about the scar because without it, his lover would have been a very handsome man. With it, he was Luke.

"God, you're beautiful," Rufus said, voice rough. "Come up here."

"Come down here."

They were in front of the fire. There was a thick rug between the two chairs, making the ancient floorboards both less creaky and less unforgiving to the knees. Rufus pushed himself out of the chair, slid to his knees, and Luke grabbed his shoulders and went backwards, pulling Rufus down on top of him.

They kissed, long and deep. Luke usually liked to talk, but all he was doing now was kissing, lips and tongue gentle but urgent against Rufus's mouth and skin. Rufus kissed him back. Pushing his hand through guinea-gold hair, not quite sure what had put Luke in this oddly silent mood but following his lead, lavishing love on his earlobe and neck for the pleasure of feeling him quiver. Bodies moving together in front of the flames, slow and gentle; mouths locked and hands entwined. It was slow and tender love-making, not just fucking but something far more intimate, and it made Rufus's soul sing.

He'd have liked to do this forever. Lying tangled together, clothing shoved up or down rather than removed, stands pressed together, rocking against one another. He almost regretted it when Luke finally wrapped his hand around both pricks, but he added his own hand, and they moved together with increasing urgency at last, kissing and stroking and gasping as the anticipation built. They were kissing as they spent, Luke first, Rufus after him, tipped over by his spasms. A gentler pleasure than the morning, but a closer one. Rufus didn't move his hand, but rearranged himself so he was curled around Luke, keeping him warm.

"I should go to bed," Luke said at last.

"Come with me." Rufus didn't want to lose the closeness.

"I need to sleep. I think I will tonight. And I really cannot get into the habit of sharing your bed or using your name, or any of those things. It's not a good idea. I don't want to hurt you."

"Hurt me? How the devil would you do that?"

"Easily, if I were careless." Luke sat up, disengaging himself. "And you wouldn't deserve it, because you're a good man. You wouldn't deserve it, and I don't want to do it."

"Is something wrong?"

Luke gave him a twisted smile. "The Marsh makes me melancholy.

That's why it needs rainbows." He gestured at Berengaria's painting, then brushed a swift kiss over Rufus's lips, rose, and left without a backward look.

The next morning, Luke was at his desk, heavy-eyed, as though he had not slept at all. Rufus would have liked to speak about that, and other things, but Smallbone, the steward, arrived on time and with an extensive list of places to visit. Rufus rode over the estates with him, armed with Luke's updated list of repairs requested and carried out, listened to yet another round of complaints on undone work that had caused wholly unnecessary hardship, and came back to Stone Manor in a state of profound irritation with his relatives.

He wanted to speak to Luke about it, but he was nowhere to be found. One of the footmen said he had gone for a walk. Rufus had perforce to accept that, but was undeniably in a scratchy sort of mood when he went to dinner. He wasn't sure how, but the glorious closeness of that Sunday seemed to have slipped from his grasp, and he didn't like it.

Matilda opened the evening's hostilities with, "We are honoured that you choose to join us tonight, Oxney."

Berengaria made a noise of exasperation. Matilda shot a look at her. "What a peculiar and unladylike sound."

"Pick a fight with someone else, Mother. You may be in the mood but I'm not."

Matilda looked daggers at her daughter, who merely returned to her soup. Fulk and Odo exchanged glances, then Fulk cleared his throat and asked, "What have you been doing today, Oxney?"

"Riding the lands with Smallbone. Spoke to Compton, the tenant at Summer Hill Farm. We'll be starting the repairs there next, and not before time. It's in a shameful state."

"You seem to have established very well that your grandfather was unable to supervise all his holdings from his deathbed, from the number of your remarks on the subject," Matilda said. "I hope that you will one day be as good a lord of these lands as dear Father."

"Judging by the state of things, that's not much of a challenge."

"How dare you—!"

"Mother, Oxney is doing as he should," Odo said unexpectedly. "It is quite right that he should make himself master of affairs. And things would have been in better order if Grandfather had handed over authority when he was no longer able to manage them. Father said so very often. Didn't you, Father?"

"He's right," Fulk said, agreeing with his brother for the first time in Rufus's experience. "If a man's not fit to drive he should let go the reins, and if he don't see that himself, he should be told."

Matilda looked between her sons, mouth open, apparently stunned by the double defection. Conrad said, "Fulk has, to some extent, a valid point. My father's age and infirmity undoubtedly led him to a state of harmful mistrust. If my assistance had been sought instead of spurned..."

He didn't specify what might have resulted, and nobody asked. Pagan, dining with them for once, took the opportunity to launch into a lengthy lecture on Norman-French inheritance law. Rufus ate, and waited for the meal to be over.

Everyone seemed in a temper tonight, as though Luke's odd mood from last night were contagious and the whole of Stone Manor had it. Even Berengaria, who cared for nothing but paint, seemed nervy. Rufus wondered what was wrong with everyone, and wondered it all the more when he went upstairs at around half past eight to discover that Luke had already gone to bed in his own room and wasn't responding to knocks.

He needed the sleep. There was nothing wrong. Rufus told himself that, and tried to believe it.

❧

Someone was shaking his shoulder, irritatingly insistent. Rufus became aware of that in the depths of sleep, and hung there for a bewildering, groggy moment before he snapped awake.

He expected Luke; his mouth was moving to the shape of that sound even as he realised he was wrong. The man waking him was Odo. His cousin was hanging over his bedside repeating "Oxney!" in a bleat that made sleep-dizzy Rufus want to punch him.

"What the devil?"

"You need to get up."

"What time is it?"

"Two o'clock."

"Are you out of your fucking mind?"

"I wish you wouldn't swear so," Odo said. "You're an earl, not a soldier. Get up, Oxney. You have to see this."

"See what?"

"Just come. You have to see; I doubt you'd believe me otherwise. Put some clothes on. You'll need shoes."

Rufus gave brief consideration to strangling him and leaving the body on the floor, then hauled his unwilling carcass out of bed. He had thought the end of the war might mean the end of night alarms, but apparently not.

Odo was quivering with urgency and looked very serious. Rufus followed him down through the dark house. It was unnervingly like the night he'd found Luke prowling downstairs...

He had a sudden and very bad feeling about this.

"What's going on?" he demanded.

"Just follow me, and keep quiet. Please."

Rufus would have liked to demand answers. He didn't. He followed, trying to push away the growing fear, until they reached a door. Odo opened it and blew out his candle. "Fulk?" he asked, low.

"Here." Fulk's voice was barely audible. "He's still there."

"I've got Oxney."

"Come this way. Keep quiet."

The moon was bright enough that Rufus could make his way. He followed the brothers, mind racing. *He.*

If they'd caught Luke with another man—say, whoever he'd had that assignation with—the first thing was to protect him. Rufus's feelings could wait; Fulk and Odo would have to be silenced. Fulk would doubtless take a pay-off; Odo might be less easily bribed, but could surely be bullied.

Rufus would do whatever it took, bribe or threat. Luke would not be delivered up to the law, and that was all there was to it.

He'd thought that through in the time it took the cousins to reach the Cathedral, so that he wasn't at all surprised to see, through the folly's excessive windows, a glimmer of light.

"Look," Odo breathed. "Look in."

Rufus didn't want to look. He didn't want to know who the other man was, didn't want to see Luke in someone else's arms when he already had that picture in his head. Refusing on the grounds that he could guess what was going on would be an incredible stupidity, though, so he moved silently and with bitter reluctance to the window and peered through.

Luke was there, fully clothed, crouched on the floor, alone.

The relief was such that it took Rufus several seconds to think of anything else. He simply stared at Luke...searching through a chest?

He *was*. He was searching a chest in the folly, with a lantern on the floor by him, and as Rufus watched, he tossed his head back with something that looked like irritation, stretched his neck to one side and the other in a painfully familiar way, and moved to another chest. He pulled at the lid. It didn't come up, so he picked up a hammer and chisel, and gave the padlock a sharp rap.

"What the devil," Rufus said aloud, under his breath. "What the hell?"

"He was at it last night," Fulk said. "Odo saw him. Didn't do anything about it, though."

"I was half asleep," Odo said defensively. "I just thought, *Oh, there's Doomsday*, and it didn't seem odd until the morning. But he asked me about the Cathedral on Saturday, and the key was missing when I looked for it on Sunday. I think he must have taken it on Saturday night."

"Odo told me so I got up to watch tonight and there he is," Fulk concluded. "We thought you should see for yourself. Didn't think you'd take our word for it."

He was right: Rufus would not have believed them. He felt oddly numb and he couldn't stop looking: Luke, in the dim light of a lantern, methodically working his way through... "What's in there?"

"I don't know," Odo said. "I thought it was all old clothes and broken furniture, and chests of things. I don't know if there's any valuables—"

Rufus held up his hand abruptly. He didn't want to hear any more. He couldn't bear to hear words like 'valuables' that told him Luke, his Luke, was a thief.

He made his way quietly round the building, Fulk and Odo trailing at his heels. If the door was locked, he fully intended to kick it in.

The handle turned with a creak and he threw the door open. "Don't touch that light!"

Luke at the end of the room, was spinning round, reaching for the lantern. He froze at Rufus's voice.

Rufus strode up through the long, cluttered room. He couldn't make out Luke's features in the darkness, could only just hear him breathe. He snatched the lantern off the floor and held it up.

Luke stared back at him, face expressionless, rigid with the effort of holding it so.

"Do you want to explain yourself?" Rufus heard the grit in his own voice.

Luke's eyes flickered side to side, to Fulk and Odo, then back to Rufus. He swallowed, once. "I doubt there's much to say."

No protest. No excuse, no perfectly reasonable explanation that would show it was all a misunderstanding. He wasn't even *trying*.

And he'd stolen the key on Saturday. He'd had it in his pocket all that joyous Sunday, playing with the children, riding with Rufus, talking, kissing in front of the fire. All that time, he'd been planning this?

"Jesus," Rufus said aloud, the word forced from him by that blow. "So what is it, exactly, that you're stealing from me?"

"Nothing." The raised tissue of the scar cast a fractional shadow, drawing a black line down his face, a mark of Cain. "I have stolen nothing."

"Rubbish," Fulk said. "He's had access to the books, the bank. We should search his room."

"Don't do that," Rufus said quickly. God knew what else Luke might have on his bookshelf, given *Jonathan*. "I'll—" He intended to say *I'll do it*, but his feelings revolted at the idea.

This had to be wrong. There *had* to be a reason, if he gave Luke a chance to justify himself. He'd be up to something he didn't want to reveal in front of the cousins, and there would be an explanation: Rufus had only to trust him. "Fulk, Odo, outside."

"Really, Oxney—"

"I want to talk to him. Wait for me."

"But—"

"Out!"

He used his command voice, and it got his cousins into rapid retreat. He waited for the door to be pulled almost shut, and said, "What's going on?"

Luke looked up at him, face deliberately blank, muscles twitching to keep it still. "As you see."

"I don't see. Explain this. Tell me what you're doing."

"I can't."

"God damn it, Luke! You must see what this looks like. I don't care to believe that you're a thief, and I will not assume it, but I need you to explain. Talk to me and I'll listen."

Luke's jaw was set solid, as if his back teeth were clamped together, and his voice sounded unnatural. "I told you that I could hurt you if I was careless. I have been careless. That's all."

It couldn't be all. Rufus refused to accept that. "It is not all. You owe me an answer. Whatever you're up to, for God's sake, just trust me!"

Luke's face spasmed as if he'd been struck, and Rufus saw the effort it cost him to pull back the expressionless mask. "I don't have an answer. Stop asking."

"What do you mean, stop asking? You're ransacking a locked room, of course I'm bloody asking! For Christ's sake, Luke!" His heart was pounding in an unpleasant, panicky way. "Can you not understand what you're doing? What is it you want to find that's worth everything you're throwing away?"

Luke flinched again at that, but all he said was, "It doesn't matter."

"What do you mean, it doesn't matter?" Rufus shouted. His voice rang off the walls, the rafters. "It matters to *me*!"

"I'm sorry." His voice was thin and wrong, and though his face was still, there were muscles jumping in his neck. "I made a mistake. I should go."

"You're not going anywhere until you've explained yourself. Fulk! Odo!" He grabbed Luke's arm and marched him down the dark room, heart throbbing like a boil, hot and tight and painfully swollen. "Put him somewhere safe for the night. Don't hurt him, just lock him up somewhere he can't get out of, and I'll deal with it in the morning. Thank you, both," he made himself add.

Fulk just nodded. Odo said, "You can rely on us, Oxney," with painful sincerity. Luke said nothing at all.

Fourteen

RUFUS WENT STRAIGHT TO LUKE'S ROOM, WHICH WAS TIDY AS ever, and stood in the doorway, hesitating.

He needed to search, he knew that, but it was such a vilely intrusive thing to do. This was Luke's space, and when he explained himself, Rufus would feel like a swine for invading it.

He *would* explain himself. Perhaps he'd been afraid of being overheard by Fulk and Odo, Rufus thought, knowing he was groping at straws. Perhaps he had a good reason to make them think he was a thief, whatever that could possibly be: Rufus didn't have the ingenuity to come up with it.

Or perhaps everything was exactly as it looked and he was deluding himself to think otherwise.

He made himself go in, and searched, feeling like a peeping Tom as he opened drawers and peered under the bed. He found no stolen goods, no valuables, nothing that shouldn't be there. Nothing that didn't suit a proper, respectable, trustworthy secretary. Somehow, that wasn't a reassurance.

He sat on the bed, face in hands, fighting an urge to curl up on the sheets that smelled of Luke. He wanted to understand this. He needed to believe there was something to understand beyond the obvious. It was getting harder and harder to hold to that.

He checked the bookshelf. There were a few novels, all Gothic trash. *Vathek, The Monk, The Italian, Melmoth the Wanderer.* Absurd but within the bounds of decency; *Jonathan* was the only piece of dubious literature.

Jonathan. That silly bit of filth carried such glorious memories, and Rufus's feelings rebelled at the sight. He couldn't accept Luke had thrown away everything between them so easily. There *must* be a good reason somewhere, if he could only get at it.

He picked up the book as if its existence was a reassurance. There was a paper folded into it, which proved to be a letter. It was addressed to *Dearest Luke.*

He ought not to read further, but he did. The writing was a clear, almost schoolteacher-ish hand, and uncrossed.

2nd February 1823

Dearest Luke,

It was a delight to have your visit. I hope I will see you again soon. George sends his fondest regards, as does Mary.

Since you ask for it in writing, I, Louisa Ann Meadows, born Louisa Ann Brightling of Fairfield, here state that I never went through a ceremony of marriage with Raymond d'Aumesty.

I wish you all success, my golden boy.

With love,
Your affectionate mother

She appended her signature.

Rufus sat down hard on the bed. The words swam in front of his eyes in quite a different way to the usual, and he had to read it twice more to understand as the full truth dawned like the Day of Judgement.

There had been no Brightling marriage. Luke's story, his whole reason for coming to Stone Manor, was a lie. Not a misunderstanding or an honest mistake, but a lie, and it had been a lie from the start. Luke had known all along that his claim had been false—his claim, with its story of a deathbed confession that only he had heard.

"He made the whole thing up," Rufus said aloud, the words falling flat in an empty room.

No secret marriage, no family mystery. Luke had invented it for his own purposes, given Conrad yet another stick to beat Rufus with, put his earldom, his future, at hazard, all to weasel his way into Rufus's trust—and perhaps he hadn't even meant to do that. Perhaps he'd meant to become indispensable to Conrad, and only switched sides when he saw Rufus would be more easily fooled.

Luke had run rings around him, just as Rufus had always known if he'd only let himself. Had used his position of trust to go where he had no right, had seduced Rufus to distract him, and Rufus had been so easily distracted. He'd done it all in order to get access to the house and rob it.

That was the reason his eyes were heavy-lidded and dark-ringed. That—oh Christ—that was why he'd been prowling around the Manor that fateful night when Rufus had caught him. It hadn't been an assignation, had it? He'd been *searching*. Even then, he'd been searching the house, and for all his claims of wanting and desiring, he'd offered himself to Rufus only when he'd got caught.

Everything had been a lie. Every word. Every smile. Every touch.

And Rufus had been so easily lied to. He'd wanted an ally, a friend in the house; he'd wanted Luke, with his wicked laughing eyes. He'd taken every crumb Luke threw his way, and counted himself blessed beyond all men. Glorious Luke Doomsday, changing his hand for Rufus, taking his side, sharing his bed: oh, he'd been so perfect. A wiser man might have wondered about that. Not Rufus d'Aumesty, the blundering oaf he was, led by the nose by a clever trickster.

Luke had lied, and lied, and lied, and Rufus had swallowed it all. That was his great love affair: weeks upon weeks of calculation and deception. And now there was nothing left but the humiliation of having been so publicly fooled, the inevitable rejoicing of Matilda and Conrad, his cousins' solicitude, which he didn't want any more than the rest of it, and the horrible emptiness of the room next to his, the study, his bed.

Rufus curled up in the darkness around his bleeding heart, and wished he'd never heard Luke Doomsday's name.

～⁌

Berengaria was at breakfast when he came down the next morning after far too long lying awake.

"Oxney." She examined him with an odd expression, almost like concern. "Did something happen last night?"

"Doomsday," Rufus said briefly. "We caught him robbing the Cathedral. He stole the key and broke open some chests. I think he's been searching the house since he got here."

"Good heavens."

Rufus glared at her. "Why don't you sound surprised?"

"Fulk and Odo told me about it yesterday, that Odo saw him and what they were planning," she admitted. "And you caught him in the act? He was doing something wrong?"

She sounded oddly urgent. "Yes," Rufus said. "I blasted well did, and he blasted well was. Look at this."

He handed her the letter. She read it over, brows creasing. "But this is dated February. We were told of this supposed marriage in April."

"He knew all the time it was a lot of rubbish." Rufus's throat felt tight, as though he were coming down with a cold. "For all I know he made it up out of whole cloth. The entire business was a sham all along."

"But Emily told me about it—told us—"

The cousin. Another Doomsday. Everyone had warned him that he was trusting himself to a man of criminal stock, and they'd been right. He'd never felt so stupid in his life. "She's in on it with him. I'll lay you a monkey."

Berengaria's face tightened. She got up, swept to the bell, and rang it in a forceful manner. "I want to know what's happened here."

Fulk came into the breakfast room at that point, with Odo at his heels. "Good morning, Oxney. You've told Berry?"

Berengaria held out the letter. Fulk read it and whistled. "Well, there goes Father's last hope. He won't be happy. And it was all a lie? So what the devil has that pestilent Doomsday been up to here?"

"Did you search him?" Rufus demanded.

"I did. The Cathedral key was in his pocket, but that was all. What about his room?"

"Nothing except the letter."

"And I asked Mother to check her jewellery and there's none missing, she says." Fulk scowled in thought. "I suppose you've looked at the petty cash?"

"I haven't," Rufus said. "I don't know what the devil he was playing at but it can't have been shillings and pence."

"No. What did he think he'd find in the Cathedral? It's a lot of rubbish that's been there for years."

Rufus had no answer, because it made no sense. Stone Manor was not dripping with valuables for a house so old and long inhabited. The d'Aumestys had apparently not felt a need to point up the glory of their ancient name with anything so sordid as expensive furnishings or valuable art. The butler guarded the silverware at night, and whatever jewellery the Countesses of Oxney and Baronesses Stone had accumulated was kept in the bank, as it was decades since a lady had held either of those positions. There was nothing lying around to be stolen.

Perhaps that was the answer. Perhaps Luke had spent his sleepless nights ransacking the premises for anything worth stealing, and eventually...what, decided they kept precious items stuffed in unopened trunks and chests piled haphazardly in an unused building?

Nonsense. Rufus had seen how Luke worked, and it wasn't by guessing and hoping. And he *liked* work. Rufus simply could not credit that he had thrown away a generous salary and excellent position on the off-chance of picking up some random trinket. No, the little bastard must have had an aim. Rufus was sure of it. He just couldn't guess what it had been, or how it could possibly be worth everything Luke had thrown away in its pursuit.

"He was looking for something," he said.

"Oh, he was," Odo agreed earnestly. "He asked a lot of questions about the Cathedral, you know. And he had the books out from the time it was built, the years nine and ten. I saw them on the desk more than once. He told me he was asking on your behalf."

"He asked me about Baldwin's works too. Send for Tallant at once," Berengaria added to the footman who arrived then.

"Why the devil would he want to know about the building of that ridiculous eyesore? What did he think was in there?"

All four cousins exchanged blank looks. Rufus shook his head. "It hardly matters. He's a thief, or at least a housebreaker, and I want him out."

"Will you bring a prosecution?" Odo asked.

"No." Rufus hadn't fully decided that until he spoke, but the question drew the answer from his lips without conscious thought. "I don't much want to look a fool in front of the wider world as well as my household. And damned—sorry, Berengaria—dashed if I know what I would prosecute for, if nothing's been stolen."

"He took the key!"

"And opened a door to a lumber room, and broke into some old chests full of rubbish, and stole nothing. If we find anything gone it's a different story, but if there was nothing in his room or his pockets, I don't know what a magistrate would make of it."

"But—"

"Oxney's right," Fulk said. "I wouldn't go through all the parade of a courtroom either, and tell a pack of rustics I'd been gulled. Give him a good thrashing and kick him out, that's what I'd do."

"And prosecute as well," Odo argued. "Make sure the wretch can't get another post in the area. That's only fair to others who might be fooled by him."

"God, you're a snitch."

"I'll decide what to do with him," Rufus said. He didn't shout, but apparently some of his feelings came through anyway, because the brothers stopped bickering. "I'll get rid of him now. And I'd rather not hear any more about what a terrible lapse of judgement it was to employ a secretary. From anyone."

"Yes, shut up, Odo," Fulk said.

"He meant, tell Mother and Father not to gloat," Berengaria said. Fulk glowered at her.

Tallant arrived at that point. Emily Doomsday, rather, and no wonder nobody wanted to employ her under that ill-omened name. Rufus had seen her around: a woman of no great stature, aged perhaps thirty, with brown hair and a likeable face, although right now

Rufus didn't like it at all. Her eyes widened a fraction as she took in the massed d'Aumestys. "You sent for me, miss?"

"Your cousin Doomsday," Berengaria said. "He was caught burgling the house last night."

"Yes, miss." Her face was blank. "I heard this morning."

"Do you know what he was doing?"

"I do not, miss. It was nothing to do with me. I'd like to know myself," she added, with a righteous tone Rufus didn't believe for a second.

"Especially since you introduced him to the household," he said. "Didn't you? Wasn't it you who let Conrad know of his claim to the earldom?"

Berengaria shifted slightly at his tone. Tallant didn't look afraid; she seemed, if anything, affronted. "I passed on what he asked me to about this possible marriage, your lordship. I said I didn't know anything of it myself."

"It was a lie. A damned lie."

"Language," Berengaria said. "But it was indeed a lie, a cruel and deliberate one." She sounded truly angry. "How were you involved?"

Tallant's face tightened. "I was not."

"You were. You told his story—"

"Like he asked me to! I didn't know what he was going to do!"

"He's your cousin!"

"Well, you've got cousins, and brothers too!" Tallant flashed back indignantly. "And you aren't responsible for them, so why should I be for mine? Miss."

"That is not the point!" Berengaria retorted. "You brought his story to us—"

"I never said it was true. And who's to say it's not?" she added, wounded. "Everyone calling my cousin a liar—"

"He *is* a liar. There's a letter from his mother—"

"You *what*?" Tallant shrieked, at such a pitch that Odo dropped the boiled egg he was taking and Fulk let out an oath. "*What* did you say?"

"Letter? His mother?"

"His actual—Give me that!" Tallant demanded, adding belatedly, "Miss," and then "please."

Berengaria handed it over, for all the world as if the housemaid had a right to it. Tallant scanned the paper, face reddening. "His mother. He found her and he didn't say? All along he's known? Oh, that brat, that merciful maggotty plaguesome rotten *brat*. Joss will be two men. Ooh." She handed it back, giving herself a shake, and slipped into her staff voice again. "I'd no knowing of this, Miss Berengaria. None at all. And I'm not happy to see it either, the little toad. What's he been up to?"

"How should I know?" Berengaria asked, and then straightened, adopting a more formal tone herself. "Well, anyway, good. Come and see me later and we'll discuss it. You may go."

"Yes, miss."

"Do I have a say in this?" Rufus asked, as mildly as he could.

"No," Berengaria said. "Leave her to me. You can get your secretary off the premises."

Luke had been locked into a cellar. That was only reasonable, Rufus reminded himself, because the part of him that hadn't kept up with current events was crying out with rage at the mistreatment. He had to steel himself before he opened the door and went down.

Luke was sitting on the floor, knees to chest, head bowed, looking very like a man who'd been locked in a cellar overnight. He raised his head as Rufus came in and they exchanged a long, silent look.

"Your face," Rufus said. There was a nasty red scrape on Luke's cheek. He'd told Fulk no violence.

"I fell down the stairs."

Rufus interpreted that as *I was pushed*, and reminded himself Luke deserved it. "Last chance," he said abruptly. "Tell me what the devil you were doing."

Luke made what sounded for all the world like an exasperated noise. "I stole the key. I broke open your chests. Stop *asking*."

"Tell me what you stole."

"Nothing."

"Tell me why you did it."

"No."

"Then perhaps you can tell me why you lied to do it," Rufus said. He pulled out the letter, and saw what little blood there was in Luke's cheeks drain away. "Well?" he said furiously. "Would you care to. explain? You knew it was a lie all the time. You made your claim, you pretended to be on my side—you said you had people searching for your mother, and gave me that Cheltenham tragedy of the poor lost woman, and all the time you were lying to me? Jesus Christ. What did I do to deserve this?"

Luke was shaking his head in denial. He looked distraught, as if he had any right at all to that. "Nothing. You did nothing at all. I never meant—I'm sorry."

"*Sorry?*"

"For everything. You deserved better."

"That's it? That's all you have to say?" Rufus slammed his hand against the ancient brickwork. It was rough and cold against his palm. "What are you, some sort of changeling? What's *wrong* with you?"

Luke's jaw tightened at that, but he didn't reply. Rufus wanted to haul him up, push him against the wall, demand some sort of answer.

Why he'd had to lie, to pretend, to pose as a friend and a lover and an ally. Why he couldn't have just stolen Rufus's possessions, and left his heart and soul and self-respect alone.

"You're a contemptible little shit. A thief, a traitor, a fucking liar, and a worthless bastard." He said that last deliberately, knowing it would hurt, and felt the flinch Luke couldn't hide. "Get out of my house. If I find you took anything from this house, if you involve yourself in my affairs or me in yours, I will break your neck with my bare hands. Don't ever let me see your face again."

He left on that; he didn't want to hear a reply. He told a footman to watch the man pack and escort him off the property: he could carry his own bags all the way to Dymchurch for all Rufus cared.

Fifteen

LUKE SAT ON THE DYMCHURCH WALL IN A LIGHT DRIZZLE, AND wondered if it was possible to feel worse than he did.

Of course it would be possible. After all, he'd thought he felt as bad as he could when he saw the devastation on Rufus's face, and his efforts at lying to himself had come crashing down. Then he'd made his miserable way back to Tench House, and given Gareth half an explanation, which was still quite enough to put a dreadful disappointment in his eyes. He'd done so much for Luke, and here he was, throwing people's trust away, again.

And *then* Joss had got Emily's note, in which she'd informed him that not only had Luke lied about the whole possible marriage business, put her position at risk by dragging her into it, and set the Doomsdays against the earl of Oxney, he'd also found his long-lost mother and not told anyone.

Joss was normally a measured, even-tempered sort of man. But he loved Gareth deeply, he protected his family, and he always knew what was going on. Those were the three pillars of his life and Luke had struck at all of them at once.

Joss had been furious beyond reasoning. Gareth had ended up dragging him out of the room, though he almost never intervened in Doomsday arguments, and they'd had a blazing row in the corridor while Luke lay curled on his bed, unable to make himself move. Joss had demanded if there was anything Gareth wouldn't defend Luke for, and Gareth had shouted back, "I'm not defending him!"

Even Gareth, who'd always stood for him. Even he thought Luke had done as badly as he possibly could; even he was giving up, and why would you not, over someone so irredeemably, perversely stupid.

He'd hurt Rufus so much, and the dreadful thing was, he'd known he would, and lied to himself more than anyone to pretend otherwise. *It won't do him any harm,* he'd thought, and *I'm working for him too, doing a good job,* as if that changed or justified anything.

So stupid, and not even the first time. He'd betrayed someone he loved before, and been punished for it hard enough that you might think he'd have learned his lesson. Yet here he was again, and for exactly the same reason. He'd had a vision of what he wanted, and pursued it, and not let himself see what the cost would be.

He hadn't slept in three nights because every time he shut his eyes, he saw Rufus's hurt, bewildered face. Rufus had cared so much for him. Done so much. And Luke had thrown it away—for nothing, he supposed, but he had a dreadful feeling that if he had achieved his goal, it would have been no better. He'd have been a man in a fairy tale, finding the enchanted gold only to see it crumble to dust in his hands.

He stared out at the sea, watching the high tide nuzzle close to the top of the Wall, dry-eyed but for the rain on his face. He didn't trouble to turn around at the crunch of footsteps; he didn't care.

"A'right, Luke." Joss sat by him with easy grace. "Thinking of jumping?"

"No, but you're welcome to push me."

"Tempted."

They sat in silence for a while, the drizzle prickling Luke's skin. You couldn't be precious about rain on the Marsh: as he had told Em, if people died of rain, there'd be nobody left alive.

Joss broke the silence eventually. "Know what I wish?"

Probably to have better cousins. That Luke had never been left on the Doomsdays' doorstep. "No."

"I wish Granda was here now. He was the man to talk to when you got something wrong."

Luke wished the same, suddenly and agonisingly. His great-uncle, Joss's Granda, had been a place of safety in his turbulent childhood. He didn't want to talk about how much he missed him. "When did *you* ever get anything wrong?"

"You're joking. I threatened Gareth in court, remember, made him call himself a liar. I'm lucky he ever spoke to me again."

Luke had accepted those events as he had a lot of things in his boyhood. Now he thought that probably had been a challenge to get over. "What did Great-Uncle say about that?"

"Not much. He never did. He'd just ask you questions till you reached an answer yourself."

"The Socratic method," Luke said. "A dialectical style of enquiry named after a Greek philosopher."

He was being a bettermy prick, and he knew it. Joss didn't rise to the bait. "I dare say. Granda was good at it. Not sure I knew how good till now, because I'm sitting here, and the only question I can think of is, what the blazes were you playing at?"

Luke stared at the grey waves. "I don't know."

"Gareth's fraped about this, Luke. I'm not pleased myself. You've done Emily an ill turn, and lied to all of us, and I doubt me the new earl's a happy man either. You want to tell me why?"

"No."

Joss breathed out. "Wasn't a question."

"It's my business."

"It's Doomsday business when you involve Doomsdays."

"Then don't be involved," Luke said. "I didn't want you involved. It's not up to you."

He thought, if he pushed hard enough, Joss would shout at him and walk away. He didn't. Instead, there was a long silence, and when Joss broke it, it wasn't with anything Luke had expected him to say. "Ah, Luke. You ever going to forgive us?"

Luke would have got up and walked away himself if he'd had the strength, and if Joss wasn't entirely likely to come after him. "We're not talking about that."

"What else is it about? You found your ma and you didn't tell us. You know how my ma feels about her going, and us not helping her. She's been guilty about that for years."

"Good," Luke said through his teeth. "Maybe she should be. Maybe everyone who let my father do as he pleased should be guilty about it."

"Luke—"

"No." This, at least, was something he could be angry about that wasn't his own wretched failure. "Yes, I found her, and one of the first things she said was that she doesn't want anything to do with the Doomsdays. Not your apologies, not your bribes, not your gifts to 'make it better'. She does not forgive you and she does not want anyone's conscience to be salved. She told me to say that."

He knew that would hurt, and it wasn't even fair. Joss had been twelve years old when Elijah Doomsday had raped Louisa Brightling, and he had, eventually, been the one to take a stand against the man at some cost to himself. But right now he was the Doomsdays' representative, and they had done his mother and Luke too a deep and unmendable wrong.

Joss took that in. "Well, it's her right. As long as she doesn't blame you?"

"That's between her and me."

Joss rubbed his face, wiping off the damp. "Fine. But you could have told Gareth. He'd have been glad for you."

"Told him, and asked him to keep it secret from you?" Luke said swiftly. "Please."

"He would have."

"No, he'd have *talked* to me about it and explained why it wasn't your fault and made me be *reasonable*—" He broke off because he was starting to feel thirteen again.

"I hear you," Joss said. "That's the thing about Gareth. I do the wrong thing now and again, don't we all. I think, well, this is what I want to do, and I go about my way. And then he'll say what I did was wrong and I'll think, *I don't know how I didn't see that.* I look back and it's clear as day I was wrong, but I don't see it proper-like till he talks to me. Like, when you were a nipper, I saw some of it but not enough, nowhere near enough. If it hadn't been for Gareth—"

"I know."

"I'm sorry we didn't do better. Me, Ma, all the Doomsdays. I'm sorry I didn't see more, and I'm sorry your father hurt you and we let him. I don't know what I can do about that now, but Gareth called me over for it last night, again. He says we've never mended what Elijah broke, in you or between us, and I've no doubt he's right. So...I love you, Luke. You're my cousin, and a Doomsday, and a sneaking bettermy wretch with twice the brains of the rest of us together, and you saved Gareth's life, and I love you. It queers me what you've been up to at Stone Manor, and I can't say I'm happy about it, but whatever trouble you're in, whatever you need to get out of it, all the Doomsdays are standing ready to help. Because I don't care what you did: nobody touches you on the Marsh while I've got my strength. Hear me?"

Luke felt a sob rise in his throat, and forced it back by sheer will. "I bet Gareth didn't tell you to say *that*," he managed.

"Lord, no. He'd want you to make amends and put things right. Granda would say that too. And if that's what you want, I'll help however I can, but if what you need is to get out of trouble or off the Marsh, or have me shut the Earl's mouth for him—"

"You can't do that!"

"Watch me."

"No, you *can't*," Luke said urgently. "You mustn't. It's not his fault. He's got every right to be angry, he should be, I was awful. Oh God, Joss. I let him down so badly and it's all my fault. It's exactly what you said—I didn't see it was wrong. Or, I did but I persuaded myself it didn't matter. I don't know. I'm so stupid."

"No, you're blinkered," Joss said. "Always have been. Once you set yourself to something, you don't think about the consequences, you don't see anything but your goal. You chased a couple of murderers over the Marsh on your own at thirteen years old because you were determined to find Gareth. Chuckle-headed thing to do, and you saved his life with it."

"And before that, I betrayed you and him to my father because I was determined to curry favour with a brute," Luke said savagely. "Have you forgotten that?"

"Haven't forgotten why you were driven to it, either."

Luke put his face in his hands. Joss dropped an arm over his shoulder, and after a moment Luke leaned against him, ignoring the wet of his coat.

"It's not Lord Oxney's fault," he said, muffled. "He didn't drive me to anything. He was nothing but wonderful, and I ruined everything and I don't know what to do."

"You tried apologising? Sometimes works, if you mean it."

"How? 'I'm sorry I lied to you from the start and threatened to make you illegitimate and burgled your house and let you trust me and even shared your bloody *bed* while I was doing all that to you'?"

"That…might take a while to get over," Joss allowed.

"He won't get over it. He's the most honest man I've ever met. He'd never take anything that wasn't his, and I— Anyway, he said never to let him see my face again or he'd break my neck."

"Can't blame him." Joss's arm tightened. "Won't let him, but can't blame him. You've dug yourself a pit here. All right, I'll tell you what I reckon Granda would say."

"What?"

"He'd say, do you need to apologise?"

"Of course I do. I told you, I *can't*."

"You can't apologise? Or you don't think he'll forgive you if you do?"

"He won't."

"Maybe not," Joss said. "But the question wasn't, can you get away with this? It was, do you need to apologise?"

Luke stared out at the sea. Joss clapped him on the shoulder, and then used it to lever himself upright. "Think about it. Come on, let's go back. Catherine's baking. You eat something, stretch your legs instead of hiding in your room, and we'll work out what to do when you can think a bit clearer. But for now, you're home and you're safe. Hear me?"

Luke hauled himself to his feet, and wiped a hand over his wet face. "Yes, Joss."

He took Joss's advice-cum-order and went for a walk, grateful that the persistent rain and the Marsh's emptiness kept him from being stared at. Probably word was spreading of his disgrace even now.

Equally probably, nobody would dare taunt him about it, as not only a Doomsday but the son of the most notorious of them. Elijah had been a brutal, heavy-handed, much-disliked man. Doubtless a lot of people would feel satisfied, or justified, by the news his bettermy son was a liar and thief.

He'd have to leave. Go offmarsh again, find another post. Hope Rufus wouldn't spread the word about him as the Graysons had done. Christ, he'd be lucky to get another job in his life. That was a miserable line of thought, but at least better than dwelling on how much he'd hurt Rufus.

He spent a silent evening, because Joss or Gareth or both had decided to give him space and time to think, and slept like the dead, worn out by physical exhaustion, too many late nights, and the sheer weight of misery.

It was still raining the next morning, in dark grey drifts that billowed over the flat land. He felt as though it might rain forever, and went for a walk anyway, letting his legs do the thinking because his mind didn't seem to be much good at it.

You can't apologise? Or you don't think he'll forgive you if you do?

He wanted to be forgiven, desperately. He wouldn't be. To go and grovel would only expose himself to Rufus's justified anger, only make him look worse in Rufus's eyes.

It would do Luke no good at all, and it wouldn't make things better for Rufus; if he knew more, he'd feel more betrayed. And he'd told Luke to stay away from him, so that was what Luke should do. He wasn't being a coward, and he wasn't shirking what he owed because it wouldn't serve his ends. He told himself that as he trudged through the long, rank grass of an ungrazed field, down past the Warren, towards Little Stone, with the question throbbing in his head, in Joss's voice and Great-Uncle's, and even Rufus's, because Rufus didn't shy away from unwelcome truths. *Do you need to apologise?*

"It's more complicated than that," he said aloud, to all of them and himself. A startled jay flurried up in a streak of blue and pink, and gave him a resentful caw.

He didn't want to go into New Romney: he might see people. He took the path to the right instead, trudging through the rain to the ruined chapel.

The chapel was Norman, or possibly Angevin, and he wished he wasn't aware of the difference. It was barely worthy of the name anyway, just a few pieces of masonry wall jutting around a mound in a field, like the stumps of teeth in an old man's mouth.

He knew it well; Gareth had taken him here a few times to look for beetles. It was called Hope All Saints. He was standing in the broken ruins of Hope in the rain, like the stupidest Gothic hero in the stupidest book.

"Jesus *Christ*, Doomsday," he said aloud, and wished he hadn't because it was exactly what Rufus would have said.

At least the chapel walls offered some slight protection from the slanting rain. Not that rain killed you, he thought again. It just hid the tears.

He'd done too much crying, too much thinking, too much arguing. He'd hurt people he loved in far too many ways, and the sorry truth was, he'd done it deliberately. Not that his aim had been to hurt Rufus, but he'd behaved in a way that could only ever have had that result, so the distinction was academic.

Elijah Doomsday had hurt a lot of people, sometimes because he wanted to, but more often because he hadn't troubled not to. He'd gone about his life without thought or care for the damage his acts would cause, and Luke did not like that reflection at all.

There were too many thoughts crowding his head. He sat on his heels, back to the wall, next to a stand of cow parsley, and just... breathed.

He wasn't sure how long he sat thinking of nothing, but eventually the rain ceased and when he looked up the sky was already streaking clear blue, in the way of Marsh weather. A couple of birds embarked on cautious song. He stood, stretched, and walked up onto the little mound in the centre of the ruins. It was perhaps two feet above ground level, but one advantage of the Marsh was that you didn't need to climb far to improve the view.

The grass was wet and fresh around his feet. The air was clean, full of the indefinable smell of rain. The Marsh stretched around him, its green-grey flatness cut with dykes, studded with thorn trees.

And over it all, a double rainbow. One crisp, bright, perfect bow that looked like it arched from Millbank to the Isle of Oxney, and above it a second, fainter streak of colours against the scudding grey.

Rainbows over the Marsh. Just as in the picture that Rufus had hung in his own rooms for no other reason than that Luke liked it.

He stood and watched the rainbows till the brightening sun faded them to nothing. He walked the hour or so back to Dymchurch with his wet coat gently steaming in what was now unseasonable heat. He went into Tench House, found Gareth, and said, "Can I borrow a horse?"

≈

It was fourteen miles, a good part of two hours, and Luke did not enjoy walking the horse up the slope to the top of the Isle. He was having very serious second thoughts about this.

He would apologise because he had to. He just hoped Rufus would listen, and couldn't shake the fear he would not. Rufus had put so much faith in Luke: there was absolutely no reason he should listen to a man who'd never put the slightest faith in him.

And that would be his choice. Luke would apologise because he owed it. If he didn't do this, he'd never have rainbows again.

Luke stared at Stone Manor's imposing door, took a moment to wish he was dead, and knocked.

The footman who answered stared at him with open astonishment. Luke said, "I need to see Lord Oxney. Could someone take my horse?"

"I... Mr. Pauncefoot!"

"Let's not trouble him," Luke said, and slithered by into the hall.

Fulk d'Aumesty was there, arguing with his brother. It felt like Luke had never left.

"Mr. Fulk," the footman faltered.

Both d'Aumestys turned and stared. "What the devil are you doing here?" Fulk demanded. "Insolent little—Throw him out!"

"Really, Doomsday." Odo looked outraged. "One might think—"

"I need to see his lordship, Mr. Odo," Luke said. "It's important."

"Who the devil do you think you are?" Fulk said furiously. "Come on, Odo, let's kick the little wretch down the hill."

"Oxney said, no violence—"

"God, don't be such a prig. I'm throwing him out."

"Mr. Odo, I need to see Lord Oxney," Luke said, louder, ducking sideways as Fulk approached.

Odo looked uncertain. "Maybe we should ask him?"

"Don't be ridiculous. Help me get this scoundrel out. You! Come here!"

Fulk lunged. Luke dodged. A very loud voice cut through the hall. "What the bloody hell is going on?"

Rufus was there, and his expression was very far from welcoming as he took Luke in. "What the—"

"He just turned up," Fulk said. "We were throwing him out."

"I need to speak to you, my lord," Luke said over Odo's stammer. "Please."

Rufus's jaw set. "Is there any reason I should listen?"

I'm sorry, Luke wanted to say. I care, so much more than you could believe. "Ten minutes of your time, my lord. You need to know."

"Know what?" Rufus barked.

"In private."

Rufus's eyes met his, hard and menacing, and it struck Luke for the first time: he'd been a soldier for most of a decade; he'd definitely killed people, with a gun or a sword. Somehow, that hadn't occurred to him before. He put his hands up in an automatic gesture, showing himself not to be a threat. "That is, it's a personal matter. I would be grateful for your indulgence."

"You won't get it," Rufus said. "You can have five minutes. In—" He stopped abruptly. He'd been going to say the study, Luke would bet, and neither of them would want to go there, where they'd laughed and learned each other, where Luke had worked out the readable hand, and Rufus had made him gasp his name against the wall.

His throat was full of thorns, and he needed his face not to show it.

Rufus's expression was stony, remorseless. "Follow me. The rest of you, be about your business," he added, in a half-shout that had everyone scattering.

Sixteen

LUKE FOLLOWED AS RUFUS STALKED THROUGH THE MANORIAL Hall, into the North Wing and the Countess's Drawing-Room. He'd only ever stuck his nose in here; it hadn't been used in four decades, and was only unlocked for the daily dusting as far as he could tell. He'd meant to suggest putting it under holland covers.

Rufus shut the door. "Well?"

He didn't sound receptive. He wouldn't *be* receptive, and Luke's courage, or his principles, abruptly deserted him. He couldn't make himself speak.

"What the hell is it?" Rufus demanded. "I told you not to show your face, and you forced your way in anyway. You're here: what do you want?"

He looked dreadful. His eyes were tired; his mouth was hard; he wasn't humming with that vibrant energy Luke was used to. He looked like a man who'd suffered a blow, or a series of them, and it was all Luke's damned stupid fault.

He needed to say something and he couldn't think what. It felt, had felt for days, as though something vital inside him had broken, and he tried to shape an answer, but his mouth wasn't working.

"Christ's sake," Rufus said. "You don't get to play speechless now. What do you— Actually, no. I don't give a damn what you want. You need to talk to me?"

"I do," Luke managed. "I need—I have to apologise. I'm sorry. I'm so—"

"I don't give a shit!"

The words bounced off the walls. Rufus had a powerful voice when he really shouted, and he'd never really shouted at Luke before. Luke hoped he'd repressed his instinctive flinch, but a flicker of something—contempt, anger—in Rufus's eyes told him he'd failed.

"Don't play the fool, or the victim, with me," Rufus snarled. "And don't come here with puling apologies. What use is an apology? What good does that do?"

"None. I know that. But I owe you it anyway."

"Don't waste my time with puffery. If you have to say something, I want answers. Give me those or get out."

"Answers," Luke managed.

"Of course answers! I want to know why you treated me like that. A few days ago I was *happy*. What the hell happened?"

So much hurt in his voice. All Luke's fault.

He did not want to tell the truth, such a petty story for such miserable consequences. And he didn't have to. He could refuse, walk out. Leave Rufus bewildered and hurt, keep his secrets for the sake of, what, his self-esteem? He didn't have enough of that left to be worth protecting.

He took a deep breath. "I'll tell you if you want. But it's not good, and you won't like it."

"Do you think I expect to?"

"No. Just—please, if I tell you, will you let me say I'm sorry?"

"You are pushing your luck to the breaking point. Tell me exactly what you came here to do, and why you lied to me for weeks on end to do it, and I'll decide for myself if I want to hear another word out of your mouth. Now, get on."

Luke set his shoulders. "Gold. That's the long and short of it. I was looking for gold."

"You came here to rob me," Rufus said flatly. "I worked that out myself."

"No. It's not your gold; it's not anyone's. It just happens to be at Stone Manor, and I came looking for it."

"What? What do you mean, it's here and not mine? Is this some damned smuggling thing?"

"In a way," Luke said. "It's complicated."

"Then explain it in simple words," Rufus said sardonically. "What, and where, and what entitles you to take it, and why you had to gull me to do it. Take your time. I've nothing better to do." He folded his arms and leaned against the mantelpiece, demonstratively waiting.

Luke walked to the dusty window, wondering where to start. The whole story was long and involved, but without it, all he could say was *smuggler's gold*, and that was humiliatingly inadequate. "It began before Gareth came to the Marsh, when Sir Hugo, his father, was alive."

"Oh, for Christ's sake. I don't want a saga. Get to the point."

"This *is* the point. Do you know about the guinea boats?"

"Smugglers, transporting gold over the Channel to Napoleon. Scum."

"Sir Hugo Inglis and his brother were guinea-runners."

Rufus's jaw dropped. "You cannot be serious. Even on your bloody Marsh, a baronet running guineas?"

"As investors. The brother, Henry, sent chests of guineas down to Sir Hugo, who passed them on to a smuggling gang—the Sweetwaters, in Camber. One day Henry sent a shipment of guineas, and Sir Hugo told Sweetwater it had never arrived, while he told Henry it had been put on a boat and lost at sea. He lied to both sides and kept the money for himself."

"Honour among thieves," Rufus muttered.

"Sir Hugo died unexpectedly, and Gareth became the baronet. Sweetwater and Henry Inglis realised that Sir Hugo had fooled them and stolen the money. And that's where it all started. Inglis and Sweetwater thought Gareth had the guineas, in the bank or hidden at Tench House. He didn't know anything about it, but they didn't believe that, and thought they could force it out of him. So they kidnapped him, and tied him up to drown."

"You cannot be serious. What the devil sort of place is this Marsh of yours?"

Luke had grown up amid running battles between gangs of smugglers, or smugglers and Preventives, and that was a generation after the really dangerous times. He didn't care to explain that now. "I found out where they had Gareth. I fetched Joss, who got him safe." That night still played out in his dreams now and then: the endless run across the Marsh, lungs burning, face throbbing, searching desperately for Joss to come and save them. "He lived. Two men died."

"And this was during the war? How old were you?"

"Thirteen."

Rufus shook his head. "Go on."

"That's the money: stolen gold. As to where it is... Gareth's father hid it with the help of a labourer named Adam Drake, who vanished shortly before Sir Hugo died. Joss thinks Sir Hugo killed him. He's afraid if anyone finds the guineas, they'll find Drake's body, and he doesn't want people to know that Gareth's father was a murderer. That's why he didn't look for the money."

"Would that stop other people?"

"Well, hardly anyone knew the full story," Luke said. "Henry Inglis was tried for embezzlement, not guinea running, and he died in gaol. The Sweetwaters fell foul of the Preventives not long after, and most of them were transported. It's been thirteen years. It's forgotten."

"But you're looking for it. You don't care about Sir Gareth's family name?"

"Sir Hugo didn't kill Drake."

Rufus rubbed his temples. "And how would you know that?"

"I tracked down his widow and asked her about Drake, what he'd been doing before the murders, where he'd worked. I've thought about this a lot, you see. Sir Hugo needed to hide it somewhere accessible to him, an old man, but not to a casual passer-by. And Mrs. Drake told me Drake had been an allworks, a casual labourer, at Stone Manor." He could feel the echo of the thrill as the dying woman had whispered her words, the realisation that he could solve this years-old mystery. "Nobody would have looked twice at a familiar man on the site carrying a few boxes. Anything he stashed on Stone Manor's grounds would be safe. And Sir Hugo and Mr. Pagan were friends, fellow scholars. Sir Hugo used to stay here when he was bug-hunting on Walland Marsh or the Isle. It was a perfect hiding place."

"From smugglers or passers-by, maybe. What about the family, or the staff?"

"Your family never throws anything away," Luke pointed out. "The place is full of ignored chests and boxes. And he didn't mean to leave the gold here for thirteen years. It was a temporary hiding place, except he died."

"But what about this Drake fellow? What was to stop him walking off with it at his convenience?"

"He was dead."

"You just said—"

"Sir Hugo didn't kill him," Luke said. "Mrs. Drake did. She confessed to me: she was badly consumptive and I think she wanted to get it off her chest before she died. She said he used to hit her and one day she hit back with a poker. She dragged his body to a dyke in the night and threw it in, then she raised the alarm as if he'd vanished. That's where he went. He died, Sir Hugo died, and nobody else knew where the money was. It's been missing ever since. I think it's here."

Rufus's lips moved slightly as he took all that in. "And you didn't think to tell Sir Gareth about his father's innocence?"

"I wanted to find it first. I wanted—"

"Yes," Rufus said. "Tell me what you wanted."

"I thought—" He couldn't begin to explain this part. He didn't know what he'd been thinking any more. "You see, it isn't anybody's money now, really. Henry Inglis embezzled it, and had to pay back what he'd stolen. So maybe it was his, but he died, and his next of kin was Gareth, who wouldn't take a penny from him. It's just sitting there. Just money."

"So you thought it should be yours."

Luke stared out of the window. "Yes. Yes, I did."

"That's a damned sordid story."

"I told you. There's nothing worth—" Worth what he'd lost. "Nothing that changes anything."

"And you had to gull me because—?"

"I had to get in here somehow," Luke said bleakly. "I'm too short for a footman, and people don't want staff who look like this." He indicated the scar. Rufus began to say something, but stopped himself. "I needed time to search."

"So you made up this fantasy about your mother marrying my father? Have you any idea what it was like proving my right, with Conrad attacking my mother's character, my legitimacy, my very right to exist, still less inherit? I spent seven bloody months of my life tied up in law and nonsense while a pack of bewigged old men deliberated over my future, and then you started it all over again!"

"I'm sorry," Luke said, throat dry. "I didn't know you then, and once I'd started I couldn't just—and you needed help, and I suppose I thought I could do some good while I was here. Earn my place. I thought I'd get things running smoothly, so when I left, you'd be in a better position. I thought that would make up in some way for, uh—"

"For lying relentlessly and shamelessly from the moment we met," Rufus said. "You do have a high opinion of your skills. And I walked into it, didn't I? I thought you were heaven-sent, and all the time you were about your own business. Thirteen years ago—that's what you wanted with the books from the years nine and ten?"

"That's when it happened, at the end of Lord Stone's works. I was trying to work out where Adam Drake put the gold."

Rufus scrubbed at his cropped hair with the heels of both hands. Luke knew exactly how that felt, could feel the phantom scratch on his palms. "And you had written confirmation that there was no marriage from the mother you claimed so movingly not to know. What was that about?"

"The truth. I picked up the letter when we visited Gareth. I was going to give it to you to silence Mr. Conrad, but I'd forgotten what she wrote, and it would show I knew her, and I couldn't think how to tell you about it. I thought maybe later—"

"When you'd found the gold?"

"Yes," Luke said hopelessly. "When I'd found the gold."

"You put my position, my legitimacy, at hazard. You lied to me, you let me—all we did—"

"Yes."

"And you also changed your bloody hand for me. Jesus Christ, Luke." His voice was ragged. "That's what I can't grasp. I understand greed, and trickery, and lies. I don't understand how you combined them with everything else."

"I won't say I didn't know it was wrong. I did. Only, I wanted the money, and I thought it wasn't doing you any harm."

"You were lying to me in my *bed*."

"I wasn't," Luke said. "That wasn't lies. None of that was ever lies."

They stared at one another for a long, painful moment, then Rufus shook his head. "You're making it seem reasonable."

"I'm not trying to. I know it was wretched and stupid. It's just that it mattered so much to find it, or I thought it did. I've been thinking about it for thirteen years. I had to look, and I couldn't find another way in, and I got caught up. It seemed reasonable when I did it. That's all."

"It's not all. Why?" Rufus demanded. "Why do you care about whatever damn fool stolen money this was? Do I not pay you enough? I'd have doubled your salary for the asking, you must know that. You're worth it." He swallowed. "I thought you were."

Luke bit the inside of his lip, hard. "It's not about the money."

"Jesus *Christ*," Rufus said explosively. "You literally just told me—"

"I meant, it's not—I don't need money in general. It's *this* money. It's what it stands for."

"I don't understand."

Luke had no idea at all how to explain. He wasn't sure he understood himself. "The thing is, this money—my father died for it."

"What? Where the devil did your father come into it?"

"He told Henry Inglis and Bill Sweetwater he knew where the guineas were. Probably he thought he could string them along and get a bit of drinking money that way. Only it didn't go well, because he was found dead in the Royal Military Canal. Just at the foot of the Isle, actually, where the Canal meets High Knock Channel, so maybe he did have some idea? But not enough of one, because he didn't come up with the goods and Bill Sweetwater broke his neck."

"Christ. Luke—"

"That's why I thought the money was mine to take. That's why I lied to you and cheated you and ransacked your house. My father was killed for it, and I wanted it."

Rufus was watching his face and the sympathy in his eyes was a torture. "I'm sorry to hear it. And I understand, I suppose—compensation, a blood price. I don't need to tell you that money won't bring him back."

"Why would I want him back? If I thought he'd come back, I'd never set foot on the Marsh again. He was a shit. He was a horrible, vicious man and I hated him, I *wanted* him dead—"

Rufus moved. Luke thought for a single overwhelming moment that he was going to be struck, but instead Rufus's hand closed round his wrist. The grip was warm, and firm rather than hard, and it was right up by his face. Because his own hand was on his cheek, he realised, fingers digging in, over the scar. He hadn't been aware of doing that.

"Luke," Rufus said, voice deep. "You asked me not to talk about it. But I asked you to be my trusted confidential secretary and you played hob with that, so: how did you get the scar?"

Luke stared up at him. His pulse was thudding against the encircling fingers. Rufus stared down. "I want to know," he said softly.

Luke lowered his hand. Rufus didn't let go for a few seconds, his hand warm and firm, then released him.

"It was," Luke began. "I..."

"Was it your father?"

Luke felt the nausea rise, a nasty dizzy sensation, smelling of blood and salt. He didn't want to talk about it: he never did. Every instinct told him to push Rufus away, with words or force, and make it stop.

He owed him this.

"I told you about me," he managed. "Ill-begot. My mother left me on the Doomsdays' doorstep as the consequence of my father's actions, and he never liked to be faced with those."

"Christ."

"By the time I was thirteen, he hated me. Really hated. Because I looked like my mother, perhaps, or because I was young and clever and he wasn't, or just because I was me."

"Luke—"

"Joss was running the Doomsdays by then, so my father had come to hate him as well. You know that line from Othello: 'He hath a daily beauty in his life that makes me ugly'? My father in a nutshell. And then—"

He particularly didn't want to tell this part. He wasn't afraid of trusting Rufus with a secret, and he wished he'd realised that earlier; simply, he didn't want to admit what he'd done.

He took a deep breath. "It was my fault. I was sneaking around one day—I was a sneaking sort of boy—and I saw Joss with Gareth."

"With— Ah."

"I don't know really what happened then." The whole period was confused in his mind, with shame and fear and blood, and the memory of feelings he hadn't understood. "No, I do: I went and told my father, a vicious, violent brute, that Joss was tupping the new baronet. I just don't know what I thought would happen. Maybe that Pa would clasp me to his bosom and tell me he loved me after all. He never used my name, you know. The others called me Goldie, but he called me 'bastard' if he spoke to me at all, and I *still* went running to him with that to use against Joss, who never did me wrong in his life."

"If you kick a dog hard enough and often enough, it will stick to your heels and bite your enemies," Rufus said. "So I'm told. Go on."

"I told Pa, and he was pleased with me. I don't think I'd ever pleased him before. He said that we'd destroy Joss, see him hounded

from the Marsh, maybe worse. He was delighted, and I saw—it was—
I'd had an idea and I followed it as though I was in a tunnel and
couldn't see anything else, and suddenly the walls fell away and I
understood what I'd done. I begged him not to go through with it, and
he lost his temper. He dragged me out to the strand where Joss and
Gareth were walking." Sand under his feet, sea salt on his lips. "He
told them he'd make me say what I saw in front of all the Doomsdays,
and if Joss didn't admit it was true, he, my father, would beat me half
to death for lying. I don't know if he'd have stopped at half."

Rufus swore, impressively even for him.

"I don't mind that so much because—because that was when
Gareth stepped in. He must have been terrified, but he said that this
wasn't a fit scene for a child and told me to come home with him.
He promised he'd keep me safe." He could feel his throat tightening
at the memory. "He didn't even know me, I'd done him the worst
possible turn, and he still protected me. Joss was going to take on my
father to stop him, but Gareth was thinking of *me*."

Rufus breathed out hard. "Good. Good."

"Only Joss couldn't stop him, and Gareth couldn't protect me.
Because I told Pa I wouldn't say it, and he pulled a knife." Luke ran
his fingers along the scar, remembering that split second when he'd
realised what was going to happen, too late. "And he—my face—and
that was that. Joss beat seven bells out of him, and Gareth took me
home. The Doomsdays threw my father out of the family, so he went
running to Sweetwater out of spite and got himself killed. I told him
about Joss and Gareth and it started everything, like a landslide,
and at the end of it he was dead. And it was my fault, but it was about
the money too, and—" He gestured, for lack of useful words. "Well.
There it is."

"You cannot believe that was your fault. Any of it. What the devil
could you have done?"

"Kept my mouth shut?"

"You might as well say you should have stood a foot to the left. It doesn't work that way."

"But it does," Luke said. "I do stupid things and I hurt people. I don't mean to, not you or Gareth or Joss, but I did it then and I've done it now. All I could see was what I wanted, and I didn't let myself think about the damage I'd do. Because I liked working for you, and we were…friends, and being with you was marvellous, every minute of it."

"Was it?" Rufus said. "That first night—you were searching. Weren't you?"

"The ice house. And yes, I wanted to stop you asking questions, but I could have done that a dozen ways. To be honest, I used it as an excuse—not to you, to myself. I knew it wasn't fair. But I couldn't bear not touching you any longer."

"Thank you," Rufus said, slightly ragged. "I was wondering."

Luke grabbed his hand, willing him to believe. "I swear it. I never lied about us. That was wonderful, you were wonderful, and I spoiled it all because of money, and a worthless man who's been dead for thirteen years." He let go Rufus's hand; he shouldn't have touched. "I'm sorry."

"Mmm. Have you considered not letting this ruin your life?"

"It's memorialised on my face. It's not something I can forget."

"No." Rufus shoved his hand over his hair again. "Well." He wandered back to the mantelpiece, and picked up one of its long-ignored ornaments, a china shepherdess, weighing it in his palm. "I don't know, Luke. I'm damned if I know what to say. What a cursed miserable tale. I don't know if it constitutes an excuse, but it's certainly an explanation. I wish you had told me before."

"So do I."

Rufus tossed the fragile ornament a couple of inches and caught it. "How much are we talking about, out of interest? I'd like to know what sum's worth killing and lying for."

"Ten thousand guineas."

The shepherdess shattered on the hearth. "*How* much? Ten thou-sand?! Are you serious? Ten thousand *guineas?*"

"Don't shout," Luke hissed.

"Jesus Christ almighty! Why didn't you tell me? Mother of God! You don't do things by halves, do you? So where is it?"

Luke couldn't find a single word. Rufus grabbed his shoulders and shook. "Oh, come on, this is an actual treasure-hunt. It can't just be lying around in the Cathedral, surely. Why aren't you looking for it?"

"I...was? That's why you sent me away. This is what I lied to you about. You're angry about that, remember?"

Rufus waved his hand in impatient dismissal. "Balls to that. You didn't say it was a sodding fortune!"

Luke looked at him, and then he started to laugh. It bubbled out of him, helpless and stupid and absurd, great choking gasps of laughter so racking that it was inevitable they should turn to sobs. His shoulders heaved violently, and then Rufus's arm was around him, warm and strong, easing him over to a settle.

"Come on, sit down. Stop. It's all right."

It wasn't all right, and Luke couldn't stop. He'd spoiled so much, gained nothing by it, and Rufus's instant, instinctive, utterly bloody predictable enthusiasm was the last kick in the teeth.

I could have told him. I could have told him and not ruined everything.

"I'm sorry." He choked the words out between sobs. "So sorry. So stupid."

Rufus didn't say anything more. He just sat with Luke on the uncomfortable horsehair seat and held him as he wept out the days of misery and self-rebuke, arm around his shoulders, body close. And Luke clutched on to him, not caring if he was making himself ridiculous, because if this was the last time he'd get to touch Rufus, he wasn't going to waste it.

Seventeen

OVER THE LAST FEW DAYS, RUFUS HAD ANNOYED AND FRUS-
trated himself with endless imaginary conversations in which Luke
regretted or justified or crowed about his wrongdoings. Some of
those fantasies had ended in abject submission, some in violence,
most in his erstwhile secretary slinking away in shame after Rufus
had read him the brutal lecture he deserved. He had not imagined
Luke weeping into his shoulder, still less himself stroking his hair
and repeating it was all right.

He was still getting to grips with the tale. It rang true, and the
details were all entirely plausible. Unfortunately, the first story had
also rung true and been full of convincing detail. Possibly Rufus was
the most gullible man in Kent. He still stroked Luke's hair because the
tears were real, and dug out a handkerchief because so was the snot.

"Thank you," Luke mumbled. He blew his nose and dragged his
hand over his eyes.

"Take your time."

Luke nodded. He also moved to sit up, away, and Rufus quashed
an entirely foolish urge to tighten his arm and keep him close.

"Right," he said. "So. I understand why you didn't want to blurt this out, but I cannot approve of how you went about things. It was dishonest, deceptive, manipulative, and has caused me an astonishing amount of trouble."

"I know." Luke's voice was small.

"That said, buggered if I can see how you should have gone about it. I like to think I'm a reasonable man, but if you'd said, 'May I take ten thousand guineas from your house?' with no proof that either it wasn't mine, or that it was yours, I doubt I'd have listened."

"No, well, that was part of the problem." Luke sniffed noisily. "And it's not honest money."

Rufus would have happily hanged the bastards who spent the war shipping gold to the enemy for their own enrichment. He wasn't sure how it affected matters that the culprits were dead. "Your family weren't involved in the gold-trading?"

"No. Joss said we were free traders, not free bankers."

Rufus rather wanted to meet Cousin Joss. "I need to think about this. I can't simply..." He gestured in lieu of saying what he couldn't do; he didn't want to voice it.

"I'm not asking you to forgive me," Luke said. "That's not why I came. I owed you an apology and I hope you believe it. That's all."

Rufus rubbed his face. "You rode here from Dymchurch when I specifically told you not to come back, purely to apologise?"

"I had to. I did poorly by you, and I wish I hadn't."

"So you've said. And you truly believe there's smuggler's gold to the tune of ten thousand guineas hidden in Stone Manor?"

Luke sniffed. "Yes."

"You'd better find it, then."

Luke's jaw dropped, then he shook his head violently. "That isn't what I wanted. I'm not asking it."

"I don't care what you're asking. This money isn't mine, is it?"

"It's not anybody's."

"But it's definitely not mine, so I don't want it cluttering up my property. I'm not a bloody bank vault for your convenience."

Luke's jaw was slack. "Are you serious?"

"Entirely serious. You have too much unfinished business. Finish it."

"But—"

"But what? You said you were owed something, and you're probably right."

"Not by you!"

"I'm not giving you anything: it's not my money. I'm not sure it's yours, and I don't know if finding it will do you any good, but that's not my affair. Go and get it."

Luke stared at him a moment longer and then put his face abruptly in his hands. Rufus contemplated him with some alarm, wondering if he was crying again.

He wasn't used to this. To tears, in general—he wasn't a man whose shoulders people tended to cry on, possibly because his sympathy was rather too bracing—or to Luke being other than the cocksure, competent secretary and friend and lover on whom he'd relied so absolutely.

Had the cockiness been another lie? Or was it armour, something to protect the hurt child within? Or perhaps it was simply Luke's defiant stance against everything and everyone that tried to tell the scarred, scared smuggler's bastard his place.

It didn't matter. Luke's feelings were his own to struggle with, and none of Rufus's concern any more. But he'd come back when he didn't have to, he'd told what sounded like hard truths, and Rufus believed him. Perhaps he was the most gullible man in Kent, Essex, or the entire South of England, but he believed Luke, and that being the case, this seemed the fairest course.

Luke was shaking his head, without looking up. Rufus put a hand on his shoulder, carefully, and felt his muscles tense.

"Come on," he said. "Why not?"

"Because I don't—because you shouldn't— Oh, God, why are you being so *kind* about this?"

"You'd prefer me to throw you out?"

"I don't want your pity," Luke said savagely into his hands.

"Fine," Rufus said. "In fact, good. You can work for it."

That got Luke's tearstained face up, at least. "What?"

"You need to look for the money. I need a sodding secretary. Look at the mess I'm in."

"You must surely have written for a new man already."

Rufus shook his head, and Luke made a tiny sound of exasperation. He cut it off almost at once, but Rufus heard, and it stabbed like a knife because exasperated Luke was so painfully familiar.

He had not written. He didn't know who to write to, and the prospect of hiring a new secretary—the delays, the advertisements and interviews, the necessary explanations about his reading, the dismal fact that this fellow, however competent, would not be Luke—had been too much to bear.

Luke could do it. Luke could clear up the mess he'd made here, keep things under control while he found Rufus another secretary, collect his money, and go on his way. They'd part on civil terms, without hatred, and get on with their lives, and if that prospect currently seemed as bleak as Romney Marsh itself, well, time healed all wounds.

You'll fall in love once and once only, and God help you if it's a mistake because you'll be stuck with it.

He shook that thought off. "Come back. Sort my books out and find your money while you're at it. You need free run of Stone Manor to do that last, and it sounds like you owe me several days' work if you've been playing the fool on my time."

"But," Luke said blankly. "Don't be ridiculous. I can't possibly come back."

"Why not?"

"You sacked me."

"I'll rehire you."

"Everyone knows I was lying about the marriage."

"Make something up. The letter was delayed and you only just received it. You were protecting your mother."

"Your cousins shut me in a cellar!"

"You deserved that. Did you carry out your duties for me honestly? Were you embezzling from my estate, or otherwise exploiting your position?"

"No!"

"Then what's the problem?"

Luke set his teeth. "You cannot simply bring me back as though nothing happened."

"If you're suggesting that a d'Aumesty, especially the earl, can't behave in an irrational and arbitrary manner, you haven't been paying attention. Are you seriously expecting me to work with Odo again? What kind of bastard are you?" He could have kicked himself as the word came out. "I didn't mean—"

"Of course you don't want Mr. Odo. So you need to hire a new secretary."

"I will. And in the meantime, you need to put this whole business to bed. To rest," he corrected himself, too late.

Luke's eyes snapped to his. Rufus put his hand up. "And, no, before you ask. Nothing more. That—we will not discuss that. I don't want anything of you except your skills. *Secretarial* skills." He was making a pig's ear of this, but Luke's brief flash of alarm had not been tolerable. "That is—our prior relations are no longer—"

"Understood."

"You'll come back, find your money, and work for me until I can get a suitable replacement. That's all, and I think you owe it to me."

"And then what?"

"You do whatever you want with your riches, I suppose." Ten thousand guineas, invested at four per cent, would bring him significantly more than his annual salary. He wouldn't need to work again. "You could buy a substantial amount of the Marsh, I expect. Or go somewhere with more scenery. But you'll need to find it first, so I suggest you hurry up and get it all done with, for both our sakes."

"Is that what you want? Really?"

Was it? Rufus didn't know what he wanted, precisely. Not reconciliation, that was beyond the pale, but he didn't want to be angry and vengeful. He had enough conflict in his life, and he hated the sick feeling of hurt and stupidity Luke's betrayal had left him with. That was somewhat eased now; it would ease further if he took control of affairs. He also didn't want hidden treasure nagging at his mind forever, as it inevitably would if not found. In fact, he wanted this whole sorry episode over and done with, concluded with decency, so that when he looked back he would not have to rebuke himself for his temper or his behaviour. If he erred, it should be on the side of generosity, and if Luke took advantage of that, Rufus would make him regret it.

"That's what I want," he said.

Luke exhaled, a long shallow breath. "Yes, my lord."

Rufus might, he realised at dinner, have overestimated the d'Aumesty tolerance for eccentric behaviour.

"You're what?" Fulk demanded explosively. "Taking him *back*? I caught the little wretch stealing! Stayed up all night to do it!"

"I, I really cannot think, Oxney—" Odo began.

"An absurdity and a foolishness," Matilda said with icy majesty.

"Are we not to forgive repentant sinners, and bring them back into the fold?" Berengaria said, with one of her alarming forays into the fray. "I'm sure that's what last Sunday's sermon was about. Is he repentant, Oxney?"

Rufus met her eyes. "Exceedingly."

"There. How Christian of you."

Matilda's lips thinned. "It is not Christian to admit a lying scoundrel into the house. It is folly."

"Lost sheep," Berengaria said sententiously.

"Be quiet, girl! To see that Oxney prefers a known cheat and thief to the assistance of my own son—"

"I'm busy with the family history, Mother," Odo said. "Of course, if Oxney wants me to stop that and help, I shall at once."

"Absolutely not," Rufus said, with more force than tact. "That is, the history is important. How long was it since we've had one?"

"Well, Arnulf, Lord Oxney—"

"Oh, shut up, Odo," Fulk said. "This seems the most extraordinary freak of yours, Oxney. I assume you have a reason."

"Of course he does," Conrad said. "It's the marriage. The Brightling claim."

Rufus bit back an oath. Berengaria shut her eyes, signalling utter exhaustion. Odo said, "Father, that has been cleared up. There was no marriage. The letter from Louisa Brightling—"

"Doomsday has no claim on the earldom, despite the Brightling marriage. He was not only acknowledged as son by another man, he was found on a doorstep in a basket. That could have been any unwanted baby. There is no proof of descent from Brightling, and thus none from Raymond. The Committee of Privileges will certainly deny his claim," Conrad said.

Rufus's cousins exchanged glances. Odo said nervously, "But, but there *was* no Brightling marriage. We know that."

"On what evidence?"

"Um...she said so? In, in the letter?"

"To whom, and in whose possession was it?" Conrad demanded. "Doomsday's! He is a known scoundrel, Brightling an unchaste woman. It is obvious. Once it was made clear to Doomsday that his claim would fail, despite the marriage, how could he profit from it?" He gestured at Rufus. "By selling his birthright. By denying the truth, falsifying that supposed 'proof' and thus allowing this man to pretend he is the lawful earl—"

Rufus slammed a hand on the table, so hard that plates jumped, and so did Odo. "My God, will you ever stop? You call me a liar, a thief, a cheat, all while you live under my roof and eat at my table, and I will not have it! I set your own son looking for evidence of this marriage, curse you, what more do you want? You have no proof at all, nothing but your own imagination, and you *will* not make up this slanderous nonsense and spout it as truth!"

"I'm the true earl!" Conrad shouted back. "Me! I earned it! Who the devil are you to foist yourself on this family, you half-bred bastard slop-seller?"

"*What* did you call me?"

"I know the truth! Why else have you let that Doomsday into the house? You are paying him to hide your deception!"

"That's not very subtle," Berengaria remarked. "Could Oxney not more easily send him the money?"

"Shut your mouth, girl!"

Berengaria gave her father a very cold look. Fulk said, "At the risk of drawing attention to myself—"

"And you! Be quiet!" Conrad shouted.

Fulk pushed on. "With respect, sir, I would remind you of the old saw that the simplest explanation is usually the best. You have proposed an explanation as to why Oxney has forgiven the scoundrel, which is perhaps a little convoluted. Is there a simpler one, Oxney?"

"Yes," said Rufus, who'd been scrabbling to think of it. "The books, the estates, the whole business of Oxney is in a condition so neglected and shambolic that, were the last earl alive, he would be liable for an action at law by his heir. You were, as you believed, that heir, Conrad, and you let buildings fall into decay and tenants' pleas go ignored, and did nothing to remedy the situation. If I am to repair the damage you ignored while you sucked at the teat of the estate, I need hard-working, competent, honest men to help me. Doomsday is two of those things. It seems to be the best I can hope for here."

Berengaria's brows were at her hairline. Fulk said, "Oof."

"I hope that I'm honest, and I did try my b-best," Odo said, voice shaking.

"You are and did," Rufus said, kicking himself. "That was not aimed at you in the slightest."

"It was, of course, aimed at Conrad," Matilda said, voice vibrating. "You have no knowledge, no understanding, of what he has done for the estate."

"Damn all," Rufus said. "That's what he's done. Doomsday has a void where his ethical principles should be, and I can *still* rely on him more than I can on people who endlessly vaunt their lineage without doing a thing to earn or support or maintain it. You have entirely ignored your duty to our people, and you should be ashamed of yourselves."

He pushed back his chair and stalked out on that. He was still hungry, and would need to ring for food to his rooms, but it felt too good an exit line to waste.

It only dawned on him an hour later, as he sat alone in his room not looking at Luke's empty chair or Luke's painting, that he'd left Conrad in possession of the field.

Eighteen

TAKING LUKE BACK DIDN'T SEEM SUCH A BRIGHT IDEA THE NEXT
morning.

Rufus sat on his bed for longer than he could justify, going over
his thoughts from the previous day. He really did not want the whole
business left unfinished. He really did need a secretary. But he wasn't
quite so sure any more that he should trust Luke.

Luke had laid out such a careful web of lies the first time—his
reluctance to be involved, his vulnerability, the sorry tale of his
mother and the marriage. Rufus had no idea how anyone could think
so many steps ahead, or remember all the details, but clearly Luke
could. It was entirely possible he'd crafted this second story to get
back into Stone Manor and search for the gold. Assuming there *was*
gold and he wasn't after something else entirely.

Rufus groaned aloud. Never mind his heart: this was making his
head hurt.

But he'd believed Luke yesterday, and for all he'd been fooled
before, he didn't think he was that easily gulled. Although probably
most gulls thought that.

Damn it. He would not sit here thinking in downward spirals: he would talk to Luke frankly, and trust his own judgement. It was all he had.

Rufus dressed, aware of a desire to look his best, and accordingly making sure he took even less care than usual, and went downstairs.

As expected, Luke was in the study. He looked up as Rufus walked in, and a smile bloomed on his lips, a look of sheer pleasure at seeing him that withered and died at once, as if he'd remembered he had no right to it.

"Uh. Good morning, my—good morning, Lord Oxney."

Rufus groped for a response, for any of the things he had wanted or wanted now to say, and came up with, "Advertisement."

"Uh—?"

"For a secretary. Replacement. Write to whoever it is you write to and get some people sent for interview."

"Yes, my lord."

Rufus turned on his heel, heading out of the house, and down the road, walking for the sake of movement rather than destination. He couldn't think in Stone Manor. He couldn't think near Luke, and especially not about Luke.

He wished he had someone to talk to, someone who knew his situation, who understood people, who would tell him he was being a fool. Unfortunately, only one person fit that bill.

God damn it. He had been a major of the 54th Foot; he *could* think for himself, and judge for himself too. He knew very well most people would call him a fool for giving the man another chance, or say he'd fallen for a tale of woe, but if he went around doing what people wanted him to do, he'd have handed over the earldom to Conrad.

Luke's story had been plausible. The detail, and more, the way he'd looked and sounded telling it, with the hollowness of a man who'd had the stuffing knocked out of him. And what could he possibly want that was more valuable than ten thousand guineas, given he had no claim at all on the title? No: Rufus was prepared to believe that was the truth.

It was also no excuse. Luke should not have cozened his way into Stone Manor, and having done so, he should have told Rufus everything before they went to bed, or very shortly after. The ongoing concealment betrayed a deep and disturbing dishonesty that Rufus would be a fool to ignore.

And yet he was obviously miserable, and striving to make amends. Surely his shame meant something. Surely he wouldn't look so wretched if he didn't understand he'd done wrong.

That was possible. Rufus had known men do stupider things, junior officers who had got themselves into extraordinary tangles. Strong passions, whether for people or gold or vengeance, could lead to terrible decisions. For example, Rufus himself had invited Luke Doomsday back into his house.

And there, in plain sight, was the real problem, which was that Rufus *wanted* to believe him. He wanted to believe the whole thing had been planned without harmful intent and run out of Luke's control, that there had been no malice, that he had cared, even if he had failed to think.

Rufus chewed on that as he walked into Stone-in-Oxney. He chewed on it as he looped around the church and the vicarage where Pagan's Mithras altar stood, a weatherbeaten block of stone that bore the vague outline of a bull. He exchanged greetings with the vicar without having any idea what he said, and headed back to Stone Manor, still chewing it over, and by the time he was walking up the drive, he'd concluded there was only one way he could deal with the whole sorry business.

He headed back, went to the study, and found Luke deep in the books. Luke looked up, this time keeping his face neutral, unreadable. "My lord. I have drawn up a letter, if you'd care to review—"

"Just send it, you know what to ask for. What are you doing?" He glanced at Luke's writing as he spoke, saw that perfect, readable hand.

"The Tenterden repairs—"

"Forget it. Leave all that. Come on."

Luke, pen in still midair, blinked at him. "Come...where?"

"The Cathedral."

"What?"

"Cathedral. Your business. We're going to get that done, right now. I've got the key."

"But I'm in the middle of—"

"It'll wait. Come on."

"No," Luke said. "That's ridiculous. I'm supposed to be working for you."

"You do work for me. That means obeying orders."

He shouldn't have said that. Luke's lips parted, and Rufus was vividly, painfully reminded of orders given, a fair few of them in this room. Luke's taste for playing with his title and position had been an erotic delight; he cursed it now. "Cathedral," he repeated, in lieu of trying to dig himself out of a hole, and stood, demonstratively holding the door.

Luke rose in silence. He didn't comment further until they reached the absurd building, at which point he remarked, "People are going to wonder what we—you—are doing."

"Think of an explanation," Rufus said, unlocking the door. "You're the one with ingenuity. God almighty, what a lot of rubbish. How do we tackle it?"

Luke went to shut the door, and planted his back against it. "Why are you doing this?"

"You're here to find the money. So we're looking for it."

"You said *I* could look. Not that you would."

"You haven't started. I want it found." He wanted proof of the whole story; far more, he wanted to know what would happen if, or when, Luke found himself in possession of a fortune. He wanted it done with, because only then, one way or another, would he know where he stood.

Luke made a strangled noise. "You're being kind. Don't."

"I'm being practical. I want this done with, so we will get it done. Move."

Luke's lips parted, then he shoved himself upright. "Fine. Certainly. My lord."

Rufus contemplated the stacks of boxes and lumber. "We'll need chalk, to mark boxes to be hauled out and thrown away."

"Here," Luke said, going to the windowsill. "I've already marked the boxes I've searched."

Rufus caught the stick Luke threw—perhaps a little hard—at him. "Of course you did. Any tips?"

"Ten thousand guineas weighs about thirteen stone, by my reckoning. That's what, something about your weight?"

"I ride closer to fifteen."

"It's still a lot to carry. You'd want to make as few trips as possible, and Drake was strong, so I'd guess the money will be in perhaps three small chests, unless it was transferred to bags."

"So we can start by pulling boxes about and discarding the lighter ones. Make sure you mark some for disposal as you go along, for the look of the thing."

Luke mumbled something that sounded like a reflection on grandmothers sucking eggs. Rufus grinned to himself and set to work.

It was a tiresome and dusty job. There were spiders, and some evidence of mice, and a lot of the boxes were heavy enough to necessitate searching, in case. They worked in silence for the first little while, but Rufus had never been very good at silence.

"It must have been a damned nuisance doing this in the dark."

"It was." Luke left that there for a few moments then added, almost reluctantly, "And trying to avoid making noise."

Rufus shoved a chest full of gently decaying dresses to one side with a loud scrape. "You must have infinite patience. If we simply burned the place down, would we find the guineas in the ashes?"

"That's the third time you've suggested setting fire to your ancestral home."

"Only the third? I'm amazed. Everyone thinks Baldwin had rats in the attic, but I quite understand wanting to pull this place down and build something new."

Luke sat back on his heels. "Are you thinking of doing that?"

"The family would murder me. Well, my grandfather estranged himself from his own son and heir over the proposal. I don't know what a child of mine would have to do for me to treat them like that, but it would be more than architectural preferences. Or an ill-thought-out marriage, even." He got another chest open. "I don't understand it. They were his sons: how would he not have sought reconciliation? Granted he cared about the name, and the bloodline, and this damn fool heap of stones, but would he not want to forgive his sons?"

"Aunt Sybil forgave my father whatever he did, including what he did to my mother," Luke remarked with that appalling matter-of-factness he had for dreadful statements. "She always had excuses for him. She was angry when he cut me, but I dare say she'd have forgiven that in time. She brought him up almost as a son, and she loved him, but people should realise when things are not theirs to forgive."

"You don't forgive lightly, I think."

"No." Luke closed the chest, pushed it to one side, and scrawled on it with chalk. "Perhaps I should. But I resent apologies. I resent people telling me once it was too damned late to make a difference that they were sorry, they should have done better. It makes me ask, why didn't you?"

There was a bite in his voice. Rufus didn't reply, and after a moment Luke added, lower, "I have no standing to complain about this to you of all people. I'm aware of that."

"It isn't comparable."

"No, it's not. I could so easily have done better by you. Whereas what happened to me was nobody's fault but my father's and mine, and I still—my family—ugh."

"You said as much before, and I still don't see how it was your fault."

Luke sighed. "Joss and Great-Uncle wanted to send me to school, but I wouldn't go because my father didn't want it. If I hadn't been a little fool desperate to please a man who hated me, I'd have been offmarsh, so my father wouldn't have cut me, so he wouldn't be dead. But I didn't want to be sent away. All of it happened because I wouldn't be sent away."

"You've got a damned high opinion of yourself," Rufus remarked. "How many dead men was it, how many adults fighting over gold, and you think a thirteen-year-old boy made the difference? What, your father wouldn't have been a stupid greedy prick in your absence?"

"He might not have died. Although, Gareth might. If I hadn't found him that night, I doubt anyone else would have."

"Sir Gareth lived and your father died, and you're complaining. You wanted it the other way around?"

Luke's mouth opened. Rufus reviewed what he'd said, and found it sound in the essentials, if a little blunt. "It seems to me you're taking a damned sight too much on yourself," he went on. "That, and carrying a number of burdens that don't strike me as yours to carry."

"I *want* to let them go. I hate feeling like this, like—" Luke clenched a fist, banged it on his chest. "I hate that I can't enjoy my family now when things are better because things should have been different before."

"What do you mean?"

"They didn't stop my father." Luke sounded very young there, somehow. "He didn't hurt me when people were around, or not much, but when we were alone he did, because he liked to and he could, in places where the bruises wouldn't show. So the rest of them didn't see it happening. Nobody saw. Nobody *looked*."

"Did you tell anyone? Ask for help?"

Luke looked up at that. Rufus put a hand out. "I'm not casting blame. I was ashamed that my father left, bitterly ashamed for years. I didn't want people to know. It felt like—well, it felt like my fault, damn it, though it was no more mine than any of this was yours. And if my father had abused me in the way you describe, I dare say I'd have been ashamed of that too."

Luke swallowed, hard. His voice was a whisper. "Yes. I was ashamed. And, no, I didn't tell. But they should have seen. I wish they'd seen."

Rufus just watched him. Luke's face twisted. "And I can't forgive it. I can't forgive that they didn't see, and then once he cut me and everyone *had* to see it, they just let me go and live with Gareth. As if it didn't matter that a Doomsday went away."

"Why did you go?"

Luke shrugged. "It was best for everyone. Pa was Aunt Sybil's little brother, and he'd died estranged from her, and she couldn't look at my face without seeing why. It was a reason for Joss to be always at Gareth's. And as for me, it was wonderful. I had Gareth and Catherine and Cecy being interested in me and looking after me and *caring*, not to mention my schooling and so on, and you'd think that would make me happy, but the older I got, the more I felt safe and loved, the more angry it made me, because why could I not have had that before? Why did my father have to hate me?"

A fellow officer of Rufus's on the Peninsula had had a knack for bloodcurdling campfire tales, including one about a sorcerer who raised men from the dead. Rufus wished that such magic was possible. He'd give anything for ten minutes with Elijah Doomsday.

Luke had his arms wrapped around himself. "It wasn't my family's fault really," he went on, voice lower. "If they'd realised, they'd have acted. But they didn't. They were busy, and my father was cunning, and I wasn't anyone's in particular, so nobody noticed me unless I made a nuisance of myself—but I resent it, even so. I wanted to find the money to show them, to *spite* them, so that they'd have to admit the ill-begot bettermy brat *was* better than them, and do you know the worst thing about that? They'd all be delighted for me if I did, because they don't understand what the problem is!"

Rufus felt a sneaking sympathy with the other Doomsdays. "I don't follow. I thought you wanted the money as compensation for your father?"

"Yes, but I—gah!" Luke flung his hands up, a frustrated gesture. "I don't know. I did a stupid, dreadful thing to you because of a lot of knotted-up stuff that doesn't even make sense. I've hurt people I love because of someone I loathed, and I just wanted—I don't *know*."

Rufus's knees were starting to hurt, but he didn't want to stand and loom over Luke now. He sat instead, stretching his legs out. "Tell me this: what will you do with the money? Are you going to spend it? Go back home in furs and finery?"

"I thought I'd give half of it to Gareth. Not for himself; he'd throw it in the sea, what with everything. But I owe him so much, and I know he thinks a lot about what he can do for Cecy's boys, and Charlotte, his god-daughter, and there'll doubtless be more Doomsday children along now Isaac's wife is increasing and Tom's courting again. Because the money was a curse to him then, but if he could use it for the children, that would—well, make it clean. Make things better. Wouldn't it?"

He sounded increasingly doubtful as he spoke. Rufus rubbed his scalp. "You can't change the past."

Luke's head came up defiantly. "I can change its consequences. Why shouldn't I? That money nearly killed Gareth, and it did kill my father. Why can't I make it do some good?"

"Sounds like it already has."

Luke's jaw dropped, as well it might. "Not Sir Gareth," Rufus said hastily. "But your father—so a scabby thatchgallows rapist bully got what he had coming. Who gives a damn?"

"I do," Luke said. "Because it left me nowhere. If I could have— well, not asked him why he hated me, he would never have troubled to answer. But if I could have told him he was contemptible, that I've made something of myself and I'm no longer afraid, or even just spat in his face as a gift from my mother, that would have been something. He was a monster in my life and then he was dead, and I am *angry*. I'm so angry, about all of it, about what people did and didn't do, about the whole wretched mess. It's sat on my life like a toad and I'm sick of it. I've been angry since I stopped being afraid, and I wanted to find the money because at least that would be some sort of exchange, and *somebody* owes me *something* for this!"

The words echoed from the Cathedral's roof. He turned abruptly back to the chest, ducking low, hiding his face.

Rufus watched him, kneeling there on the dusty floor, then clapped his hands. "Right. Leave that, come with me. We're going for a walk. Lock up here and I will meet you at the front door."

⌘

Rufus set the pace as they left Stone Manor on foot, striding out along the path that led down the hillside.

"Where are we going?" Luke asked after a few minutes.

"Down to High Knock Channel."

"Why?"

"You said your father died there. Show me."

He could feel Luke's gaze, but he didn't say anything. Rufus strode on. This might be a good idea or a dreadful one; it was the only one he had.

The Isle of Oxney was really just a hill with waterways around it. The Royal Military Canal ran past the Isle, straight and wide; High Knock Channel formed a loop that briefly ran alongside it just by the bridge down from Knock Hill. Luke led the way over the bridge to the thorn tree that grew between the waterways, a gnarled, hunched mass of aggressive twigs.

"They found him here," he said. "In the Canal. I don't know where he died exactly, so this is where I think of it."

"That'll do, then." Rufus came to stand by him, shoulder to shoulder, inches apart. "So. I've seen a lot of people die. Men I knew well, good friends, but also men I couldn't abide. We developed a sort of informal ceremony. The idea came from a fellow who'd been a Classics scholar, but it caught on in my regiment. I thought it might be worth doing now."

"A ceremony? For my father?"

Luke did not sound enthusiastic. Rufus pressed on. "The idea is, a funeral is for the best in a man. You say he was a good soldier even if he wasn't, that people will miss him even if they don't; you wish him the best for where he goes next, even if you expect the worst. We all need that last charity; none of us look good on a close accounting. But sometimes you need to say other things too, so we had what the classics fellow called libations. Drinks for the dead."

"He liked a drink," Luke said. "I have no idea what you're getting at."

Rufus stepped forward to the thorn tree, fishing out a hip-flask from his pocket. "Elijah Doomsday." He spoke formally, in a carrying voice. "You were a disgrace, as a father and a man. You failed your son in every way; you took what wasn't yours to take; you had a dog's death and deserved it. I thank the man who snapped your neck because he saved me soiling my own hands. It's a good thing you're gone, and past time you were forgotten. Here's your drink, now sod off."

He poured a measure from the flask onto the ground as he spoke, and stepped back. Luke stared at him, speechless.

"You might want to say other things, of course," Rufus said in his usual voice. "Kinder things. Forgive and forget, if you care to: that's your right. That was how I felt, which is what this is for. Getting it said." Luke was still gaping. Rufus felt a stab of uncertainty. "And the last line is traditional, our tradition, no matter how one felt about the fellow, but I see you may not—"

Luke took the flask from his hand. "Elijah Doomsday." His voice sounded thin. He cleared his throat. "If you'd treated other people properly, I wouldn't exist. If your aim was better, I'd be dead. I'm sorry for my part in getting you killed, but if you didn't want all that to happen, maybe you shouldn't have cut my fucking face open!"

He took a moment there. Rufus stood, back straight, waiting.

"I wanted you to love me," Luke went on at last, quietly. "I would have loved you if you let me. But you didn't, and that's not my fault. I'm not going to forgive you, ever, because you chose to do it all. But I am going to forget you, because I'm tired of having you in my life. Oh, and on Louisa's behalf: burn in hell." He tipped a generous slug of brandy onto the wet grass. "Here's your drink—"

"Now sod off." Rufus said it with him, softly, like a prayer.

They stood in silence for a moment, watching the water. Then Rufus retrieved the flask, took a ceremonial swig, and passed it back. Luke drank, then made a dramatic grimace. "Gah."

If he wanted to pretend the tears in his eyes were down to the fiery spirit, Rufus would too. "All right?"

"Yes. Yes, I am. That was—odd, but thank you."

"It seemed the right thing."

"It was. I don't know if it would catch on in general."

Rufus shrugged. "Sometimes you need to have the last word."

"I usually like to." Luke rolled his shoulders. "Unless you have any other dead people to abuse, shall we go back up?"

"Back to the Cathedral. I want that finished today."

Luke breathed out, long and slow. "Yes, my lord. You should get your brandy from Joss, by the way. His is quite a lot better."

"I prefer to pay duty, thank you."

"He declares most of it now," Luke protested, and they set off on the climb back up Knock Hill together.

⁓♋

On the whole, Rufus felt the day was a partial success. Luke was quiet for the rest of the afternoon, but in a better way, he thought, without the quivering tension of before. He looked like he was thinking about things, which had to be an improvement.

On the other hand, they didn't find any trace of the guineas.

"Damnation," Rufus said, shoving the last box out of the way. The light was evening gold; he'd need to change for dinner soon. "Damn."

"The Cathedral was a guess," Luke said. "Well, the whole idea that it's at Stone Manor is a guess."

"There are plenty more places to search, God help us. Where do we look next?"

Luke gave him a look that tried hard to be exasperated. Rufus said, "Don't you dare deny me this. I want to find it. I'd prefer if there was a map, of course, ideally written in dried blood."

"You're ten years old at heart, aren't you?" Luke muttered, and Rufus took the casual jibe like a gift.

He had acquired an amazing amount of dust. He ended up tipping water over his head in an effort to get it out of his hair, then had to change all his clothes, and ended up sprinting down the stairs when he heard the dinner gong. Matilda gave him a frozen look at his lateness and doubtless his dishevelled appearance, but forbore to comment; Conrad merely grunted. It was as much as Rufus could hope for.

Fulk, apparently feeling himself a licensed commenter, said, "What on earth have you been up to, coz? You look positively damp."

"Moving boxes," Rufus said. "I want the Cathedral cleared out. It's absurd to use that building for rubbish and moth-eaten clothes. It might not precisely fit with the rest of the Manor—"

"It's an abomination," Odo said.

"But it's here now, so either we demolish it at vast expense, or we use it."

"Dear Father did not want it used," Matilda said. "Dear Father found it an offence to the eye, only fit to use as a lumber room."

"He and I would have disagreed on a lot of things," Rufus said. "Berengaria, could you use it as a studio? It gets plenty of light. I'm told you need that."

Her head came up. Matilda's nostrils flared. Fulk opened his mouth and, with unusual good sense, closed it again.

"I might, perhaps," Berengaria said cautiously. "If it's not damp. Goodness knows what the roof's like."

"It seemed dry to me. Needs a good clean, of course. Have a look, say if it's no use to you, but I'd have thought your work would look good in there. Could you make it a studio-gallery?" He could imagine the high walls covered in Berengaria's bright colours. "We could get everything hung properly. Framed, too."

She was pink with pleasure, and her expression made Rufus realise how infrequently he'd seen her smile. "I...that would be... Thank you, Oxney, that's extremely kind of you. I'll look at it tomorrow."

"Do that. I'll have it cleared and cleaned and the rest as soon as you give the word."

Odo beamed at them both. "That's a wonderful idea. Stone Manor's own art gallery. Yes. If we must have the Cathedral—"

"You propose to put those daubs on display?" Matilda enquired. "Where people might *see* them?"

Berengaria's colour went from pink to a dull red. Rufus said, "What a cursed unpleasant remark."

"I will speak as I choose to my daughter. If she had not wasted her time and her youth in this foolery with paints, she might have been married by now."

"Hardly," Berengaria said. "You must recall I had no portion, Mother. You paraded me around as though our surname alone should secure me your idea of a good match, kept me from any society where I might have discovered a like mind, and have never ceased to blame me for the results. Do you not know, if you want to place an unattractive daughter, you must pay someone to take her?"

"I gave you every chance, which you failed to take! Sir James Wingard—"

"He was forty years my senior!"

Rufus met Fulk's eyes. Fulk casually let his hand drift across his neck in a throat-cutting motion which economically conveyed that the evening was, once again, doomed.

"—wasting your time and your father's generosity with this nonsense—"

"My grandfather's generosity! *You* never gave me anything!"

"And look where his favouritism has brought you! An old maid, nothing but an ape-leader—"

"I never asked for a Season!" Berengaria said. "I never wanted to be married! Can you not just leave me be?"

"And what would you do if we did?" Conrad demanded. "You live on our sufferance, miss, and if you don't wish to lose that, you will mind your tongue, speak with due respect, and do as you are told!"

"She does not live on your sufferance," Rufus said, with some volume. "She lives on mine, just like you, and I will trouble you to remember that. Berengaria has a home here as long as she cares for it, and she will speak as she pleases in it, so this barracking will stop."

Matilda was white with rage. "*My daughter*—"

"Yes. Not your whipping-boy."

"We are her parents, and we shall direct our children!" Conrad shouted.

"They're grown adults," Rufus said. "And it's past time they and you behaved like it. I don't know what the devil the old man did to you all, but I've had my fill of this dictatorial nonsense. They have their own lives, and frankly, Conrad, if you'd claimed your own life when you should have, things might be a great deal better for everyone."

"Claimed, as Raymond did?" Conrad demanded. He was an ugly red. "You think I should have rebelled against my father, married a common slut, committed bigamy—"

"Oh, for Christ's sake!"

Odo had been watching with his head turning from side to side. Now he swallowed noisily and said, "I want to get married."

That landed with the thud of a mortar. Rufus, Conrad, and Matilda all gaped, silenced by shock. Fulk said, "Does she know you?"

"Be quiet," Berengaria said. "Who to, Oddy?"

He licked his lips. "Miss Colefax. Laura Colefax. From Fairfield."

"Colefax the curate?" Matilda said. "You want to marry a *curate's* daughter?"

Odo went bright red. "She is a marvellous—charming, intelligent—so very kind—"

"That old fool's old maid? That gawky, patched bluestocking?"

"Don't, Mother," Odo whispered. "Don't be unkind about her. Don't."

"A curate's daughter," Conrad said contemptuously. "As if it is not bad enough to have a draper's son foisted on us, we are to have a provincial girl of no account? Do you propose to bring a vulgar bride here, to this house? Absolutely not. No."

"Father—"

"No! I will not hear this absurdity. I refuse my permission."

"He doesn't need it," Rufus said. "He's a grown man."

"With nothing! What do you propose you and your commoner bride live on, you fool? Well?"

Odo was scarlet. "I—uh—"

"His salary," Rufus said loudly. "That's what."

Everyone turned. Conrad's eyes bulged. "You dare not."

Rufus locked gazes with him. "Odo, see me tomorrow and we will agree a fair wage for your work as family historian. You will have a salary, and a place here if you want it, or I dare say we—I—own a cottage or some such you could have. If the lady says yes, I'd be honoured to meet her."

The subsequent explosion from Conrad and Matilda was the most unpleasant yet, but Rufus felt it was worth it.

Nineteen

LUKE LAY CURLED ON HIS BED, LEAFING THROUGH *MELMOTH THE Wanderer* for the miserable parts, which was most of it. He was deep in Alonzo's agonies of despair as he lay in the Inquisition's dank, amphibian-infested underground prison when Emily came in. "What's your man doing now? All hell's broken loose down there."

He sat up. "What's happened?"

She gave him a quick summary of events, as shamelessly eaves-dropped. "Mrs. Conrad has always hated Miss Berengaria painting, the old misery. Thinks it's too much like honest work or not ladylike enough, or maybe it's just that Berry enjoys it. She's livid. And Mr. Odo and the curate's daughter! Mind you, Laura Colefax is just right for him, now I think of it. She's a kind soul, and she doesn't half go on about history. Mr. Conrad's in middling order about all of it: with any luck he'll have an apoplexy. The servants' hall is in uproar and Mr. Pauncefoot's fit to be tied. This place hasn't been so much fun in years."

"I'm glad you're enjoying yourself," Luke said. "Em?"

"Mmm?"

"Did I make you much trouble?"

She gave him a look. "Just a bit. Miss Berengaria likes your man; she wasn't happy to think I'd been in on fooling him. And she thought I'd hoaxed her, too, and that— She doesn't have enough people she cares for to lose one. It wasn't kind."

"I'm sorry, truly. I didn't think how wrong this would all go."

"Seems to be going all right from where I'm sitting," Emily observed. "I wouldn't have thought even Joss could talk his way back from the twitter you caused, but here you are."

"Not for long. Not to stay. He's having me send for another secretary." Luke had written several letters, with prompt attention and bitter reluctance, all of them now waiting for Oxney's frank. "And I didn't talk my way back in: it was all his lordship. He's—" Luke could barely manage the word. "He's being *kind*."

Emily considered him, then sat on the bed, shoulder to shoulder. "He told Mr. Odo and Miss Berengaria they could live here as long as they like, and to blazes with Mr. and Mrs. Conrad. She was near crying when she told me. They've always harped on at her, but since the old man died it's been like you wouldn't credit. She's a useless mouth, can't get a man, she wastes her time painting—and now he's giving her a gallery. And he's giving Mr. Odo a proper job with money, and he's sat with him right now, calming him down because of what Mr. Conrad said about Miss Colefax. That's a merciful good-hearted man, that one. Why shouldn't he be kind to you?"

"I don't deserve him to. I wouldn't be if I were him."

"That's true enough," Emily said. "Good thing he's the earl and not you. But as for deserving—if we all got what we deserved, we'd be in trouble."

"He said that today."

"See? I must be right. Chin up, bettermy. This isn't like you, glooming around."

"I haven't made a mess like this before."

"You've made a fair few," Emily said. "Always had other people clear 'em up, too, Joss and Sir Gareth and me, even. And now you've got his lordship clearing this one up. Nice for some."

"It's not like that!"

"Sounds like it is."

"It isn't. I'm doing what he wants."

"That right? Funny how what he wants sounds an awful lot like what's good for you." Emily clambered off the bed. "I've got to go, I've work to do. I'd say look out for yourself, but you don't have trouble with that, mostly."

Clearly he was far from forgiven. "I'm sorry, Em. I won't be here much longer."

She paused at the door. "I don't mind you here, bettermy. I mind you causing havoc, or the wrong kind of it. Mr. Conrad's been in a merciful dobbin with all that's happened, and when you had him thinking his lordship might not be the rightful earl, and then he got disappointed *again*—you've no idea how he's been taking it out on Berry, and everyone else. If you're going to make trouble, make it for the right people."

Luke sighed. "I'll do my best."

It was another half hour before he heard Rufus's heavy tread on the floorboards. He tracked the motion: into the Salon, a brief hesitation, then into the bedroom.

He spent another few minutes staring at the wall, thinking about rainbows, and what people wanted. Then he went through the anteroom, knocked on the door, and walked in.

Rufus had pulled off his shirt and stockings and was sitting on the bed bare-chested and barefoot, and the sight stopped Luke in his tracks. "Uh. Excuse me."

"If you didn't want me in deshabille, you should wait for permission to enter. What is it?"

"I heard about this evening. I wanted to see if you were all right."

"Of course I am. Odo isn't. I had to escort Conrad out of the room: he was frothing at the mouth, as if he ought to dictate every act of his offspring. What's wrong with this bloody family, keeping people on leashes? The old man did it to his sons, Conrad's doing it to his children—"

"Control," Luke said. "After fifty years under his father's thumb, of course Mr. Conrad wants to do the same to his children. It's his turn."

"If someone hurts you, find someone else to hurt? That's a wretched way to go on." Rufus leant forward, propping muscular forearms on muscular thighs, powerful shoulders rounded. Luke's mouth went dry. "God rot it. Why must we make each other miserable?"

Luke braced himself. "That's what I wanted to talk to you about."

Rufus looked up. "Go on."

"I—" He licked his lips. "I don't expect you to forgive me. I behaved shockingly and you've been nothing but kind about it, and you shouldn't be."

"Why not?"

"Because I don't deserve it! I cannot keep taking like this. I was supposed to be here to work on your books, and instead we've looked for the money and you brought me out for that ceremony, and I *can't*—" His voice cracked. "I feel a hundred times worse than I did before, and that was bad enough. Please, I'm begging you. Please be angry, or, or have some ghastly thing you need done, or just send me away if you want me gone, but stop being kind to me! I'm a grown man who made a bloody stupid decision, *series* of decisions, and can take the consequences, and you're treating me like I'm going to break!"

"You looked like you were!"

That shut Luke up for a second. Rufus went on, "I don't know what you think I should be doing, but if it includes kicking a man when he's down: no. You're unhappy, damn it. What do you want me to do about it, sit and watch? Christ, you're confusing."

"*I'm* confusing? You ought to be furious with me!"

"You really are an unforgiving son of a bitch. Do something about that. You might start with yourself. And don't think I'm not angry because I'm not shouting. What you did was dishonest, and callous, and it bloody hurt, and I am struggling to reconcile that with the man I thought you were. I don't know what I think about that yet. I can't say it doesn't matter. But Christ, Luke." His voice was suddenly aching. "Don't ask me not to care. Don't ask me not to act when you're in pain. You asked me for my protection when we first met and I promised you'd have it. I don't go back on my word."

Luke's ribcage was too small, and full of jagged shards. "I was *lying.*"

"I wasn't."

Luke put his face in his hands. He heard the ancient bed creak, and then Rufus was with him, powerful arms closing around him. Luke leaned in to him, burying his face in the broad, bare chest, feeling his warmth, his solid bulk. Skin to skin.

Rufus was stroking his hair, a gentle, absent motion. "Luke, Luke. What the devil am I going to do with you?"

You're going to send me away as soon as I find the money, and I don't want to go. I don't want the bloody money. I want what we had, what I threw away.

He could say that, and Rufus might even listen, and there he'd be, doing what Luke wanted.

If he wants me to stay, he'll say so.

"I will do whatever you want," Luke said into his chest. "Just, please, make it *be* what you want. Because you're looking after everyone in this house and you ought to have someone thinking of you."

Rufus started to say something—Luke felt the movement of his ribs—and stopped. He let go, instead, and Luke reluctantly stepped away. "Everyone in this house is thinking of me, for good or ill. I'm the damned earl. And if you want to do something for me, make it what I ask: find your bloody money, and put an end to this business."

"Right," Luke managed, feeling his stomach sink. "Yes."

"Do it tomorrow. Where is it if it's not in the Cathedral? You must have an idea. Someone said Baldwin built the ice house."

"I've already looked there, and through the North Wing," Luke said. If Rufus wanted to talk about this, that's what he would do, no matter how much he wanted to step back into those brawny arms. "The last of Mr. Baldwin's works was the mithraeum."

"The what?"

"It seems Mr. Pagan built a mithraeum, his own personal Roman cult temple, in the undercroft."

"Of course he did. What's the undercroft?"

"I've no idea. Perhaps a cellar? Whatever it is, Mr. Pagan has the only key."

"Ask him for it tomorrow, then. He's a late riser when he appears at all, and I've to go out with Smallbone early, but tell him it's my orders. Now go to bed. And stop fretting about this: it's not doing you or me any good."

Luke was in the office at an ungodly hour the next morning. If Rufus was adamant about him finding the money and putting an end to everything, then at least he would leave matters in good order.

KJ Charles

It was quite astonishing how much chaos Rufus had managed to create in his brief absence. Luke set himself to getting things straightened up, and resented that he did so with one ear twitching for footsteps. Rufus had gone out on a long inspection of several properties; he wouldn't be back soon, and there was no point listening out for him.

That didn't stop him jerking to attention when a set of feet came to the door at mid-morning. Unfortunately, they belonged to a footman, with an order for him to attend on Mr. and Mrs. Conrad in their drawing room at once.

He went through to the New Wing. He'd been in here before to be shouted at; he had a feeling this wouldn't be very different.

Conrad and Matilda were both waiting for him. She sat with her lips pursed in an expression of distaste; Conrad stood with his hands behind his back like a schoolmaster about to dispense punishment, his chin up and a slight sneer on his face.

"Doomsday," he said. "Close the door."

Luke did so and turned back to the pair. "You summoned me, Mr. Conrad?"

"Yes. I wish to discuss the matter of your continued employment in this house."

"That is a matter for Lord Oxney."

Matilda sniffed. "And as such, he has permitted you to return to Stone Manor despite a disgraceful exhibition of outright dishonesty. Why?"

"Again, that is a matter for his lordship."

"I asked you a question. Answer it at once."

Luke met her gaze. "I have. If that's all, Mrs. Conrad—"

"Rubbish," Conrad said over him. "You're a thief, caught in the act, yet he's given you your post back out of the goodness of his heart? I think not."

"We know not," Matilda added venomously. "We know *exactly* why not."

Luke felt cold snake down his spine, but as a Doomsday, 'never admit anything' was branded into his soul. "There is no 'why', Mrs. Conrad. Lord Oxney very graciously offered me a chance to redeem—"

Conrad snorted. "Enough of this flannel. We know what you are doing for Oxney, and why he is permitting a gallows-bird Doomsday in the house."

"And may I say it is shameful," Mrs. Conrad added, mouth tight.

Conrad took a step closer. He was quite a lot taller than Luke. "I say, we know what you're doing for Oxney." He paused, glanced at Matilda, and went on, "I want you to do it for us."

It took a second for that to sink in, then the sheer horror of the proposition dawned on Luke in full, appalling, vivid colour. He took a deep breath to voice a strongly-worded refusal, and only just managed to stop himself as his brain jolted back into life.

Of course Mr. and Mrs. Conrad weren't suggesting three in a bed, though he was going to need a drink to deal with the idea they had been. They didn't know he'd slept with Rufus, either, or things would be a great deal worse. They thought he was up to something else.

And they wanted that something very badly. Luke's finely honed instincts for skulduggery began to flare. He tipped his head on one side, not confirming or denying, but letting a little bit of calculation slide into his expression. "What is it you believe I can do for you?"

"You are conspiring with my nephew," Conrad said. "Your mother married Raymond and you found that out. He is paying you to conceal the fact."

"My mother has attested there was no marriage."

"Of course she has," Matilda said with contempt. "A woman of that sort would say anything she was paid to."

Luke didn't know his mother well. He'd found her three years ago; they had met four times not counting his birth. But she had welcomed him, and wept with him, and schemed with him too, because Luke hadn't got his brains from Elijah Doomsday any more than his looks, and the mental tally mark he added to his score was drawn with force that would have cracked a slate.

"There *was* a marriage," Conrad said. "All the facts go to show it. The Brightling man's testimony, my father's letter. And you—why would the draper's boy permit you to set foot in this house, except that you have a hold over him? You are blackmailing him because you have proof of his bastardy. I know it."

"By 'draper's boy', do you mean Lord Oxney?" Luke enquired.

Matilda stepped in. "Doomsday, we know the truth. You will attest it whenever required, and so will the Brightling woman. You will swear to the marriage, and he will be removed."

Luke looked from one to the other of them. "And why, exactly, would I do that?" He let his voice carry a world of meaning, and saw satisfaction in Matilda's eyes.

Conrad lifted his chin. "You will not find me ungrateful. He's paying you to keep the secret. I will pay you to share it."

Luke nodded slowly. "How much?"

Matilda's lip curled. "As I told you, Conrad. Quite without morals."

"Mrs. Conrad, I will work for Lord Oxney until I leave his employment for a better offer," Luke said. "For that, I need to know the terms."

"There will not be an offer of employment," Conrad said. "Your association with this household will come to an end. I shall pay you"—he glanced again at his wife—"five hundred pounds."

Luke lifted his lip in a hint of a sneer. "Not enough."

"I beg your pardon?" Matilda said furiously. "We do not barter with servants. How dare you—"

"My dear," Conrad said. "Doomsday, you cannot expect to maintain this position indefinitely. My nephew is a bad-tempered, vulgar man; he once offered *me* violence. You would be well advised to consider that. I am prepared to propose, in recompense for your full assistance, one thousand pounds. That is final."

"That's very generous, Mr. Conrad," Luke said. "Do you have a thousand pounds to give me?"

Matilda's nostrils flared. Conrad reddened. "I will when I have the estate!"

"So I help you take it, and you then express your gratitude with a thousand pounds?"

"Precisely."

"And, forgive me for stating the obvious, but once you are the earl, what's to stop you deciding you aren't grateful to me after all?"

Conrad swelled. "Are you doubting my word, sirrah?"

"Mr. Conrad, I would be foolish to exchange a comfortable situation now for a promise of future reward. I'd need a more immediately tangible inducement." Conrad blinked at him. Luke said, "Cash up front."

"But I cannot—"

"Of course we can. Or, you can, Doomsday," Matilda said. "You manage Oxney's books, don't you? The man is barely able to read."

"There," Conrad said, with satisfaction. "The matter can easily be resolved."

"You are instructing me to embezzle money from the estate?" Luke asked.

"Of course not. The property is rightfully mine."

"It is lawfully Lord Oxney's."

"*I* am Lord Oxney, damn you!" Conrad bellowed, making Luke jump. "I! Not he! By right, by birth! I earned it, and I will have it, and you will give it to me!"

"And if I can't?" Luke said, though his shoulder blades were twitching with the desire to take a step away. "Because I don't know if my mother's word will suffice to convince the Committee for Privileges with no evidence to support it."

"But there will be evidence," Matilda said. "A special licence was issued; there is the word of the Brightling woman, which you will provide; and we will have the testimony of the man who performed the ceremony."

Luke took that in. "You've found the parson?"

"We will have his testimony."

"May I ask who—?"

"You may not," Conrad said. "You will do as you are ordered. Support our right, give your word in court, and ensure your mother does the same."

Matilda clicked her tongue. "She is not his mother."

"I beg your pardon?" Luke said.

She pointed a pale finger at him. "You are *not* the Brightling woman's child. You are a foundling, a nameless bastard of unknown origin. When Raymond's first marriage is proven, you will have and make no claim on the earldom. Remember that."

"Ma'am," Luke said, bowed, and got out of there.

Luke wasn't entirely sure what next to do. He wished Rufus were here. His nerves were running high and he didn't want to sit on that conversation any longer than he had to.

But he wasn't here, so Luke considered his options.

He wasn't sure what they meant about the parson's testimony, or what they could possibly have found. And why 'we will have'? Given a bit more information, he'd have set himself to getting in their way, but he was at a loss as to what they might intend.

There wasn't anything he could do about Conrad now, and meanwhile Rufus had given orders. The second last thing Luke wanted was to listen to Mr. Pagan, and the absolute last to find his money and be given his notice of departure, but what he wanted was not relevant, so he sloped off to the Chamber Block to seek out Mr. Pagan d'Aumesty.

The Manor was not generally a comfortable place but the Chamber Block took that to extremes. He couldn't begin to guess when it had last been refurbished; he'd swear the stone staircase was original to the Norman building, and what with the tiny windows, a man could break his neck in here.

It was deserted. Mr. Pagan lived in here; nobody else had reason to set foot in the place except the maids, resentfully carrying meals up winding stairs.

Luke made his way up, passing a dozen rooms as he went, most of them empty, some holding ancient furniture, thick with dust. Sir Hugo could have left his chests of gold in any of these rooms and nobody would have noticed. Luke was fairly sure he hadn't, because he'd spent three long, frustrating, and really quite nerve-wracking nights searching the Chamber Block.

He knocked at Mr. Pagan's door several times, and let himself in.

The old man was in a chair by a fire. It was the middle of a pleasant early summer day, but the room wasn't overly warm, which indicated how cold this place must get in winter. He said, "Mph? What's this?"

"Mr. Pagan?" Luke said. "I'm Lord Oxney's secretary."

"You are not."

"I am, sir. Luke Doomsday."

"Doomsday? The bastard branch? But that was not his name. And he was dismissed."

"I was, yes. Lord Oxney took me back on."

"Nonsense. My brother's secretary was..." Pagan waved his hand vaguely in the air, indicating height. "And he's dead."

"The secretary?" Luke asked.

"What?"

"The secretary is dead?"

"Lord Oxney is dead. You should know that if you're his secretary."

Luke took a deep breath and started again. "I am the new Lord Oxney's secretary, Mr. Pagan. *New* secretary, to the new earl. Rufus, Lord Oxney," he added, for complete clarity. "He would like to see the mithraeum."

"Who would?"

"Lord Oxney."

"He would not. He ordered it shut. Locked. Said he never wanted it opened again." Pagan paused. "And he's dead."

Christ and all his angels. Luke could only see one way through this maze and he didn't want to take it. But he was going to be in here forever either way, so he set his shoulders and said, "Rufus, Lord Oxney wants it opened. He is very interested in Mithraism. As am I."

Pagan's rheumy eyes lit up. "You are a scholar?"

"The merest amateur, sir. I would be most grateful for your wisdom."

He got it. Pagan launched into a lecture about someone called Zarathustra, Roman mysteries, Greco-Roman practice, levels of Mithraic initiation, the Roman remains at Lympne, and the conclusive yet nonexistent evidence of a thriving Mithras cult at Stone. Luke nodded with his most sincere face on, and counted in his head until it was over. He got to eleven hundred and sixty-two.

"Fascinating," he said once Pagan ran out of breath. "I would be most honoured to be admitted to your mithraeum."

"Well," Pagan said. "A scholar such as yourself—I suppose the earl would permit it."

Luke didn't bother with the argument. "I'm sure, Mr. Pagan."

Pagan hauled himself out of his chair, a lengthy process, and went into his bedroom. He returned with a key, which he didn't offer to Luke, instead leading the way out of the room.

Oh God. "There's no need to show me," Luke said. "If you direct me—"

"No, no. It will be my pleasure. I don't have many visiting scholars."

"Like Sir Hugo Inglis?"

"Ah, yes, Hugo." The old man made his slow way down the steps. Luke hovered, poised to grab him if he slipped. "Hugo showed a great deal of interest in the project. He has not come to visit in some time. I wonder why not."

Being dead, probably. Luke decided not to break the news, which had doubtless been broken before, more than once. There was no point: he didn't think Pagan was troubled so much by memory as by a profound lack of interest in other people.

They reached the ground floor, and Pagan took him along a short passage to where a flight of stairs led down to an obvious cellar door. "Down here," he said. "The mithraeum is a replica, of course, but I flatter myself, an effective one. Where is the lamp? We must have a lamp. What were you thinking?"

Luke went back up the several flights of stairs to get a lamp, hoping Pagan didn't wander off. He returned to find the old man waiting with obvious impatience.

"Good, excellent. It has been too long. Come."

The door was of thick, ancient dark oak secured with blackened iron bands. Pagan unlocked it with a hand that shook, and led the way inside, and down.

Luke followed him down the steps, noting the dry chill, the absolute silence, the dark. He reached the archway and the floor, and raised his lamp high.

A temple loomed before him.

Luke stared, astonished. The room was full of thick, squat pillars, each far wider than a man and with stone arches springing from its top, like the leaves of cocoa-nut palms he'd seen in pictures. The low roof was entirely made of those connecting, interlocking arches, the spaces between filled with brickwork. It was quite empty as far as he could see, just the pillars and arches over and over again, a glory of repeating patterns which, with only the light of his lamp, seemed to stretch on forever. It was the loveliest thing he'd ever seen.

He walked forward, columns on either side of him, their pale stone repeating as though mirrored. Like being in a petrified forest or a perfect equation, he thought, and felt the cool beauty settle over his soul.

"It's glorious," he said.

"Hmph? Typical Norman undercroft. Come." Pagan walked forward, whispering under his breath as he did so. Luke followed reluctantly. He didn't want to know what blasphemy had been perpetrated on this beautiful place.

It was at the end of the cellar. The two corners of the end wall had been built out to create a rectangular alcove—apse, he thought you'd call it in a church. In the apse was an altar, about six feet long and three high, made of grey stone topped with a large slab. The front was carved with a sharp, clearly new representation of a man in an odd cap stabbing a bull, which was echoed by the unframed painting that hung on the wall behind it.

It was Berengaria's work, a finished version of the Mithras image he'd seen before, with the white bull and the man killing it, the dog and the snake and the scorpion. Somehow it looked a great deal less absurd in here, with the fading rows of columns and the flickering light, and the dark that pressed around them like velvet.

Pagan's whisper was a little louder now, becoming a mutter, and Luke made out the syllables now. *Nama Mithras. Nama Mithras.*

"Ah, the tauroctony," Luke said, mostly to make him stop.

"The sacred symbol," Pagan agreed, breaking off his chant. "What was your name?"

"Luke Doomsday."

"Luke." Pagan's voice curled around the word. "An interesting name in a mithraeum, wouldn't you say?"

"Why, sir?"

"Luke, the gospel-maker. The Christian evangelist whose symbol is—?"

"The bull," Luke said, wishing he hadn't asked. The painting loomed in the corner of his eye.

"Indeed. The bull. And here we stand before the tauroctony: Mithras, Lord of the Contract, God of the Exchange, killing the bull to the glory of the sun." He raised his hands. "Nama Mithras. Nama Mithras!"

Luke's memory brought up, with unnecessary vividness, the frontispiece of a Gothic novel he'd once read. It depicted an ancient white-bearded druid wielding a sharp sickle, preparing to offer sacrifice. Pagan was eighty years old at least and Luke was young and healthy, so he didn't turn on his heel and run, but it took an effort of will as the invocation to a dead god hissed through the surrounding silence. "Nama Mithras!"

The picture Berengaria was working on began to take on a lot more meaning, too, now he thought of it. A bright-haired god facing a foursquare soldier, in a dark space studded with columns and blurred by incense smoke, stalked by men in masks and robes who chanted to their subterranean deity. There could easily be robed worshippers in here, hiding behind the thick pillars, waiting to step out...

If Rufus wanted him to spend *one more minute* down here, he could bloody well come too, with a great deal more light, and preferably armed.

"It's marvellous, Mr. Pagan," he said. "His lordship will have the greatest admiration. I shall go and tell him all about it immediately."

"No! He has forbidden any use of the room, and you must not mention it to him. He called it a cursed and ungodly place." Pagan's voice dropped, as if trying to conceal the words from someone listening. "He did not want to hear of it again."

"This was when the Cathedral was built?"

"What? Cathedral? It is a mithraeum, not a place of the usurping heresy!"

Luke had absolutely no intention of pursuing that line of discussion. "I beg your pardon, sir. Shall we go?"

Twenty

RUFUS DIDN'T RETURN UNTIL THE LATE AFTERNOON, BY WHICH point Luke's nerves were twanging like an overstrung violin.

The day out looked like it had done him good. He was thrumming with energy, as he always was after activity, or seeing things go well, and the last thing Luke wanted to do was spoil his mood.

No choice.

"May I speak to you?" he asked. "In private."

Rufus closed the study door. "I trust you're going to tell me you found the money."

"There's something else. More important."

"I told you—"

"Your uncle tried to bribe me," Luke said, and launched into the story.

Rufus listened in silence, the exuberant look fading to be replaced by thunderclouds. At least Luke could blame Conrad for that. He gave the whole account as best he could, concluding, "I realise I'm asking you to take my word for all this, but it's the truth. If you confront Mr. Conrad, he'll tell you I agreed to his proposition." He braced himself. "I did."

"You agreed," Rufus repeated. "Keeping your options open?"

Luke tried not to wince. It was a fair jibe. "I wanted to find out what they were after, and what evidence they might have. But they only said *the parson's testimony*, and wouldn't tell me more."

"Meaning, the parson who performed the ceremony." There was a pulse ticking in Rufus's jaw. "So my father did marry Miss Brightling? But she denied it in the letter. What the devil is going on?"

"The Conrads are operating entirely by wishful thinking," Luke said. "Mr. Conrad has convinced himself that I am holding the truth about the supposed marriage over your head, and Mrs. Conrad insists I am not my mother's child, as if some other baby boy might have been left on the Doomsdays' doorstep that night. They can't bear the truth, so they're making their own. I wouldn't believe their so-called testimony if the parson in question is anyone less than the Archbishop of Canterbury."

Rufus shoved both hands over his hair. "I suppose not. Christ. And they want you to pay yourself for your services by stealing from me? God damn it, how much more of this must I tolerate?"

"None," Luke said. "Why are you not throwing them out? Bribing your staff to conspire against you, by stealing from you—"

"If Conrad has actual evidence, I will respect it," Rufus said. "But he can bloody well put it on the table for examination instead of skulking around like this. If he has proof—"

"If he had proof, he wouldn't need to bribe me. He's got nothing."

"I will ask him what he has. And you will not pretend to accept his propositions again. I don't want Conrad claiming you took his bribe. Your reputation matters too."

"I think I've put paid to that in this house."

"No," Rufus said flatly. "I will not have you do this. I will tell the Conrads you made that pretence on my behalf, and from now on, you consign them to the devil. You will not debase yourself on my account. I will not have it."

"I don't feel debased by lying to the Conrads. I feel as though it is the sensible way to find out what's going on."

"I don't want you lying for me," Rufus said through his teeth. "Will you understand that? I do not want it, and I will not have you compromised, or compromising yourself, in my name. Leave the Conrads to me."

But you can't handle them alone! Luke wanted to say, and bit it back. Rufus was a grown man and a perfectly capable one. He might be utterly useless at skulduggery, or too fair-minded for his own good—in fact he was both—but it was his decision, even if Luke felt, once again, that he'd been slapped in the face.

Rufus didn't want him working behind the scenes, because he knew Luke's shiftiness and hated it. Because he no longer wanted Luke as right-hand man; because those days were over. That was what it came down to, and if Luke didn't like it, he should have made a lot of different decisions.

"As you wish," he said.

Rufus went off to speak to the Conrads and didn't come back. Luke worked until past eight, fuelled by bread and cheese at his desk.

He went up to bed, since he had nothing better to do than read alone, and was deep in *Melmoth's* gloom when he heard exceedingly firm, not to say angry, footsteps heading up the stairs and into the Earl's Salon. He got up by sheer habit, and stopped himself outside the door, wanting to go in, wishing he could.

Rufus called, "Luke?"

He went in, hovering in the doorway. "My lord?"

"Don't—" Rufus began. "That is, uh. I just wondered if it was you. What have you been up to?"

"I went to the mithraeum today."

"Find anything?"

"I couldn't look around: Mr. Pagan was with me. I think he's anointed himself a Mithraic priest."

"Oh *God*."

"It was actually quite terrifying. He refused to give me the key, but he may give it to you, if he remembers who you are. Is everything all right?"

Rufus jerked his head, inviting Luke to come fully in. He did so, but didn't take his chair. That would be presumptuous. "The Conrads, of course. I wanted to speak to them but they were out until almost dinner time, they ate in their rooms, and when I went up there just now, they were having a sodding great row with someone. I could hear them shouting from half way across the New Wing. I dare say I shall find out what's going on tomorrow, but I'm so damned tired of this. If they can't do better, they might at least stop making things worse."

"I'm sorry."

"Not your fault."

"It is," Luke said. "Mine, and the Conrads, and more or less everyone in this house except you. You have done your best by so many people, and you ought not always be thinking what people want who never give a damn what you want."

"Nonsense. I'm doing my job."

"That's not true. Or, yes, you are, but you do so much more than that, and never with yourself in mind." He saw Rufus about to wave that away in the brusque manner that entirely failed to hide his heart, and Luke's own heart twisted unbearably. "You know you do," he said. "You always ask—asked—what I wanted. We always did what I like."

That landed like a stone in a still pool, ripples spreading outward. Rufus's lips moved silently before he managed, "Luke—"

"Let me say this. Please." Doubtless he shouldn't. Rufus had said they weren't lovers any more. But this needed to be said, all the same. "When we were—before, you never said what you wanted, you always let me tell you my pleasures, and I did. That wasn't fair."

Rufus blinked. "Are you under the impression I was denying myself?"

"You always put my wants, my desires first. You give, so much, and I just took, and that isn't right, and—" He threw caution to the wind. "And if you want something, anything, I want to give it to you."

Rufus was watching Luke's face, eyes searching and hungry. "What are you saying?"

"I miss you," Luke whispered. "I wish I'd done better. I know this won't change anything between us, I'm not trying to do that, but if there's anything, anything at all, you want of me, could I give it to you? Just tonight? Whatever you want, whatever you might need—"

"Luke." Rufus's voice was deep. "Giving you what you want *is* what I want. Hearing your desires and making them happen. There is—*was*—nothing that pleased me more in bed than when I pleased you. I would never do anything you don't care for, and if you're offering that as some sort of penance, don't do that to me. You should know I wouldn't do it to you."

Luke shut his eyes, wondering if he had anything left to get wrong. "No. I know you wouldn't."

Rufus gave a half-laugh that held no mirth. "And I don't have your imagination. I don't know how else one should do things."

"No other way," Luke said. "You do it perfectly. Do you recall, our first night, I told you to fuck me like you own me?"

Rufus's lips parted. "Uh. Yes."

"Then the truth—the real truth—is, I wish you did. I wish I was yours. And I'm not, and that's my fault, but still, I wish you would. Just once more."

"Luke..."

"It won't change anything," Luke said again. "I don't expect that. But I miss you so much, and it's the truth, and that's all I've got left."

Rufus reached out. He slid his fingers round to the back of Luke's skull, into his hair, staring down with unreadable eyes for a long, silent moment. Then he tugged Luke's head back, and kissed him.

It was a hard kiss, a reminder that there was no weakness in his kindness, and Luke opened to it with desperate thanks, feeling stubble rasp on his lips and chin. He didn't try to grab on, just let Rufus kiss him, until his earl lifted his head away.

"Lock the doors."

Luke darted to do that, the inner and outer ones. By the time he was back, Rufus had stripped off his shirt. "Get those clothes off."

Luke made short work of his shirt and breeches, kicking them away, and Rufus grabbed his arse, hoisting him up. Luke wrapped his thighs around Rufus's waist, arms round his neck, skin against skin. Coming home.

"Seigneur," he whispered.

Rufus carried him the few steps to the bed, and half fell onto it with him. Luke was on his back, legs still wrapped around Rufus, fingers digging into his shoulder blades, kissing with hunger and urgency, his whole body a howl of need. He could feel Rufus's stand, smooth and hot against him, and he rocked his hips for the pleasure of the moan it won him.

This might be the last time. The loss was unthinkable.

Rufus pulled his head away. "Luke?"

"Yes?"

Rufus stared down, eyes dark in the dim light. Luke stared up, lost. "Luke," Rufus said again, and put a very gentle hand to his scarred cheek.

Luke took a long, slow breath, let it out. Put his own hand to Rufus's and covered it, letting himself feel the odd lack of sensation around the hard, curved ridge. *No shame in scars.*

Eyes locked, fingers twining, bodies kissing from calf to shoulder. "Move up."

Luke squirmed obligingly up the bed, while Rufus grabbed the oil from his drawer. He kissed his way up and down Luke's body, along the dark gold trail of hair, taking his time. Luke had both hands on his scalp, fingers clutching and releasing.

Rufus was tracing his fingers over the inside of Luke's thighs, where the skin was smooth and near-hairless. He dug in, splaying his hands to grab as much as he could, mouthing the tip of Luke's stand in a gratuitously taunting way before taking him down.

Luke jerked underneath him, spluttering broken blasphemies. Rufus went to work, licking and sucking, and this wasn't at all what Luke had had in mind when he'd suggested Rufus do as he pleased, but if it pleased him... He lay back, relishing Rufus's lips and teeth, the ridges of his mouth and the press of cheek, the fact that he had this again. "Oh, Jesus God, so good. I'm going to—argh!"

That was because Rufus had pulled his mouth up and off, leaving his prick standing stiff and untouched. "Son of a—"

"Language." Rufus dripped oil into his palm, slicked a finger. Luke's head flopped back on the bed, and he shifted his legs apart. Rufus knelt over him, circled his entrance with a slippery fingertip, pressed in gently, pushing through the ring of muscle.

"Christ. More."

"Patience." He eased his finger all the way in, so the heel of his hand was against Luke's balls, his fingertip brushing the pleasure-point inside. Thank the Lord for big hands.

Luke jerked underneath him. "Fuck, fuck, Rufus, *please.*" His prick was weeping, a drip of viscous liquid sliding slowly down. Rufus leaned forward to lick it up, and Luke sobbed out a breath. "Jesus Christ."

"I'm going to do this until you're begging," Rufus said. "And then

I am going to fuck you, and if you can walk tomorrow it won't be my fault."

Luke stuttered enthusiastic assent. His whole body felt hot and tight, and Rufus's hands caressing and pressing were glorious and unbearable. "Oh God, please!"

"Please what?"

"Anything. *Please.*"

"You are mine, Luke Doomsday," Rufus said, a low rumble. "Mine by right. Mine by conquest."

Luke arched under him, urgent and needy, and Rufus leaned in and kissed him fiercely. He was hard and hot, pressed against Luke's skin. "Tell me you want this."

"So much. Please, Rufus. All of you. Jesus *Christ*, will you just fuck me?"

Rufus shifted, hauling Luke up onto hands and knees by main force. He knelt as Rufus grabbed the oil, cursing as he spilled it, slicked himself, grabbed Luke's shoulders. "You beauty. You beautiful— ugh—" He pushed in. Luke grunted at the entry, shifting to accommodate Rufus inside and over him. Rufus trapping him, or the pair of them trapped together in this beautiful, grotesque wooden cage.

Rufus was taking it slowly, whether for Luke's comfort or his own self-control. He got one hand round to Luke's prick, and Luke gasped pleasure at the weight that transferred to the other hand. He could take Rufus's weight forever.

"Christ. My Doomsday. End of my world."

"Hold me," Luke whispered. "Have me."

Rufus did both. They moved wordlessly together, only the sounds of pleasure: gasping and panting, flesh slapping, Luke's own unstoppable whimper at each thrust, Rufus's grunts of effort, until the timbre of those changed in a way he knew well, and Luke let go his restraint and gave himself up to sensation. "Jesus. Rufus, yes. Oh Christ, I love you, *yes—*"

He bucked violently, prick pulsing in Rufus's hand, emptying heart and soul and seed at once, and Rufus fucked him through the climax, fucked him as he spent and collapsed forward, and then kept going, harder now, driving into his prone, helpless body exactly as he'd needed, so that Luke was the one sobbing pleasure as Rufus came.

Rufus flopped down, flattening Luke to the bed so he could barely breathe. He was sweat-damp and boneless, his nose full of musk and dust. It was perfect.

Except he'd said—

Shit.

Rufus propped his forehead on the back of Luke's skull. "Do you need to move?"

He needed to run away, except that he was pinned on a medieval bed under fifteen stone of earldom and also, there was nowhere else he wanted to be. "No."

Rufus sighed, long and deep. "You said that wouldn't change anything."

Luke opened his eyes into the sheets, lashes brushing the linen. He didn't look round; he didn't want to make Rufus look him in the face.

Maybe he hadn't heard. Maybe he was pretending he hadn't heard. Luke wasn't sure which was worse.

He needed to answer. "I know it hasn't."

"No. Find your money. Tomorrow, if possible. We need this over with."

"Yes," Luke said, stifled.

Rufus kissed his neck. "But, for tonight…thank you."

⁂

Find your money tomorrow, Rufus had said. As though it were that easy. As though he even wanted to.

No, he did want to. He knew very well that if he turned down the chance to find ten thousand guineas now, he'd kick himself for it later. It was just...

It was just that, for all he'd said *This won't change anything*, he'd hoped it would. Not that Rufus would forgive him or ask him to stay, exactly, but that he might at least give Luke a little longer, instead of pushing him to find the money and get out.

You should have begged for his forgiveness rather than his prick, then, he told himself, and went off to find Mr. Pagan and ask for the sodding key of the sodding mithraeum, since that was what sodding Rufus wanted him to do.

He went through the New Wing to reach the Chamber Block, which meant he heard the shouting.

"Utterly disgraceful!" That was Rufus at full volume, and as angry as Luke had ever heard him. "Corrupt, dishonest, criminal, and cruel. How dare you? How bloody *dare* you?"

Luke fought the urge to stop and listen: he'd doubtless find out what that was about soon enough. He made himself walk on, fast enough that he couldn't be accused of eavesdropping, and up to Mr. Pagan's rooms to ask for the key.

Pagan gave him what in another man would have been short shrift—the monologue took about twenty minutes—flatly refusing to part with it. Luke contemplated stealing the thing, but decided Rufus would not like that, and in any case, his desire to explore the mithraeum alone was very close to zero. He retreated back through the New Wing, in which ominous silence now reigned, and encountered Emily.

"What's going on?" he demanded.

"You missed it? Ooh." She made a dramatic face. "The Conrads have been acting about, and no mistake. Seems like they went to Mr. Colefax—curate of Fairfield, Mr. Odo's lady friend's father—and told him to swear that he married Mr. Raymond to your ma."

Luke's jaw dropped. "They ordered a parson to perjure himself?"

"You know the Conrads," Emily said. "They said if he wanted his daughter wed to their son, a d'Aumesty, he'd do it. You know what they're like, probably expected him to kiss their feet while he was at it, and Mr. Colefax didn't like that one bit. He threw them out, so they told Mr. Odo he's never to see Miss Colefax again. They were barracking and hectoring him all last night, and you know Mr. Odo, poor man, he can't never stand up to them. He was crying all night, Miss Berry said. And then he got up this morning and went and told Lord Oxney the whole thing. Which is a lot more sense than I'd expect from him, but can't have been easy."

Luke remembered all too well the desperate, clawing need to please a parent who could never be satisfied, the dreadful shame of admitting that you were unloved, worst of all the sense of treachery in exposing any of it to others' scrutiny. "No. Not easy at all. Good for Mr. Odo."

"And your man went *off*," Emily said with immense satisfaction. "Oh, he was in merciful bad order, and talk about calling them over: I've never heard language like it. He was middling angry about you too. Said they'd tried to bribe you, is that right? Mr. Conrad started up about you taking money, and his lordship said you'd told him everything. He said you were a true and loyal friend, and Mr. Conrad was a rancid thieving shitbag. And you want the best part? He told them they've a month to pack their bags and get out."

"*Finally*," Luke said. "He's really done it?"

"Oh yes. Mrs. Conrad kept saying he couldn't, and Mr. Conrad started bellowing about the law, and his lordship wasn't having any of it. Berry said that was when she really understood he used to command an army. Or a regiment or whatever it is majors command. He's run out of patience, anyway. And he's taken Mr. Odo down to Fairfield to see the Colefaxes."

"God, I wish I'd seen it. Thank the Lord. I've thought he should kick them out since I got here."

Emily snorted. "Haven't we all."

Luke went back to the study, feeling decidedly fretful. The Conrads' eviction was long overdue, but he couldn't avoid the fear that Rufus was in a mood to get rid of people he didn't want.

He'd known that. Last night had changed nothing; he hadn't done it to change anything, or if he had, then he should have spelled it out to Rufus. Who would have doubtless refused him on those terms, so perhaps he should be grateful for that one last fuck and stop wishing for more than he was entitled to.

The thought of what he was entitled to came back with some force a little later, when Mr. Pauncefoot arrived.

"Mr. Doomsday," he said with distaste. "The undercroft key, with Mr. Pagan's compliments."

Luke blinked at the heavy iron key he deposited on the desk. "Why?"

"I understand you requested it earlier. It appears that we must all now bow to every one of his lordship's whims, or be deprived of home and livelihood. It seems that only servile obedience will do." Pauncefoot's voice vibrated with feeling.

"Very much like the last Lord Oxney, then," Luke said. "Everyone who's complained my lord is too different must be delighted."

Pauncefoot made an expressive noise and departed. Luke considered his options.

Rufus would have enough on his plate today, and for the near future. If Luke could put an end to his own business, as Rufus had repeatedly asked, perhaps he might then offer to help him through what would doubtless be a very unpleasant month of argument and high dudgeon.

That would be an excellent outcome. Whereas the opposite

course of action—avoiding the frightening underground temple—
might seem obstructive, and perhaps also a little bit spineless.

"Get on with it, then," he told himself, and set off to find what he
needed.

He met nobody on the way to the Chamber Block, which was
a relief: he didn't want the Conrads asking what he was doing. He
found the ancient door, and put the key in the lock. It turned with a
little difficulty because of the weight, but no stiffness. Clearly Pagan
kept the lock oiled. Probably he visited regularly. Luke was *not* going
to examine the top of the altar for bloodstains.

He was hesitating about going in, he realised. Nervous.

That was reasonable. For one thing, he might finally find the gold
he'd been dreaming of for thirteen years, in sufficient quantity to
weigh down his father's ghost for good. For another, there was that
fraction of a chance he'd find Adam Drake's body, which he'd long
discounted, but which came back to him now. For a third, it was the
subterranean temple of an ancient cult and he read too many Gothic
novels.

He pushed open the door and stood at the top, wondering if he
wanted the door open or closed behind him. Open would be an invi-
tation for anyone passing to walk in and see what he was up to, not
that anyone was likely to pass. Closed meant he wouldn't have a
clear exit.

Clear from what, he asked himself irritably, the monster in the
dark? The spectres of ancient Mithras-worshippers who hadn't even
worshipped here? Idiot. Nevertheless he left the door a little ajar,
ensured the key was safely in his coat pocket, and went down the
steps, lamp in hand.

The undercroft was as lovely as he recalled, and he concentrated
on appreciating the beauty, and not on the shadows that sprung and
danced from every column with every movement. He walked briskly

up the central aisle to the altar, and checked behind and around it to make sure he wasn't missing anything obvious.

He knew he wasn't. Pagan had been worshipping in here for Lord knew how long; even he would have tripped over a pile of gold by now.

Luke moved to the altar. The stone slab on top was relatively thin, though still massive. He could give it a try. He put the lamp down at a good distance so he didn't accidentally knock it over, examined the vertical slabs on which the top rested until he found a gap, got a good grip on the crowbar he'd brought, wedged the end under the slab, and heaved.

The slab didn't move. Luke put his full weight on it, lifting himself off the ground, and felt a shift. He leaned in hard, working the wedge end into the gap, and felt as well as heard the slab move three-quarters of an inch with a grinding screech.

He'd never be able to get this back on by himself, but he'd worry about that later. As long as it didn't fall off and shatter. He worked on, stripping off his coat after a few minutes because this was hard labour, moving the slab a little more each time. Screech. Grind. Screech. Grind.

It was the devil of a job. He couldn't help reflecting that Rufus would have managed it easily, with his bulk and strength. It took Luke at least half an hour to shift the slab so that there was a gap of something close to a foot, by which time he was exhausted. He sat on the brick floor to catch his breath and calm his thundering heart. Then he fished a candle end out of his pocket, lit it at the lamp, and leaned over the black hole that was inside the altar.

There was no obvious corpse, thank God and Mrs. Drake. He leaned in a bit further, awkwardly angled, trying to squint to the other end of a six-foot-long box while not dropping the candle, burning his hand, or falling in, and saw...something. Some huddled shape, something that the jerking candle flame picked out as not just empty space.

Hell and damnation: he'd started at the wrong end, and he'd never be able to push the slab back the other way. If he tried to turn it sideways, perhaps? No: the leverage would be near-impossible, and also his shoulders sobbed at the idea of more work.

If, on the other hand, he climbed into the altar...

Luke took a moment to reflect on how little he wanted to do that. Then he reminded himself that this was not a real altar and Mithras not a real god, and also that being trapped in stone sarcophagi was a thing that happened in *Melmoth the Wanderer* rather than Romney Marsh in 1823.

The altar was not quite two feet wide, a little over three high. He had pushed the slab to create about eleven inches of clear space. If he got in and squatted down as low as he could with his back to the end, he should be able to duck his head under the slab. He could then crawl forward, find out what was stacked at the far end, reverse the movement, get back into a squat, and work his head up again.

He went through it in his mind a couple of times and found it good, or as good as any plan that involved crawling into a stone tomb would ever be. He tried out the motion with his back to a pillar, hunching low and then leaning forward to crawl out flat.

It would work if he had enough room to get his head under the slab. If he didn't, he'd just have to move the stone another couple of inches. His arms screamed at the thought.

He stepped into the tomb—altar, damn it—squatted low, and ducked his head. There was very little sideways space, and his hair rasped against the slab at the top, but he just managed to get under. He reversed the movement immediately to be sure he could get out, because he'd feel stupid if he trapped himself in a Mithraic altar and died.

It worked. It was tight, but he could do it. Thank heaven he wasn't bigger.

He retrieved the candle stub that he'd left on top of the altar, then squatted down, and worked his head under the slab. He folded down to his knees and slid forward, candle in one hand, weight on his forearms and elbows.

At the far end of the altar's interior was a heap of canvas sacks. Luke reached out and touched. His fingers pressed against thick, rough, dusty material, and felt hard edges. He pushed harder, and heard coin shift and clink.

He'd found it.

He'd found the fortune he'd dreamed of for thirteen years. The guineas his father had been killed over, and Gareth nearly murdered for. The money for which he'd betrayed Rufus.

He'd once thought this moment would be triumphant. Instead, he flattened his hand against a dirty old sack of metal that had cost him everything, and grief hit him like a runaway horse. He lay on his front in the cold stone darkness of the desecrated altar, shaking with sobs that rang dully off the encroaching walls, for himself and Rufus, for a future without the ambition that had driven him all his adult life, for all the misery this damned money had caused and everything it couldn't buy.

He heard nothing else until the voice.

"Good God. He's in there."

Luke opened his wet eyes, as a sharp voice called his name. "Doomsday?"

It was Conrad and Matilda. Hell's teeth.

"Doomsday, I say!"

There was absolutely no way to explain this. "Mrs. Conrad," Luke said, trying for his blandest, most secretarial voice, from inside a pagan altar. "If you'll give me a moment to come out…"

He hunched himself up to start inching back. There was a frantic low-voice conversation outside. Then the stone slab over him scraped and moved.

Luke jolted up without thinking and cracked his head on the stone. He swore through a whirl of stars, and the slab scraped again, over him, making the tomb perceptibly darker. *Closing.* "Hey! Stop! I'm in here!"

"Indeed," said Conrad.

Shit. Luke wriggled onto his back, with a panicked urgency that knocked the candle-stub over. He could see light through the gap at the end of the altar, but that gap was perceptibly smaller than it had been.

He wouldn't be able to get out.

"*Stop!*" he screamed.

The stone screeched again. The gap was down to barely eight inches. A low voice said, "My lord, I don't think—"

"Quiet, Pauncefoot." That was Matilda, coming closer. "Doomsday, you *will* tell me now. What proof have you of the marriage?"

"*What?*"

"A marriage certificate. The name of the parson," Conrad said. "You have something. What is it?"

"Let me out of here," Luke snarled. "I'll tell you if you let me out."

"You mistake," Matilda informed him with cold pleasure. "We will not bargain. You will tell us what you know about Oxney, at once. Or…" She let that hang.

"Or what?"

"Or we will leave you here." Conrad's voice. "In the dark, underground, alone, for as long as we choose. And nobody will hear you, nobody at all, not if you scream and beat your fists all night. You will be alone, and you will die alone, in the dark."

There was a dreadful quality to his voice. Luke didn't know if it was glee or horror or something else; he could barely hear for the blood thundering in his ears.

"You're mad," he managed. "You can't do this. People know I'm here."

"Pauncefoot," Matilda said. "He will not help you. Have you found the key, Pauncefoot?"

"In his pocket, my lady."

Jesus Christ, they were going to lock him in. "Lord Oxney will be furious," he tried, trying to bite back the panic in his voice.

Conrad made a noise of contempt. "He has conspired with my son against me, the rightful earl. He denies my birthright. This is *war.*"

"Give us the information we need. What is it you know about the draper's boy? Where is the proof?" Matilda's voice rose high. "Tell me the proof!"

Luke gave a frantic second's thought to a plausible answer. *I have evidence of the marriage, but I got my mother to write a false letter claiming it never happened as part of my plan to steal a fortune...*

It was too damned convoluted. They wouldn't believe him. And, he realised, they wouldn't release him, no matter what he claimed or promised, because they already knew that he would cheerfully lie to them and stay loyal to Rufus. Because Rufus, with his bloody, bloody honesty, had told them so.

"Let me out and I won't say anything to Lord Oxney about this," he said, keeping his voice calm. "It's the best I can do. Really, you can't just leave me here indefinitely. What would that achieve?"

"This is your last chance, Doomsday!"

"I've nothing to tell you," Luke said. "He's the true earl. And he will have your skin for this."

"You are a fool," Conrad said.

There was another dreadful scrape. Pauncefoot made a noise

of protest. "Put your back into it, man," Matilda ordered. "Push. Together."

Stone screeched, and the light was gone.

Luke could see the faintest possible glimmer from the gaps where the slab didn't rest quite level. He could hear urgent voices in quiet argument. Then the voices receded, and the last light went, and he was alone.

Luke wasn't generally afraid of the dark; he'd done many a run on moonless nights, but that had been outside. This was different. It was so utterly black that he could almost see shapes, as though his mind was trying to create something out of nothing. He shut his eyes in case that helped. It did not.

He was entirely helpless, trapped in a stone box under a slab far too heavy to move. He tried anyway, squirming back round to his knees and bracing his shoulders against the slab, pushing with all his might until he saw stars, to no effect at all.

He slumped forward onto the hard, worthless sacks of gold, entombed in stone, and silence so absolute it made his ears ring, and the choking darkness of the grave.

Twenty-one

RUFUS WAS HAVING AN EXHAUSTING DAY.

Odo had come to him that morning with reddened, dark-ringed eyes, blurting out his sorry tale. Mr. Colefax had refused to oblige Conrad and Matilda with perjury, and they had forbidden the match in contemptuous terms. The curate had sent Odo a note, stiffly declining to link his family to the d'Aumestys under any circumstances. That showed a deal of courage, Rufus felt: he had heard more than enough about his grandfather's vengeance when his family was crossed.

There was courage, too, in Odo's plea for help, fighting off a lifetime's subservience, refusing to accept what his parents had done in a way he must know would incur their hatred. Luke had had that courage, Rufus found himself thinking, and it spurred his wrath to the point of explosion.

After the hurt and confusion and tangles, it was a relief to have a straightforward and unequivocal wrong to be angry about. Conrad and Matilda had gone a great deal too far, and Rufus could do on their victims' behalf what he'd hesitated to do on his own.

He'd given Conrad and Matilda their notice to quit, in no uncertain language. If consequences pushed them into an understanding of their wrongdoing, he would give Conrad use of some property, something far enough away from Stone Manor that he need not see them again. He had no desire to put them into hardship, but they could not be permitted to carry on this course.

That decision made, and communicated at full volume, Rufus took Odo off down to Fairfield to seek reconciliation. It wasn't immediately forthcoming, since Mr. Colefax was highly offended: Conrad had assumed he was so desperate to marry his daughter off to a d'Aumesty that he'd perjure himself to do it, and Mr. Colefax rightly took that as an insult to them both. But Miss Colefax lit up like a candelabra when she saw Odo, winning a smile from him that made him almost handsome. She was earnest, awkward, plain, and took a great interest in ecclesiastical history. They would be happy as sandboys, Rufus thought, and added an extra fifty pounds to Odo's salary on top of his apologies and assurances.

It worked. The engagement was resumed; Rufus stayed for luncheon, and listened with goodwill to Odo and Laura's mutual account of how they fell in love over the parish records of thirty-whatever years ago. Mr. Colefax then turned the discussion to current affairs, and gave Rufus some enlightening insights on affairs at Woodruff Farm, one of his nagging problems. It was a highly successful mission, if a tiring one, and left Rufus, as he rode back with Odo, in a state of bitter envy that someone wouldn't come along and solve *his* problems for him.

Of course, Luke had done that, until he became the problem.

Luke, Luke, his apocalypse. Half of Rufus wanted to shake him till his teeth rattled; the other half to hold him close and tell him it was all right, he was forgiven, he was wanted, he belonged. Rufus had no idea which course of action would be better. Maybe he should do both.

He'd never had much truck with shades of grey. A man was honest or dishonest; a course of action was right or wrong. Luke Doomsday had upended all his certainties. Rufus believed in honesty as the bedrock for relationships of whatever kind; Luke had lied to him consistently, deliberately, and outrageously, over weeks, drawing a poisoned line through friendship and intimacy. It was the worst betrayal of Rufus's life, and he wanted to forgive it so much that he had to curl his toes inside his boots to set his will.

Because Luke had also been true to him. He'd done so much, worked so hard, was still working on Rufus's side. He'd made himself vulnerable, and Rufus understood enough to appreciate what that had cost him.

He'd also said *I love you*, and Rufus was not even going to consider that now.

They could not slide back into their previous relations as though nothing had happened. When Luke found his money, he'd be able to do as he pleased, and Rufus would decide his own course based on what Luke pleased to do. And if a part of him didn't want Luke to find the bloody money because a man with ten thousand guineas had no need to drudge as a secretary in a damn fool draughty ancient shack on the edge of Romney Marsh—well, that was Rufus's shame, and to be kept firmly to himself.

All that said, he needed to speak to Luke on his return. To tell him about the events of the day, to hear whatever observations he'd make that would doubtless bring events into startling clarity, and also because of last night.

Won't change anything, indeed. Balls. They'd needed one another with a clawing urgency, and Luke had said—what he'd said—and Rufus had pretended not to hear because he hadn't known how to respond. And then he'd been occupied with family affairs all morning and not so much as spoken to Luke, after he'd laid himself bare—

Shit and derision. He should have spoken to him, shouldn't he? Even just to say *Good morning* and *we'll talk later*. Not just tupped him, and told him it changed nothing, and left him alone, stewing over what must feel like a rejection.

The thought of it clutched at Rufus's heart. He took the last part of the ride to Stone Manor at a canter, and found himself striding through the hall to the study at some speed, as if a few seconds saved now would make a difference to the fact he'd slept with Luke last night and then not spoken to him all day. Mother of God. Idiot.

Luke wasn't there and, somehow, it didn't feel as though he'd just popped out. The books on the desk were closed, the papers neatly stacked. Rufus nevertheless waited long enough for it to be clear he hadn't gone to the privy, and emerged to find Pauncefoot in the corridor.

"Have you seen Doomsday?" he demanded.

Pauncefoot's head reared back. "I, uh—the secretary?"

"Who else?"

The butler recovered himself. "I understood he had left the house."

"Left? Where for?"

"I could not say, your lordship. I believe I heard one of the footmen mention that he had gone."

Rufus waved him off, frowning, and headed round to the stables, where the grooms assured him all the horses were accounted for, and Mr. Doomsday hadn't passed by all day.

Perhaps he had gone for a walk. But it was hard enough to make him get fresh air in the working day, and he'd been doing punishing hours since his return.

Well, Rufus had told him to find the money. Maybe he was looking for it.

Maybe he'd found it and gone. The thought came on Rufus

suddenly, and with it, a rush of fears. Suppose his agonised confession had been as much lies as his initial parade of honesty and vulnerability, just another way to get back into Stone Manor, and this time with Rufus's blessing to search the place. Suppose he'd initiated last night as some sort of farewell fuck, and gone without a word because he had only cared for the money, all along—

No. He would not persuade himself of Luke's guilt just because he'd been guilty before. If you gave a man a second chance, it should *be* a chance. He was making a wild fuss about nothing, and Luke was probably upstairs in his room for some reason that would seem perfectly good once explained. Rufus headed to the Manorial Hall accordingly and hurried up to the second floor.

Luke's door stood open, and his room was a mess.

Gone, Rufus thought again, but that wasn't right. His clothes were there, and a handful of books, but they were scattered over the table and even the floor, with papers in drifts across the desk. That was not how Luke kept his things.

There was something damned odd here. Had someone searched his room? Or had he gone in a hurry? But he could see *Jonathan*, splayed on the floor; Luke wouldn't have left that behind. And he'd have needed a handcart at least to take the money. Someone would have noticed.

What else might he be doing? Rufus cudgelled his brains, and came up with two thoughts: either he was in the undercroft, searching for his treasure, or Berengaria had got hold of him for a sitting.

Yes: one of those was surely the answer. Simple as that, he told himself, ignoring the matter of Luke's room, and strode down and along to Berengaria's studio. He walked in without knocking, which was an error, because the maid Tallant—Emily Doomsday—was sitting on a stool, naked to the waist.

Rufus spun around, too late, to a chorus of high-pitched feminine ire. "My apologies," he repeated several times, his back to the ladies, hand over firmly shut eyes. "I beg your pardon."

"Never mind that. Don't just walk in when I'm drawing!" Berengaria said furiously. "I'm so sorry, Emmy. I should have locked the door."

"Not to worry, miss," Emily said. "I beg your pardon, my lord."

Given she'd just shrieked at him to fuck off, Rufus had to admire her poise. Probably that would be a sacking offence for most masters; he felt she'd expressed herself with admirable clarity, and wasn't about to argue with a bare-breasted lady in any case.

"Entirely my fault," he said. "I beg your pardon. Let me know when I can turn round."

"Keep facing that way and leave," Berengaria suggested acidly.

"I need a minute of your time. It's important."

Berengaria made the hissing noise she'd used on Fulk. Emily said, "I'm decent."

Rufus turned cautiously. "Miss Doomsday. Do you know where your cousin is?"

"Luke? Not in the study?"

"No. He's not anywhere he ought to be."

"I saw him this morning," she said. "He wasn't up to anything I know of."

"Mph. Where's the undercroft?"

Berengaria blinked. "Why?"

"He may be there. I want to find him. I'm concerned."

Berengaria and Emily glanced at one another. Berengaria said, "We'll show you."

They took him down to the Norman Chamber Block, and a flight of steps down to a great, dark door. Rufus tried it, to no effect.

"It's always locked," Berengaria said. "Pagan has the key."

"He might have given it to Luke. But would he have locked himself in?" He banged on the door with his fist. "Curse it."

Emily gave him a sharp look. She wasn't like Luke in appearance, but the expression was oddly familiar, all the same. "Is something wrong, my lord? With Luke?"

"I don't know. I want the key."

"I'll go and get it if you think it's important," Berengaria said. "Pagan will give it to me; he won't remember who you are."

She went off. Rufus glowered at the door. "I'm going to feel a blasted fool if he wanders round the corner asking what I'm up to," he muttered.

"That's Luke all over," Emily said. "He's a right one for turning up."

"Would he—" Rufus began abruptly.

"My lord?"

"When he left you, your family. After his father cut him, and he moved in with Sir Gareth. Did he say goodbye?"

Emily stared at him. "He told you about that?"

"It, uh, came up."

"Came—up," she repeated. "Of course, my lord. Well, it wasn't goodbye really, then, he was just at Sir Gareth's. It was when he went to school he did that. Just went away, gone. We knew he was going off but not when and Joss didn't warn us. Said that's what Luke wanted." She paused. "Reckon he was wrong. *I don't want goodbyes* is the sort of thing Luke says, but it's not what he means."

This was the kind of thing that left Rufus, a straightforward man, hopelessly adrift. "Because he means instead—?"

"He means, *I'm scared you don't care, so I'm not giving you a chance to prove it,*" Emily said. "He's that way, Luke. Aunt Sybil says he's hard to love but it's not true. What's hard is making him see it when you do, because he's already decided you don't."

Rufus stared at the solid door in front of him, not really seeing it, because all he could see was Luke, last night. The whisper of *I know this won't change anything*, and his own stupid bloody agreement that it hadn't.

"Shit," he said, and then, "I beg your pardon, Miss Doomsday. Tallant. Which do you prefer?"

"Emily's fine. My lord, I want to know where my cousin is. You're putting me in a twitter."

"If that means you feel anxious, so do I." Had Luke gone to prevent Rufus sending him away? "He hasn't taken a horse. Where would he go on foot?"

"On the Marsh? To Sir Gareth, and he's not walking there, lazy wretch," Emily said, then turned as quick footsteps approached: Berengaria, scowling. "Got the key?"

"I do not," Berengaria said. "Pagan says he gave it to you, Oxney."

"Nonsense."

"No, I thought you'd remember. He then said he gave it to your messenger."

"You mean, to Luke?"

"I couldn't tell. He started rambling about a fellow who used to work for Grandfather, and I couldn't get any more sense out of him. But it's not in the accustomed place, so he gave it to *someone*."

"Then why isn't it open?" Rufus thumped the door again, producing a dull thud. "And where the devil is he?" He slammed his fist against the door a third time, this time with real force. "I will—"

"Ssh!" Emily said sharply.

Rufus turned to her, astonished and not a little outraged to be ordered about by the housemaid, and saw her face, sharp and tight. "Hear that?" she demanded.

"What?"

"Hit it again, hard as you can, and keep your mouth shut this time."

Rufus contemplated her, and then took a step back and gave the door a powerful kick, foot flat to the wood. He held his breath as he did it, and this time he thought he heard something. A faint, very faint, sound.

Emily shoved him out of the way without ceremony. She knelt, lips close to the keyhole, and let out an owl hoot, astonishingly piercing. A second later, Rufus could swear he heard the faint sound again, two distant, barely audible notes.

"He's in there," Emily said. "And in danger. Not trouble: *danger*." She pointed a savage finger at Rufus. "You, kick that door in, right now. Hear me?"

"Don't be ridiculous," Berengaria said. "You'd need gunpowder. Or a locksmith? If we send to Rye—"

"I said right now!" Emily snapped. "Or I'll send for the Doomsdays to do it!"

"I can break down my own doors," Rufus said. "Get me an axe."

Berengaria rolled her eyes. "For goodness' sake, both of you. The wood will be hard as iron, not to mention those iron bands. Breaking it will take forever."

"Then I will start now," Rufus said. "Axe!"

Emily ran. Berengaria looked after her, shook her head, and said, "I've a better idea."

She hurried back towards the New Wing, leaving Rufus alone for the longest few moments of his life. He restrained himself from kicking and shaking the door, knowing it would be a waste of energy. He wanted to shout down to Luke, didn't know if he could be heard, called anyway. He intended to get his hands on whoever had locked this door.

Emily was back first, panting as she heaved an axe that wasn't much shorter than herself. "Here."

There wasn't much space to swing in the stairwell. The fear and frustration flowing through Rufus's muscles made him feel like he'd have the door down in three strokes, but Berengaria had been right: with the ancient wood and iron bands, this would be the very devil of a job.

He hefted the axe to begin it, and heard a cry.

"Oxney!" Berengaria was approaching at a very brisk walk, dragging a bewildered Odo with her. "It's all right. I've brought Odo."

"You..." Rufus was momentarily speechless. "*Why?*"

Odo looked nervously at him. "Uh, can I help?"

"Doomsday is locked in the undercroft," Rufus said, with all the calm he could muster. "Have you a spare key to this door, at all?"

"Oh—ah—no. No, I don't think there is one."

"Then bugger off and let me break it down!"

"Well, if you like," Odo said. "Or you could take the other way in?"

⁂

"Is this a priest's hole?"

"We're not Catholics, Oxney."

Odo had brought him into the New Wing, to a dusty lumber room. In that was an unassuming door that opened to reveal a cupboard, which had a hatch at the back. Odo had lifted it and they were both crawling through, Rufus second. They both had lamps; Rufus had brought the axe.

"Well, what is it, then?" Rufus demanded.

"It was built in the Civil War. We were Royalist and Kent was mostly Parliamentarian."

"And who knows about it?"

"Me. And you, now. To be honest, I liked having somewhere that nobody could find me."

Rufus followed him down a narrow, creaky wooden staircase that did well to take his weight, along a passageway that had him bending double and cursing. He wanted to ask where they were going, but the silence felt very heavy.

They came to a door. "You can barely see it from the other side," Odo said. "Not if you didn't know it was there. Awfully clever." He unlatched it.

They emerged into a higher space, though the ceiling was still low, a mass of thick stone pillars. Rufus called, "Luke?"

There was a muffled, echoey cry. Rufus hurried forward, and saw what looked for all the world like a pagan church. There was Berengaria's absurd painting of the bull business, a stone altar before it, and a pile of cloth. He picked that up, and saw it was Luke's coat, discarded on the ground.

"Luke! Where are you?"

A ghostly, echoing voice called back, "The tomb!"

Odo gave a squeal of fear and clutched Rufus's arm. Rufus shook him off. "He's not dead, you bloody idiot! Where's the tomb?"

"There isn't a tomb!" Odo yelped. "It's a cellar!"

"Rufus!" Luke called, and he sounded desperate. Trapped. In—

"Christ alive." Rufus strode to the altar, ignoring Odo's "But that's not a tomb," and banged on the stone slab. "Luke?"

"Rufus! Help!"

"What the— I'm opening it."

Now he looked, the top was a little off centre. He wedged the axe blade under it, hoping the metal was well forged, and leaned hard. The top shifted with a squeal.

"Rufus!" Luke almost screamed from within. "Get me out!"

"I am. Move down, if you can: the blade might snap. Cover your face. Odo, help me!" He applied more force, all he had, jammed the axe handle into the gap he levered up, and then pushed like hell, grunting breaths, muscles bulging and straining.

The lid scraped again and moved an inch or two, aided by Odo's spindly efforts. Not enough. Rufus dropped the axe and put everything he had into pushing, bellowing like a bull until his muscles strained against his shirt and he felt the slab begin to tip. He shouted a warning as it slid and crashed to the floor.

Luke was curled on his back in the stone coffin, hands over his face. "Luke!"

He moved his hands and looked up, and Rufus simply grabbed him, heaving him out of that accursed box and into his arms by main force.

"Odo," he said over Luke's shoulder. "Get out. Go and tell Emily Doomsday he's safe. Now! No, leave the fucking light!"

Odo fled. Rufus barely waited for him to go before he slid to his knees, gripping Luke hard, kissing his hair because it was all he could reach. "Jesus. Jesus Christ. Are you all right? What the *devil?*"

"Oh God, oh God, don't let go. Rufus. No, I am not all right. It was so dark," Luke said into his shoulder. "So dark and so quiet and they left me in there—"

"Who?"

"Conrad, Matilda, Pauncefoot. Don't let go!"

"I won't." Rufus was trying to hold all of Luke in his arms at once. It wasn't physically possible, but he didn't let that stop him. "I will not let you go, I will never let you go. I have you. You're safe."

Luke made a tiny noise, and burrowed into Rufus's chest. Rufus tightened his grip. "Did they hurt you?"

"They trapped me in there. I don't know how long it's been. I didn't know if they were going to come back, and I didn't know if you'd come. I waited for hours and you didn't come!"

Calm, Rufus told himself through the roaring in his ears. Shouting and swearing wouldn't help. "I'm here now. Why did they do that?"

Luke took a shuddering breath. "They wanted information against you, to prove Conrad's case. That's what he said, at least, but I think it was mostly spite. I'd fooled him, and he's lost, and he doesn't like it."

"He'll like what I'm going to do to him even less."

"Same," Luke said savagely, and sounded like himself again in that vengeful word. "I will make them *regret* this."

Rufus kissed his hair. "That's my Doomsday. My own—Christ. I thought you'd walked out. Left me without saying goodbye."

"No!" Luke looked up sharply at that, twisting to see his face in the lamplight. "Rufus, no. I would not."

"I know. I thought it anyway, and I couldn't bear it. God damn it, I'm putting my foot down. You invoked droit du seigneur: well, I am exercising it. You asked for my protection, so you are mine to look after, and I am taking no more nonsense from you, Luke Doomsday."

Luke's lips parted. "Uh...how?"

"Last night, for one thing. 'This won't change anything', indeed."

"It didn't. Did it?"

"No," Rufus said. "Because I loved you before, and I wanted you before. But also yes, because you told me the truth. I think you've been telling the truth all along, even when you were trying not to."

Luke's eyes were huge. "I lied. You know I lied."

"You said when we first met that you needed a place. You do, don't you? A place you belong, and that's here. You made this house somewhere I could live. You made some of my family people I could live with."

"You did that, not me."

"But I didn't see how to do it without you. We make things work together. This is your place along with me, and you ought to be here. You ought to be here and safe and loved, and ruling the roast like the overreaching little swine you are, and I will do anything in my power to give you that if you just stay with me. That's an order. I'm begging you. *Please.*"

Luke swallowed. "Truly?"

Rufus cupped his face. "My Doomsday. The end of my world."

"Oh God." Luke gave a little hiccuppy noise. "This is dreadful. I only meant to seduce you so I could find the money and look what you did."

"What?"

"Seduced *me*. You've got my balls and my spine and my heart and my soul in the palm of your hand, and I love you desperately. I wish I'd said weeks ago, I wish I'd told you—"

"And instead you re-invented your handwriting to make my life a little easier. For God's sake, stop talking."

He enforced that with a kiss. Luke strained up into Rufus's arms with glorious urgency, twisting and clutching, wrapping himself around Rufus in the way he did, ivy on oak, and Rufus kissed him until Luke was no longer shaking and his body was warm in Rufus's grasp.

Luke nestled against him. "God. I heard you, you know. It was so dark that I was seeing things, and so quiet that I kept thinking I heard your voice. And I'd call out, and realise I hadn't really heard, and that was—"

"Stop. You're safe."

"I am now. How did you find me? Was that Emily?"

"Yes. What was the hooting about?"

"That's our night-call, the Doomsday signal. It carries well. I heard her calling out for Doomsdays, or I thought I did, so I replied."

"She heard you say you were in danger."

"I was. And you came. Christ above, Rufus, you came for me."

"I always will, but never get yourself into such a situation again. How the blazes did they put you in there?"

"I was already inside. Pauncefoot gave me the key: he said it was on your orders, though I suppose they had wind from Pagan that

I was searching in there. I thought the gold might be hidden in the altar, you see. But I couldn't move the slab far, so I had to get in to look, and it was too tight to turn round, and then they pushed the lid back, over me—"

"Ssh. It's all right. Was it in there?"

"Yes."

"What?"

"Yes. It's there. I found it."

"You found your *gold*?"

"Don't expect me to be excited," Luke said. "I already lost you over it, so to discover I was going to die for it—Joss was right. It's ill-omened."

"Nonsense," Rufus said. "You never lost me, and you're not dead. You read too many novels."

"I'm not reading another Gothic novel as long as I live. At least there weren't amphibians in there."

Rufus didn't ask, just kissed him. "I don't know what best will help you—if you want to talk about it, or not talk about it, or what-have-you. Tell me, and I will do what I can. But what would make *me* feel better is to go upstairs, find every one of the bastards who did this, and throw them all out of my fucking house."

"I think that would help quite a lot," Luke said. "Let's."

Rufus gave him an arm to get up, dusty and crumpled and tearstained and perfect. He straightened his own clothes, and picked up the axe.

There was a patter of light feet, approaching fast. Luke looked round sharply. "Who's there?"

"Goldie!" It was Emily, sprinting along as best she could with a lamp. "Luke, thank the Lord." She dumped the lantern and leapt at him for a violent hug. "You rotten brat, you put the heart across me. You all right?"

"Fine. I'm going to murder Mr. Conrad."

"Why?"

"He shut me in that thing."

She looked at the tomb-altar. "He what? Oh, that son of a— Ooh, Joss'll have something to say about *that*. Want me to get the Doomsdays?"

Luke flicked a glance at Rufus. "No. I've all I need."

"Thought you might," she said. "Best get on, then, acause Berry asked me to say, my lord, you should come up quick. It's all going d'Aumesty up there."

Twenty-two

RUFUS HAD MANY TIMES HEARD THE PHRASE 'HE CAME OUT swinging'. It generally referred to a boxer's fists, but there was a lot to be said for an axe.

The family were all in the hallway. Conrad and Matilda were standing tall, facing off against Berengaria and Odo, all of them shouting. Fulk, lounging off to one side, was looking around in a disgusted fashion, so he was the first to see Rufus, Luke, and Emily arrive.

Rufus held the axe in one hand. It was a very large axe with a long handle, extremely well suited for making a forceful point, and he enjoyed the excellent balance as he swung it. Fulk's face changed. "What the—"

"Everybody, be quiet." Rufus gave the swing a little more power. "I am out of patience. Conrad, Matilda, explain yourselves."

"I have no idea what you mean." Conrad sounded blustery.

"Don't give me flannel. First you tried to bribe my secretary, and then you shut him in a stone tomb to, what, die?"

"Of course we did no such thing," Matilda said.

Rufus choked. Odo spluttered. "Mother, I saw him!"

She waved an irritable hand. "A fuss about nothing. Merely a warranted chastisement. He would have been released already, had you not interfered."

"Liar," Luke said clearly.

Her jaw dropped. Conrad shouted, "Mind what you say!"

"I know exactly what I'm going to say." Luke sounded unnaturally calm. It gave Rufus the sense of something imminent, a storm cloud moving in. He instinctively shifted his grip on the axe. "I wonder if you do."

Matilda gave him a disdainful look. "What a to-do over a jest. Oxney, your behaviour and language—"

"A jest?" Luke said over her. "Jests are funny. I wasn't laughing when you shut me in the undercroft." He looked at the Conrads, from one to the other. "Do you think Lord Stone laughed when you did it to him?"

Conrad's lips parted. Matilda said, coldly, "Ignore him."

"As you ignored your brother?" Luke was dirty and dishevelled, his bright hair dulled by dust, the scar livid against his pale face, but his brown eyes were predatorial and his lip was savagely curled. "You ignored him when he screamed, didn't you? When you locked him in and he begged you to let him out, when he wept with terror. You said to me that you'd leave me in the dark, underground alone. *And nobody will hear you*, you said, *not if you scream and beat your fists all night.*" He extended his hands, dusty but unbloodied. "Did he beat on the undercroft door all night, begging to be released? Did you listen from the other side? Did you hear the silence when he stopped?"

"Oh, bettermy," Emily said softly, with an anticipatory bite in her voice.

"You dare not say that." Conrad's face was white.

"He hated this house, and darkness, and you let them kill him for you. Didn't you? Was that a jest? Did you shut him in there to hammer on the door and scream till he died of fear, and tell your-selves it was a *jest*?"

"He was a coward and a fool," Conrad said through stiff lips. "Afraid of the dark, at his age. Contemptible."

"Conrad!" Matilda barked. "You will be silent, Doomsday. This is slanderous. Nothing of the kind happened. Why would Conrad harm his brother?"

Everyone present gave some variation on an incredulous noise. Luke grinned with teeth. "Because he was ordered to. Weren't you, Mr. Conrad?"

"Ordered? Who by?" Rufus demanded.

"His father," Luke said. "Mr. Odo asked the old Lord Oxney why he treated Mr. Conrad with such loathing, and he said...?"

"Henry the Second." Odo's voice was thin. "He said—Grandfather—he said he was Henry the Second."

"And you believed he was talking of the king's trouble with his sons. But he wasn't, was he?"

If Luke developed a taste for obscure historical references, Rufus might run screaming. "What does that mean?"

"Henry the Second was the one who fell out with Thomas à Becket, the Archbishop of Canterbury. He said, in anger—" Luke gestured at Odo.

Odo moistened his lips. "He said, in anger, 'Who will rid me of this turbulent priest?' Henry's knights took it as instruction, and they went out, and k-killed Becket. Doomsday—"

Luke swung back to Conrad. "What did Lord Oxney say to you about the heir who planned to destroy Stone Manor? 'Dear God, would that I were rid of him'? Is that what you thought he wanted, really? Because you did it anyway. You rid Lord Oxney of that tire-some son who just happened to be a tiresome elder brother standing in your way, but you got no thanks for it. He cut off your funds, he put the son you despised in charge of your money, and *that's* why you didn't act when he wouldn't give you the power to run the estates. That's why you did nothing as he neglected the lands. He hated and despised you for what you had done, and while he lived, he could punish you. And you thought you could just wait for him to die and claim your prize, but he had one last vengeance up his sleeve. The best of all."

"Me," Rufus said. "That's why he didn't tell them about me over all that time. Because he *wanted* them to have that shock."

"To live in the expectation and have it snatched away," Luke said with terrible pleasure. "To think you had won everything and lose it at the last hurdle. He wanted that misery for you, Mr. and Mrs. Conrad, because you murdered his son and he hated you."

Conrad looked like a standing corpse. Matilda said, "You may not repeat these lies. I will have the law on you. Baldwin died outside, in the storm."

"No, his body was found outside. You could hardly have him discovered in the undercroft: nobody would believe he'd gone down there of his own accord. Did you drag his corpse out, and leave it to get wet, and hope the rain kept up?"

"Nonsense."

"No—but—" Odo's voice was shaky. "The morning we found Baldwin, I saw Father and Pauncefoot come in from the rain, soaking wet, and Mother wiped the floor after you. I didn't know why she didn't leave it to the staff. I didn't understand. But I saw."

"Oh God," Berengaria said on a breath. "No. No. Father?"

"He was a fool!" Conrad shouted. "A damned cowardly fool! He would have destroyed Stone Manor! We had to do it!"

Berengaria put both hands over her mouth. Fulk looked as though he'd been slapped. "But surely— Mother, no. Surely it is not true."

"We did nothing wrong. A mere jest, a temporarily closed door. And if the consequences happened to be—" Matilda gestured dismissively. "It was best for the Family. For you."

Fulk turned away. Berengaria stood like a statue, arms drawn in on herself, white-faced. Odo gave a breath like a sob.

Matilda glared round at her children. "I will not be judged. How dare any of you comment on my actions! This man is a scoundrel—"

"Silence," Rufus said, in a tone that brooked no argument. "I've heard enough. Someone bring Pauncefoot to me, now. Doomsday, a word." He pulled Luke off to a corner. "Are you sure, and can I prosecute?"

"His heart gave out," Luke said. "I don't know if frightening a man to death is murder, or how we could prove it. Unless they confess, but I doubt Mrs. Conrad will let Mr. Conrad do that, once she gives him a talking-to. I don't see it working, and I think it would be very messy for them." He nodded at the cousins. "But if you want to try, I'll do my best."

Rufus considered that, then turned back to the room in general and clapped his hands. "All right. Conrad, Matilda? Get out."

"What?"

"Out. Now. You are not welcome in my house or on my land. I will order the carriage for you in three hours, which gives you time to pack, and that will be supervised, so don't take anything that's not yours. It will carry you to, oh, Ashford, and from there I don't give a damn what you do. Leave, forever. Don't come back."

"Oxney—" Fulk said.

"No. Nothing about this house or family is good or healthy and I am cleaning it out. Ah, Pauncefoot," he added as the butler arrived. "What did he do, Doomsday?"

"Brought me the key to lure me down there. Helped shut me in the tomb."

"Altar," Odo murmured, as if compelled.

"And then lied about it to me," Rufus said. "You're sacked, Pauncefoot. Give Doomsday the keys unless you want them taken off you, you treacherous lickspittle."

Pauncefoot was stuttering. "It wasn't—my lord, I didn't intend—"

"You helped shut him in an airless stone box in an unused cellar, and you helped conceal the manner of Baldwin's death. Get out of my sight and be grateful for the clemency. You can share the carriage to Ashford or walk." He glanced round. "I don't know why you miserable swine are all still here. Go!"

"Wait," Fulk said. "What do you propose my parents live on?"

"Mrs. Conrad has a hundred a year," Luke said. "There's many families on a great deal less."

"But you cannot expect—"

"They will not have another penny from the estate, and I have no interest in their objections, their well-being, or their future," Rufus said. "Come on, shift."

"No!" Matilda shouted it. "We will not be abused by this ill-bred impostor! We will go to the law. To Lord Lympne. We will bring a suit for slander and theft of our property, of our title, we will teach you what it is to threaten a d'Aumesty—"

"For God's sake!" Berengaria cried out. "We all heard Father. We all know now, and—stop this, stop shouting and bullying, please, just *stop!*"

Matilda turned on her with a savage look. "You treacherous slattern, you were always a viper in my bosom. Currying favour with the draper's boy—do you hope he'll wed you? Is that it, you ridiculous scarecrow, that you have finally found a man with sufficiently poor taste?"

Berengaria flinched back from her stabbing finger. Rufus said, "Doomsday."

"My lord?"

"I recall you mentioning that if you were imprisoned in the castle dungeons, your family would take it poorly."

Luke's eyes widened. "I—may have said that, my lord, yes."

"Well? Get on."

He'd often thought Luke looked like a fallen angel. The expression on his face now was of one with no remaining tint of heaven. "Thank you, my lord. Yes, I expect the Upright Man will want to know."

"I'll fetch him now," Emily said, with a lethal snarl in her voice. "I'll tell Ma Doomsday myself. Oh, we'll *pay* you, for every bit of this."

She took a pace toward the Conrads, which Luke mirrored. It looked extraordinarily menacing, somehow, a pair of stalking polecats.

"Two hours down, two back," Luke said. "Four hours at most till the Doomsdays come, and that brings us close to nightfall. If I were you, I wouldn't be anywhere near the Marsh by then. Because if you think Lord Stone was a fool to be scared of the dark..."

"You wronged a Doomsday." Emily's voice was soft. "My little cousin, you thought you'd harm. If you're still here by nightfall, we'll come for you."

Matilda looked more baffled than anything. "What? You dare not touch me."

"We'll do anything we like," Emily said. "Who's to stop us? Take you on a skimmity ride through the Marsh. Backwards on a donkey, Mrs. Conrad, with people throwing mud and clanging pots at the pair of you for brother-killers. How about that?"

Matilda's jaw dropped. Conrad shouted, "You insolent wretch!" and raised a fist. Rufus hefted the axe towards him. Conrad lowered the fist.

"Life's more fun on the powerful side, isn't it?" Luke said. "No more of that. The Earl told you and the Doomsdays are telling you: get away from the Isle, and stay off the Marsh. There won't be another warning."

"For God's sake, Oxney!" Fulk said. "You can't permit this!"

Rufus shrugged. "They picked this fight."

"I am the rightful earl!" Conrad shouted, his voice very shaky. "I am Lord Oxney! I earned it! I *deserve* it!"

"They stopped rewarding murder with titles a while ago," Luke said. "And very few titles go by desert. And, Mr. Conrad? You will never, *ever* be earl. I will not let that happen, as my name is Luke Doomsday. Trust me for that." He grinned nastily at the gaping man. "Help Mrs. Conrad pack, Em. I'll come with you, Mr. Pauncefoot. I'd hate the silverware to go missing."

Conrad and Matilda left on time, after all, with a number of hastily packed trunks, which Emily and a couple of allied housemaids had searched with enthusiastic malice. They hadn't troubled to send to Dymchurch. The threat, or the realisation that they could be threatened, had knocked the wind out of the Conrads' sails.

Rufus and Luke watched from the windows of the Earl's Salon until they'd gone, until the bustle in the hall emptied, and the door shut, and the sound of wheels and hooves moved off down the drive.

Rufus breathed out hard. "Is this right?"

"I don't see what else we can do. It's so long ago and we can't prove anything."

"I was thinking of how I'm foisting them on some other unfortunate town."

"That too," Luke admitted. "But all their privilege and power and their inflated self-worth hung from their position. Once they're out of the Manor without wealth or connections—they're not young, a hundred a year, no family to call on, and I can't imagine they'll make friends. They'll turn on one another soon enough, and it won't be pretty."

Rufus gave him a sideways look. "You did say you'd have your revenge, didn't you? Apocalypse. How did you find out, or guess, about Baldwin?"

"The story never felt right, but I only realised when I was in that blasted cellar. I was imagining being locked in—I'd been reading *Melmoth*—and I thought I would die of fear if that happened, and it came to me then that perhaps Baldwin had. And then of course they actually locked me in there, which rather confirmed it."

"Though you didn't die of fright." Luke had been trapped in the stone box for close on two hours, they'd worked out. Christ alone knew how long it had felt, not knowing if he'd be rescued or released. "Whereas poor bloody Baldwin—what an end."

"I blame your grandfather," Luke said. "And the years of inbreeding, obviously, and Conrad and Matilda's grotesque overweening pride, but in large part your grandfather. You can't keep people under your thumb like that and not squash them out of shape."

"True. I'm going to ask Berengaria if she's interested in travelling. Meeting artists. Getting out of the house."

"With Emily as chaperone?"

"If you think so."

"I do, and I'd also suggest you promote her to lady's maid with immediate effect. Miss Berengaria would appreciate it."

"Do it. God, this is a bad business for her, and Odo, and Fulk, too. Do you know, Fulk apologised to me earlier? Said he'd felt the earldom had been stolen from him by my appearance, and now he was grateful for the fact. To know his mother had connived at Baldwin's death to clear his path—"

"I wouldn't feel too guilty, were I him," Luke said. "She wanted to be countess a great deal more than she wanted Fulk to be earl. But it's good he said that."

"Yes, there's hope for him yet. Christ alive, there's a lot of damage to be repaired in this house." Rufus reached for Luke, resting an arm round his hips. "I don't know what I would have done through all this without you. I wonder if I might have ended up in a stone coffin myself."

"Not without a fight, I'm sure."

"Remind me: you did find the money? I wasn't dreaming?"

"I did. It's in the tomb. Altar."

"Damn fool thing. How on earth did you work that out?"

Luke gave him a look. "It's a big stone box that's hard to open. What better place to leave valuables?"

"Not now the top's off," Rufus said. "We'd better go and make sure it's safe. I want you to have it."

"Why?"

Rufus turned to him, and ran a gentle thumb over the face that turned up to his. "You wanted control of your life. You want a home, and a safe place, and to put the past to rest, and to help Sir Gareth. I want you to have all of that."

"You've already given me most of it," Luke said. "Everything except Gareth, and he can look after himself. Truly, Rufus, the money stopped mattering a long time ago. I hate to sound like a bad Gothic romance, but I came to Stone Manor searching for treasure, and found—"

"You sound exactly like a bad Gothic romance."

"I could sound worse. Remind me to tell you about the ruined chapel sometime. I love you, Rufus, unspeakably. I know I hurt you, and I'll always be sorry, but I'm not going to forget how badly I hurt myself doing it either. I felt like I'd pulled my heart from my chest. I want you to love me, and me never to make either of us feel like that again, and if I have that, I've got everything."

"I'm sure I made myself clear on this subject," Rufus said. "Droit du seigneur, remember? You're mine, Luke Doomsday, and I'm keeping you. I love you. I've never loved like this before, and I'm not sure I could do it again: it's only you, for good or ill. God help me," he added.

Luke leaned into him with a little satisfied sigh. "That's all I want. I don't need the money."

"I know."

"But, since you *do* love me, and there *is* that ten thousand guineas just lying around—"

Rufus grinned at him. "Let's go."

Luke had already regained the key. They went together to the Chamber Block, armed with lamps, and Rufus stayed by Luke's side as they went down the stairs. They stopped under the arch, looking around.

"Good God." Rufus hadn't paid attention to the architecture on his previous visit. "This is quite the place."

"It's beautiful," Luke said. "I think it's the loveliest part of the house. Or it would be, if—"

"I doubt there's a stone of this building that hasn't seen pain and death," Rufus said. "Eight hundred years of d'Aumestys: God knows why we don't have ghosts. Could we bring light in somehow? Dig one side out, put in windows? That might make it more useful, and enjoyable."

"And nobody would be trapped down here in the dark ever again," Luke said, which was indeed what Rufus had meant. "I could find out if it's possible. Also, Rufus?"

"Mmm?"

Luke grabbed him, tugging his head down, and kissed him. "I adore you, seigneur."

The tomb, or altar, whichever, stood gaping open. Rufus had feared to find the guineas gone, but there they were, a set of canvas bags. Luke untied one, took out a handful of gleaming gold, and let the coins run between his fingers.

"Thirteen years," he said. "Three dead men. Four, if you count Drake. Five, if you hadn't come for me. I could have died with the guineas in my hands, and I'd never have lived *that* down."

Rufus hoisted a bag out with a grunt. "Ten thousand guineas. That's a hell of a sum. What does a rich secretary do?"

"I should think he goes back to work. There's so much to be done."

"Really?"

"Well, in the long term," Luke said. "He might take a day off, I suppose, here and there. If he had someone to take a day off with, and perhaps a bed worth taking it on."

"Is my bed worth taking it on?"

"Considering how often I've taken it on your bed," Luke began.

"Vulgar," Rufus said sternly. "Why don't you have a day off now, or two? I think we need to breathe."

"Oh, but the Woodruff Farm repairs," Luke objected, with a great deal more provocation than sincerity.

Rufus dropped the gold and grabbed him. "Day off. Now. That's an order."

Luke let himself be pulled over, falling willingly into Rufus's arms. "Yes, seigneur."

Epilogue

TWO DAYS LATER, THEY WENT DOWN TO VISIT GARETH.

Partly this was to deliver the money. Five thousand guineas to be invested for Cecy's boys and Gareth's goddaughter, little Charlotte Doomsday. It would be a start in life for the children, and a weight off Gareth's mind, and a fraction of what Luke owed him.

Luke would keep the other five thousand. He'd earned it, in a way, and it made Rufus happier to know that his lover and secretary was a man of independent means who could stay or leave at will. A choice, he'd said, as if Luke had a meaningful one of *those* where Rufus was concerned.

He'd flipped a single golden coin into the Canal where the thorn tree grew, and hoped his father's shade enjoyed it.

And now he was here to collect his things. Tench House had been his home a long time, so he'd left a lot here when he went offmarsh. He'd be moving it all to Stone Manor tomorrow.

Catherine and Gareth made Rufus welcome downstairs while Luke packed. After a while, he heard footsteps.

"His lordship is in the garden frightening the children, as you may hear from the shrieks of glee," Gareth said, coming in. "We've acquired Simon and Charlotte as well."

"Did they smell Catherine baking all the way from Globsden Gut?"

"They usually do. With five of them on him, it's starting to resemble a bear-baiting." The two Doomsday children, Tom's son and Sophy's daughter, were inseparable from Cecy's boys, and had a knack for appearing at any hint of fun, or cake. "That's an exuberant man you have there."

"He's had a hard few months," Luke said. "And a hard few weeks, and frankly not a wonderful few days. He deserves a bit of fun."

"I think he's having it. How are things?"

"Emily is keeping Miss Berengaria steady. She didn't like her parents, but this has hit her hard. Mr. Odo is being strong for Miss Colefax, and she's letting him, bless the woman. Actually I don't think he's as shocked as all that. When you spend most of your time in the eleventh century, possibly you expect people to behave in an eleventh-century way."

"Good God."

"Stone Manor," Luke said with a shrug. "Mr. Fulk's taking it worst: his mother had a hold on him. But at least he's not blaming Rufus. Oh, and Rufus's family, his real one, will be coming to visit, we hope: he wrote to invite them, so things will be livelier then. It's going to be all right, I think."

"I'm very glad," Gareth said. "It sounds as though Oxney deserves a rest. I do like him, and I've waited a very long time to see you happy, you little wretch. Er, you should know Joss is also downstairs, allying with Oxney against the children."

Luke dropped the papers he was picking up. "You're joking."

"Let me get those. No, not at all. They hit it off at once."

"Really? Thank God. I wondered if they might, actually. They both like people who get things done."

"Quite. I foresee an unholy alliance." Gareth stooped for the papers on the floor as Luke stacked books in his trunk. "You're taking everything?"

"Rufus wants the Manor to be my home."

"Good. There will always be a room here if you need it, but... good. Also, you owe the Revelation a visit."

"I know, I know. I'll go soon."

"So you always say," Gareth observed. "As a gentleman of property—are you going to tell everyone about that?"

Luke had been considering that himself. "Did I tell you, Emily was set to have the Doomsdays storm Stone Manor when I went missing?"

"Of course she was, and thank the Lord she didn't. I had to sit on Joss to stop him going after the Conrads as it was. Did you doubt they'd act for you?"

"No. No, I knew they would. Only—what Emily said—she was going to do it for me. Not just for a Doomsday, for *me*."

"Of course she was," Gareth said again. "For a clever man, you can be remarkably obtuse sometimes."

"I have realised that. Joss said the other day that the Doomsdays had never mended what Elijah broke between us, them and me. And that wasn't wrong, but...well. The truth is, I wouldn't let it mend either."

"No," Gareth said, very much as if this was not new information to him. "That's true. It wasn't your fault, or not entirely, but it's true."

Luke sighed. "I've spent a deal more time thinking about what I wanted to gain, and resenting what I didn't have, than noticing what I actually had. *That's* obtuse."

"It's a not uncommon habit of mind."

"Rufus doesn't do it," Luke said. "He lives in the moment. I suppose it's a soldiering sort of habit, but it means he's ready to let bygones be bygones in the most astonishing way. I'll have to keep track of all the slights and grudges for him, otherwise Lord knows what people will get away with."

"I feel quite sure you're up to that task," Gareth said, grinning.

Luke stuck his tongue out. "Anyway. No, I don't think I want to flash the money about." He turned back to his trunk, and heard Gareth shuffle papers together. "To be quite honest, I mostly want it to sit quietly in my bank where it can't cause anyone any more trouble ever again. Rufus says that's rank superstition."

"It probably is, but I agree with you," Gareth said. "If you ask me—"

He stopped there. Luke, who was trying to make two stacks of different-sized books be the same shape, didn't register that for a moment. "Yes? Ask you what?"

"What is this?"

His voice sounded different. Luke turned and saw Gareth was holding a paper. He reached for it.

I, Louisa Ann Meadows, born Louisa Ann Brightling, married Raymond d'Aumesty on 26th July 1789. The marriage was conducted by special licence, carried out by a parson from Winchelsea named Dr. Topher, with the permission of my father. It was a lawful and consummated marriage. I can produce the licence, and will testify to that effect.

Louisa Meadows

"What," Gareth said. "*What.*"

"Oh, that. I got her to write two, that's all," Luke said. "One saying she did marry him, one she didn't. So I could play my hand as seemed best."

"For heaven's sake. You really are entirely unethical, aren't you? And clearly you get that from your mother, if she—" He paused, then said slowly, "If she was going to make that claim. Which would mean committing perjury, for which she could be gaoled...and the claim would be worthless in any case if she couldn't produce proof... I don't believe you. Or rather, yes, you had her write two, but—God above. This one is the truth. Isn't it?"

"Gareth—"

"Don't lie to me," Gareth said. "Don't you *dare*."

Their eyes locked. Luke set his shoulders. "Suppose it is true. What then?"

"It would make you the earl!"

"Maybe, maybe not. Maybe they wouldn't want a smuggler's bastard in the House of Lords and they'd find a way to give the estate to Conrad, who set his brother to die in the cruellest manner imaginable. Or maybe they would give it to me, and what sort of earl would I be?"

"You would be perfectly good," Gareth said hotly.

"I'd be efficient. Nothing like Rufus. He cares, he wants things to go right, he gives people chances. He deserves the title and he'll wear it well, so I'm going to make damned sure he keeps it." He ripped the letter as he spoke, into long strips. "And he doesn't *ever* find out about this, hear me?"

"You aren't going to tell him? Do you not think he should have the choice?"

"There wouldn't be a choice," Luke said. "He's honest, Gareth, in the deepest sense of the word. He'd renounce the earldom on the spot. If I tell him, either I will enrich myself at his expense, or I will give Conrad all that power over the estates, and their people, and his family. Well, I'm not doing the first or risking the second, and especially not so I can bleat, *But I didn't want to lie to you.* I *don't* want to lie to him, but that's my problem. Sod the truth."

"And the marriage laws?"

"Sod them too. You and Joss can't marry, and I'm nothing because my parents didn't marry, and Rufus should be dispossessed because his father married for five minutes. What's the good in any of it?"

"Underpinning the entire system of inheritance on which our society is based?" Gareth suggested. "Don't tell me: sod that as well. Lord Oxney is having an effect on your language, you know. What if this comes out?"

"It won't," Luke said. "Nobody else knows. I already wrote to Louisa to burn the licence. And I will deny everything on a stack of Bibles if I must. This never happened."

They stared at one another. Gareth was silent for a long moment, then shook his head. "I said you had no ethics. Clearly you don't. But you do have morals, albeit very Doomsday ones, and—oh, come here." He gave Luke a hard hug. "I'm proud of you."

Luke hugged him back. "Thank you. Thank you for everything, Gareth, always."

"Just keep living up to yourself." Gareth let him go. "And come down soon. From the sound of things outside, the children are winning. Your earl needs you."

Luke paused to listen, heard Rufus's deep laughter mingling with Joss's rich, warm chuckle, and Charlotte's high-pitched shriek of, "Charge!"

"They're hopelessly outnumbered," he said of the earl of Oxney and the smuggling prince of Romney Marsh. "I can't let that stand."

The packing could wait, he thought as he ran down the stairs, preparing to launch a surprise wolf attack. Everything could wait. Because Rufus, unquestionable earl of Oxney, was outside laughing in the sun, and Luke's place was gloriously, perhaps a little unethically, but quite irreversibly at his side.

Go back to where it all began with
The Secret Lives of Country Gentlemen, *available now.*

One

FEBRUARY 1810

KENT WAS STILL THERE.

Gareth had tumbled into the Three Ducks with his lungs burning from walking too fast in the cold night air, his face instantly reddening as the warm fug of the taproom assailed him. He didn't even know why he'd hurried: he was over two hours late and he'd told himself the whole way that Kent would have left already. If the situation were reversed, Gareth would have decided his lover for the night wasn't coming and left cursing the man's name. He'd fully expected Kent to do the same or, even more likely, find another warm body to go upstairs with.

He'd come anyway because...well, *because*, that was all. Because it was rude to miss an appointment, because he had nowhere else he wanted to go, because he hoped against hope that just this one thing might not be taken from him today.

And there Kent was, unmissable, the only man in a room crowded with men. He was sitting with a mug of ale and his feet up on a stool, chatting to the landlord without a care in the world. Then he looked round at the door and smiled, and the sight of him took Gareth's remaining breath.

The landlord slouched away as Gareth came to the table. "I'm so sorry I'm late."

"Watcher, London." *What cheer,* Gareth had worked out that phrase meant: Kent's version of *good evening.* Gareth would have been furious in his place, but the smile in Kent's warm golden-brown eyes looked entirely real. "Thought you weren't coming."

"I didn't mean to keep you waiting so long." *Thank you for staying,* Gareth wanted to say.

Kent waved a hand before he could go on, dismissing his failure to appear as though it didn't matter at all. "You look fraped. Everything all right?"

Gareth didn't know what *fraped* meant, but he had no doubt he looked it. "Not really. No. It's been rather a bad day. Terrible, really."

"Here, sit down. I'll get you a drink and you can tell me about it." He rose from his seat.

"No, don't." Gareth regretted the words as he spoke them. He would have liked very much to have a drink with Kent, to pour out what had happened and the bewildering uncertainty that now surrounded him. Except that if he tried to explain anything he'd have to explain everything, and he didn't want to do that. To present himself as a pitiable object, an unwanted thing, to easily confident Kent who didn't look like he'd been rejected in his life, then to watch him be repelled by the stench of failure, as people always were—No.

Anyway, Gareth had better ideas of how to spend the evening than brooding about his dismal situation. He had the rest of his life for that. "It doesn't matter. Could we go upstairs?"

Kent's thick brows angled. "In a hurry?"

"It's late. And I was looking forward to seeing you."

Kent frowned, just a little. Gareth probably didn't seem a particularly desirable prospect, sweaty and flustered as he was. Fraped, even. He reached for Kent's mug of ale, watching those glowing brown eyes watching him, and took a long, deliberate swallow.

"Thirsty?"

"In need," Gareth agreed, and dragged the back of his hand over his mouth in a meaningful fashion.

Kent's lips curved. "Better?"

"Getting there."

"Suppose we might as well go up, en."

The Three Ducks made the back room and the dark covered courtyard available for illicit fumbling and spending. Gareth knew the spaces well, having come here many times over the years. He'd always assumed the upstairs room was private, but Kent, who he'd never seen in here prior to this week, apparently had the privilege of using it. Perhaps he was an old friend of the landlord. Or perhaps it was just that smile of his, that wide, irresistible grin that sluiced you in happy anticipation and confidence and sheer joy of living. Gareth had gone down poleaxed at the first flash of that smile. He wasn't surprised the Ducks' taciturn landlord couldn't resist it either.

They crashed into the upstairs room together, already kissing wildly. Kent was strong, with broad shoulders and taut muscle, several inches under Gareth's height but a lot more solid, and he moved with all the confidence of his smile. He planted a hand on Gareth's arse, pulling him close, and Gareth sank into the sensation with a flood of relief.

Fingers grasping, lips and tongues locking, the press of thigh against thigh—Gareth got both hands into Kent's long, loose curls, the strands so thick and strong by comparison to his own flyaway hair. He held on hard as Kent kissed him, and felt Kent's smile against his mouth.

"London," Kent murmured. "I want you bare."

Gareth let go with a touch of reluctance: he liked Kent's hair. But Kent liked him undressed, so he stood as Kent pulled first coat then waistcoat off his shoulders; raised his arms obediently as Kent tugged his shirt over his head.

He'd worn trousers and shoes partly because the Three Ducks was not a place to dress well, partly because Kent dressed like a working man, and mostly because they came off easily. He kicked off his shoes, inhaled as Kent unfastened the buttons at his waist, and bent to peel off his stockings.

And there he was, exposed to Kent's gaze in the golden lamplight. It had felt very odd the first time he'd stood naked like this under Kent's scrutiny. He'd never been fully bare with a lover before Kent. Surreptitious fumblings in dark corners didn't come with the luxury of time, or of more undressing than necessary. And he had no idea why Kent liked to look at him so much. Gareth was nothing special: tall but thin, pale and uninteresting. He wouldn't have noticed himself in a crowd, whereas a man could look at Kent's firm, fit body and that outrageous smile for hours.

Yet there was no mistaking the heat in Kent's eyes when he stood back and examined Gareth, and the frank appreciation tingled like a touch on his skin.

"Hearts alive, you're a pretty one," Kent said, voice a little deeper than usual. "Ah, London."

Gareth breathed the feeling in: naked, exposed, offering every inch of himself up and waiting for Kent's touch. His prick was stiff at the thought. "Christ," he said. "I love it when you look at me."

"Makes two of us."

Kent moved forward, slid his hand over Gareth's chest. It was narrower and far less impressive than Kent's own broad muscles, but Kent didn't seem to mind. His fingertips were light. Gareth quivered under the feathery touch as it roamed his skin, and couldn't help a gasp as Kent's hand finally closed around his jutting prick.

"Eager," Kent murmured. "You ready for me, London?"

"Whenever you are." Kent was still fully clad. "If you're joining me, that is."

"Oh, I'll be doing that."

Kent was smiling. Gareth smiled back, and his heart was pounding every bit as hard as the blood in his groin.

He'd only come into the Ducks last week for a drink with like-minded company. Of course he'd have taken a bit of pleasure if any offer came his way, but he'd have been perfectly happy with a mug of ale and a chance to breathe out from another day. He'd looked around to see who he knew—and then he'd seen *him*.

A working man, by his dress, in a long dark leather coat. Tawny brown skin; thick, wavy black hair loose to his shoulders; a faint shadow of black beard; a generous mouth. He was talking to a pretty youth of very similar colouring, and as Gareth watched, he had thrown his head back and laughed.

Yes, Gareth had watched. Stared, even. Very well, he'd gaped like a hopeless fool, but one didn't see a man, a smile, like that every day. He'd still been looking when, unexpectedly, the man had glanced over, and their eyes met.

Gareth had looked away at once, embarrassed and annoyed at himself for the needy display. He'd carefully stared into the opposite corner of the room to mark his lack of interest, until a throat was cleared close to him, and he realised someone was standing by his chair. Not just someone. *Him*.

"Watcher," he'd said. Gareth's cheeks instantly flamed because he'd unquestionably been watching, but the man went on without a pause, "Wondered if you might be wanting company."

That was bewildering. Was he being mocked for gawping so obviously?

The man gave him a quizzical look. "Did I startle you? You look like a sighted hare."

Gareth had no idea what that meant and it sounded oddly bucolic for a London alehouse, especially in that country accent, with broad vowels and a roll to the 'r'. It didn't matter, because the man, this man, was *talking* to him.

He managed a smile that he hoped didn't look too idiotish. "I beg your pardon, I was in a brown study. I'd love company, if you'd like to join me."

The man took a stool. "I will, en. What's your name?"

Gareth winced. "Uh. Um, I don't usually, here—for discretion, you know—"

"No names? Got you, beg pardon. I'm Kentish."

"Well, hello, Kentish," Gareth said, pure instinct. At least part of his brain was still working.

The man's eyes crinkled responsively. "*From* Kent. I meant, we're friendlier down there."

"I don't know. Londoners can be quite friendly, in the right circumstances."

"I bet you can." He smiled, and the dazzling force of it close up rocked Gareth in his seat. "You're London, then? Nice to meet you, London."

Gareth smiled back, hopelessly enthralled. "You too, Kent."

They'd left the question of names there; they'd had better things to do. Kent had obtained the luxury of the upstairs room—private, comfortable, no unexpected puddles of stale beer, drain-water, or worse—in about five minutes, and Gareth had been naked for him two minutes after that. Naked and delighting in it, as though Kent's physical confidence and frank enjoyment were contagious.

They *were* contagious. He rejoiced in his own body and in Gareth's. He laughed, he set out to please them both without shame, or fear, or second thoughts, and Gareth, who was usually consumed by shame and fear and second thoughts, all but forgot them in Kent's company.

They'd met every night since and it had been the most joyous week of his life, this unexpected, gleeful, frank pleasure. Kent's admiring looks, his capable fingers and strong arms. His smile.

Gareth stood now, bare and erect, as Kent stroked and kissed him till his prick was leaking and his knees were weak. He undressed Kent with shaking fingers, in awe of the magnificent solid muscle, loving the rich look of Kent's warm brown skin against his own city pallor. He went to his knees on the bed, and cried aloud as Kent held his shoulder and fucked him with little urgent whispers—"You're lovely, London, so lovely"—and when it was over he buried his face in the rough mattress to hide his sudden urge to weep.

Kent's arm came over his waist. "You all right?"

"Yes. It's—I'm very well."

Kent stroked Gareth's spine. "You've a nice back. Nice arse, come to that."

"Well, you certainly came to it."

Kent chuckled. "So I did."

Gareth stretched luxuriously. Kent's breath came hot against his back in an exhalation. "London?"

"Mmm?"

"I've got to go."

Gareth's stomach plunged. "Already?" he said, and hated the plaintive note he heard in his own voice. "Sorry. Of course. It was my fault for being late."

Kent gave him a little squeeze. "Not right now. I meant I'm going home."

Gareth's eyes snapped open. He stared at the wall. The heat of rutting was fading from his skin and he felt quite suddenly sore, and sticky, and stupid. "To Kent?"

"To Kent. I've finished my business here, and I've a lot to do there that won't wait."

Of course he did. Of course he was going back. Gareth could feel his cheeks heating, not so much at Kent's words as at his own foolishness in not anticipating this. He'd lived in a continuous present of *see you tomorrow* without thinking about when it would end—how had he not thought about when it would end?—and of course that wouldn't carry on. Of course Kent had been planning to walk away all along.

"Yes, of course you must. Have a safe journey. It was good to know you."

The words were well enough, but the tone sounded horribly false in his own ears. Kent, lying against his back, went still, and then took hold of Gareth's shoulder and tugged until he was forced to roll over and face him. "Good to know me? What's that mean?"

"Well...goodbye? Isn't that what you were saying?"

"I was saying I've got to get home. Doesn't mean I can't come back. I have business here, regular-like. I'll be back in April, reckon." He brushed a finger over Gareth's cheek. "Wondered if you'd care to meet again."

Gareth's chest clenched tight. "Meet? What do you mean? How?"

"The usual way? You tell me your name and how I reach you. I write you a note and say I'll be here on such-and-such a day. You turn up. I turn up. Maybe we make a bit more time for a drink and a talk first. Have a bite to eat." He cocked an eyebrow, lips half smiling, eyes full of easy confidence: a man who absolutely expected his week-long lover to be waiting for him in two- or three-months' time.

The enraging thing was, Gareth wanted to. He could already imagine the heady anticipation as April approached, the thrill of unfolding a note with shaking fingers and walking into the Ducks to the greeting of "Watcher, London"...

That was easy to imagine. Fantasies always were. But he could also imagine the slow-dawning realisation as April ticked into May and no note came, or ever would, because Gareth might have amused Kent for a week but that meant nothing. He wouldn't write; he wouldn't come, and Gareth didn't wait for anyone any more.

"I don't wait," he said aloud.

Kent blinked. "I didn't mean you should save yourself for me. Just, if you wanted to meet again, I'd like to see you."

"Why?"

"Acause we get on? Or I thought we did till about two minutes ago. There something wrong?"

There was everything wrong. Gareth could feel it building in his gut. He knew this dance, being constantly put off by assurances of a future that would never be fulfilled, where he'd plead and cajole for scraps, crumbs, any attention at all, and it would never, ever come.

He was being pushed away with promises again, told to wait for a little while that meant forever, *again*, and his stomach knotted on the thought.

"I don't think so." The words came out hard and clipped, but not needy. He *wasn't* needy. He didn't need this.

"Don't think—?"

"I don't think we should meet again. This was all very enjoyable but we both have things to do." He sat up, swinging his legs over the side of the bed, turning away.

The mattress shifted under him as Kent moved too. "Enjoyable? London—"

"That's not my name."

"You didn't want to tell me your name," Kent pointed out. "I asked."

"Yes, well, perhaps you should take that as a hint." The roiling in his gut was getting worse, and he needed to leave. Leave, not be left. He rose and reached for his clothing. "I didn't tell you my name then and I don't intend to now. I doubt we'll be crossing paths again, so thank you for a very pleasant week's diversion. Let's leave it at that."

"Hold on. Wait. You mind telling me what's got you in a twitter?"

A *twitter.* The word sounded belittling, as if Gareth was making a fuss about nothing. "I am not—whatever that means."

"You seem middling upset to me. What's wrong?"

He sounded as if he meant it. As if he didn't understand what he'd done and wanted to make things right, as if Gareth could sit back down on the bed and explain it all, and give him his name and tell him about today—

No. Absolutely not.

"I'm not upset," Gareth said. "Why would I be upset? I'm leaving, and so are you, so there's nothing more to be said."

"Is this acause I said I had to go back? London, if I've put you in a dobbin—"

The betraying blood rushed to Gareth's cheeks, bringing anger with it. How *dare* Kent assume his leaving would upset Gareth? Who the devil did he think he was, the cocky swine? And if he thought that, could he not have the decency to keep it to himself instead of piling on added humiliation by making a great fuss about it? "I have no idea what that word signifies, and it might be easier if you spoke the King's English. I am leaving, since you ask, because your proposal of exchanging names—rather, my trusting you with my identity—isn't terribly appealing and I consider matters are best left here. I'm trying to do this without causing offence," he added, in the coldest tone he could manage, "so I'd prefer not to spell it out further."

He heard the thump of Kent's feet hitting the floor. "If that's you trying not to cause offence, I don't want to see you pluck a crow. What the blazes do you mean, trusting me with your identity?"

Gareth pulled his trousers up with a jerk and fastened them with shaking fingers. "All I want is to leave without any more trouble."

"Who's making trouble?"

"Well, I'm not." Gareth dragged his shirt over his head. Putting clothing back on was a lot more troublesome and less enjoyable than taking it off. "So if you're not, there's no more to be said, is there? I hope you have a pleasant journey back."

"You said that already. Are you always this maggotty and you were just keeping it quiet before?"

"There's no need to be rude."

Kent made a choking noise. No, Gareth told himself, not 'Kent'. That wasn't his name. Nobody was called Kent, any more than they were called Somerset or Hertfordshire or Devon. It was a false name, a falsehood, a lie like the whole of the last week had been, and he'd been a fool to name a man whose whole purpose was to be anonymous. No wonder Gareth had let himself care a little bit, giving him a name. That had been his mistake, and he was putting it right. He told himself that furiously, pulling his shoes on with jerky movements, not looking round. Absolutely not blinking anything away.

Hat. Coat. He had all his things and he looked more or less acceptable, if not precisely well turned out, so he could go. "Goodbye," he managed, because he wasn't going to be ill-mannered even if other people chose to be unreasonable.

"You're just going like that," the man said. "Right. As you please."

Some people couldn't part with decency. Gareth straightened his shoulders and left the room. He didn't look back, not even at the last, muttered, angry word he heard as he opened the door. It sounded a lot like, "Arsehole."

Two days later the letter arrived, and everything changed.

Acknowledgements

Huge thanks to Mary Altman and the whole Sourcebooks team, to Jyotirmayee Patra for the wonderful covers, and to my marvellous agent, Courtney Miller-Callihan.

As ever, Lis Paice did a merciless first read. Thank you!

I owe a great deal to my in-laws, Vincent and Christine, who have always been an invaluable support. Love you both.

Thanks again to Charlie and the kids. One day I'll set a book in the Bahamas, I promise (if we can expense the research trip).

About the Author

KJ Charles spent twenty years as an editor in British publishing before fleeing the scene to become a full-time historical romance novelist. She has written over twenty-five novels since then, and her books have been translated into eight languages. She lives in London.